A
BEWITCHING
SMILE

Novels by Christopher G. Moore

His Lordship's Arsenal

Enemies of Memory

A Killing Smile

A Bewitching Smile

Spirit House

A
BEWITCHING
SMILE

Christopher G. Moore

WHITE LOTUS

Bangkok

White Lotus Co., Ltd
G.P.O. Box 1141
Bangkok 10501

Published 1992. First edition

Printed in Thailand

Editor May Dikeman
Typeset by COMSET Ltd., Part.
Cover Design and Illustration Graph-East Services Co., Ltd.

ISBN 974-8495-57-4

For Max and John

and Julius

Chapter 1

Crosby was only fifteen when his penis swelled in a series of red blisters that made walking painful. He hobbled around doubled over with the stooping gait of an old man. Breach spotted the boy walking into the gambling room in the back of the pub off Harley Street in London. The boy slid into an empty chair, stuck his hand deep into his pocket and removed a fist of pound notes which he laid crumpled on the table. He grimaced as his hand brushed inside the pocket grazing the side of his penis. Beads of sweat formed on his forehead. He swallowed hard, pulling his chin into his neck. He looked around the table with that kind of look everyone there had seen on many faces before. A look of serious determination. Young Crosby had arrived to play a game of poker. He had skipped his train back to public school and had spent four hours looking for the Boar's Head Pub in Nottinghill Gate.

"What's wrong. How did you get the gimpy leg?"

"Bangkok Nightshade. A ripe whore."

"Bangkok? A lad like you screwing whores in Bangkok? Who ever heard of such a thing?"

"Can you afford the English ones?"

"And you've a smart mouth on you," he grinned at the other players around the table. "So tell us. How a lad like you came by the money to play at this table?"

"An honorarium from King's Hospital."

"Next you'll be telling us you're a doctor, now."

"Not exactly. But I have extensive experience with tropical VD."

"Extensive, he says. Well, well. And with a deck of cards?"

Crosby nodded his head.

"Is that so?" asked Breach, winking at one of the gamblers across the table. "I've a ten-pound note that says you're bluffing. You've never been to Bangkok. Never slept with a whore. You made up the whole story." Breach slid two five-pound notes across the table.

Crosby shifted, smacked his lips, staring down at the bet.

"And here's another tenner that says you're lying," said one of the other gamblers.

The three other gamblers peeled off two five-pound notes. One gambler raised the stakes to twenty pounds. By the time the bets had been laid down, there was nearly one hundred pounds on the table. That was a slight problem since Crosby only had fifty pounds to cover the bet.

"Let's have a look now," said Breach.

Crosby slowly rose from his chair, unfastened his belt buckle and dropped his trousers. The silver belt buckle struck the floor with a thud. Crosby pulled down his underpants. But he was so short that the gamblers, even leaning over the table, had trouble seeing. Breach jumped out of his chair and picked up Crosby from behind and set him feetfirst on the table. An empty silence followed as no one around the table moved. With his trousers and underpants draped over his scuffed shoes, Crosby stood, as he had done before the interns at King's Hospital, hands on his hips, explaining the spatial relationships between the blisters, the dermatological background of his VD, and how a country doctor near his school had misdiagnosed it as a dermatophyte—a kind of skin fungus—and prescribed the medication for a fungus. This flowed automatically from the mouth of a fifteen-year-old boy who could have easily passed for eleven or twelve years old.

All eyes were on the hugely swollen red penis that looked like spoiled meat and had a damp, dull, and evil smell. The smell of something that had been punctured and left to rot. One of the punters, his face white, sweat beading on his forehead, fainted. The remaining three sat without swallowing, blinking or apparently blinking at the sight of Crosby's grotesque organ. Breach, who had been standing behind Crosby, walked around and did a double take, twisting the expression on his face as if someone had thumped him between the eyes.

"A whore gave you that dose?"

Crosby blinked. "Her name was Noi. We always went to the Playboy short-time hotel and checked into room 9. Mirrors on the ceiling and walls. We undressed together and she crawled onto the bed on all fours. The arch of her back was perfect; each vertebrae a work of art. I pulled the mallets out of my schoolbag and sheet music. My father forced me to take xylophone lessons. Why? Because his father forced him. I practised the xylophone on Noi. She loved it. She said it was better than a massage. I would lose my place in the music about the time I slid myself into her. When I stuck it inside her Noi moaned, and threw back her head. And with my little mallets I ran the chords up and down her back, pumping her as I played. It almost made the xylophone tolerable. Only you don't get a dose from a musical instrument if you are holding it properly. That's what my last doctor said. And I said what instrument can compete with a Noi? With her small cherry-coloured mole above her collar bone, the narrow firm hips, and the backbone any orchestra would have killed for? He didn't have an answer."

"Stop, stop! We don't fucking care about your xylophone lessons with Noi. She just cost us about a hundred quid," said Breach, looking away.

"Can I pull up my trousers?" asked Crosby.

Breach gestured in disgust for Crosby to dress. He fumbled with his belt buckle. Then he eyed the men around the table as he reached out for the pile of five-pound notes. One of the gamblers grabbed Crosby's wrist. "And where do you think you're going, laddy?"

"No muscle," said Breach. "The kid won it fair and square."

There was a tense moment when Crosby thought the barrel-chested man who squeezed his arm was going to break it off at the elbow. He tried to show no pain or fear. But his lower lip began to quiver slightly.

"The kid might be contagious. I wouldn't be touching him."

That did the trick. The gambler's grip snapped open and he withdrew his hand. Crosby scooped up the money, stuffing it in his pockets, wincing each time he knocked against his penis.

Two hours later in Trafalgar Square, Breach found Crosby waiting for him. Breach smiled, walking up to the boy. He hadn't been certain whether Crosby would be there.

"You did a fine job." He wrapped an arm around Crosby's shoulder. "When we get back to school I don't want you flashing around your winnings. You understand?"

Crosby understood from the sudden shift in Breach's tone of voice from co-conspirator to history master where he stood before the class lecturing twenty-six boys on eighteenth century European history. Breach had gone from public school to public school like an Arab on camelback riding from oasis to oasis looking for the gambler's perfect watering hole. A brilliant teacher, his services were usually terminated in the second or third year of his appointment after a complaint of gambling reached the headmaster's ear. Crosby was still shaking from his brush with potential violence. The gambler with the arms of a dockworker had nearly snapped his wrist in two.

Crosby leaned back against Nelson's Column. A police constable strolled past, the strap of his helmet pressing against his fleshy chin. Breach leaned forward out of the wind and lit a cigarette. He made the gesture of throwing the match away, his hand making one of those well-executed turns of a fighter pilot snapped beside Crosby's windblown hair. The match appeared as if taken from Crosby's ear. He had seen the trick before; with coins, eggs, pencils, and a length of piano wire. And he knew from experience of going on capers with Breach before that one of his illusions followed close on the heels of some request that he wished to disguise.

"I dropped twenty quid before I left. I've thought about it. As a moral issue. Not as an ethical issue. And I say we share the loss, like the winnings, fifty-fifty."

A line of clear snot dripped over the top of Crosby's upper lip as he slowly shook his head. "I had the indignity of dropping my trousers before a group of total strangers and—"

Breach cut in. "You had no complaint dropping them at King's Hospital."

"Before doctors and medical students. In the name of medical science. They were at my gong to improve their knowledge. Not some crew of beefy longshore workers with dirty minds. And, that bastard nearly broke my arm. Fifty quid each. Besides, how do I know you really lost twenty quid. You might have won twenty quid. Would you have split that with me?"

"They weren't dockworkers. Two worked the floor at Top Hat; other two work the door at the Pink Willow."

"Which makes them lower in the social order than dockworkers. Thugs in suits. For a history don, you know some very creep sorts. So why should I trust you. I only have your word that you lost twenty pounds."

The major objection Breach had to extremely gifted students in second-rate public schools was their ability to unearth the practical limitations of their school, their education, and their future; they knew exactly when they had been taken advantage of; they were very difficult to deceive. "Right you are, fifty-fifty," said Breach, taking the fifty pounds from Crosby and stuffing them without counting into his pocket. He turned and walked off across the square, scattering flocks of pigeons in a machine-burst of feathers beating at the sky.

"Where you going?" asked Crosby, moaning from the pain between his legs as he tried to run along.

"To find a suitable partner. One who understands that gentlemen's agreement covers assets and liabilities from the joint venture. Who recognizes that in cases of dispute, the senior calls the shot. Not the junior."

"All right, here's another bloody ten pounds. Just slow down. I can't run. You know I can't run. Not with what Noi did to my cock."

Breach stopped abruptly and waited for Crosby to amble alongside, panting, and holding out two five-pound notes. Breach slipped them into his pocket. "Horse racing. Do you like going?" he asked Crosby.

Crosby smiled widely. "Do I ever."

"Next week you're on. You see, I know this trainer who knows an owner I once played poker with in Tunis. And on Saturday, there is a horse named Roger Dodger running in the fifth. I say we put on hundred quid on him. The odds should come in at five to one."

The Friday before the big race Breach was called into the headmaster's office and asked to resign. A ritual that Breach had seen coming and had been attempting to accumulate some capital to tide him over. He vanished from the school without saying goodbye to anyone, including Crosby. Sunday morning, Crosby read in the racing results that Roger Dodger had won at Ascot, paying out on five to one odds. Three weeks later, an envelope arrived postmarked New York City. Inside was two hundred and fifty pounds.

"Your half of Roger Dodger is enclosed. One, remember to use a condom when you screw Noi. Two, remember when you get to call the shots you have to keep your word." The note was signed "Breach."

❖

She stood erect, arm half cocked, her mouth frozen in a state of absolute concentration. Beneath her jeans, the firm line of her hips was taut. One foot was pushed slightly ahead of the other. She did not blink; from her chest there was no sign of breath entering or leaving her body. All the background noise had been filtered out of her mind. At the exact moment of release, her hand whipped forward in a perfect cantilevered motion. The lids of her eyes closed slightly, a smile crept over her lips, and slowly the end of her tongue flicked across the ridge of her upper lip.

Ross was half drunk. He was a large man with a lion's head balding with advanced middle age. Cold blue eyes with irises that dilated for hours; eyes with a haunted luster, as if they had spread open to receive a lover. He set his drink down hard, spilling *Jim Bean* over his hand. Ross licked the webbing between his finger and thumb. He stared up at her and smiled, exposing teeth that looked like a permanent set of baby teeth.

"Goddamn, Noi, you are one helluva of a dart player." He watched her proudly walk to the target and pick her darts out. "You see that last dart?" he asked Crosby, who sat next to him at the bar.

Crosby nodded. "On the money."

"You bet your ass she's on the money."

"It's up to you now," said Crosby. Making a half-turn, he winked at Breach who sat forward on his elbows, watching Ross in the bar mirror.

"I know, I know. Don't fucking put pressure on me. The more I drink, the better I throw. And I'm pretty drunk right now. But I don't need any goddamn pressure when I throw."

Ross rose up from his stool. He wobbled, belched, sucked in his belly, and walked over to the line with a fistful of darts. Crosby waved to his partner, a Thai woman in her early thirties; the first signs of creases fanned out from her eyes. She wore round gold earrings and a two-baht gold chain around her neck. She smiled back at Crosby.

"Noi, I'd like you to meet a colleague of mine. Richard Breach," Crosby said, wrapping an arm around her waist and pulling her closer.

She smiled at Breach and extended her hand. Several gold chains on her wrist reflected the lights from the bar.

"About fifteen years ago, she taught me how to play the xylophone," said Crosby, in a half whisper but loud enough for Breach to hear. "And rewarded me with a dose."

"It was you who gave me a dose," said Noi, stiffening against Crosby.

"That was another time. Two years later."

"The first time, I got it from you."

She half-closed her eyes, watching Ross's second dart find the target. "Yeah, yeah. The dose I got from Tuttle."

"From Tuttle," repeated Crosby, arching an eyebrow. "I didn't know that you gave him music lessons."

"There's a lot you don't know, Bobby."

"I wouldn't dispute that. But here's a little fact that I've never told you. You see this man. Fifteen years ago in London we won nearly five thousand off your dose."

Noi glanced over at Breach, who gave a faint nod of agreement. The wheels were in motion inside her head. "So you owe me two thousand five hundred baht plus interest."

Ross came back with his darts.

"I fucked up. Your turn, Noi. We still got second place wrapped up. If I were a little more drunk, I could throw better." He caught the eye of the bartender. "Give me another *Old Crow*."

The bartender looked confused. *"Jim Beam?"*

"Give me a fucking drink. Booze. I don't care what you call it. Fill this glass. I need fuel. We are losing first place. Can't you see I'm desperate for a drink."

Noi translated into Thai for the bartender who set a full bottle of *Old Grand-Dad* beside Ross's glass. "That's better," said Ross. "Throw us some big numbers," he said to Noi, as she walked over to the line.

Checker's Bar off Sukhumvit Road was filled with people. Dart people, as Crosby called them. Their main preoccupation after work and family was darts. Tournaments, practise, pickup games, along with T-shirts advertising their bar and team, trophies, newspaper clippings framed on the bar walls of past champions, clipboard with individual and team rankings. Ross, a lawyer by day, was a dart person at night. Noi was one of his whores that he had picked up five months earlier in Zeno's coffee shop and trained to be his partner.

Ross was also a businessman. He poured himself a drink from the open bottle of *Old Grand-Dad*. He narrowed his eyes and jutted his jaw out at himself in the mirror across the bar, picking up Breach's eyes. "There's some interesting games going on upcountry. Crosby tell you about that?"

"I thought it best if you explained it," said Crosby.

"Mae Sai mean anything to you?" asked Ross.

Breach grinned and turned, facing Ross. "It's near the golden triangle. There's a bridge link into Burma. That exhausts my knowledge."

"Guys are showing up their flashing bags of hundred-dollar bills. Crosby says you used to be a pretty good poker player. I always lost my ass at poker. It wasn't my game. I like throwing objects with sharp points; especially when I'm drunk. The more I drink the better I throw. Fuck it. Fuck it. I keep losing the track of my thoughts."

"Mae Sai," said Crosby.

Crosby arched an eyebrow as Breach looked his way.

"So I was thinking if you wanted a game. I could make an introduction. One of my clients flies up there once a week. I'm a lawyer. Didn't Crosby tell you I was a lawyer?"

Breach grinned. "He told me."

Ross stalled out again, filling his glass.

"Mae Sai," coached Crosby.

"He's an ex-Air America fly-boy. A true patriot. One of those guys who bombed the shit out of the Commies and smuggled opium with CIA bag money stuffed inside their boots. He was stationed in Korat during the war. He made some good connections. Now this guy. Shit, I forget his name and he's a client."

"Francis Harmon," said Crosby.

"That's it. Francis. With a name like that, he had to drop bombs on people to prove he was a man. You think this guy knows shit about cards? He don't know shit. He comes back with ten grand last week. If Francis can take home ten grand, you could probably double, triple that."

"You need a minimum of two thousand to sit at the table," said Breach. "I don't have it."

Ross grinned. "I put up the money. We split the winning."

"And if I don't win?"

"Negative thinking," said Ross. "I don't want any negative thoughts. Think win. Win. Win."

Crosby eased off his stool as Noi strolled back. "We lost," said Noi.

His eyes grew bigger and his face flushed. "You mean those dickheads beat us?"

She nodded, smiling, rolling the gold-plated dart shafts between the palms of her hands. "Have a drink, Ross."

"You mention that negative word, and what happens?"

Breach wasn't particularly impressed by Ross's performance. "You want me to pick up some quick cash for you," said Breach.

"Split. Fifty-fifty. Cash for yourself and for me. You know how many *farang* would love this chance? Hundreds. They would jump at it. The only reason I'm asking you is because you're Crosby's friend." Ross pointed a finger at Crosby's nose. "I've known him since he was a kid. If he says you are the best, then you must be."

He massaged the back of Noi's neck. She leaned forward over the bar squeezing a fistful of darts, keeping beat to the music as she tapped the points into the bar counter.

"Bobby's seen them all in Bangkok," said Ross. "But I ain't drunk enough to get down on my knees and beg you. Please take my money and play poker, sir. Either you want a game or you don't."

Crosby pulled Noi onto his lap, brushing the hair away from the nape of her neck. With the tip of his finger he traced the gold circle inside her left gold earring. He looked over at Breach. "You wrote me a letter once. You said only bet on a sure thing. Pretend it is a loop. Ask yourself is there a gate where you can fall through and break your ass."

Breach watched him playing with Noi's earring. "And you think this is a certain win?"

"Just about," said Crosby.

"These Chinese guys don't know dick about cards," said Ross. "It's a big macho deal to drop money in a game so they can go bragging to their Chink friends. Some hotshit *farang* won ten grand off me at cards, and I didn't bat a fucking eye." Ross slipped climbing off his chair, recovered his balance, pulled his shoulders back and walked toward the washroom. "Order me another drink," he said to Noi.

A moment after Ross had staggered away, Crosby leaned in close to Breach and whispered.

"Suda does business with a couple of Chinese traders," he said. "Tang and Gim. She doesn't know it. But they are big stake players. You go along with her to the North. She buys antiques. Everyone thinks you're her friend. A tourist. Someone in town to buy silver bracelets by the gram. You flash some heavy cash. The Chinese love the color of money. They see opportunity in money. It's perfect. It's like dropping my pants in London. Showing what Noi did to my dick."

Crosby waited for a response but Breach cleared his throat, reached around and grabbed Noi by the waist and pulled her in close. He looked at her for a couple of seconds. Eyes, makeup, lipstick, gold and more gold; long, black braided hair, and smoothed, polished skin. "You trust this guy?" Breach asked her.

She glanced over at Crosby.

"Not him. I already know better than to trust Crosby. I mean Ross. You trust him?"

"That's a bit hard, Breach."

Breach ignored Crosby's attempt to display hurt feelings. Noi puckered her lips; licked the upper lip like she had done concentrating on the dart board. Breach liked that. She just didn't fly out with an answer. She was reflecting, weighing up Ross's treachery and the possible penalty for telling the truth.

"The first night I go back with Ross he was very drunk. We go upstairs to his bedroom and roll on the bed. He's drunk and stoned. All the change spilled out of his pockets. He goes and takes a shower. I go. We make love. Then rolls over and see all this money in the bed. You know what Ross say to me? 'Too bad the tooth fairy came and we didn't have anything to leave for him.' I think he's a good man. He makes me laugh. I not trust man who never makes me laugh."

Breach was hired by Robert Tuttle, an expate American who ran a low-budget private English language school on Sukhumvit Road. Breach knew the basics about Tuttle: ex-journalist, father of a beautiful daughter, partner in a stormy business relationship with a Thai police colonel; and all Tuttle knew about Breach was that he was broke, had an unstable work record, had not been in a classroom for five years, and had once been a first-class poker player.

Approaching forty, Breach had been in Bangkok for three months and four days, and had returned from his first visa-run on the international express to Penang. Before travelling to Thailand, Breach had wandered in ever smaller circles through Tibet and Nepal, studying Pali and Sanskrit. He lived the life of a Dharma bum. Each night he folded out his bedroll, lay on his back and stared at the ceiling at the bats above. Jet-black wings pulsating in the dusky dark. He watched them flying in and out of the cave like messengers linking day and night. By the end of his stay, he saw the flutter of the bat wings in his sleep. In his dream the bats came in a torrent like ejaculated sperm searching for a target in the depths of total darkness, guided by sonar, crying in desperation.

The monk who had lived in the cave before Breach had lasted six weeks. He was found yammering that he was enlightened. When questioned, the monk raptured that he discovered his true nature in the cave with the bats: he was a clitoris. Not only was he a clitoris, but the entire human species was a single clitoris for the entire universe. The flow of the bats in and out of the cave had given him cosmic multiple orgasms—day and night; his member, constantly erect, tracked the bats like a kind of smart bomb. He was diagnosed as mad and had to be shipped by air freight to Columbus, Ohio in a straitjacket, and later appeared on local talk shows about his experience and theory.

After Breach moved into the cave, the authorities kept a close eye on him for several months. All they ever found was Breach stretched out on his bedroll, legs crossed, humming to himself and staring at the cave ceiling as if he had a box seat to an event. He never once felt like a clitoris. Visitors came and left him food, and asked him for the answers to life and the universe. "Bats. They fly in and they fly out. They breed and they die. They eat and they shit." That was his standard answer. Then, one morning, a bat shit on his head and he received a message from Crosby (though not necessarily in that order), and he sensed it was time to leave the cave life and return to the world. He washed the bat shit out of his hair and walked straight to the airport with a shoulder bag containing one change of clothes and a spare upper bridge plate. The same day he left the cave outside of Kathmandu, the cavity he had called home for almost two years, and he had an insight: enlightenment was like trapshooting—clay pigeons shooting clay pigeons. The dead splitting the dead in entertaining ways and usually before a live audience.

The upper dental bridge which replaced his four front teeth—rattled as the plane left the runway. He stared out the window at 35,000 feet and wondered why he had allowed Crosby to interrupt his meditation. Airplanes were these awful mixed metaphors: a machine with wings like a bat with signs reading "Toilet Aft" as if it were a boat and "Exit" as if it were a cinema, and flown by people in military uniforms. All that was missing was a monk who thought he was a clitoris, Breach thought. He fiddled with his bridge plate and felt a sudden sharp pain in his forehead. He remembered the last time he had the original teeth in his head; he had scooped up the winnings in a poker game outside Vancouver, where he taught in a rundown private school for girls.

Fragments of news about Breach, mostly conflicting, and mostly fabricated, had reached Crosby over the years. That he lost the tip of his left little finger in a gambling house brawl outside Kyoto. And had been stabbed in the left buttocks by an irate Philippine barmaid in Hong Kong one Sunday afternoon. One of Breach's girlfriends had killed herself swallowing live gold fish on a fifty-dollar bet. That he had become a Buddhist monk and had sworn off sex, drugs, and rock 'n roll, lived in a cave, spoke in multiple tongues, and had a band of followers from Boulder, Colorado who sent him packages containing shoes, underwear, socks, and satin pillowcases. Nowhere was there a rumor that he had washed bat shit out of his hair on his way to enlightenment.

Breach had reached the age where cosmetic reassembly had been required to patch over the bit-by-bit that had worn out or broken off. Crosby had discounted as lies the unconfirmed rumors of wives and mistresses abandoned in several countries. It seemed that in each place Breach had left some original part of his being at each port of call.

Nonetheless, several mutual friends had confirmed that Breach had sworn off gambling and, given the poverty of the people in Tibet and Nepal, it would have been difficult to find a high stakes poker game. Crosby had gone to Robert Tuttle, the expate American who ran the school, and recommended that Richard Breach, his former history don, should be given a teaching job. He didn't tell Tuttle the full story about Breach. Or that Crosby had once dropped his drawers on a card table in Nottinghill Gate as a con with Breach. He felt that might give the wrong impression of Breach. Besides, that was all in the past.

"You wanted a gambler," said Crosby.

Tuttle stared out the window of his office at an unmarked police car and said nothing for several moments. "We go easy. One step at a time."

"He can do the job," said Crosby, with heavy emphasis on "the," knowing that Tuttle's office was wired for sound. "He can improve your game." They often used golf lingo in the office. Tuttle played golf with Colonel Chao twice a week, and the competition had spilled over into their personal lives. The stakes had increased. Colonel Chao had decided to make a play for Tuttle's daughter, Asanee: diamond bracelets, gold chains, designer clothes. After the second week Asansee had stopped sending back the gifts.

Tuttle grinned. "But is he any good on the back-nine?"

Crosby didn't have an immediate answer but in his gut he felt this was the one job Breach had been waiting for his entire life.

Breach had appeared out of a hazy cloud of gray Bangkok pollution and a week later was teaching English to upwardly mobile whores. Crosby quite liked the idea that he ranked senior at the school to Breach. Something had always been different about Breach. Crosby had not decided if this difference was a matter of age, class, upbringing, or intelligence. What was clear with Breach's arrival at the school was that Crosby was no longer the schoolboy and Breach the English master. He felt that Breach had come to Thailand for a specific reason; he felt that Breach had come and gone according to some pattern or design that had never been fully revealed even to his closest friends. What he had forgotten was Breach had an aversion to patterns and designs. Along the way, Crosby had convinced Tuttle that Breach might be the one man who could recover his daughter from the Colonel; take her out of the rough and put her square on the fairway of life. That was what Tuttle had wanted to hear. Whether Breach was up to the poker game upcountry was anyone's guess. Crosby bet that Breach could pull off the old magic. Though he wouldn't say exactly how much he was willing to bet on the final outcome. All that was certain before the cards were dealt was that Breach was in Bangkok and that, mostly for his own reasons, he was heading in the right direction. Even if he didn't fully understand what Crosby had in mind for him.

Chapter 2

Sunday night Breach fell asleep on the vast marble floor of the public waiting area at Hualamphong Railway Station. Suda, who waited on the platform, paced back and forth; all she knew was that he was late and soon they would miss the train. She had an immediate decision to make; go without him or go back and look for him. Suda had not made up her mind. She started to question Crosby's judgment. Time was running out, and she doubted whether Crosby had carried out all the arrangement which had been planned to link her up with Breach. Crosby could be irresponsible, she thought. She felt a heavy sense of responsibility. She was annoyed with herself. Perhaps it was a mistake to have become involved at all? She clenched and unclenched her fist, and felt her stomach tighten into a dense coil of anger.

Breach had not intended to fall asleep; he had promised himself to be punctual and arrived at 5:30 p.m., more than two hours early. But as he eased back into a chair in the midst of hundreds of other travellers, his eyes snapped shut. Slowly they opened. Exhaustion and boredom overwhelmned him as he stared vacantly at an English-Thai dictionary. He sipped a Coke and fought off the fatigue of the previous sleepless night spent with Crosby, Ross, Noi, and the dart people. At six o'clock the national anthem blared over the loudspeaker system. People jumped to their feet or stopped walking. Everyone stood at attention, including monks, half-facing a couple of police officers dressed in their brown uniforms. Breach dropped his dictionary on the floor. No one moved. No one noticed him smiling to himself. Breach tried to read the book on the floor. Finally as the anthem ended and the buzz of conversation returned, he squatted down and collected the book. The word he had been trying to make out from a standing position was *ah jahn*—teacher. Minutes later, Breach, his head tipped to the side and mouth ajar, was fast asleep with the dictionary clutched over his chest.

He dreamed of Asanee, a half-Thai girl whose father, Robert Tuttle, operated the English language school. She had emerald-green eyes, a mouth that looked like it was in mourning, hair arranged in waves which tumbled down her back. Her manner and appearance encompassed more than sexuality; below the surface was the hint of something forbidden, unclaimed and unrestrained. Six months earlier, she had almost died. Asanee had been held at gunpoint by a deranged Thai worker. He threatened to kill her. The police had rescued her, breaking into the house and killing her attacker. She had trouble sleeping and often arrived late for a class. Breach discovered they both had the sense of motion and of creatures howling through their dreams. He told her about the bat that had shit on his head. And for the first time, he heard her laugh. They liked each other's company, and a friendship began. Twice a week they ate lunch. Sometimes she broke into tears. Once a car backfired as they walked on Sukhumvit. Another time she lost her temper when Breach asked her about the rumor that she had become Colonel Chao *mee-uh noi*. "It's not like that at all," she had said angrily. "You sound like my father. Besides, *some* people think you and I are having an affair."

"That's stupid," Breach had said. "We're friends. Can't a man have a Thai woman as a friend?"

"Someone thinks you like me too much," she had said.

"What? Your father?"

She had nodded her head. "Colonel Chao."

24

"So you are involved with him!" said Breach, squeezing her hand. "And he is as old as your father."

She quickly pulled her hand away. "A year or two older than you," she said, watching the reality hit home. He wrinkled his nose and sighed. "I think it's better for you to go upcountry," she continued. "At least for a while. If something happened to you, it would be my fault."

Her sense of concern for his safety touched Breach. It had been a long time since someone had expressed the slightest concern for his well-being or welfare. "And what could happen? I haven't done anything to anyone. I've just come out of a cave."

"That's the point. You don't know how people think in Bangkok," she said.

The next evening, crossing Sukhumvit, a motorcycle cut over the line and nearly ran him down. The motorcycle came out of nowhere. After missing, the driver turned around and came back around for a second attempt. Breach, who had renounced worldly interest for the spiritual pursuits had forgotten that in re-entering the world the only safe places for ascetics were caves, forest, and mountaintops. Places largely inaccessible to motorcycles.

In most schools where Breach had taught he had dreamed of sleeping with the headmaster's daughter; and when he succeeded, as he often did, the affair was discovered, Breach was summoned for an interview with the headmaster, fired, and sent on his way. In his dream, Breach had a massive erection; Asanee, who stood naked before him had erect nipples that were as large as Breach's erect member. He explained how misunderstood he had been. This wasn't a sexual act, Breach heard a voice instructing Asanee inside the dream. His mission was to chart the size, coloration, texture, smell, and taste. He wanted to stare at them for hours. Hold them, stroke them, suckle, lick, and massage them. He loved the soft brown hues and delicate pinks as the breasts gained a personality of their own, asserting themselves and announcing a promise—these are yours. She dissolved into tears. The sound of gunshots pierced the void, then police sirens which faded into the gong of a bell.

A bell rang out as a station guard announced the departure of a train. Inside his dream, Breach thought the muffled noise came from a police car outside. He buried his face inside Asanee's breasts as if putting an ear to a seashell. The ringing bell sound grew louder. At 7:25 p.m.—he had agreed to meet Suda between 7 and 7:15. From behind, a hand shook Breach on the shoulder. His eyes opened wide. The bell was still ringing. He was in the train station. Breach turned around but whoever had awakened him had vanished. He looked down at his watch, grabbed his bag, and ran to the platform. As he ran through the departure gate, the Chiang Mai train was at the platform, engines running. Suda sat, worried, hands folded, resting forward, elbows on her knees. She sprang up and ran over to Breach, touching his wrist with one hand and her heart with the other. Her two bags were dropped at her feet.

"I was so afraid. I think you forget. Or you get lost. Or you change your mind. I not know what I think," she said, stopping herself from expressing her fear someone on a motorcycle had finished the job.

"I fell asleep," said Breach. He didn't tell her about the dream in which Asanee surrendered herself to him and his instruments of measurement. It was not the right way to begin a journey with a stranger, he thought.

"I very worried."

"The bell woke me." Nor did he tell her that he thought the bell was the sound one heard with king-sized erect nipples stuffed into his ears.

"You too tired. Maybe you go Chiang Mai next week."

"You thought I stood you up?"

"What mean stood up?"

"The train's about to leave."

"Stood up mean in English train about to leave?"

"That's about as good a definition as I've heard."

❖

As the train pulled out of the station, they sat on benches opposite from one another. She was still rattled, and leaning forward in the second-class sleeper, Suda gave Breach a small slap on the wrist, smiled, and sat back. Her eyes flashed a look that women often give: Men, God, they take you to the edge every time. You wait and wait. Maybe they show up; maybe they won't. You can never be certain.

The air conditioner blew a steady hiss of cold mist out of wall vents as young porters glided back and forth along the narrow corridors, carrying trays of orange juice, water, watermelon, bananas, and evening meals such as curried shrimp and beef and pork, together with rice or noodles. The ultimate question in Breach's mind on that first night lacked a context for framing, no chance of being asked: would they make love. The law of train car physics decided the answer in a powerfully silent way. Suda occupied the upper berth and Breach bunked below in a coffin-shaped enclosure screened off from the corridor by a curtain. Suda sat crossed-legged below a small light and read a pirated Jeffrey Archer mystery that had been translated into Thai. She had brought three books on the trip. Breach was restless in the lower berth; he stared at the ceiling, running the possibilities of what Suda might be doing or thinking, and what her state of dress or undress might be at that moment. She had small rigid mounts for breasts, he thought. The breasts of a child.

He had agreed to make the trip for several reasons. After the motorcycle incident, he felt Asanee might have a point. And also Suda held out the possibility of being that rare, if not entirely original kind of woman, one who lived inside her own culture as an outsider; but an extraordinary kind of outsider who did not fit within the usual categories: whore, drug addict, lunatic, emotional cripple, or gangster. From country to country, the women Breach had talked with, slept with, walked, ran, and drank with in shops, small hotels, train stations, or restaurants along the road fell into one of those categories; living on the outside of a household, the family, the society was not a choice most women contemplated as desirable. It was an alternative thrust upon, a status which seized them without much choice by lethal combination of defective genes, crazy parents, and daytime TV. Suda challenged Breach's theory. He liked that; he wanted to be proved wrong. He had made a side bet with himself somewhere along the line that with Suda an edge would be reached and Suda would be snared like all of the other women he knew. Finally, he swung his legs over the side, climbed up the chrome ladder, and stuck his head into her berth. She had reached page 29 of the Archer novel.

"Someone woke me up at the stage. I thought it might have been you. Someone put a hand here. On my shoulder. When I was in the middle of a dream. That's why I was late."

"*Mai bpen rai*—never mind."

"A Jeffery Archer comic book," Breach said.

"You like him?"

"I not know him."

"You don't really know me," said Breach.

"I not read your book."

Breach liked that answer. "Cannot," he said, tapping his forehead. "It's in my private library."

"Maybe it is boring. How do I know?" Suda smiled and stuck a book marker inside the paperback and closed it.

"You don't," grinned Breach. "Indians were once afraid if you took their photograph, you would steal their soul. But you steal a man's soul by taking his words and making them your own. So I only let a few out at a time, and when I speak, so that I can call all my words home, I keep the listener occupied."

Breach took a five-baht coin from his pocket, showed it to Suda in the palm of his hand, closed his hand, clapped his hands together, slowly opening both to reveal the coin was gone. Suda stared from hand to hand, then looked up at Breach, who grinned. He reached forward and brushed against her right ear. He opened his hand and showed her the coin.

"How did you do that?" Suda said.

"Magic," he whispered, wide-eyed. "So no one can steal my soul."

As they said good-night, Breach left the five-baht coin on top of the Archer paperback; there was a slight moment of awkwardness. Partially because Breach wasn't fluent in Thai; partially because they were strangers; partially because magic caused contemplation; but mainly because everything important was left unsaid or discovered between them.

Breach dreamt one of his favorite recurring dreams at three in the morning. A skinny ten-year-old with a dirty face and torn dress was holding up a bunch of flowers. A gust of wind blew the leaves. People walked, pressing against the storm, passed her without looking. Her lower lip quivered, making her face look rubbery. Tears filled her eyes. A man in a double-breasted gray suit, touched by the display of tears, stopped and bought the flowers. As he pulled out his wallet, a man with white hair in a soiled, baggy blue suit jumped out from behind a door and stood before the flower girl.

"Hallelujah!" he shouted several times, holding up a Bible bound in white calf leather. The startled customer backed away.

The little girl fell to her knees and wrapped her thin arms around his leg. "Don't go, mister. He's me dad. He only wants you to look at his Bible. You don't have to buy unless you want to."

Whenever Breach had this dream, he was interrupted before the customer, looking down at the tiny flower girl, made his decision to stay or leave. Sleeping on the train, it happened again. A hand clutched Breach's shoulder and shook him. His eyes popped wide open and in the darkness of the narrow sleeper, Breach made out the form of a man.

"I was feeling slightly guilty," said Crosby.

"So it was you at the train station." Breach flicked on the night light near the window.

Crosby nodded and shifted his weight forward, half turning and sitting on the edge of Breach's bed. "You were sound asleep. Snoring. Disturbing the peace actually. Ten minutes more and you'd have missed the train. You would've slept straight through a perfect payday."

"Go away, Crosby. I was dreaming about my mother."

"Incest dreams on a train? I thought only the French had those kind of dreams."

"She and my grandfather were running a con on Fleet Street—right behind the Law Courts. That was back in the 30's. Their flowers and Bibles con."

"Your mother was a childhood criminal?" asked Crosby. He was impressed. In most of life the man was always less than the legend; in Breach's case, the myth and legend had not overtaken the full story locked inside the man.

"What are you doing here, Crosby?"

Crosby opened a brown bag and produced a plate, napkins, silverware, two glasses and a small bottle of claret. He handed the claret to Breach, who examined the label under the dim light.

"Nineteen-sixty-three. A rather disappointing year."

"This is Thailand and not Oxford, Richard," said Crosby, as he took back the claret and opened it.

"Where's Ross?" asked Breach.

Crosby poured a glass of claret and handed it to Breach. "How do you know Ross is here?"

"Because of the pâté."

Crosby looked puzzled.

"The pâté and claret are from the first-class car; and you never travel first-class unless get someone else to pay."

"Ross passed out in his berth two hours ago."

"Why didn't you tell me before?" asked Breach, raising himself up on his elbows.

"When you buggered off from my school did you tell me?"

Breach chewed a piece of French bread and pâté, thinking for a moment. "That was an emergency. Headmaster's daughter, the headmaster, and the police not far behind them."

"Ross's afraid you'll change your mind."

Breach sipped the claret and made a face. "He passed out on this?"

"On *Old Grand-Dad*."

"On his grandfather?"

"*Old Grand-Dad* is a cheap whiskey."

"How did you make out with Suda," whispered Crosby, arching his eyes toward the ceiling.

"She likes comic books and magic."

"I figured you'd have a lot in common," said Crosby, before vanishing a moment later.

❖

Monday morning, a barefoot train porter, with a flutter and rattle of cloth and metal, pulled back the curtain of Breach's berth at 6:00 a.m. An empty bottle of claret rolled off the bed, hit the floor without breaking, and careened down narrow corridor, shattering against a luggage rack. Breach blinked at the porter and rubbed his eyes. It was first light outside. He looked at his wristwatch. Then he lay back on the bed, closed his eyes, and thought about the flower girl pedaling bunches of wilted red roses to barristers and clerks and solicitors all those years ago in London. Forty-five minutes later the train pulled into Chiang Mai station.

Outside the station, Suda bargained with two young samlor drivers. The Riverside Guest House was about two kilometers from the station. They eyed the size of Breach in settling on the fare. The drivers flipped a coin for Breach. Then they set off in separate samlors. Suda's driver, his leg muscles knotted, the surface rippled with thick coils of veins, set off. Breach's driver followed behind, cursing his early morning bad luck on a flip of the one-baht coin. He pedaled through the busy streets, waving at motorcyclists, tuk-tuk drivers, cars, and buses to give way as he moved across lanes. Breach, once or twice, looked behind, trying to make out faces inside taxis and samlors. But he saw no sign of either Crosby or Ross. So this would be the tone of the journey, thought Breach. Suda somewhere ahead, alone, leaning forward, and shouting directions, suggestions, and orders. While he looked over his shoulder wondering at what odd hour of the day or night another mediocre bottle of claret might appear.

From Bangkok, Suda booked the guest house off a narrow sub-soi with large, green grounds that sloped down to the muddy banks of the Ping River. Modern rooms and plumbing, freshly mowed lawns with beach chairs, a restaurant beside the river, and three or four dogs that pranced around the grass, driveway, and nuzzled guests as they strolled past the main desk.

Another unasked question between Suda and Breach was answered at the check-in desk. Suda booked separate rooms on different floors. The simple act of filling out the form cleaned the air. Separate train berths, samlors, and hotel rooms. This woman was more than able to communicate her intentions. Breach thought about asking her about Crosby and Ross. Had she known they were on the train? But he sensed his timing was wrong. He hated early morning explanations, suspicions, and lies. He felt Crosby and Ross would force Suda into one of those predictable categories.

Above all, Breach sensed the truth was some distance away, and it would find him, as it always had.

He shifted through the possibilities that could be excluded: midnight shifting around rooms, romance and promises, and preoccupations and disillusionment. Sex had not been his reason for the trip, he reminded himself. Staying out of the path of Asanee's colonel had been one reason. He might not have gone if Suda had not held out the promise of something he wanted. She had showed him some rare, fine ancient artifacts from hilltribe shamans; she knew shamans living in the old way in remote northern villages. He told himself he had signed on for the trip because he wanted a set of ritual knives. An old mentor and friend, Thomas Pierce, had requested the ancient shaman knives—not for fighting, for cutting food, or for self-protection. The shaman knives had a different, wholly mystical purpose: slaughter at a fixed time and location, to discard a life to catch the attention of the gods beyond a horizon which no one could enter. An urgent request had come through Pierce's wife in Oxford. The ritual killing knives spooked Suda. When she spoke of them, Breach could see the fear in her eyes. They evoked ghosts, for good or evil, they sliced a wound, opening a seam for those in one world to see and speak with those in another.

Suda had not slept well on the train. She tossed and turned in her berth. The noise and motion, and a mind that she would not shut down. The tracks curved, the car pitched, and she felt her heart beating in the dark. She heard voices; smelled food and wine. She had dreamed of ritual knives, ritual slaughter, and bodies that fled away into darkness with the loud clack of wings, hairy limbs, and a bright-red plumage. She opened her eyes in the morning soaked in sweat.

❖

Her father had nicknamed her Suda: his inspiration came from a Thai medicine for fever. As far as she knew, she was the only girl with that nickname in Thailand.

"It could've been worse," Breach said. "You could've ended up as penicillin."

Suda shrugged. "Or aspirin," she said.

"I never met anyone named after a drug before."

"My father like very much. Also its the name of a flower."

If women were thought of as a commodity, it was an easy extension to name them after a product, drug, or flower thought Breach. He kept his thoughts to himself. There was an invisible hard edge where humor ended and criticism began; one was the surface, the other the core below the surface; and, in Thailand, the culture placed a barrier beyond the surface. Even with someone like Suda who from an early age had been a "rebel"—a word she found in her Thai-English dictionary.

From age seven she sold water and juice in plastic bags at the train station. She was one of travelling band of young faces racing along the train platform, tugging at passengers' sleeves, eyes large and clear, and begging in the way only a child can evoke sympathy. At age thirteen, a turning point in her life occurred. There had been a family crisis. Her aunt, her father's sister, had a baby who had become very ill. Suda was sent to her aunt's house in another town. A few weeks later the aunt's baby died. When Suda asked her father to return home, he looked at her long and hard: "Why don't you like my sister? You want me to lose face." The message was clear. "You are disposable like toothpaste. I can always buy another tube. My sister needs you to brush her soul clean. So you stay as long as she wants. What you want does not matter and cannot matter."

Suda lived at her aunt's house through her teens, picking up her love of antiques, and finally leaving to attend university. She never recovered from the loss of her family; that her own father had refused to allow her back into the sanctuary of childhood. She had lost something in the fashion that women often lose in their relations with men, beginning with their fathers and continuing on the back of bedroom promises. Her exile was the first sign of what waited in the shadows, thought Breach. She hovered at street level leaning against a fast-moving storm like the little flower girl in his dreams.

Breach's mother had doubled up her bet by marrying his father, who was reputed to be the best card player in postwar England. The war had killed off his competition, his mother had joked. For better or worse, his father had failed in the grand style. The old man had gambled and lost the house, the furniture, wife and children, and his marriage. His mother cut her losses and left him. The loss did not break her; she was strong, ambitious, and calculated that she would find better odds at another table. She had been the same age as Suda, twenty-seven, when she made the break. And like Suda, his mother threw herself into her work which had been to find a new husband. Suda simply threw herself into her work as if it were her husband. She consumed silver with a sexual fervor, touching the bracelets, necklaces, stroking the long, silver chains, rubbing the hairpins until her finger pads knew only the sensuality of metal.

Suda had perfected a silent-movie walk; a scuttling movement that threw her carriage from side to side. She was schoolgirl-slim—the body of a teenager—a Thai Peter Pan who had refused to ever grow up. Her face bore the features of a teenage Mao and Burmese Buddha. She had Mao's little facial mole and round face, and the Buddha's oval-shaped eyes. Crosby had called her "an ancient girl" which had said more about Crosby than Suda. It had been difficult to image that Crosby had ever been a young child.

As they checked into the guest house, for the first time, Breach thought Suda's face and body possessed the perfect combination for her work. She moved unnoticed in dangerous places. She rolled across the landscape like a shadow belonging nowhere. She was like a Trojan horse waiting to be pulled inside the gates. He followed behind her, carrying his case, up the flight of stairs to their rooms. As she stopped to unlock her door, she looked at him, smiled, and quickly disappeared inside. He had a strange feeling that she was like a long fishing line towed by someone manning a boat in the distance; with pilots like Ross and Crosby in constant radio control. Ross and Crosby were like Breach's grandfather in the old days in London, lurking in the shallow waters for the big fish, half hidden in the shadows with a fistful of Bibles as bait.

Chapter 3

That first morning in Chiang Mai, Suda led Breach through half a dozen temples. In front of the last temple, two old women sold small brown birds caged in crude straw baskets. A person made merit—an installment payment on a ticket to a better life next time around—by purchasing a basket containing two or three birds and setting them free. Breach bought a cage, opened the door. He watched the birds fly out, circle in a wide arc over the temple gate. A few moments later they flew back into another cage on the vendor's table.

"Two minutes of merit is better than nothing," he said, watching the vendor close the cage. "They are like bats."

"You can pay again," said Suda.

"Until the birds are too tired to return?"

"Or until you have no more money."

They drank coconut water and ate the wet soft white flesh of coconuts broken open by a peasant woman bringing down a large knife four or five times. The temples bored Suda. She liked one or two of the traditional motifs on the exterior but they did not hold her interest for long. She was too restless to stand in one place for more than a minute. She was like the birds looking for a cage to fly back into.

At Wat Chedi Luang, under a blazing noonday sun, Breach walked toward a five-hundred-year-old chedi; weeds grew high from the tumbled down ruins; the chedi stones jutted out like tiny stair steps to an invisible room. Toward the bottom a dozen or so damaged Buddhas had been placed.

"Thais don't throw away broken Buddhas," she said. "It's very bad to throw away a Buddha."

"So they dump them on the chedi ruins," said Breach, thinking of the surface reality and the core truth. He knew that a person's perspective determined what was a garbage dump and what was a temple in ruins; what is throwing away and what is storing.

At Wat U Mong they ate noodles outside the main gate at a road stall. Suda knew the owner and chef, and went back and cooked her own lunch. She like launching surprise invasions into other people's kitchens. Once inside, she reached for a knife, cut up vegetables, pieces of chicken on a wooden cutting board, and exchanged gossip with the owner. Six years earlier, Suda had been with a puppet troupe, taking a roadshow throughout the north. She had once lived near Wat U Mong. Her old teacher still lived in a house near the main gate.

"Why did you leave the troupe?"

His direct question produced a direct hit. "Because teacher said he wanted to marry me."

"And you didn't?"

She tilted her head, and smiled. "I worry that maybe I become another of his puppets."

Inside the temple grounds, Suda steered a path toward one of the old caves. At the end of the cave, garlands of flowers were draped over a golden Buddha. The sweet smell of incense was in the air. Suda prostrated herself, bending forward from her creaking knees, then raising up, bent over touching her forehead to the cold stone three times. Breach waited a few feet away, cocking his head to the side, as he examined a framed painting—famous in Buddhism—of the Buddha's renunciation. The image of a man with a halo looking down at his sleeping wife and infant son a moment before he turns and walks away. He thought about the puppet master living in a house near the temple. The man who had proposed marriage to Suda. Looking at the renunciation he wondered if Suda had acted to beat the puppet master to the punch. There had been nothing risked and nothing that could be renounced. Standing in the cave beside Suda, it was as if he had never left Nepal.

Breach had seen this painting a thousand times; he had the scene on postcards which he had kept under his bedroll. The vision was the essence of Buddhism. Once he believed the picture had been drawn from his own life. Once he dreamt his life had been taken from art. But morons believed all kinds of strange things about the world, convinced themselves they were a clitoris, a genius and an immortal, and confused art and life until they went batty. In Tibet, travellers came to the mouth of his cave: Breach's home for six months—usually Canadian, English, Americans, carrying a backpack and asking him for the truth. Breach grinned each time, scratched his head, spit on the floor, and pointed at the bat shit.

"Tell us, friend, the meaning of life?" someone would ask.

"Any time a stranger calls me 'friend' he usually has a criminal record or, even worse, he turns out to be some kind of missionary."

They stared at Breach standing up to his ankles in the bat shit, then at him, and sometimes he would quickly remove his bridge plate, show them a postcard, and flash a wide, toothless smile. Most never understood what he had told them; most looked at the art with a vacant, unknowing stare. The message was there in every temple in Asia. A single image that separated Buddhism and the East from Christianity and the West, thought Breach.

The answer was clear from a glance at the religious paintings. The Christian image of the baby Jesus gently held in the arms of his mother; his father looking on with adoration. The Buddhist image was of the renunciation of the family. Without that first step, there could be no enlightenment; while the Christian art affirmed the family as the way to salvation. Each celebrated a sacred act. Each believed they had the right vision. Breach never looked at the painting without remembering his father's abandonment. Breach had been a boy. His boyhood was filled with a large pool of shame, hurt, rejection, and fear. The usual emotional boils of a broken home. He waited for something to happen. His mother, no longer a tiny flower girl, answered personal advertisements placed by Canadians seeking an English mail-order bride. Ordering women like toothpaste. England had been ruined by the war; everyone wanted a fresh start.

"What if the Buddha hadn't left his palace and family?" he asked Suda, as she rejoined him. "And he invited his disciples around to the house and had his wife bake cakes for afternoon teas?"

"Not possible. Buddha cannot have a woman. Cannot be touched," she said.

"Your father abandoned you," Breach said, looking at the painting.

She didn't reply.

"My father abandoned me when I was seven," added Breach. "He gambled me away in a poker game. I was another chip on the table. He thought it was a sure bet. Only he was wrong."

Suda thought about his explanation; she glanced at the painting again. "Okay for Buddha to go. Not good for ordinary man to leave family. Unless he become a monk," she said.

Breach smiled, thinking of his father as a monk. Of course, that never happened—or could it have happened and he never knew it? When Breach turned eight he had a new name, father, school, friends and lived far away from England in a small village on Vancouver Island. Thirteen years later, he returned to England as a student at Oxford.

40

He placed personal messages in the newspaper for his lost father. He never got a reply.

After they left the cave—Breach had wanted to spend the rest of the day inside and left only when promised a surprise of unusual beauty—Suda dragged him across the grounds to a bronze statue of Buddha racked with suffering and pain; the ribs showed, the veins ran up and down the arms, and the eyes were large and hollow holes. The impression was more of a Nazi concentration camp victim than the serene smiling Buddha. This was a skin-and-bones Buddha with wild eyes.

"I like it very much," said Suda. "It is extremely beautiful."

"First you axe the family, then starve yourself," Breach said.

"It's very beautiful," she whispered.

There was in this state of starvation a sense of beauty that was strangely moving for her. Something akin to hope rose from that image.

"This is it? This is what I left the cave for? The thing of usual beauty?" Breach asked her, as she circled the Buddha image.

"I bring myself. You come along. I come to remember. The puppet teacher asked me to marry him on this spot. He knew this place make me happy."

"Are you happy you told him no?" asked Breach.

She smiled, turned away from the Buddha. "Now we see the shaman about the knives."

Under an intense afternoon tropical sun, Suda negotiated with the driver of a small red van. The plan was to drive to a mountain hilltribe village. With a worn-out suspension system the red van bounced up and down over a dusty road eroded by deep horizontal gullies; as if a giant hand had thundered down with hundreds of karate chops breaking deep into the earth. Doi Pui, a Hmong village, was five kilometers above Doi Suthep temple. The dirt road had been cleaved out the forest leaving a brutal brown scar, wide, ugly, and naked as a ski run in mid-July. Halfway up, a jeep with the steering rod broken was disabled along the side. A *farang* who turned out to be Crosby stood on the side as the driver fiddled with the engine of a jeep. Ross sat in the driver's seat, his hands clutching the steering wheel, his mouth twisted into massive rebuke. The jeep was pulled off and tilted at a sharp angle to one side as if it might fall off the mountain.

Crosby saw the van and waved. Breach waved back, turning in his seat. "Stop," Breach ordered the driver, who pulled ahead of the disabled jeep. Suda told the driver to back up and pull alongside. As the jeep approached, Ross had a look of bemused surprise and shouted at the Thai driver. "Fix this machine immediately. I have an important appointment. My clients hate lawyers who are late."

The van stopped and Breach leaned out of the window, Suda sitting on his left. "Car trouble?"

"Can someone explain to this man in Thai," began Ross, who suddenly broke off. "Jesus Christ. This asshole can't distinguish a busted distributor from a water pump leaking piss."

"I can't say that I can," said Breach, smiling. He glanced over at Suda. "He's a lawyer from Bangkok," he whispered, as if that explained everything.

"Mind giving us a ride?" asked Ross. "Crosby will pay you. Clients always picked up the expenses."

Breach glanced at Suda who nodded her assent. "Legal business in the mountain, Ross?"

Ross ignored the question. "I need a drink. I assume these hilltribe people sell booze as well as illegal drugs."

"But the quality of pâté is low," said Breach, catching Crosby's eye.

On the way up the mountain, Suda spoke Thai with Crosby.

"She says finding these knives may be difficult," said Crosby. "Collectors have picked Thailand clean."

Breach turned around and looked at Crosby sitting in the back with Suda. "She means expensive."

"You may not speak Thai, but you are starting to think in Thai," said Crosby, laughing.

Robert Tuttle, who ran the English language school, was another friend and customer. Several times she had delivered a spirit lock or other hilltribe silver piece. Crosby had known Suda for years; he had introduced Breach to her.

"What kind of lawyer are you, Khun Ross?" she asked as the van reached the top.

"Commercial law. The law of merchants, gamblers, and professional con artist. Law's really my sideline, if you insist on knowing the truth."

"What is your main line?"

"Darts and booze and extremely cooperative women," said Ross.

At the crest, a wide, level dirt parking area was congested with red vans and jeeps. Hilltribe kids and women hawked crafts out of trays as the tourists streamed into the village or circled back carrying native handbags and carvings to cars and coaches parked in the large, dusty gravel lot. A paved footpath led from the parking lot and into the village. Both sides of the path were lined with rows of stalls selling cheap carpets, shirts, baskets, fake silver, and trinkets.

"It's like a Disneyland theme park," said Ross.

Hmong merchants came around from the back of their stalls, called out, and chased after tourists. Two Hmongs approached Crosby and spoke to him in Thai; he waved for Ross to follow them.

"But do they have a bar?" asked Ross, smiling.

"Stocked with *Old Grand-Dad*," said Crosby. "But no darts."

"Tell them they won't be big-time until they get darts. And don't forget. Cooperative women. That's very important, too."

"I'll tell them," said Crosby. He walked over to Breach, patted him on the shoulder. "See you later."

"We should have a talk."

"Later," said Crosby, walking away.

"Booze," shouted Ross. He clenched his fists.

They had disappeared into the crowd. Breach and Suda carried on walking uphill through the village which was terraced on the side of a mountain. An old shaman with a weathered face dressed in a tan shirt and black trousers appeared; a *maw pee*—as the Thais call their witchdoctors—approached her from a side lane. The Hmong man emerged from a crowd and walked straight toward her. No more than two minutes earlier, Suda had asked one of the vendors leaning over the stall if they might talk to the village shaman. And a moment later, a shaman, chewing a plug of tobacco, tapped her on the shoulder. He looked Breach over, then motioned for them to follow; he led them away from the tourist area, down the back lanes, and along a narrow dirt path cut in the back side of the mountain. The real village, hidden away, private, secluded; the Hmong village for the Hmongs. A place without any foreigners shopping. There was nothing to sell. Small children with caked snot streaked across their faces played with bottle caps in the dirt. Women nursed babies and sewed.

The shaman and his family lived in a wooden house above the village. His wife, swatting flies, squatted on the bamboo veranda outside the front door. Her tired, wrinkled face watched Breach. When she smiled, a red rim of betel-nut stain that began on her lips spread back to her gums and the red turned to a dusky powdery brown forming a paste over what remained of her teeth. The shaman showed them inside the house. There was no electricity. A hard, damp red earth floor disappeared into darkness at the edge of the room. Right of the door glowing embers burned in a charcoal pit. A circle of black enclosed the fire; and in the center, metal grills held a heavy, thick kettle and a couple of pots. Opposite the fire, built into the wall, was a long, wooden platform covered with straw mats—the family sleeping quarters. The center of gravity of the room was a corner near the fire. Breach sat on a fold-up chair at a small wooden table. Suda squatted close to the fire as if to warm herself.

Rays of afternoon sunlight pierced the thatched roof. Laser-thin shafts of light struck the earth floor here and there. Small circles of dusty light never bigger than a thumbprint tailed off into darkness in the place where the shaman stored his ceremonial equipment. In that place, the earth sweated, leaving damp rings. The shaman spit out his chew of tobacco and took out a pack of cigarettes. He offered Breach a cigarette. Breach took one and held the cigarette between his fingers; a moment later, Breach had made the cigarette disappear. He had Suda open her shoulder pack and, much to the Shaman's amusement, she produced the missing cigarette. Breach returned it and with a flip, the end suddenly glowed red and a column of white smoke rose.

"I don't smoke," he said.

The shaman patted his own chest. He took a long puff from the cigarette and slowly exhaled, speaking in rapid Thai.

"He smoke since boy," Suda said, translating for the shaman. "He says, he cough all the time now. Too old to stop. He chews but it's not the same. He always goes back to the cigarette. It's a devil for him. And he like your magic very much. Now he want to show you something."

The shaman walked over to three shelves five feet off the floor. Each shelf held the instruments of his trade, which included acting as the village medicine man. There was no sign of the traditional staff, or ceremonial knives, or book, or special clothes. He dressed in a regular cotton shirt with large white and gray stripes. He wore traditional Hmong trousers. His specialty was chasing out evil spirits from village children who had become ill.

"Ask him how he heals the children," Breach said, looking directly into his eyes as he spoke to Suda.

He nodded as Suda took time to explain. "He says that a secret. But he may joke. *Farang* think healing a secret. Healing is catching spirit. Finding what he want. Why he attack you."

The shaman rose from his chair, walked over to the shelves, and pulled off a set of worn water buffalo horns. On the wall next to the shelf was a calendar turned to March. The photograph nailed to the wall was not another piece of temple art; it was the annual Patpong wall calendar. Twelve months of nude go-go dancers filmed on beaches, in bars, in cars, tuk-tuks, and on beds. One of the Patpong girls, large, firm breasts, balanced against a polished silver pole on the dance platform as she smiled into the camera. Miss March stared into the dimly lit room with a frozen smile beside the shaman's shelf. Crosby had claimed he once had played *Hey, Jude* on her clavicles with drum sticks and that Miss March had once attended Tuttle's English school in Bangkok.

The shaman caught Breach looking at the calendar.

"He say," said Suda, "maybe you make her appear like cigarette."

Breach looked the old shaman in the eye. "Tell him I'm working on toothpaste."

Suda blushed, turned and told the shaman, "Next life, maybe possible."

The shaman demonstrated his method for predicting a child's chance of survival. He picked up several water buffalo horns—which had been cut in half—and tossed them on the floor. He knelt beside the halves.

"He say, position of pieces determined the fate of the child. If halves side by side, child have life."

46

"And if they land this way?" asked Breach, switching the direction of the horns.

The old shaman scratched his chin and studied the new alignment. "He say, this position—see halves are crossed—means the bad thing. Maybe not have more life."

He sucked on his cigarette and nodded as Suda explained to Breach. His wife, who had slipped unheard into the room, quietly sat in the far corner, watching what she had witnessed over thousands of betel nuts. The old woman was absorbed in the ceremony. Breach saw her staring at the pieces of water buffalo horn. Suda would never make it as a shaman's wife, he thought. The awe of magic and the awe of selling objects for magic acts were different realities, different worlds, and different ground rules applied. Rarely, if ever, did the talent for both reside in the same person. The talents stood in contradiction, and so it became a choice that ultimately had to be made between them. It came down to show business or business-business.

"He ask if you want to wear Hmong clothes," said Suda.

He held out a pair of baggy black cotton pants. Breach slipped them on over his jeans and stood with his hands on his hips; he glanced up at Miss March—hearing the tune *Hey, Jude* go through his mind, then leaned down and picked up the water buffalo horns. One by one he made them disappear as the shaman sat, smoking cross-legged in the metal chair next to Suda.

"Where are they?" asked Suda, who had translated the question from the old shaman, whose eyes searched the room.

Breach nodded toward the shelf below Miss March. The old shaman ran over and discovered the horns lined up side by side beneath the calendar.

"Good luck?" Breach asked.

He laughed, looking up from the horn pieces, as Suda translated. "He say you can come back and stay in his house if you want. You can sleep there. No problem. He show you much more. You have much to show him. He wants you to keep his clothes. He thinks good luck for him if you wear."

"Tell him we are the same size."

The shaman grinned; he didn't need a translation. He spoke without stopping for several minutes to Suda. His hands squeezing the buffalo horns. The old woman cut another slice of betel and slipped it into her mouth, rocking back and forth, listening to her husband speak.

Finally, he stopped, cocked his head, and waited for Suda to translate. "He say he have friend with knives you want. His friend a Mein. He do this because he like you and think you have powerful magic. He want to help you. This Mien married to his mother's cousin. And he has stall in Chiang Mai market. You go there tonight and he sell you." Suda paused for a second, and leaned closer to Breach. "I know this friend. I buy from him before. Sometimes he has very good things." A smile crossed her face. "I think your magic work very good for you."

Chapter 4

In the evening Breach and Suda walked east of the *Mae Kha* Canal through the Night Bazaar. Ross and Crosby had not reappeared and presumably remained on the mountain with their disabled jeep. Breach made an educated guess: Ross was slumped over a table, sleeping beside a tipped-over bottle of *Old Grand-Dad* and Crosby was curled up into the fetal position, smoking opium in one of the long, wooden houses overlooking a sea of poppy flowers. Neither Breach nor Suda mentioned their absence. The two men had fallen—angels was not exactly the right word—out of memory.

The market in Chiang Mai was a maze of cheap restaurants, and floors crammed with small craft, antique, and clothing shops. Hilltribe teenaged girls sold women's handbags, skirts, shirts, blouses, and bedspreads. Suda darted from stall-to-stall, knowing each vendor by name, their sisters, brothers, mothers, fathers, and cousins. Commerce in the north had a kinship connection; a web of interconnected and overlapping networks of family and friendship. Thais disliked doing business with strangers. Outside the network you might be cheated, lied to, or taken advantage of. The "yellow pages" culture had not arrived; it was a word-of-mouth culture—and whatever that word was about you or your family stayed with you for life.

"He just friend. Not lover," Suda said, glancing back at Breach. Given Breach's odd appearance—the black hair, odd-looking front teeth, skinny arms and neck, no one doubted her disclaimer. Within one or two days, Suda knew, word would have preceded her about her companion. She laid the groundwork carefully, taking the initiative, making disclaimers, and keeping a professional distance from Breach.

"He's a teacher," she said. The Thai admired and respected teachers; they were an acceptable kind of companion.

"What he teach you?" one of the shop owners asked her, with a giggle.

"I teach her magic," said Breach. "She's learning how to make me disappear." Her friend smiled at Breach and translated for a couple of other friends who had gathered around the stall.

Suda slapped his arm, shot him a hard look, then looked back at her friend. "He make a joke. Always joking."

"Tell them you like my magic," he said, smiling as he pulled a large one-baht coin from her ear.

Suda's friend squealed with delight; in an automatic reflex, like a child front-row at the circus, the friend covered her mouth with both hands, her eyes as large as the full moon. As they walked away, Suda was unusually quiet. She stopped near a stall stacked with jeans and tank tops.

"How you do that? With the coin?"

"All it takes is practise." Breach said.

"You teach me?"

"Maybe," he said, eyes staring directly into hers.

"Thais don't like maybe."

"Most people don't. That's why most people are unhappy. They like the promise magic makes; that you can master the art of making a thing disappear and reappear. It's called power. Most people need three things in life: control and certainty and predictability. What they get are cheap tricks and a lot of maybe's."

"Maybe you think too much," said Suda.

"So I've been told."

Hunger had overtaken them. Before dinner, Suda spoke with an old man, a Mien tribe member, thin neck, large head, and deep gun-barrel-blue eye sockets. The old man stood stoop-shouldered beside a table of blankets. Three women huddled in a semicircle on folding beach chairs eating rice mixed with pork rind from a common bowl. He had been expecting her; the message about the strange *farang* had reached him from the hilltribe mountain village.

A week earlier she had sent a message through a friend that a *farang* was interested in buying a full set of ritual shaman knives. The *farang* was Richard Breach. She whispered to one of his relatives that she could signal the old Mien to go ahead with the sale. It was a long-drawn process; never a straightforward, this is what is wanted and this is what it costs. Always the dance among the interlocking circles of families scattered over mountains and through valleys.

Thomas Pierce, who had been Breach's tutor at Oxford, lay dying of stomach cancer. Breach received a distraught letter from Pierce's wife, Marianne—Pierce was too ill to write. With Breach's mother long dead, and a father long gone, the Pierces had become his surrogate family. In her letter, Marianne described a break-in at their North Oxford house. Thieves cleaned out Thomas Pierce's collection of shaman artifacts. The collection had been fully insured and a claim had been made. With Thomas dying of cancer, the insurance proceeds could not replace what had been lost. He grieved over the loss of the ritual knives; they were sacrificial instruments, priceless possessions for a dying man with certain mystical beliefs and wishing to communicate with the gods in the next world.

In the old folklore of some hilltribes, it was believed that when a shaman died, if he were buried with his knives, then

51

in the next world he could present them to the gods who would show their pleasure at the gift and he would return in the next life as a great shaman. Pierce had lived with the myths and legends long enough that they became infused with his own beliefs about death. Pierce had meant to be buried with his shaman's knives. The letter had been a factual report of what had happened. Neither Marianne nor Thomas had asked Breach for anything. He loved them for that. Through Robert Tuttle, he was introduced to Suda and, within three weeks, she had a couple of leads but she warned him that finding a full set of genuine ritual knives was difficult, if not impossible. Collectors had descended on Thailand, and had carried away most ancient shaman artifacts. What remain in the markets were second-rate reproductions which were aged with chemical. But there was always a chance one or two pieces had been overlooked.

On top of the old Mien's stall, Breach saw a shaman staff: the kind shaman's used in various burial rituals. He recognized it as similar to one in Pierce's private collection. It had hung on the wall behind Pierce's desk in his rooms in college. Breach saw that beside the staff, the old Mien had laid out like fish' n' chips in old newspaper four ritual knives for animal sacrifice. The knives appeared genuine. Breach rushed over and picked up the largest of the knives. It was caked with rust as if it had been buried in the core of the earth. He held it to a naked light bulb which hung from a cord above the stall. The knives had red and blue ribbons tied through a hole in the handle; they were large-bladed and heavy. He imagined such instruments being used for ritual killing. The two kilos of sharp metal slitting the throat of a goat or water buffalo. He pulled out photographs he had taken at the museum in Bangkok. Carefully, he examined the knives against the photographs. The knives in the market matched the ones in the museum.

Breach gripped one tightly, lifted it from the newspaper, and studied the contour of the blade. He thought of Thomas and his suffering. Stomach cancer was a hard way to die. Opening the throat was much easier; it was over fast. Slowly Breach laid the knife back, and turned to the old man who had not removed his eyes from his examination of the knives.

"They're genuine?" he asked Suda.

She wrinkled her nose at the knives. Arms folded beneath her breasts, she stepped forward. Then she picked up one of the smaller knives, examined the blade, handle, and touched the tip of her tongue to the blade tip.

"I think real." She spoke to the old Mien in Thai. He nodded and grunted as she cross-examined him closely.

"What did you tell him?" Breach asked.

"I said you very powerful man. You can make things disappear. And if he lie to you, maybe you make him disappear. Might be a good idea to show him your coin trick."

After the illusion, the old Mien swallowed hard, his yellow, broken teeth frozen in a nervous smile. His wife's cousin had sent word about Breach's magic. He was a believer in an invisible world—a location outside of time and space where worldly objects and people mingled, exchanged energy, and returned to earth looking the same but radically changed. Sacrificial knives were of that other world and this created risks and dangers. Selling such objects, like selling Buddha images, was always mixed with elaborate taboos and fear—it was not a standard commercial transaction. No one involved wanted to think too deeply about what was being sold, what the selling might trigger elsewhere or in another life. The unseen forces of that place might be offended by a transaction mediated by cash. To cause offense was to risk revenge in this life or the next.

The old man's name was Kaeng, and his index and middle finger were yellow from smoking cigarettes down to the filter. He reached over and picked up the staff. He handed it to Breach, then lit a cigarette, coughing and speaking to Suda in Thai.

This was an avoidance technique. The old Mien was playing for time, offering the ritual staff. Something in his eyes suggested he was afraid. Suda pressed him again about the authenticity of the knives. He coughed, a deep-hacking, smoker's cough, half turned, and spit in the dirt. His eyes rested on the knives for a long moment. Slowly he looked away from the knives, finding Suda's eyes, and then Breach's. He nodded. Breach needed no translation.

"He says he wants three thousand for the knives," Suda said, turning away from the old man. "I think he come down to two thousand for the knives. But we eat first. *Hue kaow*. I'm hungry. Then come back. I think better."

Breach had a strong feeling in his gut that it was the wrong moment to break off the negotiation. He did not wish to bargain over price. He nearly pulled out three thousand baht, handed the money to the old Mien, and walked away with the knives. They were in better condition than the ones Thomas Pierce had lost in the house break-in. Suda had laid her judgment on the line; she thought it was better to come back after dinner. She had gone to elaborate trouble to set up the deal. Another hour mattered little, thought Breach. He owed her some respect. Her face was on the line. If he contradicted her, she would lose her face. She had brought him this far; and without her, he could have run around in circles until Pierce had died. He played it over in his mind. Suda was asking him to trust her. If he didn't, she would take his rejection to heart; and Breach had decided breaking hearts to play for a hour or so of time was hardly ever worth it. And it wasn't worth it now.

"Tell him we're be back in thirty minutes." Breach made the coin disappear and reappear as Suda translated to the old Mien.

She spoke to the old man.

"You told him to wait?" asked Breach.

Farang did not understand business, she thought. "I tell him. Now we go."

What Breach saw in the old man's eyes as he glanced back was relief. The old man appeared to exhale as if his old, smoke-filled lungs had stopped from the moment they had arrived. The outstanding matters of business, the spirit world, and the unspoken link between the intermediaries of that world and this one were left suspended for a meal break.

It was important to Suda that her customers thought of her as honest; and trusted her sense of timing. She wanted people to like her; to think of her as a fair, honest person who had a good heart—*jai dee*. And, perhaps, above all, she liked thinking of herself as competent in her work and about human behavior. Breach had struck a sensitive chord in her.

Having invested a couple of days trailing along after her, Breach had observed how small her profit margin was on most sales. Nonetheless, once or twice, she would take advantage of a customer, who was a stranger; selling off a second-rate piece for more than it was worth. Or palming off earrings made of plastic as tortoiseshell. She was not perfect, in other words, yet she wanted to come close to perfection in the eyes of people she accepted into her life for more than a single transaction. Breach was not an ordinary customer; he had been introduced by Robert Tuttle, and she owed Tuttle a great deal.

Suda headed in a straight line for a dingy outside restaurant run by Thais from the northeast. She greeted everyone. The cook immediately recognized her with a big smile, looking up from the pieces of fish and chicken cooking on an open grill above a bed of red-hot coals. Pots of white steamed rice and small bowls of red peppers were stored next to a stack of plates. Suda ordered, pointing at each piece of fish or chicken. The smell of fire and fish and garlic mingled in the heavy night air. Waitresses with sweat-streaked faces broke into wide smiles as Suda inspected the food.

Breach sat across from Suda at an old card table with uneven legs. Above the table a color television set was tuned in to a nighttime soap opera. A baby in a nappy slept in a cot an arm's length away. Tiny toes twitching, the small head turned towards the fan, her front locks blowing back.

As the food arrived, Suda looked up words in her Thai-English dictionary; her mind could not stop for food. She had a fierce desire to learn English, and above all to make herself understood. By the time they had finished dinner and returned to the bazaar, the old Mien, Mr. Kaeng, had vanished into the night with his blankets and shaman's staff and ritual knives. Breach looked visibly upset; he said nothing, as he clutched the edge of the empty table, his knuckles going white. He looked away from her.

Showing anger was the one single thing Thais avoided at just about all cost. Breach knew this. It was something Robert Tuttle told him the first day he arrived to teach at the school. "Never lose your temper with the Thais. Never show impatience or anger. Or you'll pay a price far greater than you ever dream possible. Always keep smiling even when you see the blade coming at you."

He tried not to think of Pierce, he waited until the image faded before he turned around and showed his face. He collected himself gradually.

"Maybe the old man didn't like my magic," he said, smiling.

"I know him. He get very tired and go home," she said. "He's an old man. No power left. He sick from smoking too much."

The world was, in his own words, an unpredictable place. "Or he changed his mind," said Breach. "He got scared."

She joked, "Maybe you should wear Hmong pants."

"A shaman fashion show," said Breach, making a joke as well. "You're right. He decided not to sell knives to someone with my tailoring and dental work."

Suda relaxed a little and her faced softened; she liked the way he handled himself. Although he was upset, Breach had let an emotion—the greed of possession and the withdrawal of the possession—pass without showing anger. He hadn't caused her to lose face by suggesting that she was to blame. Suda ran over to another stall. Two Hmong girls greeted her warmly; she gave one of them a 100-baht note. When Suda returned to Breach, she was not smiling. A non-smiling Thai is a sign something has gone wrong.

"They tell the Mien to keep staff till we get back Friday."

"What about the knives."

Suda flushed, her mouth turned hard. "She say *farang* buy them. Never mind. I find you another set. Can do."

For an uncomfortable moment, Breach said nothing. He had a feeling when they returned and the old man had fled into the night that the knives had been lost. He reached into his pocket for a large one-baht coin. He flipped it in the air and made it disappear.

"The knives are in the same hole as the coin," said Breach.

Suda tried to smile. "You a very smart man. I think you know where to look for that hole."

The need to possess, the greed of holding, touching, and collecting had, for a brief moment, bored straight through him, and he hated himself for the way he reacted as if the loss of the knives meant anything real. He hated that Thomas Pierce was dying; that thieves broke into his house; and that, in the end, Pierce had it in his mind that going to his grave with a set of rusty knives would make a difference. Breach had been persuaded to come along on the journey for a set of objects fused with magic; he had never travelled to gain an object before. In his mind, it had been this fixed destination that had been the purpose for all of his actions. But had it been the primary reason? Someone had tried to kill him in Bangkok? Crosby had asked to go upcountry as well. Tuttle had wanted something in the north—as secret and magically as anything Pierce had lost. Ross wanted him to play cards. Breach felt the fool because his actions were beginning to fracture and lose meaning. In the cave, the meaning had remained constant, fixed; nothing was lost or forgotten, fake or real, scared or assured. In the market, Breach learned in that doing the best one could, it was easy to find and lose what he was looking for all in the space of an hour. Nothing was anchored. Having been deprived of what he sought, he wandered off down the corridor of empty stalls. Suda let him go; he needed to be alone. She started to call after him, but stopped herself.

When she returned to the guest house, she found him sitting alone halfway up the staircase that overlooked the river. She stood above him a long time before she said anything.

"I'm very sorry," she said. "You look so sad."

Breach looked over his shoulder. "I miss the bats. I should have stayed in Nepal. Besides, they were a set of old rusty knives."

"But they for your friend."

Breach thought about the mental and emotional disorders that overtake people who know they are dying. In England, dying had to be staged; makeup, lighting, props—everything but a rehearsal. In Kathmandu, the bodies, wrapped in white cotton, were cremated on a concrete platform beside the river; the ashes swept into the water upstream from where people bathed, washed clothes, and drank.

"The knives wouldn't help his pain."

"He sick?"

"Dying." He pulled a lit match out of thin air, leaned forward and blew it out. "That's dying. Nothing more."

She stood on the step above him looking at the moonlight on the river for several minutes, and then without saying anything left for her room. In the morning, they were setting out early for a Lisu village about sixty kilometers north of Chiang Mai. By the time Breach picked up his room key, it was after two. In a few hours it would be dawn. He thought about the old Mien's lined face in the harsh light of the naked bulb. The look of surrender on the tired old face after he had performed the coin illusion. It was the surrender to the unknown; the surrender to death. Whoever had come into the market and bought those knives must have paid a great deal of money to the old Mien to override the fear Breach had instilled in a single flash of a coin being and then nonbeing.

When Breach turned on the light in his room, he found Crosby sitting in a chair near the window. Crosby lit a cigarette, inhaled deeply, and watched Breach close the door and throw the room key on the bed. "You arrived without wine and pâté?" asked Breach, crossing in front of Crosby and walking into the bathroom.

"No, but Ross has some interesting cutlery," said Crosby, listening to Breach splashing water on his face. "A bit on the rusty side. Not exactly meant to cut into Oxford high table fare."

Breach came out of the bathroom stripped to the waist, drying his face with a hand towel. An image of a Buddha swung from a gold chain in the center of his chest. He threw the towel on the bed and stood over Crosby like a schoolmaster. Crosby was the kind of man who never completely shed the fifteen-year-old kid face, thought Breach. Only average in school, Crosby had been turned down by Oxford. In the last three months, Breach figured that Crosby had fitted an Oxford allusion into a conversation about twice a week; he wondered if Crosby held him, as a former teacher, partly responsible for his failure. A teacher who had gone to Oxford should have known how to get his student inside the gates of at least one of the more obscure colleges. No dice. Breach disappeared into the bathroom, spit in the sink, and emerged with a bottle of scotch wrapped in a towel. He walked over and sat on the edge of the bed opposite Crosby and poured scotch into two glasses.

"Why has Ross developed a sudden interest in ritual knives?" Breach asked. "Is this a new twist to the game of darts?"

Crosby snubbed out his cigarette in the glass ashtray and took one of the glasses. "I'm afraid they suggest the act of a desperate man. I tried to talk Ross out of it. But have you ever tried to talk a Yank out of anything?"

"I don't play poker. Doesn't he understand?"

"He understands he can't force you."

"But using extortion is okay."

"Richard, he has hardly resorted to extortion. The knives were there for anyone to buy. You could've bought them. Ross was faster. It was a legitimate transaction, and I assure you he paid more than a fair price."

Breach held up his hand for Crosby to stop. "You're beginning to sound like Ross. Why is Ross so keen about me playing cards? Can't he play himself?"

Crosby lit another cigarette, coughed into his hand, his face turning reddish. "Ross play poker? You must be joking?"

"I'm not who the joke's on."

"Ross is tired of being a lawyer," said Crosby, swallowing the rest of the scotch. "Mid-life crisis, you might call it. He hates his life. One day he woke up with a massive hangover, looked at himself in the mirror, and puked. A middle-aged, overweight, balding lawyer whose life was basically no different from your average ambulance chaser in L.A. or New York. He had this middle-class life, job, and clients. In Bangkok, everyone he knew was making a great deal of money in the stock market, land deals, joint ventures. And Ross is fed up looking in at the gold from the outside. The game is his way inside. And you are the key."

"And betting ten grand at a poker table is going to put him on the inside?" Breach refilled Crosby's glass, and sat back on the bed. "What else has he got working?"

Crosby smiled. "Ross always has something else."

"For instance."

"The game is for a lot of money."

"How much?"

"Hundred thousand. Half a million. That range."

"Forget it, Crosby," said Breach, rising from the bed.

"You play a couple of hands. You can fold whenever you want. No obligation to stay in. You get the knives and 30 percent of the winnings; he foots the losses. You've got nothing to lose, Breach."

"What's your end?" Breach watched Crosby collect himself, looking down at the ash hanging on the end of his cigarette.

"A bit of cash," he said.

"Why do I have the feeling there's more than cash involved?"

"Remember at school you told us about the difference between great and good card players? You said each generation produced one or two great players; sometimes none. You told us that your father was one of the greats."

Breach remembered this lecture. It was at a school outing and he and Crosby wandered off to a pub. A card game was going in the back. Crosby confessed that he had, during a music lesson, acquired a nasty, resistant strain of VD. Breach saw an opportunity; he told Crosby about his father, and together they planned a trip to London for a game of cards and show-and-tell.

"Ian Howard was one of the great English card players during the 40's," said Crosby. "And Richard, his son, threw away his talent. He went on to Oxford D.Phil and a career of spreading dissent and rebellion among private schoolboys in a half-dozen schools. Richard had perfected his execution and had the rare ability to count cards. Am I getting warm, Richard? And for the last two years in a Nepal cave, in between watching the bats, you played cards. Thousands and thousands of hands. Maybe millions of hands. Who knows?"

"I should have never told you," Breach said.

What Breach had withheld from Crosby that afternoon in the pub of was of greater importance. In Bangkok, he had withheld the same information a second time. Beyond such a large talent loomed something far darker, more difficult to surmount; the next step was a quantum distance—the great player had an inherited trait; one that enabled them to bring a degree of unpredictability to the table. They could make the cold-blooded decision to risk a substantial sum to throw the opponent off; to cause the opponent to distrust his own judgment, to destroy the confidence and faith in his own reason, rattle him until he no longer trusted himself. The great player understood the need to create chaos and confusion; then the range of his play was beyond expectation. Any card was possible; anything might happen. At night in the cave, when he dreamt someone was calling his name, he would wake up sweating in his childhood bed and seeing his father's shadow leaving the house for the last time.

Ian Howard, his father, had this rare quality. He placed the house, the furniture, the kids' toys on the table. With such a man one could never be certain whether he was bluffing or he held the cards. Without that ability to carve rough-edged doubts into the mind of the opponent, the player might be technically brilliant but a great player would defeat him every time. Breach as a child dreamt of his father sitting in the back of a pub holding his cards. A tall man who sat expressionless, no sign of sweat, emotion, no tricks up his sleeve, slowly pushing a signed piece of paper which carried the family house with it.

"Tell Ross to keep in touch," said Breach.

Crosby stood in the door as if he were trying to remember something. "Ross is a little crazy."

"People trying to buy themselves a new life usually are."

The next morning Breach knocked on Suda's door. He waited, staring down at his feet. There was a long pause followed by the sound of bare feet on a wooden floor. Finally she opened the door a crack, her hair matted, a blanket wrapped around her.

"No sleep. Sorry. Suda get ready. Wait."

"Thought you'd be awake."

Her hair was a mess and she tried to brush it with the one free hand not holding up the blanket. "Meet you in restaurant." She closed the door without waiting for a reply.

It was hard enough for Suda stumbling around a foreign language when she was wide-awake; half asleep, her words became disjointed and sprayed with faulty vowel sounds; the syntax self-destructed; and she referred to herself in the third person—a very Thai way of talking. She was translating Thai into English inside a head still half asleep. There was a translation problem in every language; in every country, thought Breach walking away. He went downstairs, crossed the courtyard, where a western woman sat in a lawn chair reading a tattered paperback mystery, and took a table in the hotel restaurant overlooking the river. He ordered coffee and waited for Suda. Half an hour later she arrived, smiling, and sat down, smoothing back a wild patch of hair. She looked the same as before.

"Sorry I woke you," said Breach.

"I was afraid to sleep last night. *Pee* comes into the room. I think he have knives with blood on them," she said. "I do something bad to upset the *Pee*—the ghost."

Suda genuinely believed that the ghost of the *Maw Pee*—or shaman or witch doctor—whatever name one gives to these people—had come for her. Thomas Pierce on his deathbed would have understood, thought Breach.

"You had a bad dream," said Breach.

"No, you not understand. Not a bad dream. Not a dream. I speak true," she said, with a capital "T." "I felt ghost in the room. I too scared to sleep."

"I had a nightmare, too. Crosby was waiting in my room last night."

"A what?" She looked confused.

"Nightmare," he repeated.

He scanned a pocket dictionary, searching for the Thai word meaning nightmare. There was none. But he found the word dream. *Kwahm fahn* and added *mai! dee*, the Thai expression for bad.

"I say before not a dream," she said earnestly, searching his eyes, as if to try and figure out how anyone who would put so much importance on buying that set of ritual knives could possibly confuse a dream with a ghost.

"The ghost spoke to you?"

She sighed as if he were a simple child. "Ghost moaned all night. He screamed in pain. He cry out many times. I can smell the blood. I can see the knives."

She had felt a presence in her room. Something strange had entered her room during the night, and whatever this combination of sounds and smells was had stayed near her bed until the first crack of dawn. She said her room had been stifling hot. She had turned up the air conditioning and fan to maximum speed but the heat remained unbearable.

Suda blamed herself for offending the shaman's spirits. Buying and selling shaman relics had this risk. Unlike silver antiques, clothes, baskets, wooden cowbells, the world of ghosts and demons intersected the world of commerce at a certain point. And the old Mien's ritual knives crossed the line. In the business of hilltribe antiques, not only were relatives and family members involved in the preliminaries to a sale, the dead played a role in the kind of merchandise bought and sold. The dead and the living required appeasement. The dead had come, so Suda believed, in the night to remind her she had made a mistake.

"I tell Kaeng the knives must be *gow*—old. And I offer him a cheap price. Shaman's spirit hear me make a cheap price," she said, leaning over the breakfast table, staring out at the river.

"Don't worry about price," said Breach. "Kaeng got more than three thousand for the knives."

"I sweat and very afraid," she said, not listening to him. A waitress brought two cups of coffee and a plate of scrambled eggs for Breach. "I hear it near me all night."

She compressed her eight-hour terror, sweat streaming down her face and neck, into a few minutes of conversation. Her bumpy, hot journey through the spirit world was a warning, she thought. Punishment for bargaining with Mr. Kaeng, the old Mien. If Breach wanted to buy shaman relics, then she would have to be more careful, straightforward. She looked at Breach, wondering if he understood magic other than his own.

"*Mai poot len*, no make joke," she said. "Not any worry. Everything all right. I little tired. But young. Not old like you," she said, tapping his wrist with her forefinger.

"I thought you'd gone off joking," Breach said.

She cocked her head to the side with one of her wide toothy grins. "Only have to worry about Thai spirits. *Farang* spirits not very springy."

"Springy?"

"Stay in the ground when dead." She must have thought that Breach looked worried—and of course, she was right, he had taken her seriously. She grabbed his arm, and as quickly released it. Suda's touch never lingered to the point of misinterpretation.

"Joke. Joke."

Something in her expression of alarm that morning on the terrace overlooking the river suggested Suda's dreams about the knives rose from a realm where Thai jokes tried to create a distance. He didn't want to say he could give a name to the person who had the knives. It was too much like the quick pass with the coin; a kind of magic that creates awe, wonder, and a hunger for the answer of how it is done. As Breach handed money to the waitress for the bill, he asked the question which had been on his mind all morning.

"What did this ghost say?"

"*Ooooooh gra dae*," said Suda. She didn't translate into English the meaning of *gra dae*—a shallow woman who loves makeup, sexy clothes and, like a child, likes to talk and laugh. It was the kind of insult only a ghost might make, and someone with Suda's background take seriously.

"Could he have been moaning something that sounded like *Old Grand-Dad*?"

Suda shrugged her shoulders. "Not understand."

"I'm not certain Ross understands himself."

Chapter 5

The morning sun rose angry and hot, the heat jabbing and hitting with kidney punches. Breach ached, looking at the river, dull, languid brown and still, motionless, wanting to sleep. Sweat rolled down his face; he leaned over the terrace and threw a stone into the river. A small splash echoed. He wanted to break the surface calm, cause a ripple. On the terrace, cushioned by the shade of tall bamboo, he thought about his dying mentor in Oxford. What was Thomas Pierce's desperate hunger for the knives? Was he planning a shaman's death? Would they give him redemption? Or would the presence on his deathbed allow him to cut through the oppressive stillness of the approaching death? Breach threw another stone, another splash. The stillness returned in a few seconds; you might go a few rounds, he thought. But the unrelenting heat and the disturbingly calm river surface swallowed every punch, kick, elbow, and knee thrown at it. Why did Pierce feel the universe was any different from the river when it came to the fate of our bones and ashes?

The circle of the living and dead existed in the objects she bought and sold. Such objects had required appeasement of the spirits which guarded some things if her business was to continue to expand. And she could not forget to appease those in the network without whom she could not buy the special pieces. After breakfast Suda decided to buy gifts for Lahu hilltribe children who lived in the mountains north of Chiang Mai. She bought silver in the village. She darted through the bicycle, tuk-tuk, and bus traffic down a side street, crossed the street under a blowtorch sun and raced with the stamina of a long-distance runner in the curb lane. His sweat-soaked shirt clinging to his body, Breach followed a half step behind her.

"I talked with a friend in Mae Sai. I think he knows someone with shaman knives," she said, as Breach pulled alongside. His Adam's apple made a strange movement as if he were about to warble like a thrush.

"Crosby and Ross," he said, out of breath.

She smiled, weaving in and out of traffic without looking ahead. "One fat; one baby face."

"The fat one bought the knives last night. He's offered to sell them to me," said Breach.

Suda stopped and blocked Breach's path; she stood with her hands on her hips, head cocked to the side. Her smile was gone. She didn't sweat, thought Breach. Why didn't the sun affect her?

"Why you not tell me?"

"I didn't want to lose face," he said.

"*Farang* not lose face."

"Maybe some teeth," he said, lowering his upper bridge and moving it forward. "It's as bad as losing face. If you want to eat corn on the cob."

She stared at the bridge plate and a elastic droplet of sweat which was suspended from the end of Breach's nose; it dropped, splashing on his chin. He popped the bridge plate back into place. She giggled; the moment of anger passed as quickly as it had arisen. In those few seconds Suda realized she no longer had to carry the burden of failure and disappointment. The problem had been solved. The frustration of finding a second set of knives had ended. Thanks to the fat *farang*, she thought. She didn't ask Breach about the complications; she regretted ever getting involved with the sacrificial knives, and now, in the street, the incident could be forgotten. The ghost would not return; or, if it did, she could plead ignorance—the knives are Breach's business. She was off the cosmic hook.

She walked off, singing under her breath. She didn't look at traffic coming at high speed behind her. As a good Buddhist, she believed her destiny was set: either the tuk-tuk or motorcyclist would find a way around her or knock her down in the street injured or dead. The choice of her life or death was not her concern. In her mind it had already been decided. She had the feeling her destiny had improved that morning.

The local drivers shot around Breach and then Suda, like running an obstacle course; half-drugged by the rising heat and liquid amphetamines consumed on an empty stomach. The margin of error was small. Breach turned, walked backwards for a few seconds, staring the drivers in the eye; finding in their expressionless faces a vague, bored look— the vacant, unconscious stare of a man watching himself from outside his body.

Suda raced two or three steps ahead, glancing over her shoulder at Breach who had removed his shirt and used it like a matador with the tuk-tuk drivers. She waited, hands on her hips, until Breach stumbled into her. Without a word, she turned, bumping along in her Charlie Chaplin walk. She disappeared down a side street lined with rows of small shops that sold fabric, thread, and knitting supplies. She shot in and out of the first shop in under a minute. Inside the second shop, she covered the front window like a bank robber, all shoulders and hip joints moving as if a takeover operation was in process.

Breach slowly slipped on his shirt, as Suda hauled over a slender assistant and pointed out knitting yarn in the window. The clerk removed three strands of blue, red, and white yarn and handed them to Suda, who turned them over, stroked them. She tossed them one at a time to Breach, and picked up three more. Suda set her jaw—a boxer's superior flex—a tic Breach had noticed when she was antique hunting—it meant she wanted the goods and was running the math through her head. She had entered the strenuous second stage, bargaining the price.

Suda had two philosophies about bargaining. Always bargain hard. And after you bargain to the rock-bottom price, demand a ten percent discount. A bargained price and a discount were two separate transactions. She coiled herself, back slightly arched, surrounded the seller with her intense eyes. They either caved in with a shrug of the shoulders or back-pedalled for protection to either their boss or in the best bus-driving tradition fled the scene. An old Chinese woman lying on a cot blinked her watery eyes as she watched her assistant lose the battle with Suda over the three parcels of knitting yarn. The clerk couldn't keep his eyes off Breach juggling the colored balls of cotton, throwing them higher and higher until they almost touched the rotating ceiling fan. The old woman, a faint smile on her lips, came to life as she fanned herself; perhaps seeing a glimmer of herself half a century earlier in Suda's manner.

The old Chinese woman with liver spots on her face rose from the cot and smoothed down her crumpled dress over her sagging breasts. Suda didn't wait for the old lady to reach her; she launched her attack, holding up the yarn, and employed a rapid-strike strategy of smiles, jokes, a running narrative on the hilltribes, the hot weather, and how her mother, sisters, aunts, and cousins had bought much better yarn at a much lower price just last week two streets away. But it was hot, and she was willing to pay the extra five baht. The entire time the old Chinese woman, flashing a gold-toothed smile, watched Breach juggling the colored balls of yarn. She glanced at Suda and nodded. That was it. Deal done. Suda stuffed the yarn in her shoulder pack, and peeled off three ten-baht notes. A moment later, she was out the door, across the street, picking up and putting down children's toys like an inspector testing for quality and fun.

A plastic dump truck with a yellow dumper and red platform caught her eye. "I like this one. Big. Tough toy. Can do many things with. Fill with dirt. Fill with..." She ran out of language or, perhaps, it occurred to her that there might be limits as to what a hilltribe child might put inside the small dumper.

"Magic," smiled Breach.

Suda handed him the dump truck. "The old Chinese woman liked your juggling."

"Crosby, the baby-faced one, was once my student. In England, a long time ago."

Suda grabbed a grapefruit-sized soccer ball. She picked it up, squeezed it, handed it to Breach. "What did you teach him?"

"History."

She sniffed her nose at the soccer ball.

"Like very much. Many children can play. They no have toys like this. Very good, I think. You like?"

"And religion," said Breach. "I taught him history and religion." He held the ball in one hand. "The ball's a good idea," he added.

"Good idea," she said, smiling. "Like history and religion for baby-faced *farang*."

"Essential subjects for a gambler," said Breach, and with a flick of his wrist the ball had disappeared; he fished it out of her shoulder bag as a big grin crossed Suda's face.

"Yeah, a good idea."

Ross pulled a crumpled, damp handkerchief from his pocket and wiped his face. Then, as if in slow motion, he lowered a brown shopping bag with plastic handles onto the pavement. He stared at the inside of his fingers. The handles from the shopping bag cut into the flesh, leaving him with the red-lined hands of a bag lady.

71

"You carry the fucking knives," Ross snapped.

"I recall buying the knives was your idea," said Crosby.

Ross sneezed three times in rapid succession. "It was your idea," he said, trying to affect an English accent. "You sound like a fucking woman. Where is the goddamn driver? He should be carrying the knives. Thais love the feel of weapons like a knife." They were near the Chiang Mai train station. Around the corner from the station and off the main road, they stood upwind from a large burnt-out building. A fire had leveled it to the foundations. Inside the charred remains were thousands of soggy rolls of toilet paper, tissue, boxes, tins with burned labels rising in small peaks. Smoke smoldered from a couple of ridges. Thousands of flies buzzed around a section of smashed tins of food. And everywhere were the brown faces tilted away from the sun, bent over from the waist, picking through the mountains of debris. Children in school uniforms, their books stacked on a ledge of toilet paper, scooped tunnels in the suffocating heat. Hilltribe women with babies strapped to their backs carried boxes of looted tins of food on their heads.

In the small side street, Crosby leaned forward over a tuk-tuk, and began talking to the driver. Ross dabbed his face with the handkerchief as he watched children climb through the wasteland. Small girls, their hair tied in braids, white ankle socks, black shoes, white blouses, and freshly pressed blue skirts, carried away a few tins of food. The children by instinct found trails through the mountains of debris, they spotted a can of baby corn or tuna, they walked without falling or getting cut by broken glass or torn strips of metal, and they could stand motionless in the sun, waiting for the right moment to unearth a tin of food under the nose of a bigger kid. They knew all the tricks.

"Christ, Crosby, we can't stand in the sun all day. Flies and stink. Smells worse, and is hotter than a fucking Chinese kitchen."

Crosby pointed at a man half hidden by a heap of debris. The man was bent over near a broken brick column. "Our driver."

"What in the fuck is he doing up there?"

"Shopping," said Crosby.

"He's looting. Fucking unreliable drivers. They're either sleeping, fucking, eating, or looting. Tell the sonofabitch we didn't hire him to dig through garbage on our time." Ross waited. Crosby had swung himself in the back of the tuk-tuk and out of the heat. He lit a cigarette and ignored Ross. "Tell him, goddamn."

"That sounds like lawyer's work."

Ross climbed into the back of the tuk-tuk and sat beside Crosby. He sighed heavily. His safari shirt was soaked; streaked with grim and dirt. From an inside pocket he removed a silver flask, unscrewed the top, and took a long drink. The tuk-tuk driver's head shot around at the smell of liquor. Ross handed him the flask with a belch.

"The tuk-tuk driver says twenty million baht went up in smoke," said Crosby, staring up at the mountain of garbage.

"Fucking chinks torched it for the insurance money," said Ross, taking back his flask.

"Forget about the money for Godsakes, look at all those girls raking through that goo."

Burning from the sun, the insect bites, the sharp clap of a baby crying; the anguished cry of a baby came from the back of a woman up to her knees in soggy trash.

"It burnt down last night," Crosby continued, ignoring the baby's cry.

"Wealth distribution in Thailand. A chink burns his supermarket, he gets a big pay cheque, and the Thais shuffle through the flies and garbage to fish out cans of beans and carrots piping hot and ready to eat."

Several boys, no more than fourteen or fifteen, their faces blackened with dust and grim, their clothes hanging in rags off their bodies, searched around part of a fire-scorched wall, smoking cigarettes. Hunting through garbage since dawn, they looked bone-weary and shaky on their feet. Crosby watched them for a long time; as if he were watching some old movie of himself moving along the terraces of garbage. He smiled to himself. After Ross and he had bought the knives at the night market, he had gone to a brothel, leaving Ross to drink alone in his room. The girl's name had been Tik, seventeen, long, dark hair, and the kind of lips that never fully closed; they rested like a hinge. She made a slight quiver when he entered her, raising her legs up and, with splayed fingers, ran her hands down his back. Her eyes were wide open; she was somewhere else. And so was Crosby, eyes closed he moved on Tik with the motion of someone going someplace else; a man looking for some destination other than sex.

A gentle snow fell outside the window of the class-room. The school buildings and playing field were covered in a white, soft blanket; and beyond lay rolling downs thick with snow, with only the shadows cast from the hedgerows like black snakes with their heads on the other side of the horizon. He was fifteen years old the winter of '75. He sat in the third row beside a boy whose parents were stationed in Singapore; his father was a political consular for the British Embassy. Twenty-seven boys watched as Breach entered the classroom for the final lecture before the start of Christmas holidays.

Breach walked to the front of the class, stood erect, chest out, then slowly removed his jacket and carefully slipped it over the back of his chair. Next he pulled the chair to the center of the room. He raised his right foot, his scuffed brown wing-tipped shoe, beads of water bubbling on the heels, and placed it on the seat of the chair; then he pulled himself up. Still he hadn't said a word to any of the boys. He folded his arms, towering above the class of boys, who exchanged embarrassed glances. A couple of inches above his head were Christmas decorations that had been strung across the ceiling. The decorations were cleverly cut paper houses. Rows and rows of tiny white paper houses with small slits for windows, doors, and gabled roof; handmade by the headmaster's wife for the boys. She had sprayed them with a silver glitter and each house sparkled when hit by the sunlight that streaked through the window. Only that afternoon, there was no sun; it was snowing, and snowing hard as Breach stood on the chair before the class.

Breach looked at the rows of paper houses; pretending to peer in the windows and doors. He lifted his arms and some of the paper houses tipped to the side in the palm of his hand. A gentle, peaceful expression spread over his face. He pulled a cigarette lighter from his pocket. A smile flickered across his face. Everyone thought that they were in for another of his magic tricks. Breach flicked the lighter with his thumb. A jet of yellow flame shot straight into the air. Where was the trick, Crosby was thinking. When's he gonna do it?

Breach slowly moved the lighter beneath the string of paper houses, setting each of them on fire, one after another. The paper ignited and, in an instant, a gray ash that no longer appeared like a house peeled off the string like dead, withered skin shed by a snake, and weightlessly drifted across the room. All the boys watched with a sense of fear and excitement. Their mouths wide open, they said nothing. But everyone was thinking the same collective thought. How was Breach gonna make those houses come back? Everyone was asking themselves that one question; and everyone believed that Breach could do it. They believed in him; even though they thought he was cracked.

Crosby reached up and caught one of the ashes that floated past; it made a black streak across the back of his hand. Breach watched the last of the houses burn, then he began to tell the class why he had done it. They were bewildered and disappointed. Hey, if this isn't magic, then it had better be good.

"You thought this was going to be magic? Right?"

Everyone nodded their heads.

"Magic asks the questions: Where did it go? How long will it stay? Is it an illusion? But I want to ask another question: where do you go from here? You need to be anarchist, not a magician, to ask that question properly. Someone with the guts to burn down your world from top to bottom," he said, pausing. No one said anything. Breach stepped down from the chair, and brushed gray ashes from his hands, face, and shirt.

"Remember me, if you remember me at all, as the one who used fire to burn down what you take for granted as life. Christmas is not the celebration of Jesus' birth; it's about paper houses strung across the earth. That's the gravity belt that pulls you from this room; the one that holds your feet on the ground. Now what will you do? Now that it's gone? Just like that. In a puff of smoke. Imagine that there are no more houses left anywhere. Nothing to pull you out of this room. And everywhere the earth is covered in snow and ice. What does that leave you with? This minute; this very second? Despair. Yes, that's the right word. A great throbbing ache of despair and hopelessness. You've got no place and no one you can turn to and ask them what you should do next, what you should be, where you should go, or what you should want. And you know that no God is going to give the answer. Nor are you going to find it in reason, logic, or art. All the time your head is bursting with questions you never asked yourself before: where am I? What is this place? Where is this place? From whence did I come and where do I go next? What compass do I use; which direction does it point? The answer is not in a book, a phrase, a word, or half-whisper. It is in dead silence. In the ashes of language. In the ashes of self."

Breach put on his jacket and walked straight out of the room. Although it was late afternoon, the rim of the sun was sinking below the horizon. The boys, all knees and elbows, gathered in a bunch at the windows, watching Breach walk with difficulty through the thigh-high drifts of snow. He half stumbled as he walked. He stopped, half-turned around, saw the faces in the window. His own face was a red mask as he looked past his students at the dying sun. He smiled, turned around, and walked on until he disappeared down the road.

❖

"*Set!*" the young woman's voice whispered from a tangle of black hair splayed over the pillow and cascading onto the sheets.

A second later, the same voice, a little louder and more firm, "*Set!*—finish." He pumped harder. She was dry inside. She wetted her fingers with her lips and inserted them, with a hiss, between her legs. Crosby inserted himself again. But her wetness did not last. The friction evaporated the interior surface and the more Crosby pounded against her pelvis, the more she cried out for him to finish.

"I still have one more movement to play," he said.

"What kind of instrument do you think I am?" she asked him.

"Sez the organ to the organ grinder," he replied, keeping beat with his foot against the bedstead.

Crosby's left eye popped open and stared into a narrow slit in the dark room. Tik's eyes were wide open; her jaw clenched as she sighed. "Why you not finish yet?" she said. "Maybe you sick? Maybe I no good girl. Not make you happy."

"You make fine music."

"I tell you I make sex for you. Girl no good for music."

"That's where you're wrong, my lovely. Enough talking back to the conductor and the musicians. Back to work."

Crosby closed both eyes tightly. A sharp finger poked him on the chest. This time both of his eyes opened into the blare of the hot sun.

"Wake up, goddamn, Crosby. Our looter has returned with the spoils," said Ross, nodding at a Thai man in shorts carrying two bags filled with tins of fruit, vegetables, and meat. "He says car wrecks and plane crashes are better."

Crosby leaned forward in the tuk-tuk and called out to the taxi driver who was all smiles. He knew Ross had made up the part about car wrecks and plane crashes. Ross understood no Thai; and the driver spoke no English. Crosby lay back and thought about his dream of getting laid. He had been happy inside his dream. In the dusty street, a dozen or other Thais reacted to the stinking stew of burning rubble, garbage, and scavengers with a noticeable absence of emotion. They might have been watching animals or a bed of flowers. The activity had nothing to do with them. Crosby shook off his fatigue and stepped out of the tuk-tuk. Ross had already followed the driver around to their taxi.

"At least you could have left it unlocked. No air-conditioning in this heat. It's savage," said Ross, as Crosby drew alongside.

"He doesn't speak English," said Crosby.

The driver opened all the doors; waves of heat rolled out.

"It's an oven," said Ross. He picked up one of the tins from the driver's cache. None of the tins had labels. They had all been burned off in the fire. "He doesn't know whether he's got dog food or horse piss in these cans."

A few feet away a young Thai man sprawled across the back of his motorcycle sleeping. Others people squatted down on their haunches, elbows on their knees, staring out into middle distance. A motorbike roared past, kicking up a small cloud of dust. Women along the path with doubled up white handkerchief pressed to their nose stood silently against the whirling dust clouds, watching the young revert to a primitive state of nature. Once the driver switched on the air-conditioning, Crosby climbed into the back seat. Ross stood beside the car, fanning himself and shaking the tin.

The strong smell of rotting food, smoke, burnt wood, and dust clung to the nose and throat. The smell lingered in the back of the Crosby's mouth. A few drops of concentrated poverty and desperation lasted a lifetime. When the car pulled away, he glanced back for one last look at those faces; eyes of a defeated enemy fighting for position, a toehold on the side of the mountain.

Fifteen minutes later, the garlands of flowers and amulets swayed back and forth from the rearview mirror as their driver leaned with his shoulder into the sharp curves. Highway 109 snaked across a vast landscape of brown fields, with scrub brush covered mountains in the distance, and in between the mountains and fields ridges and gullies charred from fires. Clouds of smoky haze blurred the sky and mountains. Palm and banana trees rose around with high arched thatched roofs and windows made from bamboo were coated with a thick layer of red powdered dust. The earth stripped bare beneath the grass and vegetation had turned the color of dried blood.

Their driver slowed down for a curve and pointed at a spot off the road. Shattered glass skittled down an embankment, spilling down a washed-out gully. They passed a shattered fence. The post ends had been smashed, half pulled out of the ground.

"*Farang* killed here," said Crosby, translating as the driver spoke Thai in somber tones. "Maybe four altogether. He says, they were driving too fast. Drunk too much Mekong. It never got in the newspapers. It's bad for the image, he says. *Farang* killing themselves upcountry all the time, he says. They get all pissed up and next thing they wake up in the next life."

Ross reached for his flask. "We hired him," said Ross, leaning over the seat. "So we could stay in this life. And drink. Tell him that. And I was about to offer him a drink. No fucking way now. Thai driver flees scene the scene of the crash. That's the Thai image. Tell him that."

The driver eyed Ross in the rearview mirror.

Crosby looked over at Ross. "What do you think about when you're having sex with a whore?"

Ross didn't miss a beat. "Darts."

"Darts?"

"Standing at the line, looking at the target, concentrating, and then throwing the dart. I can fuck for hours thinking about darts. And what do you think about? Horse racing?"

Crosby's teeth showed behind his smile. "Burning houses."

Ross took out his flask. "I'm travelling north with a pervert and driver with two bags of dog food. And fifteen pounds of rusty knives. I've gotta be insane."

Lighting a cigarette, Crosby laid his head back and slowly watched the smoke leak out of his nose. "At five in the morning, when I got back, you were moaning *Old Grand-Dad*. I wouldn't call that a valid visa stamp in a sanity passport. You could've awakened the dead with the way you were carrying on."

Ross pulled the flask from his lips. "Piss up a rope, Crosby."

"Only if you hold both ends."

Chapter 6

Breach, who had hiked five kilometer up a narrow, dirt mountain path, stopped and waited. Suda fanned herself, resting and trying to catch her breath. Chunks of rock split through the red skin of the earth. Breach was tougher than she thought. She watched him touching the slender green bamboo shoots on the side of the road. The shoots slanted through the ravines scorched black by fires. He climbed over a ravine and picked a handful of long elephant grass; he returned to the road and handed the grass with round-topped, feathery and fluffy blades to Suda. The grass was still in her hands against the windless sky.

"Nature's magic is perfect," said Breach. He collapsed a piece of elephant grass in his hands, and held them out for her to examine. His hands were empty.

"Maybe it's better not to play tricks on nature." She dropped them along the road and continued her climb.

"My tricks are always played with nature," he replied. Breach stared at the elephant grass in the road. He thought about the water buffalo horn parts the shaman had thrown like dice on the damp, dirt floor. The stalks of elephant grass crossed. Would the child die or survive, he thought. There was never an answer in elephant grass on a rocky mountain path or in waterbuffalo horns. Reality never stopped anyone from finding answers in an arbitrary alignment of nature, he thought. Whatever or whoever was waiting at the top could be answered by going there.

This time Suda waited for him to catch up. Behind her a ribbon of banana trees rimmed a ridge halfway toward a bank of mountains. As Breach reached where she stood, Suda passed him the plastic canteen. A trickle of water ran down the corners of her mouth. She reached into her backpack and removed an envelope.

"Tuttle asked me to give you letter."

Breach slowly lowered himself on the side of the path. "A mountainside promotion?"

"He say important I give you halfway up." She glanced towards the top of the mountain.

Breach opened the envelope and read the letter.

Dear Richard,

Suda has delivered this letter at my request. She does not know the contents, but is generally aware of the seriousness of the situation. You have a choice. You can go back down the mountain and return to Chiang Mai. No hard feelings. Or you can continue on to the top. Several months ago, a friend of mine, an American, George Snow, was taken hostage. He's held by a small group of armed men in a Lahu village on the mountain. These men are heavily armed and should be considered extremely dangerous. They are political types. The government sees what they call the "incident" as a highly embarrassing loss of face. Demands have been made and deadlines expired. We have heard nothing from Snow for almost two weeks.

Suda knows people in the village and thinks she can help. You can trust her. She will need all the help she can get. And luck, too. It was impossible to explain this in Bangkok. The city—amend that, the entire country is too small. Naturally you would have checked it out. At least, I would have done so. In checking it out, everyone and their cousin would know why you are on the mountain now. The Lahu would be waiting. More than likely they would have killed Snow. If I had gone, they certainly would have killed him.

By now the word will be out in Chiang Mai and the north that you are a *farang* on a buying trip with a well-known antique dealer. Someone who is looking for shaman knives. The Thais are used to this kind of traveller. The knives are your cover; your protection. They will allow you to get close to Snow. That is, assuming you decide to go ahead. Snow is a good guy, a good friend, who made a stupid mistake. He's worked at the school for years and, like you, he is a fellow magician; unlike you, he took his magic and himself far too seriously. What started as a joke backfired on him. He was auditioning for the role of Lahu Godman and not Lahu hostage. But that's the way it has turned out. It's no longer a joke. This isn't standup comedy. His balls are in a sling.

If you find Snow, and he is alive, tell him, "Betty wishes him a happy birthday, and many happy returns." Betty's his mother, and the happy return part means help is on the way, or may be on the way, depending on what Suda can do and what you are willing to do to help her.

As the Thais say, it's up to you.

Sincerely,

Robert Tuttle

❖

"Maybe the *farang* Tuttle wants isn't on the mountain," she said, as Breach looked at her over the letter.

"Maybe not," said Breach. He glanced at the letter again, then folded it, slipping it into his pocket. "There is only one way to find out. We keep on climbing."

Suda groaned, took another long drink from the plastic canteen. "What's that word for water—" She broke off and made a gesture of water rising skyward.

"Water fountain."

"Fountain," she said, then repeated the word a dozen times. "No water fountain in the mountains. But two more kilometers. A steam."

"Stream," Breach said.

"Steam."

"Stream," he repeated slowly. She started walking ahead, repeating "steam" to herself.

"Why help Tuttle?" he asked, as she paused to catch her breath.

She thought for a second. "He has a good heart."

"And Crosby?"

"Same-same," she said.

"And me?"

"Time to go."

The earth roiled with a reddish brown skin that wrapped around the mountain like a bad sunburn. Twelve- to fifteen-foot banana plants arched over the rocky dirt road. Breach looked down a narrow ravine where fire had destroyed the vegetation, leaving charred stumps struck together by an explosion of cobwebs. He wondered if Snow was on the mountain, what kind of conditions he was being kept in. And if he were dead, what was the condition of the body.

"Stream," he said, calling after Suda.

She turned from a point on the path up ahead, crinkled her face.

"What is it?" he asked, picking up his pace.

Breach knelt down beside Suda along the edge of the road.

Sweat streaked down his back, as he followed her eye line. Red dust and a massive ball of spiders. And together they stared at the spiders, saying nothing. There was no sound on the mountain for a moment. A dead space of silence; a interval for forgetting what lay behind or ahead; a moment separate from Tuttle's letter, Snow, Crosby, Ross, Bangkok, and the rest of his life.

Three kilometers up the road, they entered a Karen village. Snarling dogs scrambled between the bamboo poles supporting the thatched houses, kicking up a cloud of thick red dust. A wild pig squealed stiff-legged across the road. Children with large black eyes stared out from porches, windows, behind a fence, watching them pass. Watching the tall, sweating *farang*, who made a length of red cotton yarn disappear and reappear as white and then blue cotton. He worked the illusion as he walked. The disappearing ball appeared an ordinary part of his progress up the mountain. That was the trick of magic: to make the extraordinary appear another routine procedure like taking a breath or putting one foot in front of another.

From a Karen village house, they heard the muted voices of people singing. Suda called out to someone near the house and asked what was going on.

"A ceremony, he says to me. We can come back tonight. Much singing. Maybe *Maw Pee*—shaman—will come too." She paused a second, looking at the colored yarn in his hands. "They like your magic. They say maybe someone know about knives. And he say you better than other *farang*." She stopped, swallowing her words.

"When did he see the other *farang*?" asked Breach.

"About a month ago. He say your magic very good," she said.

"Snow," whispered Breach.

The village dissolved into a chorus of barking dogs, grunting pigs, children playing and running, and adults singing inside the headman's house. Along the road outside the village, a middle-aged man in shorts, T-shirt, and shoeless sat on the edge of a wooden porch. Beside him was a large pile of ginger roots. He cut the ginger stalks into pieces with an enormous knife.

"Money from ginger is not so much. Opium better. Much more money. But planting ginger is a better idea," she said. "Not so many problems." The man with splayed toes sat, his legs stretched out, wiggling his toes to music from a radio. He didn't look up as they passed. A Mazda truck caked with red dust was parked next to the house.

"That's a lot of ginger," Breach said, nodding at the truck.

"Maybe still grow a little opium. Hard life getting up and down mountain. Need—"

"Truck or van."

"Wan," she said rapidly twenty times. "Neds wan. Neds wan."

"Needs. Two e's. And van, not wan. 'V' not 'W'," said Breach.

"Wan. Needs. Needs Wan."

"You're batting fifty percent."

"Wan cost *mahk, mahk*—very much."

"Selling a *farang* might buy a Mazda."

"*Farang* like smoking opium. Many problems and dangerous."

The old villager looked up from the ginger and coughed, a long hacking cough of bronchial tubes lined with that red earth, betel, and opium. It was an echo of her own cough, thought Breach. In the mountains, the villagers lived close to a land, explained Suda. Disease and infection grabbed them with a quick fist as they went about drinking their water and breathing the mountain air. Needs a van to get the hell out of this place, Breach thought.

The people in the first village stayed a safe distance away. Framed in a door or window. Distant, cautious glances before the face turned away. Or had Tuttle's letter made them appear remote, distant, suspicious? Breach was not certain how his judgment had been colored by the letter, by the knowledge there was trouble, by the feeling he was looking for some basis to make a decision. He thought back to the market when Tuttle introduced him to Suda. Her four-year-old nephew ran past where Breach sat, suddenly turned, stopped, stared at Breach, and then rattled off a question in Thai.

"He say why don't *farang* stay in their country. Don't come to Thailand." That had been Suda's translation.

"There goes his career with the tourist board," said Tuttle.

Suda laughed. Breach remembered the young boy's eyes watching him. He wondered if Snow had seen those eyes on his way up the mountain?

The eyes of those first distant villagers silently spoke the same question. Why come here? What do you want from us? If you belonged here, then you would have been born in Thailand in this life. What are you doing with your destiny? And why have you come to interfere with ours? Leave us alone with our red earth, boiling sun, and ginger, betel, and opium. That swell of instinctive distrust toward foreigners ran deep. Strangers and foreigners were like soldiers, police, and tax collectors. They always came for something that left them poorer in the bargain. Something in the villagers' faces hinted that they would be happy to see a tall fence around their lives. One that would protect them and keep the others out.

Suda acted, as Tuttle's letter suggested, as a kind of amulet on the mountain trail. That first Karen village was no exception. Hair under arms, her short-cropped hair, and Mao face with chin and cheek scars suggested a woman bulletproof, sharp, skilled, and connected to the way they measured their lives. She was from their side of the fence. She had lived among communities which were united generation upon generation by a common struggle to stay alive, by the danger of invading strangers, and by the shaman ceremonies for births, deaths, and sickness. Suda came and went as one of them. She belonged to a small group who had an invitation to share what was hidden on the other side of their doors and windows.

❖

A kilometer outside the Karen village, a small column of hilltribe teenagers in dirty work clothes marched in pairs along the road. Sweat and red dust covered their faces and clothes. Some of the boys carried wooden-handled hoes with large blades. Boys and girls were between twelve and sixteen years old; about the same age as Breach's students in England. It was closing in on three in the afternoon. The children looked exhausted. One of the boys, his lips cracked from the heat, broke ranks, stopped, and asked Breach, with a gesture of drawing his hand to his lips, for a cigarette.

Breach, with a flick of his wrist, pulled one out of the air. He lit it, then pulled a second cigarette from the void—this one was already lit. Breach stuck the first cigarette in his mouth and handed the second one to the boy.

"Smoking no good," said Suda, as the boy inhaled deeply on the cigarette. "It make him sick."

"It may kill him," said Breach.

The hilltribe boy with cracked lips smiled as smoke curled out of his nose. Breach recognized something familiar in the boy's face; something he remembered from Crosby's face when he was a fifteen-year-old. The large capacity to accept what came down the road in life; to break ranks and ask for what you want; and to take as the natural order of things that strangers pull the object of your dreams out of thin air. Intelligence rose from the boy's penetrating, searching eyes; the kind of intelligence that knows it is doomed, that knows there is no way out, that understands no one is coming to the rescue. An intelligence that takes an act of magic on the trip down the mountain as no different from the larger illusion of calling this existence life with meaning and purpose.

The boy shrugged, then shuddered, his eyes half-lidded as he sucked in hard on the cigarette. He nodded to Breach and continued walking down the mountain road. Breach watched him walking along with a friend. A powder-gray column of smoke drifted from his head. The boy handed the cigarette to his friend, who inhaled, and passed it back. A sharing of the spoils that came from nowhere. These were the same kind of people who held Snow, he thought. Snow was somewhere on the mountain, scared and alone, waiting for another piece of magic to free him. That was the ultimate act of faith: to believe what had broken him, condemned him, would save him. Breach found some element of himself in Snow; Tuttle, he thought, had banked on this.

Suda watched the head of the column disappeared the road curved around the ridge of the mountain.

"They are very tired," Suda said. "They work in the fields since six."

The other children shuffled past. They wore an expression of a road accident victims; swollen faces gone into shock, hair full of red-brown dirt, blank eyes, sweat-beaded brows, fighting hard to stay upright, and on the edge of coma. Casualties in a harsh, demanding, brutal life, the children had not been broken. They were going home to wash, eat, and play games. They had survived another day in a life which almost ended unpleasantly.

As the last child had disappeared, Suda stopped, drank some water, and nodded through the trees at a distant mountaintop.

"That's where we go."

Breach looked at the distant ridge. A dry river gorge cut through the mountains like an old war wound. They had hiked about six kilometers from Highway 1019. Suda's pace had slowed. Her energy exhausted, she stopped again after a hundred meters to drink water from the canteen. In Chiang Mai, she hadn't slept; she had heard voices. A Mien shaman's spirit coming after her with sharpened knives? Or a Bangkok lawyer moaning for his favorite whiskey in his sleep? Breach stopped beside Suda. She squatted along the side of the road, coils of sweat trickling down her flushed face. She bent over coughing, turning away from Breach. Her cough had a deep echo. Suda had lost steam.

"Maybe I'll carry you across," Breach said. "Old man, carrying young woman. Seems like good idea."

"You are starting to joke. I like joking. *Farang* talk too serious. Joke more. Better, I think," she said, ignoring the full weight of her exhaustion.

"The question is, who is the joke on?"

She leaned forward, stretched, and, coughing her guts out again, looked up the road. "I think there might be trouble. Maybe you go back now."

"The joke's on Snow. That's my guess." He wanted to ask her what was wrong with her lungs; the rattle of that cough had an awful familiar ring.

She picked up a handful of dirt and let it run out through her fingers. "I think they will kill him. Maybe already killed him."

"You told Tuttle this?"

She nodded. "He say, never mind, you afraid. Don't go."

"He wrote me the same thing," said Breach, watching her pick up another handful of dirt. "You don't sound so well, why don't you go back."

Suda smiled and stretched back on her hands, throwing her head back and looking at the sky. "They kill him five hundred percent. And kill you."

"One thousand percent?" asked Breach.

"Two thousand percent plus," said Suda.

"And if I'm with you?"

"Then only five hundred percent." She coughed again. "Like Snow?"

She nodded, her eyes watery from coughing.

He rose back to his feet, and began walking up the road.

"Why you not afraid?" she called after him.

He stopped, and turned. She was back on her feet, hooking over her shoulder her backpack with the dump truck and ball inside.

"Because of something the children in the road reminded me of something I had once tried to teach myself, and had nearly forgotten. To survive you must never show fear to your enemy. When he sees how bad your odds are, knows he would turn and run, but sees you still keep on coming, he becomes unnerved, worried, and confused. Then the odds shift. And gambling, like magic, are about playing the odds with creative illusions."

❖

Ten minutes later, they came across a middle-aged Lahu villager and his four-year-old daughter squatting under the shade of a banana tree. Suda greeted the villager, and as she struck up a conversation, the laughter and joy flooded over her. She was herself again; something had snapped back into frame. She gave the little girl an orange and helped her peel it.

"Lek say we can ride with him. Wan—van—come. We go. Okay? Good idea?"

"You know this guy?" asked Breach, nodding at the villager.

"His cousin have minor wife who know my aunt. Before they go to school together."

The kinship connection, thought Breach. Fifty million people related in one way or another to each other; feeling out the nature of that connection in the first few minutes of conversation, establishing the link, the relationship, and then a sigh of relief which comes from the comfort of knowing another person has been located on a branch of the family tree.

Waiting for the minibus to arrive, Suda squatted beside the Lahu villager, watching him load a thin, curved, silver tube. He loaded it with tobacco, passed a flame from a lighter over the bowl, and took a long hit.

"He say he smoke tobacco," said Suda, looking over at Breach.

"And what do you say?" he asked.

"He give us ride," she said. "My aunt's family know only tobacco smokers." Her crooked grin and wink disappeared as she turned back to the villager.

The minibus turned out to be a Toyota pickup truck packed with disheveled and dust-caked children, women, and men who looked like they had been freshly dug out of the earth and loaded in the truck. Several dozen twenty-pound sacks of rice lined the bed of the truck. Suda climbed on the bumper and squeezed into a small hole between two girls. Breach stepped on the bumper, looked at the dirty faces turned toward him, nervous and uncertain, as he searched for a space. There was no room left except for an odd-shaped space on the rice bags where vegetables had been piled. Breach shrugged his shoulders at Suda.

"Maybe it a sign for you to go back," said Suda, smiling.

"Or a sign to take a dive," he said.

His response mystified Suda. There was one possible configuration. He slowly turned himself around on the bumper, his back facing the pickup and, using the bumper like a diving board, made a humiliating back flip onto three bags of rice, with his calves coming to rest over a box of vegetables. A small Thai raked the air with dirty fingernails. He spoke in rapid-fire Thai and pushed Breach's legs spread-eagle over the vegetables. Breach was wedged in; he was stuck. A couple of the girls behind him began to giggle.

"He say, maybe they eat you for dinner. *Farang* taste good with rice."

"Ask him if he's seen Snow," Breach said.

She spoke to the villager in Thai. "He says too hot today. Never have snow here."

She had translated Snow into a weather condition. He trusted her judgment enough to know that she had her reasons. He watched the greengrocer's face. "Okay, tell him they can roast me like duck."

Breach pretended to pull a long length of red and blue yarn from his ear, handing the end to Suda. There was a gasp from several of the passengers, and a broad smile on Breach's face. "Better warn him I'm on the stringy side," he said to Suda.

The truck passed through three villages on the journey to the top of the mountain. At the top, in the last of the Lahu village, Snow had last been seen alive. Slowly, following each stop, the truck began to empty. In the second hilltribe village, the distraught greengrocer unloaded his box of semi-crushed greens, and four bags of rice, explaining to his wife, who had come running out of the shop, wiping her hands on her apron, that a *farang* with magic string had been sent by the evil spirit of snow to ruin his business. He gestured, using his hands to demonstrate Breach's appearance out of the clouds and his back flip on the vegetables and rice.

"*Poo-chai jai-dee*—Man has a good heart," she said to him in Thai. And then rattled off several sentences in Thai that Breach didn't understand, but which caused considerable mirth and excitement among the villagers huddled in the truck. The greengrocer's wife flashed a knife from under her apron and waved it above her head. The greengrocer backed away and the villagers laughed. As the truck pulled away, leaving a cloud of red dust behind, Breach edged over and whispered to Suda.

"What else did you tell them? I had a good heart, and something else I didn't catch."

"Stone bottom. Last life you a water buffalo. Come back to see owner who beat you. And you pay him back by sitting on his vegetables."

"And the wife pulled a knife on him."

"She tell him before bad luck to beat water buffalo. She say, why he don't listen. He think *mahk-mahk.*"

The truck stopped near the top of the mountain where the road overlooked a wide, flat savannah, a surface gleaming with a silky sheen. Several water buffalo grazed below a splash of cream-colored clouds.

"In my last lifetime, this was my favorite restaurant," Breach said, nodding toward the water buffalo feeding in the foreground.

"Maybe you sleep with water buffalo tonight," said Suda.

"And break her heart when I leave in the morning?"

Suda broke into a smile, turning away from the fields. "I think maybe you good at breaking hearts," she said.

"First we should find Snow before it gets dark."

"I think better I talk to some friends first."

There was little argument which Breach could muster against her request to make contact with friendly allies. She had talked them this far up the mountain, and there was no reason to believe she would fail to talk them straight down the main street of the village.

After the truck had gone, Suda walked across the road and onto a building site. The wood platform and skeleton of freshly nailed walls stood opposite the Trekker's Lodge. One of the workmen put down his hammer. He exchanged a few words with the other two workers. He climbed down from the concrete foundation. On his right hip he had a well-worn brown leather carpenter's belt slung low in the best tradition of the American gunfighter. With the clatter of metal bouncing against metal, he walked over to Suda. She took the dump truck out of her shoulder bag and handed it to him, explaining it was a present for his son. It was an offering which carried an implied request for protection. The Lahu worker who received the gift lived in the servants' quarters of a teak house outside the main village.

❖

Breach wandered alone on the road. He felt relaxed, secure, his mind dancing in the unfocused clutter of objects, feelings, and desires; to the toy dump truck, to the grazing water buffalo, to his thirst and hunger, to the letter Tuttle had written. A spiral of random thoughts that led nowhere. Lost in his thoughts, a few minutes down the road, out of the corner of his eye, he saw a movement. He looked again. This time he saw three heavily armed Thais and a fourth man on a horse. The Thais had automatic rifles strapped over their shoulder; rows of brass shell casting crisscrossed their chest in ammo belts. The casting reflected the sun, bouncing light off the rocks. Two horses without saddles followed behind the armed men. And between the unsaddled horse, a man dressed in black, his face and head covered except for a slit for his eyes, rode with his hands overlapping the saddle horn. Breach felt the rush of panic. It was too late to run or hide. So he waited as the riders picked up their speed.

Breach recognized their weapons; old M16s, he thought. The rifles had been smuggled into Thailand from Cambodia; taken off a Vietnam soldier, who had been issued the rifle not knowing that sixteen, seventeen years earlier it had been clutched in the mud and heat in the hands of a dead American soldier.

The only sound of movement came from the horses' breathing; their hooves on the hard, dirt path. Breach tried to read the faces of the men quickly and accurately. Were the muscles in their faces tense? Even at a distance, eyes gave a supreme insight into intentions. The first Thai had the eyes of a tiger; nervous eyes, no-nonsense eyes, suspicious eyes, eyes that avoided other eyes. The man wrapped in black who was on horseback had sleepy eyes, and drugged eyes.

When the purpose behind the eyes yielded no answer, he fell back to reading intention from their hands. The hands were more obvious of a man's wish than his eyes; especially when they were holding an automatic rifle. A man used his hands to play cards, to make illusions appear as magic, he used his hands to kill. Breach watched the location of the fingers holding the rifles; how the thumb of one man was hooked around the leather strap. Another tapped his index finger on the trigger guard. A tensed hand instinctively fell into a fist, the knuckles turned the color of chicken bone against a brown hand. If one of the men was going to kill him, his hand would communicate his death a moment before it happened. The lead man's hand was in that indecisive half-ball shape. He had a great deal of time to decide. Breach was unarmed, there was no ground cover near where he stood, and the armed men occupied the high ground. The horses kicked up dust that drifted over the road and into the fields as they walked behind them. They spoke to each other in Thai, reining their horses in and circling around Breach.

"I'm looking for a *farang*. His name's Snow. You see him?" asked Breach, turning around in a small circle.

The horse five feet in front of Breach reared up. The men with rifles quickly brought them into a firing position.

"Who wants to know, man?" asked the man wrapped in black.

"Robert Tuttle in Bangkok," said Breach, looking at the rifles. This was precisely the wrong time for an illusion. Magic was to be avoided at all cost in front of people pointing guns. Any strange movement of the hand might startle a horse, and the rider. Breach stopped turning, keeping his hands at his side.

"Tell Tuttle everything's cool," said the unarmed rider.

"And you tell Snow, there's a message on his service. Betty wishes him a happy birthday and many returns."

The man on horseback unwrapped the black scarf from his face. He leaned over the saddle horn, shaking his head. "I am Snow. Go back to Bangkok. The situation is under control. My people are looking after me," Snow said. His sunburned face breaking into a wide smile. He spoke in Thai to the men with rifles; they relaxed, lowering their rifles.

Someone was lying, thought Breach. "You look sick," said Breach. "Why don't you come back with me."

"Sick? You must be shitting me. I've never felt better," said Snow. "Fresh air, Thai food, Thai women. . ."

"Tuttle thought you were going to die."

"Of happiness? Fuck, we are all going to die."

"Some sooner than others."

Snow coughed and spit into the dirt. "Thanks for the message from Betty. I gotta go."

Breach held the rein of Snow's horse. "Tuttle says you know some magic."

"Know some what, man?" His eyes were wet and narrowed as he talked into the sun. "Don't ever confuse illusions with magic. You get your ass in a sling doing that. Besides, it's part of the magician oath of office. An audience knows when it's been had. That's the end of the act."

Snow's eyes were impossible to read. Breach waited for him to finish his thought, but he broke off, as one of the men began pulling the horse forward.

"How about a drink later?" said Breach.

"Can't make it tonight," Snow shouted, turning around in his saddle. "Tribal duties to look after. You get the picture."

"Tomorrow, then."

"No time, man. I'm fully booked until the end of the century. Wish I could help you. But I gotta go."

Breach cupped his hands around his mouth and yelled after him. "Have you seen Crosby?"

Snow turned around in his saddle and shook his head. "Crosby's here?"

"He'll be here, if he isn't already."

Then Snow and the armed escort were gone, and only the dust kicked up by the horses swirled along the path.

When Breach walked back to the construction site, Suda was drinking coffee with the Lahu workmen, squatting in the Asia squat along the foundation of a new house. She had a sixth sense that Breach had lost his sense of humor somewhere down the path. She walked over to him standing in the road.

"You see the army on horses?" asked Breach.

"No problem. Guns for hunting. Little animals. Small birds," she said.

"Must be the water buffalo in me," Breach said.

"Good. You make good joke."

"They didn't think I was funny."

Suda leaned forward and whispered to him. "My friend knows about George Snow. He arrange for you to meet him." She waited for a reaction but none was forthcoming. "What you think?"

"That Snow's got himself a shitload of trouble."

She went back to tell the workman about how Breach had sat on the villagers' greens and how she had convinced the villager that Breach had a stone bottom left over from a previous life.

The encounter with Snow had left him uneasy. That wild look of someone who had been cut off from himself for a long period had been on Snow's face. Breach had seen that look before in Nepal. Usually on the face of people who claimed to have found the truth and had been taken prisoner by it. Snow's expression was like that of the monk who claimed he had awakened to the reality that he was a clitoris.

Chapter 7

Ross tossed the double shot of *Old Grand-Dad* straight down his throat; a gasp caught, like a shirtsleeve on a nail, in the back of his throat. He looked over the top of his glass and belched. The ice rattled in the glass as his unsteady hand held it out for a refill. He shook off the shiver, braced himself against the table, and gave the young Thai girl who served as the waitress a fish-eyed stare.

"Another *Old Grand-Dad*," he said, his face flushed from the heat and four rounds of doubles.

Crosby nursed his second Kloster. They had climbed ten kilometers up the mountain. They had survived the dirt, the rocks, village dogs, wild pigs, a tropical sun that baked the earth and peasants like a roast potato over a camp fire. The experience made Ross irritable. Slightly drunk, his mood shifted from self-pity and anger to mirth. Crosby had enjoyed the walk; it gave him a sense of satisfaction, of winning, of having scored on a bet. Not unlike the feeling he had achieved in successfully performing in a game or an auction. He drew strength from the walk as he forced himself to the edge of unpleasantness and discomfort. It was his English love of country and nature; a place where beauty and peace naturally existed. And, unlike Ross, he knew the danger waiting at the top; and this made him want the hike to last for days and weeks.

"Another cold beer for my friend," said Ross.

They drank at a table inside the veranda of the Trekker's Lodge. The lodge was built on a small knoll overlooking what might be described as a savannah. Wooden stumps marked a path leading up from the road. The over-logging had created these large African-like savannahs. Behind the veranda were the front desk and guest kitchen. Two long tables with benches were positioned near the railing. Crosby drank his beer beneath a bulletin board with maps, brochures, and half a dozen letters extolling the virtues of a guide, written in English by people who had gone to hilltribe villages or three- or five-day treks.

At one table, two young New Zealand women in their early twenties stretched out their legs and drank beer from the bottle. Both had long blond hair, shorts, and sleeveless tops, and had sunburns on their necks and the back of their arms bleaching the hair on their legs a furry white. They were from Nelson, New Zealand.

"Just arrived?" one of them asked.

"Arrived?" said Ross. "We climbed a fucking mountain."

"Lucy and I walked up yesterday. It only took three hours," said the other New Zealanders.

"Four," said Lucy, correcting her friend and wrinkling her nose. "Pleasant enough walk, wasn't it, Alison?"

Ross sat with his safari shirt unbuttoned to his navel; sweat-matted hair streaked in whorls across his large, naked belly.

"Pleasant enough walk," said Ross, narrowing his eyes. "Fucking is pleasant. Drinking is pleasant. Throwing a perfect dart is pleasant. Winning is pleasant. Being rich is pleasant. Pissing on ice is pleasant. But walking up a mountain? That is a pain in the ass. You have to be very motivated to walk up the side of a mountain with a bag of rusty knives."

One of the women slapped a mosquito dead against her calf. A smear of blood streaked across her pink flesh. So much for a man's determination; a man's strength, and will, thought Crosby.

"Sorry, we were just trying to make conversation," said the girl, wiping the blood off her leg with a tissue she licked wet with her tongue

"It's been a long day," said Crosby.

Ross cut in. "Jesus, I'm sorry. Can I buy you girls a beer. I say fuck too much after a few *Old Grand-Dad's.*"

Lucy bit her tongue on hearing the word "girls." She gave Alison a knowing glance. "He's drunk, Lucy," Alison whispered. Then she smiled at Ross and said. "We're drinking Kloster."

"Alison," whispered Lucy, pulling up her long legs and folding her arms around them in a kind of defensive posture.

"Join us," said Crosby.

"You're English," said Alison.

"See, they're English," said Alison, turning back to her friend.

"I'm an American," roared Ross. "A real American."

Alison sat down across from Ross. "What do you do?"

"Deals," said Ross, sucking on an ice cube.

"He's a lawyer," explained Crosby.

"An international lawyer?" asked Lucy, who slowly sat down beside her friend across from Crosby.

"I help generals, armies, politicians buy and sell dirt. Advise them on selling and buying plantations and serfs," said Ross. "That kind of shit."

Alison laughed as the Klosters arrived. "You're funny. A right one, you are," said Alison.

"Ross has talent," said Crosby.

Ross sucked in his bare stomach, puffing out his chest. "I practice international law. At law school I had this New York Jew professor who said, Ross, forget about practicing international law. You're not in the club. You didn't go to the right private school. You won't get an Ivy law degree. You have no family connections. Ross, you are totally fucked, he said to me. He was an alcoholic and said fuck too much. And you know what?"

Both New Zealanders shook their heads.

"He didn't know dick shit. I liked him because he liked to drink. But he knew nothing. He served two years on an insider trading charge. He's a felon now. They won't let him back in the land of golden parachutes, golden handcuffs, and golden showers. Now he's totally fucked. While I am the author of the new feudalism in Southeast Asia. Feudalism. You know what that is?"

Again both New Zealanders shook their heard as if they were one synchronized movement. "New what?" asked Lucy.

"What existed before the Big Mac."

"Oh, that," said Lucy. "Bad hamburgers."

"My clients machine-gun lawyers."

Crosby leaned forward across the table. "After they get the bill."

"I'm talking Burma," said Ross.

"Burma," whispered Lucy. "That's exciting."

"I'm dividing it like a housing estate. Carving it up like a Christmas turkey. Generals and politicians and their relatives. That's a real club. You think they ever heard of this dickhead Jew professor from New York? You think what he said means fuck all here. You can bet your young sweet asses it doesn't."

"Are you rich?" asked Lucy.

"I'm famous," said Ross. "In Rangoon, a hundred years from now there will be a bronzed statue of me on horseback. I'll have a bottle of *Old Grand-Dad* in one hand; and a dart in the other. And on a raised bronze plaque these words will appear: He never said it can't be done, and he did it fast." His eyes glossing over in an unfocused way stared, unblinking, over the railing beyond the savannah as if he were looking in the future.

Crosby took a drink from the bottle of Kloster. "You forgot something," said Crosby.

"What was I talking about?" asked Ross.

"That bronzed statue of you in Rangoon a hundred years from now. And how the Burmese are going to write, 'and Ross did it on his own; he was never a member of the club.'"

Alison poured the beer from the green bottle into the small fruit juice glass with a hair crack down one side. The suds boiled up, reached the top, a tiny trickle spilled over the side following the path of the crack to the table. Crosby handed her a paper napkin. She folded the damp napkin in two and pushed it to one side. She ran a finger around the rim of the cracked glass, glanced at the half-empty bottle. No one said anything. One of those awkward silences screamed from the void.

"What are you doing here?" asked Alison, looking at Ross and then Crosby.

"*Set laa-oh*—I'm finished," Crosby said to Ross.

"He speaks Thai. That kinda impresses the girls."

"Let's go, Ross. We should have a talk before it gets too late." What he meant was he wanted to talk to Ross while he was sober enough to listen.

"She asked what are we doing here. We're going north to clean a bundle of cash off a couple of Chinks in a card game," said Ross, brushing off Crosby's hand.

Crosby exhaled slowly, lowering his glance from the two women.

"So what do you really do?" asked Alison. "I don't believe you are a lawyer."

"I'm an artist," said Ross.

"He's a lawyer," whispered Crosby.

"An artist. A wordsmith. A craftsman of short stories."

"Would I have read your work?"

"Read my work, she asks. Impossible! They are contracts, my dear. Joint venture agreements. Technical service and license agreements. Inside each one is the story of great international personages moving through time and space gathering force and power, dividing up the world for money and pleasure. I'm a writer of the future. I may have created you and you don't even know it. I created the modern. We have seized control of the vocabulary. Words are our weapons. No other so-called writer can survive our monopoly. Yes, you may be right, these other writers are famous and I am not. But it doesn't matter. We've kicked their asses. Kicked out all the intellectuals. Forget assholes like Shakespeare, Conrad, Henry James, Updike, and the rest. No one understands them or likes them. Maybe no one ever did. We overturned history with a pen. With the merchants as our allies we control the world; the governments, the laws, the United Nations. They have submitted to our will."

"Wow," she said. "That's heavy."

"Very heavy. Shakespeare was right. Kill all the lawyers. But it's too late now. They have no words left to fight back with. And we have infiltrated their ranks. They are us."

"Lawyers write stories," Lucy said, laughing. "Get serious, Alison. He's pulling your leg."

"Don't laugh. And yes, I would like to pull your leg and other parts of your body. But that's not the point. The story of how to divide the spoils is not a laughing matter. These are serious stories."

"Banal, I'd say," said Crosby.

"The banality of power," said Ross. "Like the banality of evil, the purpose is not entertainment. These are serious stories."

"Okay, Ross, what about the army," said Crosby, letting himself be drawn into the debate. "There are no lawyers in the army. They are the artists. They write the stories. Why? Because they have the guns."

"Fucking wrong. Yes, merchants used to go into business with the military. Not anymore. Guns, tanks, and bombs are crude weapons. Why did the Burmese come to me? Because they wanted me to draft a smart bomb. A contract which can inflict damage for a hundred years. I predict terrorists will go to law school and join our fraternity of scribe knights. Merchants and lawyers are the new American world order. Fuck art, books, paintings. Destroy the libraries and museums. They only take up space for an office tower. Nothing inside them has any importance. Books say nothing and no one can read them anyway. And if they could, they wouldn't care."

"*Mao*—you're drunk?" said Crosby.

"Of course I'm drunk. It's my permanent state. An artist must suffer." He paused, tugging his chin down, gave Crosby a long stare. "Just explain to me, Crosby, why the fuck you are speaking Thai. Do you see any slant eyes at this table? We are all white. We all speak English."

Because *mao* carried the full load of every fear and despair moment of life in a Bangkok bar. It was the question often asked at three in the morning in HQ. The girls feared drunken *farangs*. Big, hairy, illiterate *farang* who could break their fragile bodies. Sex that was alcohol-assisted was like highway-driving in the passenger seat with a drunk; only the driver was on top of you, not knowing or caring if he went off the edge. Crosby rose from the table and walked away without finishing his beer.

Suda hiked her shoulder bag over her shoulder and stepped the pace as she passed the savannah wedged between a ridge of the mountain. Banana and ginger trees dotted the green belt. Breach caught Crosby's eye; Crosby was leaning on the railing. Ross was waving his arms and talking to two blond girls. Crosby nodded and raised his Kloster. This awful feeling of connectedness flowed over Breach, seized him, shook him, held him tight until he could no longer breathe. Breach wondered how long Crosby would wait until it gripped him; or had it already taken him long ago, and Crosby no longer struggled or cared that where he stepped his foot touched some part of a larger web and the reverberations ran in directions beyond his knowledge, awakening alliances and relationships he never dreamed possible. Breach stared at Crosby for a moment. Did he understand what it was like to be carried on the shoulders of invisible forces up a mountain? Was he aware what had prepared him up the mountain was more than his own will, his own physical strength and desire?

❖

Less than a kilometer walk, Suda followed the narrow dirt road flattened by tire tracks onto a small footpath. The path led through a hilly terrain and to a clear blue pond with white lotus blooming like a fairy-tale armada floating toward a small stream emptying into the pond. Breach stopped on the wooden footbridge above the stream. Below the surface of the pond, the tangled vines of the white lotus ran deep into the mud. Out of sight, out of mind, wrapped one over another, anchors keeping the blooms still and quiet in a harbor from which they could never leave. He thought about Snow on the horse. "Go away," had been Snow's message. What anchored him to this place? thought Breach. Why had Tuttle wanted to cut him free? Why had Snow wanted to stay? What possible reason could Suda have for helping him? And Crosby and Snow appearing again on a mountain without warning, without an announced purpose.

"Coming?" cried Suda, from the otherside of the pond.

Breach looked up. "Your friend's house?" he asked, knowing the answer. "It's better than a cave."

On the opposite side of the narrow bridge, he followed her along a steep ridge. Above them, with a commanding view of the pond, stream, and pathway, was a traditional Thai-style house made from teak. Three village dogs, barking and snarling, ran out from the side of the house. They recognized Suda, broke off their attack, disappeared up the hill. Breach quickly climbed up the hill to find Suda already inside the house.

Running off the central entrance corridor were two large rooms. On the right, space had been divided into two bedrooms, with the back room used to store blankets, sleeping mats, and pillows. Wooden shutters opened inward, and light and fresh air streamed into the main bedroom. Suda immediately found a broom and swept out the bedroom. Shoes off, Suda rummaged through the odd collections of polyester-filled duvets and thin mattresses rolled up like sleeping bags.

She threw one of the bags to Breach. "Catch," she said.

The bedding had all the taste and charm of the bedding in a rundown guest house. "Which relative owns this?"

"My friend build this house. I know him twelve years."

"He was part of the puppet troupe."

She grinned. "You guess good."

"Where did he get all this stuff?"

"Abroad."

The items had little apparent connection with one another; the designs and patterns gave the appearance of being bought in haste, at discount, and in foreign airports around the world. The house was owned by a friend of Suda's who worked for Thai Airlines. He had bought the land as an investment from the Lahu. One of the first of the outsiders to built a retreat at the foot of their village.

Suda repeated three or four times—a rare kind of emphasis for her—that her friend was gay, and all his friends were gay. She knew many of his gay friends. She had come to this house every three months for conversation; for a break from collecting, buying, transporting, storing, and reselling antiques. A place where she could disconnect herself from the web. She looked up from a pillow, the tip of her right elbow nestled in the center.

"In Roma. A bar in Patpong. You know?"

The Roma in Patpong II was a meeting ground for both gays and heterosexuals. "I know Patpong. One of the better illusions I have ever seen performed."

"*Farang* who go to Roma might like you. Many are *farang* bisexual. *Farang* come up to me at Roma and pinch me here," she said, demonstrated, gently kneading her ass. "And I turn around and say. But I not boy. I girl. And he say, oh sorry. I thought you were a boy."

"And if he wasn't gay and pinched you?"

"Thais never do that."

"Only *farang*?"

She thought about the generalization and the person making it. "Some *farang* not understand about Thai woman. I think they are confused in their minds about us."

Suda had used the Roma club as her segue into explaining the sleeping arrangements; she would sleep with Breach in the same room, which was not the same as sleeping with Breach. He understood her Thai conversational doodle, and shrugged. He had no expectation about sleeping with her; not since their first night on the train. He was distracted by the thought of Snow's horse being led away by three armed men. One had tugged at the reins of Snow's horse, pulling the horse around and leading it away. In that movement, again, there was something of the Thai indirection at work; the twisting of words so that they never cause the other person to lose face; a vagueness on the surface, but a fine work of art underneath.

There was Suda's message to consider as well. She had let go with a double-barreled blast: Breach was to think of her as a boy, and himself as being bisexual; and after he had digested that rich blend, he was being asked where he stood sexually. But she was asking him a lot more as well. For a split second that afternoon, he had felt doomed as three armed men had encircled him—so ask yourself how your magic works inside the kind of circle he had been invited to play in? He was confused about Crosby and Ross—so ask yourself how you feel about being set up for a fall?

Breach spread his bedroll on the floor. He rested on his knee, hands on his hips, looking out of the window at the small pond and bridge below. A man and woman made a decision at the very beginning about having sex. Either desire ignited into a blaze or snuffed out after a flicker; what followed from either decision inevitably created the blueprint for all future expectations and reactions. Suda wanted some sign from Breach that he understood what decision was being made, and that she could count on him. He was strangely removed as he stood in the window. The image of Snow, turned in his saddle, his eyes wide and fearful, searching Breach's face.

Breach stood with one foot wedged against his mattress in front of one open window. Suda rolled a mattress out six feet away directly in front of the second window. She tucked the ends of a sheet around the mattress, threw a duvet with pink, yellow, and orange floral arrangements over the top, and crossed the bedroom, passing out onto the porch. A few minutes later, Breach found her sitting in the chair. He looked through the palm fronds at the placid surface of the pond. Not a ripple or movement. He sat on the edge of the porch some distance away, half facing Suda, half facing the pond. She rocked in a restless way, her hands cupped around one knee.

"Don't worry about tonight. *Wy! jy!*—trust," Breach said.

She craned her neck around and saw him sitting on the porch. Here was a young woman whose father had sent her away at thirteen and refused to let her back, and Breach was asking her to trust him. And Breach recognized what had been in Snow's eyes: that tension between the fear of trust and the anxiety of not trusting. He looked out at the pond.

"*Wy! jy!* you," she replied, after watching Breach's face for a long time. Looking for some trick, some cooked-up scheme that would enable him to produce a pack of cards from the air.

With only an hour and a half to nightfall, Breach rose to his feet and leaned forward on the railing.

"I want to see the Lahu village," he said.

"No problem," Suda said.

"I want to talk to Snow again."

"May be problem for you to go alone."

The suggestion snapped a smile on her face; her sense of excitement translated into a flurry of activity. But she still suffered from the lack of sleep, haunted by the ghost whose presence she still felt—she never said *pee*—winging around her room. And she had trekked five kilometers up the mountain trail with an early afternoon tropical sun blazing overhead.

"*Bpy!*—let's go," she said, rising to her feet.

"You look worn-out." The word "worn" didn't register on any level of comprehension. "Tired, sleepy."

"Sleep later. Go now. Maybe you can't walk no more." The uneasiness between them had passed. Breach had once again become a target for her jokes. That was a good sign. To be the object of humor was to be trusted by Suda.

"Snow told me to go back. It is a funny way for someone to ask for help," said Breach, thinking aloud.

As she frowned, Breach wondered how the jagged scar along the right side of her jaw had come about. Was she pushed into something sharp? Fallen off a porch as a child? Struck her face into the metal flashing of a tuk-tuk?

"So what do you want? Go back to the Trekker's Lodge or go to the village? Up to you," said Suda.

"I've never seen a Lahu village before."

"You want me to help Snow?" she asked. The burden had been cast onto Breach. She had been clever, waiting for him to commit not only himself but her as well. It was a Thai way of shifting responsibility for action.

"Up to you," said Breach, using the Thai way to shift responsibility back.

He smiled, walked down the stairs leading from the porch to the lawn. He had thought Suda might be the right person for Tuttle to have chosen to help. As she had proved herself in the ride up the mountainside alongside the villagers' fresh produce. He looked back at her sitting on the porch.

"I smell a bluff." Breach had the feeling there was no middle ground. "I have a feeling Snow was never any good at cards."

"Tuttle say, he liked *poot len*—making jokes," Suda said.

"The Lahu I saw weren't falling off their horses with laughter."

Suda thought about this possibility. "Maybe it's better if Snow goes back with us."

"The Lahu carrying the M16s may not like that."

"Lahu are always laughing."

Breach felt something on his hands. A column of small brown ants crawled over his hand. He held his hand still, watching the marching ants climbing around the hair on his hand. "*Paw moht and maa moht*," he said. "In English, wizard and witch. The Thai called their wizards father ant; and their witches mother ant."

Suda cocked her head to the side; as if she had seen him perform a magic trick and couldn't believe her eyes. Only it was her ears she mistrusted. *Farangs* could easily pickup a few words in Thai. But the words for wizard and witch existed in the realm of expression restricted to native speakers or longtime residents who occupied the position of insiders.

"How do you know this in Thai?"

Breach shook the ants off his hand. He grinned and said nothing for a moment. As he let the silence accumulate, he watched the broken column of ants reunite.

"How much cash do they want?" he asked.

He had struck the mother lode. Suda smiled. "I think they want a lot of cash. My friend work on house. He from village. He say maybe ten thousand dollars."

Breach shook his head. "Why didn't you tell me before?"

"I not know you *paa moht* before." She smiled and walked off the porch.

"What else haven't I asked that you can tell me?" asked Breach, following her down the stairs. "For instance, Ross's card game."

She pursed her lips. "We go to the village now."

Suda breathed normally again from the moment they left for the village. She liked the idea that she held back the information from her friend and sprang it on him. Breach had been shocked. There was something powerful in Breach's illusions that disturbed her; his use of Thai for wizard and witch was another sleight-of-hand trick—one that frightened her. Perhaps he understood everything she had said in Thai? Perhaps he had pretended ignorance for his own purposes. The prospect unsettled her. Joking had the opposite effect on her. Tricks with cards, a coin, the thread, and the perfect use of the Thai words for wizard and witch did not play like a joke.

She walked ahead over the fields. She said nothing. Her mind worked over the possibility that the joke might be on her. Joking was a serious business in the covert network of connected families. It smoothed hurt feelings, it allowed face to be saved, it provided relief from boredom, and created a playful atmosphere in the midst of deadly business. Why did he think the Lahu had lost their sense of humor? Did he really want her to help? He walked like a *paw moht*. The ants had come over his hand and were not afraid. Who was this strange *farang* wanting shaman knives? And what— or whom—did he have in mind for a sacrifice?

Breach calculated the odds. How strong a hand was he holding? It was difficult to read: first he didn't know who was the dealer and who else was playing. He still was unclear exactly what the stakes were. Everywhere he had gone, some new, unexpected connection had been created. The feeling made him paranoid; he couldn't tell whether these invisible lines that tied one person to the next were being used to rig the game. He assumed a fix of some kind was at work. What pulled him along after Suda and toward the Lahu village was a strange curiosity to discover what game everyone was playing. He felt once he found Snow again, then maybe, he thought, some order, some control of information might let him understand why he had been dropped into this network.

Farangs were always getting into problems with the locals, he told himself. Too much money, too much interest in drugs; and too little common sense, knowledge of language, and the suffering of the people living in the mountains. The *farang* intruder affected their mood; shook the network up and down the spiral of coiled webs, waking the sleeping, stopping conversations, making them think about routes of escape, old hurts, and grievances.

The *farangs* caused the locals to meditate on the seriousness of their own captivity. It caused malfunctioning in the network, messed up alliances, and let pain sealed inside an old scar spread to the surface. The wizard or a witch had been burnt, drawn, and quartered, or hanged in the West and the East; and for roughly the same reasons: they confronted the layered networks with a direct protest or challenge to their authority. They suggested rebellion. They arrived with tricks up their sleeves, they turned the tables, and they seduced power they had not earned. They mastered the local languages of witchcraft and searched for the local tools used in rituals of birth, death, planting, coming of age, and marriage. They were opportunists who saw the defect, who saw the opening, and who marched forward with the same smell of victory as an advancing army.

Tuttle had deciphered this message from the message of Snow's abduction: that another wizard was needed to rescue the one in trouble. Someone who understood the correspondences between magic and evil, whores and nuns, gunmen and saints, and could reconstruct the equilibrium which had been ruptured. Evil wizards and good wizards, wise wizards and stupid and clever ones, bounced off the same web, penetrating the same boundaries as they rose and fell. The only difference between them was some actually believed they could control the place where they would land—someone like Snow—and then there were wizards like Breach who had learned one lesson in his travels and search for the webless place, the place of the soft landing: intentions, good or evil, were no guidance system in the fall, and because every place corresponded with another, it made no difference whether one landed on one analogy or another.

Chapter 8

The Lahu villagers toiled on the sloping fields beyond the sight of their village. They cleared the land by setting the fields on fire, burning off the undergrowth, and then the real toil began: breaking the hard surface of the rocky mountain sides with hoes. Suda led the way, climbing along the narrow trail that snaked through the fields, around the mountains, and wound into the village. On the trail, there was no shade from the sun As far as the eye could see, the earth in all directions rippled and pitched like a gale-force sea of liquid red soil and rock had frozen solid. It was the kind of alien terrain that inspired a belief in a world of invisible spirit, hidden forces of good and evil, all related and interconnected with the people working the land. Such beliefs and illusions were the inexhaustible resource of the *maw pee*, the wizard, and the magician. The Lahu landscape made Breach smile; made him feel more at ease.

"I'm going to like it here," he said to Suda.

"Why you like it?" she snapped back, not quite believing he was sincere.

"The land is like an erotic milkshake you want to drink straight down before making love."

Suda stared out trying to see what in the land had caused Breach's outburst. She saw scrub brush, scrawny trees, and, in the distance against the horizon, small forms bent forward hacking at the earth. Nowhere did she see evidence of an erotic milkshake or any other dairy product.

As Breach and Suda arrived, the Lahu had gathered up their tools and headed either alone, or in small groups of two or three, back to the village. They were dots crawling over the surface. A line moving in the distance. Like the ants running on the railing at the house. The *maa moht* and *paa moht* figures churning the soil underfoot as they raced home. A Lahu woman sang in a sweet, liquid voice; half plea, half celebration, creating a sound that seemed to come from every direction. She wore a black dress with white-striped sleeves and she walked with a baby strapped to their back. Her voice, high, rich-textured like a fine musical instrument, echoed off ridges and carried through the gullies. Another voice picked up the song. Soon a chorus of voices, clear and strong, shook off the heavy burden of the day. Tracks of playful, hopeful sounds vibrating across stretches of cracked, broken earth. Fields from which they retreated in song as if they had awakened from a long slumber.

The Lahu villagers were framed for a second like a deer moving on a slope, knowing every foothold, ducking around rocks and trees, stopping with wide eyes to observe the *farang* man and Thai woman across a small gully from them. Explorer or exploiter, one and the same had invaded before. Who Breach and Suda were ultimately made no difference to the Lahu who hurried along pathways which slanted against the slopes like a lifeline thrown into the sea. A splash of a voice raised in song, then silence, as the Lahu crept away along fields turned into a sea of cut earth, earth folded like skin back on itself, as if a bulldozer had gone out of control, stripping and disconnecting the surface from the mountains.

"Such sweet music," he said, thinking these were the people holding Snow and threatening to end his life.

"Lahu always singing," replied Suda.

"When it was just me and the bats, I used to sing. I sang morning and night. You know why I sang all the time?"

Suda shook her head, listening to the Lahu singing coming closer. "Why you sing all the time?"

116

Breach smiled. "Not to make bat soup, my ducky. In the morning I tried to translate the world to myself. And at night, I tried to translate myself to the world. It was my way to see if I still existed."

"And do you?" Suda taunted him. "Still exist?"

"If not, then to whom are you asking the question?"

Suda did not reply and walked off in the direction of the village. He watched her climb above him. With his foot, Breach pushed over a clump of red clay; it split apart as it rolled down the steep incline. He thought about the land when the rains came. With the trees gone, whole mountains would liquefy into mud. Mountains of mud with the speed and force of a tidal wave would make the motionless sea come alive, washing over villages, roads, livestock, and people.

But the rainy season was months off. All that washed over the mountains were the distant soprano voices of Lahu women, singing strange songs as they walked the rim around their fields. Women singing themselves home. Singing about destination beyond the fields and home. Lahu men calling across the expanse of hand-turned fields to one another.

When he caught up with her on the trail, they came across a group of three young Lahu boys. The boys, who looked like the ones they had seen earlier on the road, were in their early teens. One had a large knife in a wooden scabbard strapped to his right hip. His friend, another boy, pulled a two-foot silver-bellied snake behind him. He had made a leash from string and tied one end three or four inches behind the base of the snake's head. The dull black eyes of the snake stared at the trail, and as the boy held the string chest-high, the snake appeared to sit up and beg. Two of the boys waited on the scarp and the third boy disappeared around the bend.

Suda asked after the headman of the village and a couple of other people. She dropped the name of her friend who owned the teak house two kilometers away. The sense of alarm left the boys and they relaxed, flashing a rare smile. They had killed the snake an hour earlier, bashing it with a stick—though, from the outside, there were no visible marks or wounds. The snake was for dinner and would end up on a bed of rice.

Breach squatted beside the snake. He made a pass beside the head of the snake and showed the boys the coin he had taken from the snake's head. The boys exchanged a nervous glance. They seemed to have stopped breathing.

"Snow," said one of the boys, sneaking a glance at his friends. A signal was exchanged, and fear filled their faces.

The boys turned and ran away, leaving the snake beside Breach tangling on the end of the string. He pulled the dead snake up eye-level and looked at the head.

"I think you scare them," said Suda.

"Look into the dead eye of a snake and see the universe as if really is," said Breach, rising to his feet and lowering the snake back to the ground. "Scared? Yes, I agree with you. But who has scared them? That is the question. Boys pulling death behind them. Who turned a child's illusion into an act of terror? That great magician, Snow?" That had been the great lesson of history: children loved wizards because they shared, with children, the faith of innocence, and used illusions to restore and redeem innocence; but one day a wizard might believe he had become sacred and turn his face another way. This was disaster.

Breach had seen in the boys' eyes something he often looked for: the state of innocence. On the mountain what he saw in their eyes were children whose innocence had been vandalized. What should have been preserved or bestowed was gone. Magic for them had turned into mugging and robbery. He wondered if this had been Snow's doing; or whether other forces had intervened. All Breach knew for certain was where there should have been laughter and joy, there had been abject fear. These were not city children; but children of the land. They had told him that something was very wrong in their village, in their lives.

A short distance from the spot where the boys had fled, they came upon the Lahu village. Grass thatching covered the slanted-roofed houses which had been baked by the sun into a dull brown. Clusters of houses rose on thick bamboo stilts from the dried and cracked ground. Black-haired sows grunted and ran across the path and disappeared around an outcrop of rock as Suda, walking ahead, approached the village gate. Constructed from bamboo posts on either side of the path, the arch of the gate was decorated with a lattice of bamboo scrolls, geometric images, ceremonial patterns and designs.

❖

"*Maw pee*—Shaman," said Suda, stopping short of the gate and pointing at the arch.

"I know the *Maw pee* is your mother's second cousin."

"He is my friend," she replied.

He assumed she would not make a cold call on a village holding a *farang* for ransom. He had begun to assume that her connection, like the universe, expanded outward, touching everywhere and everyone in her path; her wide band of friendship stretched from the cities through the mountains, friends of the past and the present interconnected, friends who called her by name.

He examined the ritual gate which led into the village from the fields. The shaman's gateway was a kind of spiritual card trick. The kind of entrance which was alien in modern cities.

"I have a friend who has one of these," said Breach, thinking of Pierce's reconstructed ritual gate.

"Where he buy?"

"He made it himself," said Breach, pausing. "From memory. In his last life, he was a *Maw Pee*. It's a homemade job in his garden. The cat uses it as a clawing post. His dog pisses on it. Robins built a nest in the top; crows robbed nesting material from it. The neighbor kids used it as a May pole. A drunken friend vomited on one side of it. And all the time, the cells inside his stomach were rearranging themselves into radically new patterns, and growing faster and faster."

"I think not the same," said Suda.

"The same, or not the same. Does it really matter?"

Like Thomas Pierce's gate, this one was an entrance to a theatre of supernatural performances. The Lahu village was founded on a share faith in magic, ritual, and illusions. The shamans were wizards; they were storytellers and magicians; the keepers and communicators of the narrative story that knitted villagers to nature, created their sense of awe, respect, indeed, reverence for the land and animals who shared it with them. They had the ability, like all wizards, to lift people out of time and out of themselves. Believe in this and find safety, relief from suffering and sorrow, believe in me and I will deliver you. Only the form changed but the message remained the same over time and place; it was found in every priest's words of comfort; inside every cathedral. Pierce thought his legacy was the same. As his gate fell into ruin, he never lost faith even though he must have known everyone had lost their faith generations ago.

Breach stared at the gate with professional interest. One magician admiring the paraphernalia of a colleague. He judged the quality of the handiwork, walking around the structure, nodding as he walked. Suda eyed him closely, feeling he sensed something she had missed.

"Bamboo and English winters don't mix well. Too much snow," said Breach. "A gate like this in Oxford might last three, four seasons, then it was bird nest soup."

She was still upset over the incident involving the village boys and the dead snake. It was not a good omen. She disliked entering a village behind advance word that some threshold of fear had been tripped by a stranger.

"I think too much Snow in this village," she said.

Breach's head snapped around. "You are quick," he said.

What had Snow understood the first time he saw the gate, wondered Breach: that these people were an audience who liked magic shows? That they had a pie-in-the-sky craving for illusions? Or maybe, laboring under the modern view of things, that the gate was another kind of McDonald's arch; another marketing miracle. Breach had a feeling Snow had made the classic mistake, taking the paraphernalia as a call for entertainment. Pierce saw it as a plea for redemption. More than one wizard had been destroyed by this kind of confusion.

Breach touched the latticework.

"Magicians don't like competition," said Breach. He raised his hands wide apart. "It makes them feel vulnerable. Nice work here. Whoever put this up is serious about his work."

"You kill that snake?"

Breach looked around from the arch. "You think I killed the boys' snake."

"I don't know. I ask you. You kill it or not?"

"It was already dead." She looked unconvinced. "Don't go weird on me, Suda."

"Why you know about *paa moht?*"

He lingered until Suda grew impatient.

Then she caught sight of one of the boys they found dragging the dead snake on the string. He quickly darted behind one of the houses. She ran after him. A minute later she emerged, smiling and relaxed. "He say they kill snake. We go now."

Each day the Lahu walked through that gate, reaffirming values about themselves, their condition, their struggle with the land. It was "the way" into the village and "the way" out. Breach had the sudden urge to push the entire structure to the ground, burn it, spit on it, kick dirt on it. There was no way in or out, he thought. It was that kind of distorted perception which had convinced a crazy monk that he was that part of a woman's vulva which experienced pleasure. And that the human species was the vibrating sensory organ that allowed the universe a climax.

"I didn't kill the snake. And let me explain what I believe about this arch. People who make them die of cancer just like anyone else. And when a bat shits on your head this is as close as anyone ever comes to the cosmic description about in and out, thrust and afterburn, penetration and withdrawal," he said.

"No problem, for you," said Suda. "You tell it to the shaman. He's over there. You want to see Snow, he can tell you where Snow is." She nodded at an old man standing next to the boy from the path. The boy no longer looked frightened. The shaman stared hard at Breach.

"Show time," he said under his breath, kicking a stone from the path.

"I asked him about your friend."

"Snow's not my friend. I only met him a couple of hours ago."

"No problem. We find him."

Beyond the gate a smoky haze painted the sky a sludge-gray, weaving a thick white mist among the thatched houses. Notched logs leaned against each bamboo veranda, making a narrow kind of staircase. Suda walked ahead, following the wide dirt path through the village. She cut behind several houses as the path sloped steeply in the direction of the headman's house. On the veranda, wearing shorts and a Mets shirt, a *farang* sat, legs stretched out, one ankle hooked over the other, writing in a notebook. His tortoiseshell-framed glasses slipped to the edge of his nose, and he brushed one hand through his investment banker's haircut.

"That your friend?" asked Suda.

Breach blinked hard; it hadn't occurred to him that besides Snow there were other *farangs* in the Lahu village. He shook his head, closed and opened his eyes, but the *farang* in the Met shirt was still on the veranda when he looked again.

"Trekkers come here sometimes," said Suda.

"Tourists. My God, the *Maw Pee* takes American Express," said Breach, doing a little dance.

He waved at the young man on the porch who looked up and grinned back. Someone else from the city checking in for a magic show, thought Breach, finishing his dance.

"Have you seen Snow?" shouted Breach.

"Mister, I haven't seen rain. This is reality. Lyricism can be found everywhere in these gentle people. They have found their spiritual selves. If only we could learn from them," he said, as if he was reading from memory what he had just finished writing.

He glanced at his notebook, then at Suda, and without a word, returned to writing in his notebook.

"You write that shit down on paper?" asked Breach.

The young man nodded, as anger crossed his face. "What would you know about reality?"

"The clitoris of the universe is in Columbus, Ohio," said Breach.

As they walked away from the thatched house, Breach kicked at an empty tin of beans in the road.

"Many *farangs* in Thailand," said Suda.

"A mini-festival of *farangs*," muttered Breach.

"Why they come to Thailand?"

"They come looking for new stories, adventure, drugs. They want to get laid."

The *farang* on the porch was another serious face looking for a narrative in all the wrong places. It was old-hat that the cities had created a bureaucratic consciousness. A consciousness which stored, shifted, and passed along information. What was information but a story with its magic and prophecy lost? Rattling around the world were a vanguard of people trying to escape (living and travelling undercover as tourists) from the hell zones of information, places of concentrated facts, events, business operations, where millions used information to produce patterns and shapes so immense and oblique that no one person, government, or think tank fully understood the random connections all these information sculptures had made.

Breach remembered them like a lost flock flying into Nepal; the data bank drones believing that in the mud, shit, and sink-hole villages buried in a fetid swamp between mountains that the secrets, plans, failures, and movements of that data could be unraveled, pieced back together to supply meaning. Or they could recover some encoded sacred vision untouched over time that might redeem them from their data jails. As if inside the primitive mind, pre-modern man had no information; as if they existed on a pure story.

People from California and England came to his cave in the early morning. Breach ignored them. He told no stories, performed no magic. He sat in the entrance and shuffled cards and sang. Sometimes he walked to the entrance and stared at the sky as tall as a man, then walked back inside, yawned, curled up and slept. Sometimes he sold them postcards. They gave him fruit, nuts, and water. After awhile, they went away. They had found nothing corresponding to the idea they had inside their own head. And that was their transcendent experience, thinking they had escaped the information sculptures that populated their thoughts and dreams.

"Tell us the truth," one would say.

"Bats sleep during the day," Breach would answer.

They would nod in agreement.

"And they fuck at night upside down," he would add.

They would reverently nod again.

124

"And when they finish fucking they go to sleep."

"It's so simple," said one of the group.

"And one more thing," said Breach. "No other bats ever come to this cave and ask them to tell them the truth."

Even a second-rate wizard could pull most of these people straight to the bottom. They wanted to be conned by illusions, magic, and story; the heart of darkness was the horrible, awful realization that con never changed. The story became sacred, then the storyteller; and everyone remained trapped in the same wilderness of patterns, connections, and information.

Snow had followed the same pattern. Like a good emcee, he probably had a basic skill, an instinct of vesting connections in the lives of others with intention and purpose. That was his undoing, his mistake. Sooner or later the audience woke up and asked some hard questions. Snow was a difficult case; such a person might not want to be rescued—or why the routine on horseback? Or had Snow been playing the same tune he had played in the entrance to his Nepal cave? Breach had been to the edge of that frontier, he knew from Crosby what Snow's rap was "Fuck the women, man. Take no survivors over eighteen. Trash cars, TV sets, and electric can openers. Take a crap under the shaman's gate."

Breach walked behind Suda and the shaman, thinking the sky looked an ash-gray; the color of cremation smoke he used to watch blow across the river from his cave.

The headman, lips bar-girl red with betel, two skinny brown dogs at his side, greeted Suda on the veranda of his house. His wife, her face wrinkled and puffy, jowls sagging, stuck her head out of the doorway. Her breasts were the texture of leather and when she walked they flopped like dried bats inside a rough cotton blouse untied to the belly.

The headman invited Suda into his house. He looked at Breach with the politician's face that gave nothing away, and said something in a low voice to Suda.

"He says we go inside now," said Suda.

"I like him, too."

"We eat first."

Breach followed Suda up the narrow—no more than eight inches wide—wooden stairs cut from a single piece of timber.

Dogs and pigs and children scampered along the splintered steps. A traffic jam of kids and animals brushing against each other, squealing and laughing. Breach removed his shoes on the porch. He ducked down, walking through the low open doorway into the house. Several minutes passed before his eyes adjusted to the darkness. A charcoal fire burned near the center of the room; pots and kettle bubbled. It looked the same as the shaman's house on the mountain outside of Chiang Mai, creating the illusion there was simply one house containing different people shifting in time and space.

A young Thai man, stripped to the waist, nodded to Suda as she sat down on the mat. The headman sat cross-legged on the floor beside Breach, smiled and began speaking in Thai. Suda saw Breach looking around the hot, damp room.

"*Kow!-jai!*—Do you understand?" she asked him.

"*Mai! Kow!-jai!*—I don't understand," he replied.

She told the headman about *maa moht* and *paa moht.*

The headman, in his early 60s, laughed, his mouth of stained, cracked, worn-out teeth looked like one of the scorned fields with tree stumps shrivelled and shrunken by fire. A slash and burn smile blazed across his face as he shook his head.

"*Khun paa moht?*—are you a wizard?" the headman asked him.

"*Chart gorn*—last life," said Breach, watching the expression on Suda's face.

"*Poot len*—you tell a joke," she said.

Breach smiled, "Last life I told jokes. This life I tell the truth but everyone thinks they are jokes. Next life, the jokes on me."

The old headman listened to Suda translation, his eyes sparkling and he nodded, smiling as he stared at Breach. He told Breach a story. A week earlier, a West German woman had been on a three-day trek; part of the journey was by elephant. On one of the mountain slopes, the elephant, either too tired, mean, or careless, lost its footing and toppled over, sending the woman curled into a frightened ball, rolling into a ravine. She had the wind knocked out of her, bruises, and a bloody nose. Nothing had been broken, except maybe her pride.

"Elephant not understand *farang*," Suda translated the old man as saying. "Maybe she kick him in ear. Elephant no like. She go back to Chiang Mai and make big complaint. Funny. Ride elephant, sometimes fall off."

As the headman roared with laugher, Breach broke into song as if he were back in the cave. The house echoed with the lyrics from an old Janice Juplin tune, "Oh, Lord, won't you buy me a Mercedes Benz, my friends all drive Cadillacs and I must make amends."

Her raspy voice pumped through his head as the young man with the tortoiseshell-framed glasses arrived with three other equally short-cropped hair *farangs*. The Thai who, stripped to the waist, had been tending the pots, spoke to them in perfect, unaccented English.

"Sit anywhere you like. The water's okay to drink. And I bought the food in Chiang Mai. It's not too spicy. Everyone who comes on the trek loves it. Just dig in. Help yourself."

Breach nodded to the man he had seen writing on the porch. "Did you finish your letter?"

"Book. I'm writing a book," he replied. "You find Snow yet," he added, after a moment, nudging one of his friends with an elbow.

"He'll turn up," said Breach, sticking his head into the boiling pot and sniffing. "In one pot of stew or another."

"I don't get the log stair," said one of the *farang*. "You could break your ass climbing down that to take a piss in the middle of the night."

The guide smiled, lowered his spoon with rice and lamb curry. "They pull the log up at night. That keeps the dogs and any wild animals from getting into the house. If you've need to take a leak, look at the floor. See the gap between the bamboo. That's your toilet. You're eating on it." He laughed in a way he liked telling this story to *farang* at mealtime; that it was one of the pleasures of his job.

Suda leaned over close to Breach. She rested her hand on his wrist. "He say, he not see your friend."

"You mean we are eating where we piss?" asked another of the *farang*, his mouth full of unchewed food.

Breach enjoyed such moments of revelation; in the search for the exotic, sooner or later most people discovered the distinctions between eating and excreting swiftly collapsed, slamming closed like a series of doors on stupidity and innocence. Unity of vision didn't come free; for every insight, there was a price to pay, and it was too high for most. They wanted to maintain the separation of functions. At each crossroad, as one shed the skin of ignorance, there was a toll booth which foreshadowed the existence of another down the road.

He watched the old headman who was eyeing him. He thought about the two boys on the trail; their panic and terror. So that was the way it was going to be.

"Tell him, no problem. There's been a mistake."

The headman grinned and nodded as Suda translated. Breach rose to his feet. He stretched and walked back onto the porch. The old woman sat in the corner chewing betel. Breach knelt down beside her. He traced his finger in the dust of the wooden slats. He pulled a ball of the yarn out of his shirt and placed it on her lap.

"*Khun hen farang Cheu Snow.*—Have you seen a westerner named Snow?" Breach asked her.

She picked up the ball of red yarn and turned it over in her weathered hands. She drew her lips together, then smiled the bright red betel smile. Coiling back, she half-turned and spit over the porch railing. She raised her eyebrows toward a house three rows away.

Chapter 9

Breach quietly slipped between a row of thatched houses. The sunlight streaked through a cloud of red dust carried by a slight wind. A fine layer of dust powdered the windows. He walked with a handkerchief tied around his mouth and nose. With only his dark eyes visible, he might have been a bandit. Heads popped around corners, a furtive glance of a young boy eating an orange, a mother breast-feeding a skinny baby. Breach saw in their movement the dance of people who wish to avoid contact with a stranger. The villagers hid in the cool shadows behind the bamboo walls; their houses raised from the earth on wood piles looked barren, ragged, like a ribcage with most of the meat picked off by vultures. Breach headed downhill along the path which led to the road out of the village. Above the rows of thatched gabled roofs TV antenna cast long spidery shadows from the late afternoon sun.

He paused in front of the house pointed out to him by the old woman. In the air was the smell of peppers and garlic bubbling on a stove somewhere close by. Breach slowly pulled the handkerchief down from his face. A skin-and-bones cat, a skeleton wrapped in yellowish scrappy fur, sprang from a pile of firewood and landed on the veranda; a small rat hung limp in its mouth. The cat, seeing Breach, froze, slowly turned, and disappeared behind two large water jars. A moment later it emerged, and ran down the middle of a van tire track. The road sloped in the direction of the Trekker's Lodge, and down the mountain road to Highway 1019.

Breach felt the tingling in his hands which told him he was being watched. He spun around, looking into the windows of the house, and then glanced at the house across the road. A woman with a gaunt, feverish face with blotchy yellow puffy bags beneath the eyes, swung away from the doorway as if she were attached to a hinge. Then she appeared back in the doorway and stuffed a fistful of rice into her gullet. Her face was like the cat, thought Breach. A hungry, desperate, ill, and frightened face etched with the corrosive furrows which came with suffering and poverty. She had a heads-you-lose-and-tails-I-win resignation, thought Breach as he watched her chew the rice.

He walked a few more steps. Could the headman's wife, the old woman, who had eyed his trick with the yarn, have been mistaken? Or, more likely, she had sent him on a wild-goose chase while pocketing the ball of yarn. He halted in front of the last bamboo veranda of the last house where he discovered a porch littered with rubbish: a yellow plastic bucket, a twenty-four-cup coffee machine with a broken cord, and a scuffed pair of white Reeboks that were like the pair Snow had been wearing on horseback. The laces were dirty and bunched up. One shoe was tipped over on its side, and Breach reached down to pick it up.

"*Hue kao*—I'm hungry," moaned Snow. Breach turned around but couldn't place the voice. "I'm starving, man. Can you get me some food?"

"Snow?" He called out. "Where are you."

Snow lapsed into silence and he sought to determine whether someone was playing a cruel joke. He heard Breach's voice call his name again. The voice was not that of a Lahu.

"Who the fuck. . .what the fuck. . .who are you, man?" The voice was in a panic of emotion.

"A friend of Tuttle. He said you might be in trouble."

"Shit, forget about the *might* bit. I'm talking human bondage, man. These assholes won't even let me watch TV," said Snow.

Breach walked across the veranda and looked through the window. Snow sprawled on the floor, his legs and arms tied. Inside the room, Snow stared at him and gave a faint smile. Breach crouched down and began untying his ropes.

"Hey, I remember you. You were on the road with the broad. The Lahu wanted to kill you, man. But after I told you to go away, they changed their mind."

"That was big of them," said Breach.

"Hey, don't think you can fuck with these guys."

Breach shrugged off his assessment. "The Lahu figured if you really knew your stuff, you should be out of these ropes in under two minutes," said Breach. The ropes were looped round Snow's shoulders and cut into his flesh.

"And they figured if you knew your stuff, you would come back for me," said Snow. "These guys enjoy fucking around with your head."

"Where are they?"

"On the other side of the village working on the van. Dirt fucked up the fuel pump. They were a little pissed off when they found me shoving dirt into the fuel injection system. I said, hey man, it's a trick. Now you've fucked with it. It's your problem. They didn't like that much."

"What are they planning next?" asked Breach.

Snow rubbed his wrist, trying to get the blood circulating again.

"They want to move me. When you saw me on the road, they were coming back from a Karen village. They went to borrow a van. But it was down in Chiang Mai."

Snow leaned forward and untied the ropes around his ankles and kicked them off. But his ankles were chained with a padlock and the chain threaded through an iron hook anchored to the floor.

"Let's get the hell out of here," said Breach, looking out through the open window at the empty path.

"It ain't that simple, man. There's a woman across the street watching this place. And she's got a gun. The entire village is armed to the teeth with fucking guns."

"You do want to go?" asked Breach.

"Does the Pope shit in the forest?"

"I don't know," Breach replied, thinking of how best to cut through the one-inch chain holding Snow to the floor.

"Now let me ask you a question. How the fuck did you get in here without getting your ass shot off? And how much are you getting paid to help me? And how much money you got to pay them off?" asked Snow. His eyes looked puffy from lack of sleep and beatings. From the four- or five-day growth of beard, Crosby had been kept on the move for nearly a week.

"That's more than one question."

"Okay, okay. How did Tuttle arrange this?"

"Through a friend of a friend who knows the headman," said Breach.

"The headman's asshole. I wouldn't trust any of his friends either," said Snow. "So who is this guy?"

"It's not a guy. It is a she," said Breach.

"Not the skinny broad with you on the road?"

Breach shrugged his shoulder, running his fingers across the length of chain.

"Oh, man, I am fucking doomed. Unless that little bitch has a flamethrower or two. Then we have a chance." He patted his crotch, his head tilted down. "Otherwise, it's good-bye amigos."

Suda knew not only the headman but the situation; of course, she had known from the moment they left Bangkok, thought Breach. Like much of what she thought or knew, she had kept it to herself; there had been no point in explaining the setup to Breach. She let Tuttle perform that task in the letter. This left her in the clear. It was Breach's

133

decision whether to go into the village, his decision to find Snow, and his decision to bring Snow back down. Breach stared at Snow, chained to the floor of a Lahu village house—he had to decide. Was this man worth what lay outside the door waiting to stop them from going down the mountain?

"Is Crosby here, too?" asked Snow, resting his head back, half closing his eyes.

Breach nodded his head. "Yeah, he's in town with his lawyer."

"Not that hamburger, Ross?"

"*Old Grand-Dad*," said Breach.

"I can't stand booze or smoke. That shit will kill you."

Breach smiled, holding several links of the chain. "A lot of things can kill you in this life."

Snow had arrived in the village three months earlier with a suitcase of store-boxed illusions and magic tricks shipped by courier from New York City. Breach had been Snow's replacement in Bangkok. When the Lahu figured out Snow wasn't in the Peace Corps, the government, the police, and had no apparent network of friends, they decided he was the kind of goods that could be sold back to his parents. Snow was allowed to send word out through Lek, a village girl, a seventeen-year-old whore who worked at the *Tiger Bar* in Patpong. His balls were on the block. He was scared shitless. She delivered his message to Crosby. The note had been short and to the point.

"I saw *Star Trek: The New Generation* on the headman's TV. That old fart is on one side and the *maw pee* is on my other side when Captain Kirk says, 'Beam me up, Scottie.' The *maw pee* loved it. Kirk goes all shimmery and shows up inside the Star Ship Enterprise. The headman says, 'You can do or not?' Man, I thought they were joking. I said, 'That's special effects.' So the *maw pee* who has hated my ass from day one sees an opportunity. 'Okay, hot shit, a Lahu godman can do or we might start to think he's just another honkie trying to jump the bones of our virgins.'

"The *maw pee* said jump the bones of our virgins?" interrupted Breach with a question, as they sat opposite one another on the floor.

Snow rattled the chain on the floor. "Or words to that effect."

"And then you were finished," sighed Breach.

"Not so fast, man," said Breach. "In between the Johnny Walker and Volvo commercials, I knew I was in the shit. If I said, 'Hey, guys, lay off. Lahu godmen don't beam anyone up,' I was toast. If I said, 'already,' and fucked it up, which of course was one hundred percent assured, I was toast. All the time I'm thinking, life is a bitch. I love *Star Trek*. I fucking grew up glued to the tube watching Spock and Captain Kirk. I'm a lifelong, card-carrying Trekkie, a Spock addict who landed on this alien planet between an old fart headman and a neurotic *maw pee*. So I played for time. I said, 'Yeah, I can do that shit. No problem. But I need some preparation time. I have to sacrifice some chickens, drink some lizard blood, smear some spiderwebs on my dick, and fuck a few virgins.' And you know what? The *maw pee* suddenly takes my side. The little shit tells the headman, 'We send Lahu Godman some virgins.'

"After *Star Trek* the old headman and *maw pee* get ripped on opium. I come back to the Lahu godman's house. This place here. And about where you are now, I find a Lahu girl in a tank top and blue shorts between two candles. In the candlelight she's all skinny legs and dirty feet and watery eyes. She's shaking and rocking back and forth, clutching a fucking teddy bear against her breasts. After about an hour, she calms down and says that her name is Noi, she's a fifteen-year-old virgin, and arrived compliments of the *maw pee*. 'Maw pee say I make with you,' Noi said. 'But I afraid.' I kiss her gently on the lips. 'Don't be afraid,' I said. 'I think cure hurt me bad.' And I say to myself, that's kind of cute, in a Lahu village, the girls thinking of losing their virginity as a cure. Not like rat-faced, fat-assed white women who believe sex with a man is rape.

"She slipped off her shorts, dropped them on the floor, then pulled off the tank top. All the time she's balancing the teddy bear which smells like rancid pineapple. Now she's naked and still on the floor, legs crossed, and she's waiting. I whip off my clothes, and I think to myself, 'This is what it is like to be a god.' After watching *Star Trek* you go back to your bunk and the local witch doctor has supplied you with a fifteen-year-old virgin. I'm squeezing those firm, ripe breasts. Heaven. Then she wraps a leg around my neck. 'Not bad, for a virgin,' I think to myself. 'The kid might have hidden talent.' Then she wraps her other leg around my neck and starts pumping my face with her mound. It has a sweet smell. Paradise. Don't ask me why because I had this raging hard-on, but I said to her, 'Baby, I'm gonna give you the cure.' And you know what she says? 'Good, then I can get my job back in Chiang Mai. No more AIDS. No more problem. You cure me now, okay?

"I'm looking straight into the hole. It's like her voice box had fallen between her legs. 'Say again?' And she obliged me, '*Maw pee* say I fuck you, no more AIDS.' I slowly unwrap Noi's legs from around my neck. I clutch her teddy bear and roll onto the floor. I start chanting. Of course, Noi's freaking out. I knock over a fucking candle and about burn down the Lahu godman's house. She puts the fire out with her shorts. I tell her this is the cure. I examined her breasts, then her mound, and chant. Bingo, no more AIDS, and now she can go and fuck the *maw pee*. 'Tell, him compliments of the Lahu godman.'

"Now the *maw pee* knows I'm hip to the village virgin scam. After a one-week deadline, we watch *Star Trek* again. Again, the old headman and *maw pee* want a demonstration from me. But I still can't beam them up. 'Smoke opium. That's how they do it,' I said. They didn't buy it. God knows, I fucking tried to think of a way to get rid of *maw pee*. The village is his turf. And I'm, of course, fucked. Being God ain't what it used to be. Since I can't beam them into a Chiang Mai whorehouse and I won't fuck their AIDS-infested virgins, they decide to un-god me. I say, 'No hard feelings. Let's shake hands. We're keep in touch. Good-bye, so long, and keep trekking.'

"But it was too late. They were willing to let this ex-Lahu godman keep his balls for ten thousand US. They wanted the cash to buy someone's older brother and an uncle out of a seven-year jail term. The government threw their asses in prison for cutting down teak trees. For ten grand the prison would look the other way. Money forgives all and the guys would walk out of jail. They give me two choices. Or the *maw pee* says, 'We give you a second chance. Can't beam me to whorehouse. No problem. Get brother and uncle out of jail instead.' If I'm God, then I can spring the two tree felons from jail or find a godlike friend with ten grand US. They said it was simple. They are waiting for me to decide. Magic or cash. Or I'm minus two balls. I write Crosby and ask him for a small favor: Advance me ten grand. Make that pronto!"

An earlier attempt to free Snow and pay the ransom had failed. Snow's parents pulled together the cash from their Visa, Mastercard and American Express credit cards. They wired the money to Crosby. Crosby collected the cash in at two in the afternoon, and by eight that night he was in a card game. A friendly game that started with twenty-baht bets. By two that morning, Crosby had lost seven grand. The Lahu villagers refused to settle for the remaining three grand.

"Why didn't Tuttle come?" asked Breach, peeking out the window. The woman across the road was still hunched over a plastic bucket of ginger. A rifle leaned in the doorway.

"I can't blame Bobby. Some asshole colonel wants to fuck his daughter. The second Bobby leaves Bangkok, Asanee is as good as screwed whether she wants it or not."

"Tuttle a hostage?" asked Breach.

"Man, we'll all fucking hostages. Except some have a bigger deck to run around on."

Snow leaned his head back against the interior wall and stared unblinking at the ceiling. "Crosby didn't lose the fucking money again, please, God, tell me he didn't lose it," Snow said to himself.

"Crosby has the money. Sort of, that is," said Breach.

"Man, these guys are sort of going to cut off my balls and dick for refusing to hammer about a half-dozen diseased so-called virgins. They are into weird shit, man. Look across the road. See a dog?"

Breach leaned back from the window and looked over his shoulder. Across the road, the lifeless body of a dog lay sprawled out on a deep bed of straw. At first the absolute stillness of the animal suggested it was dead and had been dumped. A scruffy white color with a smudge of brown over one ear; the dog could have passed for any feral soi dog in a Bangkok dead end soi. Breach walked over, stood beside the dog. The lid of the dog's eye flickered with flies. Its testicles had been cut off and stuffed in its mouth. Breach pivoted around as two villagers came up the road. He recognized them. They had been with Crosby earlier on the road.

"You see it?" called Snow from the thatched house, unaware his captors were returning.

"Your horse trainers are back," said Breach.

"Fuck, man. Tonight it's my turn. That piss-ant *maw pee* wants to fuck me up bad. The deadline is midnight." Breach flinched and dropped the chain. "They didn't tell you that, man?"

"I'll be back."

"Cash. No traveller's checks or green stamps," said Snow.

A few feet behind the two villagers, Breach spotted Suda, hands on her hips, glaring at him. She ran up to him as he stepped off the veranda.

"I thought you get lost."

Breach shook his head. "Just having a look around. Sightseeing. Sorry I didn't bring along my camera."

"Maybe we go now. Okay? *Hue kaow, mai?*—are you hungry?" asked Suda.

"Starving for lunch meat," Snow's muffled voice rose from the thatched bamboo house. "Send Jack Flowers. It's kinda hot, ain't it?" Snow babbled into the wind.

The remote Lahu village had a different feel along this path: the one leading toward the highway and Chiang Mai. After a last look at the house where Snow was being held, Breach hurried down the path. He glanced over the road again—house after house in poverty, broken-down squalor—he saw the rotting teeth in a woman's mouth as she, balancing herself on one foot, leaned in a doorway, a baby planted on one hip with a snot-streaked face. She was joined by a man whose tight-lipped face stretched back to reveal black gums; the man removed his silver opium pipe and pointed at Breach and grinned.

Ten thousand dollars would be a lot of money here, thought Breach. And he thought about the American trekkers eating dinner back at the headman's house; they had arrived by this road with their own food supplies and guide. They would leave behind about ten dollars each. The following morning they would depart along the same road. It would be an experience of a lifetime. Tourists came and left under an escort. They submitted to control as a disciple submits to his teacher. Above all they came to see the illusions performed by the Lahu as a kind of spiritual, magical overnight roadshow. A Woodstock weekend for the 1990s. They left never knowing a Trekkie who had beamed down with a pack of illusions which had not played well in the village.

Breach thought of the young man in the tortoiseshell-glasses. Thinking of him glancing back with a sigh as he spotted the skinny old woman whose dark areolas had shriveled like mushrooms left in the sun. What a beautiful, gentle people, the tourist would think. Would they take the same road out? It was unlikely because they had not taken the same road in. What Breach saw, looking back at the last few houses, were hilltribe people overloaded with the ugly scattering of modern junk, TV antenna everywhere, pickup trucks, and coffeemakers.

"It's like an English council house estate," he said.

"Lahu live in England?" asked Suda.

"Anglo-Saxon Lahu," said Breach.

The villagers had surrendered a long time ago to belief in the Almighty Tourist God. This god promised them their share of the goodies from the cities. They could beam up like everyone else. Snow found out that the Lahu tradition of messianic movements was over—killed by the Star Ship Enterprise and Captain Kirk; this God was a historical oddity, a creature gone extinct in the age of television, computers, and fax machines. The Lahu godman was dead, only no one had bothered to inform Snow before he set out with his magic tricks. His timing had been all wrong; the last Lahu godman died before the world had invented Spock.

Suda waited restlessly, hands nervous on her hips. She stood like a bar girl leaning against her pole, peering over the edge of the stage at a customer; a girl who suddenly was pure body language transmitting the common question from a woman to a man: "Can't you make up your mind about your own appetites?"

"Go now. *Hue kaow*—I'm hungry." She walked briskly ahead.

Breach stood anchored to the ground looking at the dead dog left on the side of the road. One of the two men who had accompanied Suda stood on the veranda of the house where Snow was being held. Breach knew he was being watched.

With a flick of his hand, he pulled a bunch of yellow flowers out the air and threw them on the dog.

❖

Ross leaned back in his chair as he concentrated his attention on a rag he dipped into turpentine. He ran the rag along the blade of a rusty knife. He rubbed the sides, stopping to admire his work and taking a drink. A table fan rotated beside the window. His shirt, damp with sweat, stuck to his chest; the collar flapped like bird wings against his neck. His forehead and cheeks were flushed red. Near his elbow was a half empty bottle of *Old Grand-Dad* whiskey. Crosby stretched out on one of the two single beds. His arms folded behind his head, he propped himself up at a forty-five degree angle against two pillows. He had been watching Ross for nearly ten minutes, during which time neither man had exchanged a word. A notched layer of cigarette smoke rose above Crosby's head; he noticed something unexpected in Ross—a strange kind of pride in the rubbing, scrubbing, and polishing as Ross continued to stroke the blade of the large knife.

"You ever drink that stuff?" asked Crosby, nodding at the large tin of turpentine.

"Never. But I've had clients who made their prisoners drink gasoline. Commie political prisoners with a gun pointed at their head drank it by the gallon. It turned them into capitalists."

"Charming," said Crosby, exhaling on his cigarette.

Ross was drunk. He stopped rubbing the knife and looked up at Crosby on the bed. "Maybe you think I was once in the army? That I know secret information about weapons. For instance, you may have heard the rumor that I can field-strip an automatic weapon." Ross paused and took another sip from his glass before refilling it from the bottle. Crosby said nothing. "I neither deny or confirm rumors. But I note

141

that I give that impression to many people," Ross continued. "I carry a VFW life membership card in my wallet." Ross pulled out his wallet, rummaged through the contents, then stopped, a vacant look coming over his face. "What was I looking for?"

"Your VFW card," said Crosby.

Ross found the card and tossed it to Crosby. It landed on his chest. Crosby picked up the card. Lifetime membership in the VFW was printed on the card along with Ross's name.

"While I never served in the army, I saw action in the Cold War. I want you to understand that."

Crosby looked up from the card. Ross's face was more flushed than before. "I wasn't in the army," said Crosby. "So what's your point?"

"That I'm a member of the club."

"Which club might that be?" asked Crosby, tossing back the VFW card.

"The club of people who give the impression they know a great deal about guns, tanks, and antiaircraft placements. That club. That's why this Richard Breach will do what I want him to do. He respects my club. He wishes his sweet ass he had a lifetime membership card."

"Maybe he does," said Crosby, rolling off the bed and buttoning his shirt.

"Where are you going?" asked Ross.

"The fumes from that shit make me sick." Crosby nodded in the direction of the table where the *Old Grand-Dad* and turpentine were side by side. "There is a good chance that you are ruining the value of the knives."

This last remark stung Ross and he reared up, sucking in his stomach, and roared back. "Ruin these! Look at this blade shine. This is restoration work. You don't know dick."

Crosby walked over and tapped the side of the blade. "It says Wilkenson's finest blade, patent applied for 1978. Not exactly an antique."

"You mean that fucking Hmong witch doctor ripped me off?"

Crosby nodded. "He was a Mien. But let's not quibble over hilltribes. Let's say the saleman took certain liberties with the truth. Not unlike most lawyers."

"The man's a common criminal. Faking antiques. Fuck, it does say 1978. That asshole. This is a criminal offence."

"If being an asshole is a criminal offence, Ross. Can there ever be enough prisons?"

"The sonofabitch faked these knives."

"We will make up the money in Mae Sai. Besides, with a little more cleaning, you might be able to use them in the kitchen."

"Fuck," said Ross.

He threw the knife against the wall, and sat back hard in his chair, holding his glass with both hands as he raised it towards his mouth. "I never thought this was going to be easy."

"But you never thought it was going to be this hard," said Crosby, as he walked out the door.

"Your fucking ex-teacher better play cards and better play well," said Ross, a sense of menace squeezed from the slurred words.

"And if he doesn't."

"A fake set of knives might find their way up his ass."

Crosby wasn't certain whether to take Ross seriously.

"They aren't exactly darts, Ross."

He looked up with his liquid blue eyes swimming in a sea of red. The lids making a snapping sound as he blinked. He had his dart-competition face: the look of total concentration on a distant target that was more felt than seen. Ross hated to lose money. He was cheap and mean when it came to paying a bill. The entire idea of the trip was to increase his wealth. As he sat looking at the scattered rusty knives, the reality had begun to filter in behind the booze. The money in Mae Sai wasn't a sure thing. Ross hated anything less than a sure thing when money was involved. He made a mental note to get the Hmong, or Mien, or whatever fucking tribe he belonged to; how or where, or by what means, he hadn't the sobriety of mind to determine, but more than anything in the world he wanted to get that bastard. And since he wasn't at hand, and Breach was, the hatred shifted from the swindler of knives to the teacher who refused to play cards.

"That bastard had better play to win," said Ross. His demand had gone from playing cards to winning at cards.

Crosby was halfway down the path when he heard the knives bouncing off the walls of their room. He stopped and listened. There was a long silence. Then a loud thump, following the sound of a bottle breaking against the wall. Ross had gone into the third stage. That stage where drink had taken him beyond the brink of reason; to the edge where he became dangerous, cunning, and without fear.

Walking alone in the dark, he thought about what Breach had once said about romantics. "A romantic is another kind of militant searching for an emotional hostage or for a co-conspirator and can never be rescued from himself." Ross romanced the bottle, darts, and women. He was on a roll but he needed money, a great deal of money, to keep those wheels turning onward in a steady motion toward some garage where he had parked his dreams.

Later in the evening, the house servant passed a flashlight to Breach so he could negotiate his way down the steep embankment, where the earth literally fell away into total darkness. They had set out together after dinner. Suda stayed alone in the teak house intending to catch up on her sleep. She had refused the servant's offer of a rifle. Not that there were bandits, he was quick to add. But a woman alone sometimes felt better with a rifle at her side. He thought about what Snow had said about everyone having a gun. She exchanged a glance with Breach as if to read his mind. "Thai people like," she said, gesturing at her gun.

He looked relieved when she declined. Her experience with ghosts and his return later contained the possibility of turning into a nasty accident.

"You come back soon?" asked Suda.

Breach didn't look at her as he lied. "Soon."

He decided not to tell her that he was going back to the village for Snow. Something told him that she already knew. But something else told him she did not want to share his plans and explicit knowledge of what would happen next; then she would have to make some hard choices—choose a side. The *farang* held hostage or the Lahu villagers who trusted and had traded with her for many years. Breach didn't want her pressed into making that decision. Perhaps he was afraid what the decision might be.

The flashlight cast a dim pale yellow light so weak that it disappeared before ever striking the ground. Trying to find the light Breach stumbled around in the dark. He gave up on the flashlight, switched off the light, and returned it to his guide. A brilliant full moon illuminated the mountains and fields in a soft, warm light. As they crossed the small bridge over the pond, Breach's eyes had adjusted to the pale moonlight, and after a couple of minutes the outline of the path, the fields, and mountains beyond emerged. And, in the ghostly light, the most visible objects on the path were Breach's white Reeboks. They shone as if attached to a separate power supply, some internal engine splashed outward revealing thick cushions moving up and down the path. A wizard's feet like pistons pushing hard against the dark earth.

The guide, who during the day had a leather construction worker's belt strapped around his midsection, and had carried the dump truck bought in Chiang Mai back to his children, spoke a kind of broken English. He scratched the back of his head, and asked Breach how much he had paid for his shoes. There must have been a premium for shoes that glowed in the dark.

"Seven hundred baht," Breach said, explaining they were expensive shoes.

"In Chiang Mai shoes two hundred baht," the guide said. Like most guides in the north he knew within ten percent the price of name-brand consumer goods.

"I saw a pair in the village. Last house," Breach said, looking straight ahead as he walked. He waited for the guide to reply. But silence followed for over a minute.

"My cousin he have," the guide said, speaking slowly. "He say pay one hundred baht. I think he tell bullshit."

"Maybe the shoes belong to a *farang*. A *farang* named Snow. Maybe your cousin told you about him."

The guide said nothing. Breach had stopped in the path and faced the guide directly. He tried to read the man's eyes in the reflected light. What emotion was on his face? Was he frightened, surprised, off-balanced, or angry? "If you help me, I'll give you my shoes."

"Men in village dangerous. They have guns. They hurt you. If you go there, they do the bad thing," the guide nodded in the direction of the village.

"Maybe you're scared," said Breach.

"How much you pay me?"

A typical Thai conversation. How much you make? How much you pay for rent? How much, how much—the category of items that generated these questions could last well into the night. How much will you pay me not to be scared?

"Depends on what bad thing you can stop them from doing," said Breach, looking out over the valley.

"Aunt me *Maw Pee* brother," he said, his syntax sliding down the wall of understanding of how to say uncle in Englilsh. "I know her. She take you to the village tonight. I go with you. Now, how much you pay?"

"How much do you want?"

The guide smiled and glanced up at the sky. "The moon."

Chapter 10

On the veranda of the Trekker's Lodge, a young, earnest Japanese student leaned forward over a table, and balancing on his elbows, his eyes followed the two blond New Zealanders like a hunter spotting game. His smooth complexion and controlled smile peered out from gold-rimmed glasses. The combination of control and determination which suggested that having mastered toilet training at an early age, he had concluded the rest of life was a piece of cake. He had introduced himself to the New Zealand women.

"Hitoshi," he said, in a half-grunt, half-sneeze voice, looking away from his book and over the top of his sleek gold-rimmed glasses with oval lenses.

"Excuse me, did you say something?" asked Alison, tilting her glass and carefully pouring her beer.

"My name's Hitoshi. I am doing research," said Hitoshi, putting a designer bookmarker in the book.

"Research for a guidebook?" she asked.

Hitoshi pulled off his glasses and rubbed his eyes, shaking his head, as to say, "No, no, you simpleton. You blond New Zealand hilltribe fool."

He cleaned the oval lenses with a crisp white handkerchief, and slowly replaced his glasses. All the while Alison and Lucy waited while the young "professor" collected his thoughts, prepared his lecture. Cradling his hands on the table, he watched the New Zealand girls for a few moments as if the word guidebook had set off an internal chain reaction of rapidly growing disquiet.

"No, I am not writing a guidebook," he replied in fluent English. I'm doing scholarly research on Ma Heh," he said. The word scholarly carried a freight train of weight; slowly, he paused at every syllable, as if it were a station. His formal style made Alison giggle. She couldn't take him seriously and thought it was a put-on.

"Oh, how interesting," said Alison, looking over at Lucy and rolling her eyes.

Lucy shrugged her shoulders against the slight chill in Hitoshi's presentation.

"We know that guy. He played drums for U2. Right?" asked Lucy, winking at Alison and letting the irony flutter with butterfly wings in her voice.

Hitoshi smiled and again removed his glasses—this affectation made Lucy burst into laughter. "You already cleaned them," she said.

"It's the dust here," he replied.

Lucy nudged Alison. "The dust. You notice any dust here? I certainly haven't seen much dust."

"Yesterday, it postively rained down tons of dust and grime," said Alison.

Hitoshi tilted a Kloster and emptied it into his glass. He relaxed slightly, seeing that they were no threat; and much as he had predicted, lightweight, uneducated, and simple. He could play their game as well. Then Alison spoiled things by asking him a dead serious question. "Okay, Hitoshi. We're having a spot of fun. At your expense, of course. But that's the world, isn't it? So tell us, who is this Ma Heh character and why did you come up here looking for him?"

This question allowed Hitoshi to indulge in his favorite pastime: lecturing a new audience.

"Seventy years ago Ma Heh led a religious movement in the hilltribe," explained Hitoshi, in the measured tones of a university lecturer.

"He was a Lahu Billy Graham," said Alison, with a wink at Lucy who sprayed beer across the table laughing.

An old Lahu woman, who had been smoking a silver opium pipe in the shadows of the veranda, rose from a chair; her loose, worn sandals flapping against the wooden floor, as she shuffled over to Hitoshi's table. An overhead light revealed a toothless, grinning face collapsed with age and self-abuse; the folds of loose, wrinkled skin avalanched down her face; and wild gray strands of hair spiralled around her ears. Her clothes, hair, and skin recked of tobacco, opium, and mekhong.

"*Ha Heh* give this to me," she said, in a dry, raspy voice emitted from her rubbery mouth.

She unfastened two buttons on her blouse embroidered with garlands of red, yellow, and blue mountain flowers and removed a silver chain. She held her gnarled hand out to Hitoshi.

"What she got?" asked Alison.

Then the old woman sprung open her fist and displayed an amulet. He carefully turned the amulet over on the old woman's leathery hand. She moved closer as Hitoshi's interest in the piece increased.

"A fish," said Lucy.

The amulet was a small silver fish etched with miniature scales, fins, tail, and a ruby eye. The slender body of the fish was arched and the silver chain threaded through an eyelet fixed to the dorso fin. Hitoshi thoroughly inspected the amulet in silence. He had forgotten his lecture, his audience, and threw himself into a microscopic examination of the object that retained the warmth from the old woman's breasts.

"I am glad someone has heard of this *Ha Heh* bloke," said Lucy loudly, from the table a few feet away. "I thought Hitoshi had made up an original come-on line."

Her comment delivered with a dramatic sigh brought a quick grin on Alison's face; but Hitoshi didn't simply ignore what had been directed at him, he appeared not to hear it; his focus on the old Lahu woman and her amulet became so complete that the rest of the world dissolved.

"My name's Hitoshi. I'm a graduate student at Tokyo University. I'm writing a thesis on Ma Heh's movement," he said, meeting the old woman's bloodshot eyes.

"May I ask you a few questions?"

The old woman nodded and pulled back the amulet.

"Please sit down," Hitoshi said.

Lucy leaned over and whispered to Alison. "Look out, here comes the bamboo under the fingernails."

But the New Zealanders no longer interested him. He waited until the old woman flopped into the chair, and ordered a bottle of mehkong on Hitoshi's account. As the bottle and a glass arrived, Hitoshi exploded with a rapid-fire series of questions.

"What did Ma Heh look like? How tall was he? Did he really cure people of leprosy? Did you ever see him perform magic? How many children did he father? Is it true one had six toes and another a tail? Did his second wife kill herself or run away? Did his mother have the gift of second sight like everyone said? Tell me everything."

What had started as a polite request for information had quickly turned, by the end of his interrogation, into an official demand. This delighted the old woman, who blinked her languid eyes at Hitoshi. He drummed his fingers on the table as she filled her glass with mehkong. She took a long drink and put the glass down, staring out into the night. "You ask many questions," the old woman said.

"But I have many more."

"I tell you what I know," she said. Her lips lubricated with mehkong, she sighed.

She had his full attention. She watched him like an old vulture as she struck a match and relit her pipe. A pig's tail of smoke rolled across the table.

"I'll write it all down. I have a notebook. You see?" The conciliatory tone crept back into his voice. "In Thailand I asked many people about Ma Heh. But you are the first person I've ever met who knew him. This is a perfect day for me. It is a great victory. Because you have chosen me to tell the story of your people."

"Oh, brother," said Alison.

"I'm not certain she said that," added Lucy, addressing her comment to Hitoshi.

To her surprise, Hitoshi smiled. "You are right. I must go more slowly."

The old Lahu woman beamed; her lips pulling back into a full gum smile, exposing a wet, pink babylike tongue slapping against the roof of her mouth. Hitoshi lapsed into silence.

"The history of his messianic movement is my work," said Hitoshi. He made the word "work" sound like a sacred mission. He explained as she stared at the moon about his computer data base. It contained every piece of known information about Lahu godmen; he had done personality, social, and psychological profiles on each recorded Lahu godman. He unloaded a large stack of printouts from his designer backpack; there were charts, profiles, directories, outlines, maps, and diagrams. Soon the table was covered with his computer printouts. His presentation had convinced two Japanese corporations and well-placed officials at the Ministry of Education to fund Hitoshi through various research grants and travel expenses. The old Lahu woman understood nothing and everything about him.

"You carried all that up the mountain?" asked Alison.

Hitoshi ignored the question.

"I bet he paid someone to carry it," whispered Lucy.

The only person who existed that night was the old Lahu who shifted in her chair like an old vulture feeling its way over a fresh kill, unhurried, waiting to find the right piece to start the feast.

❖

"I ten year old. I go to see Ma Heh with mama. He give me." She removed the silver chain and lowered it slowly into Hitoshi's hand.

He brushed his fingers along the edge of the silver fish as if it were the shroud of Turin. The Lahu godmen had first appeared about two hundred years ago in China around the time the Lahu rebelled against Chinese central authority. A template for a Lahu godman emerged during that historical period, according to Hitoshi. He spoke like a man possessed; like a man afraid that if he stopped talking, he would wake up and the entire setting would have vanished; as if he needed to demonstrate to this disciple of Ma Heh, that he, Hitoshi, had learned everything there was to know about godmen. There hadn't been a corner he had not gone into, swept out, inspected the dust, recorded it, analyzed it, put words and images to it.

"I learned two weeks ago there is a new Lahu spiritual leader. A white man," said Hitoshi, glancing in the direction of Alison and Lucy. "I have want to meet him. Interview him. But I have failed."

"You see, it is Billy Graham," said Alison with a giggle. "I was right."

"May be in one way yes, and another way you are wrong," said Hitoshi, turning back to the old Lahu, the smile returning to his face as if she and he knew the secret and the New Zealanders were fools.

"We are interested," said Lucy. "Really."

"Really, we will be good and listen. I know we've been very rude. We meant no harm. But if you'd rather not tell us then it would serve us right for being such bores," said Alison. She glanced over at the old Lahu woman who figured the silver fish.

Hitoshi edged forward in his chair. "I tell you a little bit," he said, clearing his throat. The thought of a contrite, friendly audience was a powerful force. And the thought of impressing the old Lahu woman an irresistible opportunity.

"Each Lahu godman follows the same career path to personal destruction. He—there were no Lahu godwomen—always began as a village priest, a *paw hku*. One day he thinks the world which revolves around the sun has shifted into a world which revolves around him. This is a breakthrough day. The *paw hku* claims to possess supernatural powers. He uses magic. The villagers believe he has powers beyond a mortal man. He can heal people. After he heals some villagers the word of his power spreads to other villages. Soon the Lahu, and members of other hilltribes, the Mien, Akha, Lisu, Hmong, and Karen come to his village. They arrive with offerings and prayers.

"They go to the *paw hku's* house and, one by one, the sick come out feeling healed. The lame walk. The deaf hear. And the blind see. The *paw hku* announces that he is the agent on earth of the supernatural *G'uisha*. His language is like poetry, he knows the right lyrical phase, and he controls the reality of the villagers. That is my thesis. But there is more. If the *paw hku* stayed in the lyrical phase, they might have survived.

"But every *paw hku* has his head turned by all this attention. He believes he has supernatural powers; that the ill and sick are cured. And before long, he is leading a religious revival. He has hundreds, and soon thousands of people telling him that he is the Lahu godman; that only he can help them fight against oppression. Then it happens. The poet becomes a politician. He no longer talks of poetry; he uses slogans of power. He is converted into a messianic king. He cures his followers of disease and promises them immortality."

Hitoshi's eyes sparkled as he said the word "immortality." Alison and Lucy had moved over to his table, and a fresh round of beers had arrived, including a fresh bottle of mehkong for the old Lahu woman who had relit her opium pipe.

153

"You mean these blokes promised people they'd live forever?" asked Alison.

"What a crock," said Lucy, sipping her beer.

Hitoshi started to pack up his papers.

"Is there more?" asked Alison. He didn't reply. "You must admit living forever is difficult to swallow. Don't be a brick, Hitoshi. We were just getting interested."

Hitoshi stopped packing away his papers, looking at the old woman, then the two New Zealand girls. "There is more."

"Then tell us before the mosquitoes eat us alive," said Lucy.

Hitoshi continued, "At the beginning of this century, the Christian missionaries and Lahu godmen fought for the souls of the hilltribes. Whomever won controlled Southeast Asia. Each promised the Lahu if they followed their own version of immortality, they would be saved. The Lahu godman threatened heretics with an invasion of tigers. He warned a tiger would sneak into the house of any villager caught near a missionary and eat his or her heart out as they slept. And the missionaries said anyone who believed in the Lahu godman would go to hell and devils would gorge on hearts ripped from their chest. The choice was between a tiger or a devil eating you alive."

Hitoshi screwed the cap onto his pen and closed his book. He leaned back in his chair, folded his arm around his chest and waited for the old woman to respond. She sat expressionless and puffed on her pipe, her lips making a smacking sound. She gave the impression of someone floating far away, lost in thought and memory. Though it was possible she had not followed any of Hitoshi's lecture; that as her eyes glossed over, and she rocked softly from side to side, she were plugged into another frequency coming from the savannah. Hitoshi nervously cleaned the silver fish with a handkerchief. He crinkled his nose as he rubbed the cloth on arched body. He was buying time. Watching the old lady, and the silver fish, he examined his work and handed the chain back to the old woman. She lowered it over her head and as she rocked back the fish moved between her breasts like a salmon struggling upstream.

"But the greatest Lahu godman of all was Ma Heh," he said, pausing. The old woman looked at him.

"Ma Heh," she repeated, fingering the silver fish.

Hitoshi watched her playing with the amulet and, although he tried to resist, she had hooked him and was slowly drawing in the line. "Ma Heh was at the height of his powers during the late 1920s and early 1930s."

"When I was a girl. See me now, you never think I was young like you. I say what I remember. No more. No less. Up to you, believe, not believe. I do not care. I'm old. And I die soon. So I tell something about him," said the Old Lahu, a spider web of wrinkles splayed out from her smiling eyes.

This descendant of the times of the last Lahu godman promised to deliver Hitoshi his Ph.D., if all went well, the next year. He gestured for her to continue. The New Zealanders slapped mosquitoes and drank beer, drifting off into private conversations about the two *farangs* from Bangkok who had been at the lodge earlier in the day. Hitoshi demanded silence. He clapped his hands. Everyone's head turned to the old woman and she began to speak in a low, tobacco grooved voice. Hitoshi unscrewed the cap of his fountain pen and began to write. He wasn't certain what flowed from his pen were the old woman's words, his own wishes and thoughts, a scattered collection of ideas ignited by the printouts, or a rush to complete the last, elusive portion of a story that he had been unable to finish. The old woman's story was later rearranged, edited, and poured into Hitoshi's Ph.D. thesis, which later was reprinted in several specialized journals, and was as follows.

❖

Like every other godman the Lahu had produced, Ma Heh claimed access to an invisible world of *G'uisha*, the most powerful of Lahu deities. Villagers imagined cures of leprosy, the common cold, opium smoking, depression, and heat rash. In those days the Lahu lived in a region along the Burmese border. The British ruled Burma, and the Lahu with a godman was considered a potential threat.

The British heard rumors that Ma Heh had jumped from religious godman to mountain politician. Fifty Indian soldiers were dispatched to reclaim authority for the British; they were led by a British officer named John Hayes. His orders were the usual colonial orders: squash Ma Heh's state of rebellion. Mah Heh learned that the troops and Captain John Hayes were on their way and gathered his followers around. Hysterical pigs scattered in the dust as Ma Heh descended from his house of fine teak and stood on the village path where the entire village had assembled.

Women with baskets on their heads and children on their backs crept close. Villagers with rifles balanced on their shoulders stood off to the side. Children yelling and running after one another came to a hushed silence as Mah Heh held up his arms. Any person who wore one of Ma Heh's amulets had the *Ne*—a spirit—on their side. A British bullet striking him in the chest would be transformed into beeswax as it struck the body and fell away harmlessly to the ground. I was in the crowd that day. I was a girl. I was one of the first to receive an amulet from Mah Heh—and others followed me, and stepped forward to received the protection from British bullets.

Captain John Hayes and his squad of fifty men arrived around three in the afternoon. Three Lahu men were on the top of the fort, they bared their chests, and shouted curses at Captain John Hayes and his men. They boasted in Lahu. One of the soldiers interpreted for the captain.

"He say our bullets can't hurt him. He has protection so he isn't afraid."

"Not afraid of bullets, is that a fact?" asked Captain John Hayes, raising his rifle and drawing a bead on one of the three Lahu men, who were spitting down from the top of the fort. Laughing and dancing on the roof like school-children. For a moment, Captain Hayes lowered his rifle.

"What's that on their chest?"

"Amulet—he says, no man can kill him. Amulet protect him."

"So after I shoot him," said Captain Hayes, squinting down the sight. "I want you to order the others to lay down their rifles and surrender. We will not come to harm."

The soldier nodded grimly, knowing what was being asked was futile. Captain John Hayes drew a bead on the chest of the sentry, aiming at the amulet. He squeezed the trigger and the shot rang out; the round hit home, striking the Lahu square in the chest, buckling his legs. The Lahu pitched forward, falling off the fort rampart and sending up a thin cloud of dust after a dull thud. He lay still. The soldier on the Captain's right cupped his hands around his mouth and shouted in Lahu for the other two sentries to throw down their rifles. But they jeered, cursed, and boasted like their dead comrade. Captain John Hayes scratched his sideburn.

"Bloody fools," he said. "You told them we'd shoot them?"

"They say we can't kill them."

"Tell them their mate isn't sleeping. He's dead."

"Lahu don't care about that."

"Shoot the sonsofabitches," said Captain John Hayes, throwing up his hands and walking away.

The Captain walked back and pulled three men out of the ranks. He pointed at the two men, sticking out their chest as if they were bulletproof. "Shoot those men," he ordered. A volley of shots rang out. The Lahu fell off the ramparts like pigeons shot from a telegraph wire. A dead fall into the dirt. Not a sound or movement.

By the time Captain John Hayes and his men entered the Lahu fort it was nearly deserted. Ma Heh and his followers had gained sufficient time to escape and hide in the jungle. He was never captured, but the British accomplished what they had set out to do. They put an end to his political movement. Ma Heh, except to a close band of personal followers, was finished as a regional power base. He had entered the ranks of another Lahu godman who had overextended himself into politics.

By the time Hitoshi laid down his pen and rubbed his hand, the old Lahu woman had once again removed the silver fish and chain from around her neck. She held it out to him. He looked at the silver fish cradled in her weather buffed hand. As a silence fell around the two tables, with Alison and Lucy spellbound, the old women cleared her throat, half turned her head, and spit over the balcony railing. Her watery eyes moved back to the amulet that Hitoshi held out against the kitchen light.

"Five thousand baht," she said.

Hitoshi didn't takes his eyes off the silver fish, as he reached back, and pulled out his wallet. Wallet in one hand, the amulet in the other, he sat there for a long moment. Then he quickly counted out ten purple five-hundred-baht notes. The old Lahu stuffed the folded notes into her blouse and relit her pipe. Hitoshi slipped the silver chain and amulet around his neck. "I will never forget you," he said. "Or your story. I will make it live as you told me."

"Are you bulletproof?" asked Alison, who was a little drunk.

"I can sleep now, knowing the truth," said Hitoshi, sitting back in his chair, ignoring her remark.

Crosby walked across the veranda and ordered a beer from a waitress standing inside the kitchen door. Lucy nudged Alison, who grinned at Crosby.

"Where's your friend?" called Alison.

Breach had climbed halfway up the stairs. He stopped looked at the New Zealand women, Hitoshi, the Old Lahu, and Crosby paying for a large Kloster. "I'd say he's just arrived," said Breach.

Crosby scratched the side of his jaw, his cheeks ballooned with air, which he slowly exhaled. He took a long drink directly from the bottle of beer. Breach's guide had gone over to the old Lahu and their heads huddled close together, whispered in Lahu, with knowing glances at Hitoshi, Breach, and Crosby.

Alison laughed. "You're not the same bloke who came here this afternoon. Unless you've lost seventy pounds and grown hair."

"I'm afraid that friend is indisposed," said Crosby.

"You mean shitfaced," said Lucy.

Crosby smiled, fingering the rim of the beer bottle. He plucked the tip of his thumb in and out of the bottle, making a hollow, dull corking sound. Breach glanced at his watch; it was nine-thirty.

"Time to bring Snow out," he said to Crosby.

"What a good idea," said Lucy, assuming that Breach was referring to Ross. "Then we can have a party, and Hitoshi can show us how he is bulletproof."

The old Lahu woman rose from her chair, knocked the bowl of her silver opium pipe against the side of the table. She slipped it into a shoulder bag. Breach's guide came back and stood on the railing of the veranda, looking out at the night.

"She wants five thousand baht," said the guide in a half whisper.

"Three thousand," said Crosby, in Thai.

The old women relit her pipe and shrugged.

"Three thousand five hundred," said Crosby, again in Thai.

This time she nodded and rose from her chair.

Breach looked at the old Lahu; her ancient eyes with the distinctive qualities of an old one who had the instincts of survival, pride, will, and enterprise. Breach nodded and the old Lahu's face broke into a smile.

Chapter 11

At the crest of the hill, the dirt road curved left through a low, flat green field. The guide and the old Lahu woman walked ahead, whispering among themselves and, a step behind them, Breach and Crosby followed. The rhythmical flapping of the old woman's plastic sandals echoed on the windless night. The moon cast luminous bands of light across the field, making the water buffalo and green plants merge in a metallic shower of light. The streamers of light struck the old woman's legs, giving them a bowed wishbone-like appearance.

"Looks like the old girl had rickets," whispered Crosby.

"Or rickets had her," said Breach.

Her form cast strange, elongated shadows among the ruts behind her. Crosby nervously eyed Breach's gait, as his foot came closer and closer to the old woman's shadow.

"Don't step on her shadow," said Crosby, lighting a cigarette.

Breach, not slowing down, was watchful as the old woman's shadow floated along the road. The flame from Crosby's lighter shot straight into the night sky.

"Bad luck, is it?" asked Breach.

"Two or three lifetimes worth." Crosby was full of awe.

Breach lengthened his stride until each step fell square onto the shadow. He looked over his shoulder at Crosby, who looked possessed as he sucked in long and hard on his cigarette. Crosby shook his head as a shiver ran through his body.

"I wish you hadn't done that."

"Wake up, Crosby. It's doesn't matter."

"It's dangerous," he said, wide-eyed.

Breach had a strong inclination to send Crosby back.

"You are afraid of the wrong things. Go back to the lodge, I can handle it alone."

"You need someone who can speak Thai," said Crosby.

"I need someone who can think in English."

Crosby walked a few more steps before replying.

"How do you know that I am wrong about the shadow? Who appointed you world authority?" asked Crosby.

"The goddess of avocado," said Breach.

"Of avocado? You're barking mad," said Crosby.

"And this comes from a man convinced of the power of an old woman's shadow."

"I'm a product of a mediocre education," said Crosby.

The tone of disbelief changed to resignation. Breach had spent a lifetime stepping on every symbol of danger, sticking his thumb in every taboo, and trying to corrupt his students into doing the same thing. One could hardly expect that he could resist shadow-dancing on the form of witch.

Breach remembered the mountain road that led into the village. He pointed a series of depressions along the road.

"From their horses," said Breach. "I ran into them earlier."

"And?" asked Crosby, stopping.

"They were armed with M16s."

"Shit."

"It's not too late. If you want to go back."

"I know it's fucking mad. But nevertheless, I wish you hadn't stepped on her bloody shadow," said Crosby, catching up with Breach.

At the back entrance to the village, Breach looked for the body of the dead dog but it had vanished. The old Lahu woman coughed, cleared her throat loudly and spit where he had seen the body. The village appeared like a gloomy spiral of witch's shadows. A deserted landscape. The doorways were dark in shadows. There was the smell of opium circulating in the air. A scattering of dogs barked a high wailing howl in the distance. The old Lahu woman clicked her tongue; and several of the dogs scattered beneath the houses. The empty doorways and verandas were silent and haunting as if someone were waiting and breathing out of sight. The dim glow of oil lamp fires illuminated a window here and there. A corkscrew smoke rose from the roofs. But most houses were lost in darkness; inside, whole families curled together on rough bamboo mats, sleeping until dawn when the cycle began again and they spilled out of the village and back to work the fields.

"Do you know we're being followed?" Crosby whispered anxiously, flicking away his cigarette.

Breach nodded. "Maybe for two minutes. Snow's guards."

"How do we know we haven't been set up?" asked Crosby. He sounded worried and automatically patted the money belt beneath his shirt.

"We don't."

Hostage taking was habit-forming; a centuries-old contagious form of behavior that periodically infected a neighborhood, a village, or a country. It was cheap and effective. The pre-capitalist way of turning a large profit from a product like Snow, a man in the wrong place, over his head, and without connections. Snow hadn't been the first man to take a joke seriously and bet his life that the punch line would make him happy, rich, and content. His audience had been waiting all along to put on their own performance, proving a smart audience can set up a performer who is stupid enough to trust his own promise of magic. That was the message Snow's backfired scheme left written on the night.

At the opposite end of the village, the house servant stopped in front of a house with a US Airforce flight jacket draped over the railing. The old Lahu woman cupped her hands around her mouth and shouted. Bent over in the moonlight, she darted up the notched log on her spiderlike legs and rang a small bell that hung from the roof of the veranda. The loud clang startled the dogs, sending loud howls from below. Emerging on the veranda was the small figure of a man dressed in black, chewing betel. He grinned at the old Lahu woman, who gestured at Breach and Crosby who had been joined by armed guards. Breach recognized them from earlier in the day when they had been on horseback.

The elderly man chewing betel nut was the village shaman. He wore a black robe opened in the front, exposing a bony chest and rib cage, black hat, and black sarong. The shaman carried an embroidered handbag on a shoulder strap. A young man emerged onto the veranda and stood next to the shaman, holding a rifle. He, too, was dressed in black, except for the pair of white Reeboks on his feet. Breach stared long and hard at the shoes. He was certain they were Snow's.

The old Lahu woman shouted down in Thai.

"She says they want us to go for a walk," said Crosby.

"Does that mean we have a choice?"

"You go with them," said the Old Lahu

"Guess that's our answer," said Crosby.

Breach looked at the guide, who was Suda's friend, and remembered him holding the toy dump truck they had bought in the market at Chiang Mai. But the guide refused eye contact and looked the other way. Such conduct was never a good sign. The other guards were nervous, restless, averting each other's eyes as well; Breach could see the tense fashion in which they held their rifles.

"No sudden, sharp movements. We don't want any accidents," he whispered to Crosby. "Tell them we have come for Snow."

Crosby's voice quavered with fear as he spoke.

The shaman grunted to the young man with the rifle. He disappeared into the house, and emerged a moment later with Snow, who was blindfolded, his hands tied behind his back and his mouth taped shut. It was time, so it appeared, to settle scores, thought Breach. From the rough handling of Snow, it was clear that there was little lost love between the shaman and Snow who had arrived as the new talent in town and sought to displace him. No one liked to have their show cancelled; especially by an outsider. It didn't take much imagination to guess that questions of face had been involved. Exactly how much face had the shaman lost? And what had he planned to regain his lost face? When things went wrong, they went wrong quickly. From the look on the shaman's face, even in the near darkness, there was a confirmed conviction of someone with a strong desire to kill.

"Snow, you look like shit," said Crosby.

"Hey, man, what took you so long?"

Crosby waited until Snow stepped forward on the veranda.

"They beat you up?" asked Crosby.

"No, man, I always look this way after coming out of the *Twilight Zone*."

Snow's eyebrows arched above the blindfold; his reply totally muffled by the tape over his mouth. But he knew one important fact; he was no longer alone. This registered as a muffled sigh beneath. If he was going to die, at least it wasn't going to be alone among strangers.

"Tell them we want to make the trade now. We don't go for a walk," Breach said to Crosby. "They hand over Snow here; we hand over the money."

Crosby, his voice again breaking, translated for the shaman and the old Lahu woman, both of whom had understood Breach in English. She slapped her thighs; a cackle of laughter broke through the night. The shaman grinned and gestured for Snow to be taken down from the veranda. The guard removed Snow's blindfold, the tape from his mouth,

165

untied his hands, then nudged him in the chest with the barrel of the rifle. The guard nodded toward the notched log leading to the ground.

"This greaser used to be my number-one man. He got into *Star Trek*, too. He called me Captain Kirk. And I called him Spock," said Snow, staring up at the guard, as he climbed down the notched log. "He pimps for a brothel in Chiang Mai. Nice kind of guy once you get to know him."

"Still have your balls?" asked Breach, staring down at Snow's bare feet.

"Intact. Just lost the shoes, man. Let's fucking break out of this popcorn bowl," said Snow.

The other two villagers raised their rifles, fingers hovering just above the trigger guard. They wanted something more than a transfer of cash. The old shaman had in mind some other form of redistribution of wealth and power. Compensation that would impress the villagers. And his decision wasn't open for further negotiation. He pulled on the US Airforce jacket and came down the steps after Snow.

The armed men dressed in black let them out of the village and to the edge of the jungle; each carrying their rifle at ready, leaving no doubt that if any of them turned, walked, or ran away down the road, before they were ten feet away a bullet would have them.

"The *maw pee* is still a little pissed off, man," said Snow. "But he'll get over it, man."

"I've got the ten grand," replied Crosby, trying to light a cigarette , but his hands were shaking so badly he couldn't match the flame to the cigarette tip.

"You haven't heard the bitching and moaning about how to divide up the fucking money," said Snow. "The *maw pee's* got a wild hair up his ass. He wants his cut. The headman wants a cut. And two of their guys got seven years for cutting logs. That's another big chunk to buy them out."

"They said ten grand," moaned Crosby.

"They say whatever the fuck comes into their head. Two minutes later they don't remember. Opium and betel and American TV reruns ain't memory enhancers."

They fell into dejected silence as the last lights from the village disappeared behind them. Breach remembered the path from earlier in the day; it was the entrance that Suda and he had used, and where they had found the two boys dragging the snake. He stumbled forward, falling onto the path where he had seen them hide the snake. One of the guards accidentally squeezed off a round. Everyone stood still, in the after echo of the rifle shot.

"You okay?" asked Crosby, helping him up.

Breach grinned; he had a snake inside his shirt. Only this one was not the same as he remembered. This one was alive.

At the edge of the forest the group stopped. In Thai, Suda's friend, Breach's guide, pointed to the ground beside a bamboo structure. On the backside a ladder ran from the ground ten feet to the top of a platform made of bamboo that had the appearance of a makeshift pulpit and altar. A place where a Lahu godman would command a view of the entire village and appear to the villagers as someone high in the sky.

"Sit down."

Breach dropped down, looking up at the tall structure and the empty platform on top. "What is this, Snow?"

"My soapbox, man. I climbed up each morning, did a few tricks, asked for—"

Crosby interjected. "Virgins?"

"So I fucked up."

The guards pushed Crosby and Snow down on their knees and came up behind, sticking the barrel of their rifles into the back of their necks, Chinese-style.

"I really don't want to fucking die like this," said Crosby through clenched teeth.

The old Lahu woman puffed on her silver opium pipe, holding a Bic lighter over the bowl. She eyed Snow, blowing out a jet of white smoke. She thought about the three Lahu warriors who stood on top of the rampart as Captain John Hayes closed his left eye and drew a bead with his right, aimed, and fired. All those years ago, and she had not forgotten. She sat on the ground opposite Snow and Crosby.

The *maw pee* knelt beside her and lit two beeswax candles. He placed them upright in the soft soil a foot from where Snow sat on his knees. From his shoulder bag, the *maw pee* pulled out a small pouch of raw husked rice grains, a handful of green leaves, and several balls of cotton string: white, red, and black. He placed all these things on a small plate, and began chanting.

"This is called *Let's Make a Deal*. It's a Lahu game show," said Snow. "He would melt the ratings in LA."

One of the young villagers made a hard jab of the rife's barrel into Snow's neck. The jolt knocked him forward and shut him up. The man who had been guarding Breach handed his rifle to the shaman. The old man smiled, ran his hand up and down the barrel and laid it across his lap. The *maw pee* resumed his selection of things, again, having the full, undivided attention of everyone in attendance; he produced a piece of white string from the plate and tied the string around the space between the stock and trigger case mounting. His chanting shifted out of Lahu and into Thai.

"May it be able to shoot, may there be luck, may it shoot without missing. May it close the eyes and ears of wild pig, wild ox, barking deer, wild elephant, wild fowl. May *aw ha* return and not leave again. May *aw ha* guide the bullet straight. May it kill the devil in this man."

When suddenly he stopped chanting, his face was frozen in a mask of pure hate, staring straight at Snow. There was no more joking. The smile was wiped off Snow's face, he had run out of jokes and lines. The *maw pee* slowly pulled a round of ammunition out of his waistband and loaded it into the firing chamber. The *maw pee* handed the rifle back to the owner. He reached into his shoulder bag, and this time removed a small, oddly shaped object with a polished surface in the moonlight. It was an egg. The string had been tied to the rifle's stock to keep the *aw ha*—the soul of the gun—in place. Like an expert chef, the *maw pee* cracked the egg with one hand, separated the albumen from the yoke into the small plate. He lit another beeswax candle and peered over the edge of the plate and examined the yellowish substance inside. There were small red flecks—foreign bodies floating on top. Whether from the egg, the grain in the plate, or a sleight of hand in the dark, blood had come forth as a sign. The atmosphere suddenly changed and the ceremony was drawing to a climax. The other villagers squatted down and looked at the spots of blood, passed around the plate, and smiled.

Breach saw it coming; he saw it when the *maw pee* chambered the round and handed the rifle back to the guard. "Pretend to die, Snow."

Snow's head jerked up; his jaw set, his eyes wild with fear.

"This wasn't the fucking deal, man." He sobbed.

The *maw pee* raised his hand, and slowly lowered his index finger until it was level with Snow's head. In Lahu, he ordered the guard behind Breach to shoot Snow.

"It's not real, Snow. Pretend to die," said Breach again.

"I told you not to step on the old woman's shadow," said Crosby, shuddering.

The guard found Snow in the sight of that rifle and squeezed the trigger; there was a loud report that froze everyone and a plume of smoke rose from the barrel. Snow pitched forward and with a thud landed facedown in the dirt. Breach, on all fours, crawled over to Snow, rolled him over, and before the shaman, the old Lahu woman, Suda's friend, who was his guide, and the three armed villagers, Breach pulled the long, thick carcass of the live snake from Snow's ear. He threw it at the feet of the shaman. All three rifles were pointed at Breach, waiting for some further sign from the *maw pee*. The old man leaned forward, spit on the snake and with a knife cut it in two.

"It's okay, the show's over. It's time for your resurrection," Breach whispered to Snow. "You can pretend not to be dead."

Snow's eyes popped open and he sat up. The villagers looked with terror at the *maw pee*. He had recovered more than his face. His authority, power, and position in the village had been re-established in that moment. The shaman rose to his feet and walked over to where Snow sat. He bent over and studied Snow carefully and touched Snow's head. Then the old man turned away and looked at the villagers and the old Lahu woman.

"His soul has returned," the shaman said. "Let them go."

"The money," said the old Lahu woman, in English.

Crosby pulled up his shirt, unfastened the money belt, and threw it to the shaman. "He ever come back, I cut his balls and dick," said the *maw pee*, pointing his knife at Snow's crotch.

Snow began to make a wisecrack, stopped himself, and simply nodded. The *maw pee's* formula had worked, reaffirming that his position as village guardian of the spirit found in those who kill and the spirit residing in the instruments of death. He had killed the demon in the *farang* and brought ten thousand dollars into the village.

Wide smiles crossed the faces of the young villagers. The shaman stopped beside Breach; he offered Breach his hand, and when Breach removed it, inside the shaman had left a silver Indian rupee. Breach's guide produced a large bottle of mehkong, and then they were gone, swallowed up by in the shadows. Crosby and Snow sat around the beeswax candles, passing the bottle of mekhong back and forth.

"How did you know?" asked Snow, passing the bottle to Breach.

"I saw him chamber a blank."

Crosby shook his head. "He bloody well fooled me. All I could think of was you stepped on the old woman's shadow. And we were all going to pay."

"How did you get that snake, man?" Snow broke in.

Breach smiled. "Magic."

Half across the fields, the horizon behind them glowed red from a fire shooting a tower toward the moon. They stopped and watched for a couple of moments in silence.

"My tower," muttered Snow. "That asshole *maw pee* torched the fucker. I hope he never gets cable TV. He's dangerous enough."

"He's going for the insurance money," joked Crosby, still shaking as he tried to light a cigarette.

"He's sending a message," said Breach. "They've got the money. Let their men out of jail. And—"

"And what?" asked Crosby, watching the thick neck of flame throwing light over the mountainside.

"The old Lahu godman's dead."

"Cremated and beamed up to the next life," said Snow. "That's what they were going to do. But they fucking changed their minds."

"There's an old Lahu saying," said Crosby. "Don't muck with a wizard bearing snakes."

Breach turned, and walked off across the field.

Ross slumped between the two New Zealanders. He scratched a half an acre of mosquito bites on his stomach. His nails drew blood trails. Ross moaned, touching his head, then rubbing his jaw.

"You're bleeding," said Lucy, staring at his large stomach.

"Blood! I have no blood left. It's been drained from my body by these evil insects. All that remains is *Old Grand-Dad* flowing in my veins," he said, reaching forward and draining his glass. "Thank god I drink or I'd could be dead." He sucked on an ice cube, closing his eyes with a long sigh.

When he opened them a moment later, Crosby and Breach were standing in front of him. Snow, a man he had not seen before, stood a couple of feet back, flicking his wrist out and releasing a child's yo-yo. Ross set his jaw, grinding his teeth, looking at Crosby and then Breach.

"I have been burgled," Ross blurted, his face flushed with sudden anger.

"He was robbed?" asked Alison. Lucy withdrew into a strange, frightened silence.

"Hitoshi?" Alison whispered to Lucy.

"No way," said Lucy. "He's a whimp."

"I was drunk. Passed out. And a crazed Jap took my money belt. Peeled off my shirt and left me for the mosquitoes. Just like in those WWII movies with John Wayne. Three more bites and I'd be dead. I'm fucking mad. I want a gun. I want to find this Jap bastard. I want to put him against a dart board. After I throw my darts, I want to shoot him. In the balls. Six rounds in the balls. I've got six mosquito bites on my balls. Did I tell you that. Six. There are probably more, but I can't see them all." He lifted up his shirt, showing off the red blotch of bites and started to unzip his pants.

Alison screamed. "We believe you."

Ross scratched his nose and reached for his drink.

"How much money did you lose?" asked Snow.

"Who is this man. I demand to take your statement. Where were you two hours ago?"

"I was tied up with a crazed Lahu *maw pee* who threatened to cut off my balls."

"A reasonable alibi. But do you have a witness?"

Snow hooked his thumb over his shoulder at Crosby and Breach.

Breach reached out and took a Kloster from the tray that had arrived. He watched Crosby, looking away and into the night. Crosby looked pale, uneasy, restless; he looked like a man who had a guilty conscience.

"I decided to play at Mae Sai," said Breach.

The New Zealander girls, in a half huddle, were talking about leaving that night. "Shut up, everyone shut up," said Ross. He turned on Breach. "Would you repeat what you just said?"

"When we reach Mae Sai, I am in the game. Until things are put right," Breach said, sipping his beer.

"Until what is put right?"

"The ten thousand dollars you volunteered to pay for Snow's ransom. Until I win that back." Breach walked over to the railing and sat back against it.

"Hey, like thanks, man." Snow stood with his hand extended. But Ross ignored him.

"Crosby, you crazy sonofabitch. You asshole. You English slime cunt hole. You set me up," said Ross, through clenched teeth, his eyes bulging out in a full rage.

"And those are his good points," said Snow.

"You fucking shut up," yelled Ross.

Crosby turned around from the railing and faced Ross. After what he had been through outside the Lahu village, Ross seemed like a very small threat. He blinked a couple of times, pulled out a cigarette and lit it. "You wanted Breach to play cards."

"What's that have to do with stealing my goddamn ten grand?"

"That was the price," said Breach.

Ross was on his feet. Weak and still drunk, he staggered, knocking over a chair, then one of the tables. He tumbled forward, cutting his lip on the way down. Slowly he raised himself up on his hands in a half press.

"I thought Breach wanted the goddamn knives."

"They were fakes. I knew that in Chiang Mai," said Breach. "If you are going to play a game, any game, there is always the same rule: make certain the odds are in your favor and what is at stake is the real thing."

The bedroom in the small isolated teak house on the edge of the Lahu village was pitch-black by the time Breach returned. As Breach kicked off his shoes in the outside corridor, Suda reached out of her blanket, found a box of matches, and lit the candle between the two mattresses. Without looking to meet his eyes, she immediately turned, facing the far wall, her back away from him, and pulled the blanket to her neck. Breach hurriedly stripped, slipping into a T-shirt and pair of jogging shorts, and crept onto his mattress. He looked at Suda in the candlelight; a look that admitted neither desire or want—having closed down those switches in Chiang Mai—but for something more rare, some understanding in the form of this woman.

"You got Snow out, okay." She didn't move as she spoke.

Breach smiled in the dark. "It fell in the mid-range between cleaning your teeth and pulling your teeth."

"Maybe you not trust me enough, so you joke," said Nail.

"It might have been dangerous for you."

"Danger is not knowing." She turned around on her mattress. Her eyes watched Breach by the candlelight. Night eyes that crept softly from floor to wall to ceiling without ever divulging their next stop or the purpose of their journey.

Breach folded his hands behind his head and looked straight at the teak ceiling and the candlelight images shifting across in uneven patterns. She was right, of course, he thought. He had put her at risk; though, he had rationalized, a small risk; and he had done so without her knowledge or permission. Such a transgression was difficult to makeup. It wasn't enough to say he was trying to protect her; because she was right, in the end, he had placed her in greater danger.

"I think about it a long time," she said. "And I think hard. And I think, maybe I would do the same as you. But I'm tired now, I sleep."

Suda rolled over and lay silently, motionless on the other side of the candle. She was not asleep. Her eyes half-closed, she was lost in thought about the people she knew in the village. She swallowed hard, clearing her throat. Breach rolled to the edge of his mattress. He wanted to say something; explain what had happened, what almost happened, and what he felt at the moment his hands touched the dead snake in the darkness. But little of that mattered now. Breach's illusion, his magic hadn't caused anything to turn out the way it did. It had been far more simple, and basic. Suda had intervened on his behalf while he had scouted out the house where Snow had been held. Her personal relationship with the headman had been the ultimate, prime cause that the three of them had been allowed to walk away.

Suda looked so small holding the blanket in a clenched fist. Her short-cropped black hair was parted, exposing a thin, pale scalp. Her head was dwarfed against the pillow. She lay on her side with her knees bent; a high diver's back-flip curl.

"Where does the money go?" asked Breach in a half whisper.

She shifted position, rolling over on her back, and watched the candlelight flicker on the ceiling.

"Major Chuan Norapon. I tell the headman he can trust Major Chuan. He will bring the two men back to the village. No more prison."

"And if he doesn't?" asked Breach.

"Why you care? You never go back. It will not fall heavy on your head."

He was outside the circles of personal relationships. She was right, how could an outsider understand the ledgers and balance sheets that were kept, added up, subtracted, multiplied, and divided in a way that every one on the inside understood instantly. The Lahu village had not held a Thai police or military officer; they had held a *farang*. This hadn't been a mistake or mere convenience; Snow had been a source of revenue in the bank, and his life had been added to the ongoing personal relationship ledger.

The rich Chinese president of the company which had organized, supervised, and profited from illegal logging had his picture in the newspapers. Three weeks later, the official judgment was he had no charge to answer; there was lack of evidence to proceed with a criminal charge. The decision, of course, had nothing to do with law, but with his personal network of friends, associates, and influential people and his relationship with them. The act—the illegal cutting of teak trees—had been committed; and with every act someone becomes responsible; someone is held accountable. Why not a couple of villagers who actually cut the trees? They had chopped down the teak trees for seventy-four baht a day. Once all responsibility is flushed to the bottom, the bottom feeders are left to cut their own deals. They ransomed Snow. So for all the illegal logging, the person who ultimately paid was Ross, the *farang* lawyer who had represented the timber company president.

A basic quality of observing another person's life was to ask the questions: When and in what circumstances does one man answer for his acts. In Thailand, the answer had little do with his acts and everything to do with the family background of the man being asked to answer. Where in the web of interconnected factions, relationships, clubs, and families did he fit in? There was one guiding principle: where possible, find an outsider to pay the full freight. The system was preserved; no one loses face, and there was no fear of retribution. The gunman waiting in ambush waits for the Thai who violates the position occupied by another. *Farangs* occupied no positions in the neo-feudalistic system of rewards and punishments.

Breach leaned over on the hard floor and blew out the candle. There was the sickly sweet smell of mekhong whiskey on his breath. His head pounded against the pillow. He went over and over again the march into the forest, the small clearing, the shaman shoving a blank into the chamber of the rifle, the loud report, Snow slumping forward, pulling the snake out of Snow's ear. It had all been a sleight of hand to distract them from the reality Suda had set up earlier in the afternoon. He wanted to say something about the *maw pee*, the gun ritual, about playing a Lahu godman, and about Snow, who lived in a windowless room and hung out in a windowless coffee house in Bangkok nicknamed HQ. But it was too late. Breach sensed she wanted to be anonymous on the floor. She didn't want to hear her name on her lips; she didn't want to think about why all this was necessary. It was easier to fall off and sleep. And hope that the ghost didn't come creeping through the windows and doors during the night and steal her soul as ransom for some god who needed an outsider to save himself.

Across the floor, Suda sighed, turned over under the cover of complete darkness. No words were exchanged, going deeper and farther down into that part of themselves where the trail of thought had deadened less in mystery than confusion and misdirection. In the same kind of place like the Lahu village gate which promised a boundary that separated yesterday and today.

"You find the snake?" she asked.

The question hung like a religious rite.

"How did you know?"

"I didn't know. I feel from the way you watch the boys. I say you leave snake for *farang*."

"The snake was alive."

She said nothing for a few minutes. "But you find?"

"I found."

As he lay in the dark, he thought about the snake, the boys, and her story. Truth was never part of the bargain with any ritual; but a well-done illusion always was. The ritual made the story magic; and the storyteller sacred. It always had and always would. But there was a limit beyond which faith was lost. If you wanted to be Lahu godman and order fresh virgins delivered at your door every night, then never disclose the basis of your power isn't magic. Never admit your word and person are not sacred. Never admit that you've been fooling people, tricking them, making an ass out of them, and stealing the innocence of their daughters night after night. People have murdered storytellers for such confessions.

If you wanted money to break your relatives out of prison, then take a Lahu godman and turn the magic around. It was better than murder. Outside the Lahu village, no more than half a kilometer out the back road, a twenty-seven-year-old virgin tossed on a thin mattress, searching for her gods. Breach thought she might have made a deal with the headman. But why? He confessed that he didn't even begin to understand. He had just begun to understand that he still didn't know what had really happened in that small field earlier in the night. When he thought he might die. He took one final look over at Suda's motionless form. It occurred to him that he might have had the desire to take her. But, now, he had none.

Chapter 12

The first light of dawn light slanted over his face and Breach's eyes snapped open with the realization that he had been dreaming in Thai and Lahu. In the play of light, he lay back remembering his dream. He had understood the dream conversation between a group of men with their backs turned towards him. They appeared to be the *maw pee* and villagers holding M16s in the firing position. But as the man, who appeared to be the *maw pee*, chambered a live round into the rifle and turned: Breach saw Thomas Pierce's face, and what had been a *maw pee* ceremonial gown were Oxford robes and hood. The hood was pulled over Pierce's head and he was outlined by the glow of flames shooting into the sky from the Lahu godman tower which was engulfed in an orange ball of fire. From the infernal, Asanee walked onto the level field, her breasts exposed to the night air. Breach watched motionlessly as Pierce, as the *maw pee* had done with Snow, lowered the loaded rifle and stared down the barrel, drawing a bead on Asanee, who approached him. In slow motion, Pierce's finger twitched as it squeezed the trigger, more a tender caress, a gentle, showing of care gesture; it was as if he were about to perform an erotic act. Asanee pursed her lips and glided across the field, turning, her arms held high, laughter pouring from her throat. Then Pierce swung the rifle around and aimed at Breach; he stared into the barrel, heard the loud report, followed by Asanee's muffled echo of laughter. Breach awoke with the terrified, disorienting feeling of having heard a loud noise, that feeling of not knowing whether the dream had ended, of not knowing where he was; what country or what time existed outside the window. He bolted upright on the mattress. For a moment, he was uncertain whether he was alive or dead.

Sunlight streamed through the two broken slats in the shutters and fell in broad shafts across the teak floor. Suda paddled around her mattress barefoot in her blouse and shorts.

"What was that gunshot?" Breach asked her, as she folded her mattress. He heard the sound of distant voices laughing and yelling.

"Not a gun. Boys are playing outside. One threw the ball. It hit the shutter. They laughed very hard. I think buying the ball was a good idea." Suda worked as she talked.

"Great idea," muttered Breach, sitting up on his elbows. From his position on the floor he could look out and see a couple of village boys kicking the ball.

"Why did you think a gun?"

He didn't have a direct answer; bringing up the dream would have further confused matters. Why had he been dreaming about Pierce shooting him? If she had been in the village the night before, she wouldn't have asked that question. If he hadn't lost the ritual knives to Ross, he wouldn't be questioning himself. He wanted to describe how he had been dreaming about Asanee's firm breasts, the erect nipples a dark brown in the moonlight, and the rifle trigger moving back, the muzzle flash, and explosive sound as the round left the barrel of a gun. About how he had been the target in his dreams when the night before it had been Snow who had been the target.

"Maybe you worry about it?" she asked. His eyes followed hers to the old rifle leaning in the corner of the room.

Perhaps that was the connection, he thought. Even if it weren't, he was grateful for the chance to deflect his thinking away from the village, the ceremony, and the *maw pee*. The villagers were her friends, her people; and no purpose would have been served in exposing his fear.

"Remember in the van ride up the mountain you suggested the locals make me into *farang* hamburgers." he said.

"I think *maw pee* has many rifles."

She folded her blankets, smoothing out the creases with her hand. She watched him out of the corner of her eye for a long minute before it became clear he wasn't going to reveal the details of his dream or what had happened the night before. She shrugged off his evasiveness with an indifferent glance in his direction. It wasn't all that important, she told herself. Her mother raised to her to believe that you never trusted a *farang* to answer with the truth. The strangeness of Breach's form upon his return during the night had vanished. He was once again a familiar presence. He was alive and nothing bad had happened; nothing had gone wrong, and this made her heady, light on her feet, bouncing around with a child's energy.

"*Wing*—run," she said. "Down mountain. I race you and win."

And most importantly, her humor roared back. When her humor dried up, she coiled up into a stiffened emotional state, and withdrew into a cocoon of silence. Breach was uncertain whether Suda wanted to talk about what had happened in the village the previous night. The outcome had been predetermined; that was enough, and they had all come out without a scratch; they had lost nothing. What had Suda gained from the successful rescue of Snow? Breach wondered, raising up on his mattress, as he watched her ready to race to the lodge. He didn't have an immediate answer; nor did he have any ready answer for what she had stood to lose if the rescue attempt had failed: if the bullet chamber had been live and Snow had been left dead.

"How did you sleep last night?" Breach rolled off the mattress and stood in the window, watching the boys kick the small football below. The pond across the grounds shimmered in the sunlight.

"*Khit mahk, mahk*—I think too much," she said. "No good."

In Bangkok, at the English school for ex-bar girls, this was Tuttle's favorite expression. It was often on the lips of the female students. As Breach looked over at Suda, he sensed what troubled her wasn't all that different than the students.

"It's hard knowing which side you belong on," he said. Suda stood, hands on her hips, and arched her eyebrows.

"Maybe there is another problem even more difficult," she replied.

She waited for him to react. She was tempting him. "Which problem is that?" he asked.

"The problem of someone forcing you to choose. Choose this side. Go here with these people. Take this back to those people. And maybe you don't want to choose them, or go with them. But you must. Because it is our way."

In her own fashion, she had summed up his feeling about Thomas Pierce. He thought about this insight into a dream he had not told her about and about a man she knew nothing about except he was dying and Breach had asked her help to find shaman knives as a gift.

"And which side did they choose for you?" Breach asked her.

She looked down at his bedding, smiled, and glanced back.

"The side that never has to ask which side."

"Because they know without words," Breach said, turning toward the window. "I know some of the same people."

She nodded. "Like Khun Robert."

"An old teacher of mine. Thomas Pierce."

"The man who wants the knives."

"He would say the knives chose him."

Suda raised an eyebrow. "Maybe, he speak the truth."

Held hostage between ghosts, shaman, headman, an obligation to Tuttle, she found it impossible to close down the gates of thought most of the night and she slept no more than a couple of hours. Another woman would have been collapsed in complete exhaustion. But Suda had that extra reserve; a capacity for life with currents that ran deeper and wider than most. An arc of fire ran through her; and no man, no thing had ever come close to breaking it. Her small frame glided across the room, sweeping up her side of pillows, mattress, sheet, and blankets and stuffing them neatly folded in the backroom.

"*Foon*—dust," she said, waving at Breach on the road, or disappearing off the porch or hurrying red-faced out of a room, as she coughed up phlegm from some underground wound deep inside her lungs. Whereever she happened to be: along the road, field, garden, markets, restaurants, or hotels, the attacks were preceded by frightened eyes and pale face and quickly a smashing dead sound from her lungs.

That morning she walked out onto the veranda, cleared her throat, with the rough, jagged modulation, gagging, that physical sensation of someone choking, in the long and difficult minutes, before, bent forward over the railing she could discharge some burning, inflamed object from inside. She leaned over the railing, panting, eyes half closed, as Breach came out.

"How long you had TB?" asked Breach.

She turned her head away. "How you know it's not a cold?"

"From the blood. I saw a lot of TB in Nepal. But if you want to play a game that it's only a cold, that's up to you."

Breach hooked one leg over the railing, then the other, jumping down to where the village children played with the ball Suda had given them. She watched him show the children how to make goal markers with stones. He demonstrated how to bounce the ball off the knees and keep it in the air; how to bounce it off the soles of each foot and never let it touch the ground; and how to use the head to punch the ball over the goal line. The boys laughed, clapped their hands, and ran around Breach, eyes burning with the hot fire she knew was inside herself. He was a strange *farang*; but they were all strange. This one, though, was different. She could see it in the eyes of the children dancing round and round, as Breach bounced the ball from knee to knee in a kind of high-stepped dance to the gods.

❖

A bashed-up pickup truck, the fenders dented and rusted, the tires with no tread left, was loaded villagers, the engine idling beside the Trekker's lodge. Across the road, at the building site, Breach's guide from the night before, the house servant who had eaten dinner with Suda and him, stood tall in the morning air. He had once again reverted into an ordinary carpenter, his leather tool belt slung low like a holster over one hip. He waved Breach over. Suda climbed into the back of the pickup.

"Not leave for five minutes," she said to Breach.

Breach nodded and walked over to the construction site. He felt like someone after a war greeting a soldier on the other side. The carpenter's face broke into a smile. There was no resemblance between the man standing before him—so harmless and friendly; and the participant in a firing squad the night before. In the warm early morning sun, he didn't look capable of shooting anyone. Yet the same man had stood with his tribe as the rifle had been lowered at Snow's head, another link in the chain of Snow's brush with oblivion.

"I kill a deer early this morning," he said, in halting English.

"You seemed to have learned English overnight."

The carpenter smiled. "Speak a little bit."

"Yeah, yeah. I get it. Glad you got a deer," said Breach, extending his hand.

"I kill it with same rifle," he explained. "I have meat if you want to take."

Breach ignored the offer of food. "What time did you kill the deer?" asked Breach.

The carpenter thought for a moment. "Think just after dawn. I see it in a gully."

Breach broke into a smile. "It was a good kill?" asked Breach. He had heard a shot. It hadn't been the kids kicking the ball against the shutters. Or the ball and the shot exploded at the same moment.

"It was a good kill. Last night the soul come back to the gun," whispered the carpenter, leaning forward. "*Maw Pee* very good. He know how to do. Your friend, he wanted to see. He asked many times. *Maw Pee* say cannot. Last night, he decide to let your friend watch you before he go. He think your friend like. He surprised to see your friend was very scared. *Paw Pee* not understand why *farang* not like. And *maw pee* very surprised you take snake from head. He still not know why snake in man's head. Never mind. *Farang* head not same our head."

Breach looked down at the dirt. "You mean Snow asked to go into the field. He wanted to see the shaman perform a *ritual*."

The carpenter nodded, looking down at Breach's reeboks. "Return of soul to gun ritual." He cleared his throat, turning his head and spitting. "You know Thai word for gun?"

Breach shook his head; he had not learned that word.

"*Bpuen*," said the carpenter, his hand brushing against his crotch. "We call this *bpuen*. And the two eggs underneath we call the same as bullet—*luke bpuen*—child of the gun."

The *maw pee* had conducted a shaman ritual for the lost soul of the hunter's gun. But which gun, thought Breach. The name of what hung between a man's legs was a story of how it belonged to the owner. He smiled at the carpenter. "Thanks for the lesson."

The carpenter wiped his mouth on the side of his arm. "I trade you deer meat for your shoes."

Breach reached down and began undoing the laces of his right shoe. He flipped it off, then he took off the left shoe. He held them out to the carpenter. "That sonofabitch, Snow. He knew all along."

"Wait, I get meat for you."

"No time. You keep the shoes. They're yours." Breach turned and walked barefoot over the road to the pickup truck. The driver was gunning the engine and Suda was yelling at him that it was time to go. The carpenter dropped to the crowd, took off his boots and put on Breach's shoes.

"They fit," he cried after Breach, who had already stepped into the van. "You good man. Have good shoes."

The pickup driver pumped the gas pedal, keeping the engine in neutral, and pistons and valves—in the same state of repair as the tires—choked out a cloud of gritty, black smoke.

Lucy, the last passenger to arrive, climbed into the back, helped by one of the villagers. She had been running and was out of breath.

"Crosby wants you to meet him," she said. She suddenly forgot where and wrinkled her nose. "If I haven't bloody well forgotten."

"Chiang Rai," said Breach.

She beamed. "You bloody well read my mind."

"No, I read Crosby's."

"He said to meet him at outdoor cafe outside bus station in Chiang Rai," she said. Breach nodded, watching the carpenter hopping around in the running shoes. He followed the carpenter's eyes up to the old Lahu woman sitting with her pipe on the lodge porch. She sat resting her elbows on the railing, puffing on her silver pipe. A glint of a smile in her tired old eyes. The Old Lahu watched them, rocking back and forth, her elbows opening and closing like an old pair of hinges.

"Goodbye, Lek," cried Lucy, calling after the old woman.

"What a grand, sweet old lady," said Alison, leaning back against the bed of the pickup.

Suda looked up from Breach's feet. "What happened to your shoes?"

"I gave them to the carpenter," said Breach, looking down at his feet.

Alison laughed and pushed a canvas bag over to Breach. "What goes around comes around."

"What is it?" asked Breach.

Everyone watched as he opened the bag. "Your friend Ross said to see they were delivered to you," said Alison.

"They aren't half heavy," added Lucy.

A smile broke over Breach's face as he pulled out one of the shaman knives. Breach passed it over to Suda, who nodded her approval. He examined a smaller one, turning the blade over; Ross had carefully cleaned the handle, restoring the metal to a fine shine.

"But I don't think he likes you," said Alison.

"Ross?"

She nodded. "He said if that bastard Breach isn't in Mae Sai ready to play; he'll have a nasty surprise in store."

Lucy giggled, covering her mouth. "I reckon hundreds of mosquitoes had the best feed of their lives last night."

"Blood and whiskey," said Alison, handing back the small ritual knife, as the pickup bumped along the uneven, cracked road.

Breach watched a young Lahu woman who was about twenty years old examining one of the knives which were being passed down the row of villagers. Alison and Lucy continued to talk about Ross and Crosby. Suda's eyes followed Breach's to the small, round-faced Lahu woman nursing a baby; her blouse pulled open. Her son, no more than three or four, sat nestled up, his shoulder resting against his mother's hip and ribcage as she rotated one of the knives a couple of inches from her baby's head. His small oval face—a tiny reproduction of his mother's—had turned a sickly pale yellow on the cheeks and forehead. He looked listless, eyes, which like the dog at the back gate of the Lahu village, moved in slow motion. Behind them an old woman whose face was creased around the eyes like a damp sheet sat next to her middle-aged daughter. Between them was a small black pig in a bamboo basket. The pig stood rigid and wild-eyed on his first and last journey down the mountain where a knife was waiting to slit his throat.

Four teenage girls wore shirts with American advertisement on the front: Coke is it! and Madonna. They giggled and teased one another by pulling at each other's clothes and hair. Two young teenage boys stood, their backs to the others, held onto the cab of the pickup, the wind in their face, like downhill skiers, their knees all rubbery as they absorbed the bumps in the road. The hilltribe teenagers were the last to get hold of the fake shaman knives. Either they didn't recognize them as ritual knives or, if they did recognize them, the knives meant nothing to them. Breach wished, for just a moment, Thomas Pierce were sitting next to him in the van on the bumpy road down the mountain. What he had wished for on his deathbed no longer had any meaning in the very place where they had been forged.

The New Zealanders talked about the exchange between Hitoshi and the old Lahu woman. That moment when young Hitoshi's glasses fogged over with emotion as he lowered the necklace and passed it over his head, had taken on a mystical quality. Especially for Lucy, who said, in her mind, it ranked as the high point of their nine months on the road from India and Nepal to Burma and Thailand.

"I'll never forget the magic," said Lucy, purring through half-lidded eyes.

That was a word Breach had hoped not to hear again. Magic. The world was too full of information and possessed too little magic. What magic was left, he thought. The crude, entertainment variety kind of magic from the travelling roadshow performer. The great wizards were all long dead, dust and ash, gone and forgotten, or turned into gods. He thought about the inferno burning as they turned and watched in the field. About the teenagers playing around with the shaman knives. Everywhere there were small brush fires of ignorance sparked by the friction of rubbing together the sticks of quick judgments and wrong assumptions. The first knife returned to Breach was medium-sized. As he remembered the dream where Pierce in his academic gown, the hood pulled over his head, aimed the rifle at him, Breach held the knife by the tip of the blade like a carnival knife thrower. As he slowly raised his arm in an arc, he brought it back fast, throwing the knife out of moving van, cutting threw the dust, and over the side of a mountain ridge.

"Hey, don't do that. You have to show respect for their ways," said Alison.

Breach half crouched in the back of the pickup, waited until the truck slowed for a curve, and then threw out another knife. The remaining two were kept by villagers who reasoned the insane man in the back obviously did not want them. "Did you hear what I said?"

Breach stared at her as they bumped along in the back. "You mean like the Japanese guy last night?"

"That's exactly what I mean," she said, edging away from Breach.

Lucy leaned close to Suda. "You should have seen her. I mean when she smiled at Hitoshi. You never have seen so much love in a person's heart. It was as if she'd been waiting from him to come up this mountain her entire life. She had waited a lifetime with that amulet. She knew one day Hitoshi would find her. It was so beautiful. The way she told about going up to Ma Heh as a child. Being so afraid. Her mother gave her a shove to the front of the crowd. Ma Heh's eyes fixed on her. She walked like in a dream. Everyone in the crowd went silent. Ma Heh reached out and placed the silver fish around her neck. How many mountains do you have to climb to find one real story that gets to you?"

If Suda had an answer, she kept it to herself. She coughed, her face flushing red, half turned, and spit over the side of the pickup.

Half of the passengers got out where the gravel of the mountain road spilled out over the intersection with Highway 1019. Breach said good-bye to the New Zealander girls who dressed like hippies in ragged clothes; Alison turned a pierced ear for a kiss. Lucy, a slender, blond pigtail sticking out of a short-cropped head of hair, extended her hand. They had been in India for six months on the road.

"Thailand's delivered in a big way for me," said Lucy.

"I'll remember to show respect," said Breach, grinning.

"We're going back to India," said Alison, kissing Suda on the forehead. Then she turned back to Breach. "Last night Crosby wouldn't tell me something about you."

"What?"

"Why you stayed in that cave for two years."

Breach looked down at his bare feet and stretched his toes, his lips pursed together. "I was trying to understand how my predecessor in the cave thought he was a clitoris," he said staring at his toes.

"A what?" asked Alison, not quite believing her ears. "A clitoris?"

Breach nodded, watching her eyebrows knit together.

"He thought a woman's clitoris was the castanets of the universe. And this one instrument connected everything together," he said, wriggling his toes.

"Connected to what?" Alison asked, in a serious tone.

Breach smiled. "He never got that far before men with butterfly nets caught him and dragged him away. Of course, if you look hard enough, everything is connected: the Lahu want Reeboks and trade deer meat for them. And the soul of the gun is connected with the sole of the shoe."

"What about the shaman knives you threw away." She looked confused and shouted after him.

"And in England I know a man who thinks shaman knives are the keys to heaven," he shouted back through cupped hands. "Another mad man looking for the castanets of the universe." He didn't really believe that Pierce was mad. He had wished his former mentor could be dismissed that easily.

Before she could reply, the pickup shot off. She watched it make a hard right turn onto the highway, and accelerated, the driver stripping the gears. Breach looked back at the two women looking so small standing alone on the road, their dirty shoulder bags at their her feet; Alison zipping up her small Mien coin purse.

He visualized Crosby wrapping his arm around her shoulder; her face tilted towards his. Crosby rolling his eyes and exhaling smoke. Ross pacing around the veranda with clenched fists, knocking into the chairs and tables; taking bearlike swipes at mosquitoes diving at his belly. She looked back and waved goodbye. The road curved and she was gone. Breach had seen her yearning before. Each time, he thought about this kind of traveller, people with no address, occupation, or particular goal whose life was consumed with hot desire for the remarkable; and in less time than it took to complete an unremarkable curve in the road, they had vanished from sight.

Suda held the Lahu woman's baby. She was from the village, and Suda knew her father. Sitting in the back of the pickup for next ten kilometers, Breach brooded. Why had Suda had been so quiet during the entire way down the mountain? Alison and Lucy had held her attention with the story of Hitoshi.

"You knew the old woman at the lodge."

Suda nodded, handing the baby back to its mother.

"For many years," she said. "She know my mother's family."

"Why you didn't say something to the *mems*?"

"They not ask me."

"She took five thousand off Hitoshi for the amulet," said Breach, leaning back and feeling the wind on his face. "Five grand for a silver fish. Good price or bad price, Suda?"

"Good price." The baby started crying and Suda took him back, rocking him in her arms, keeping the wind out of his face.

"For him?"

"For her. She bought fish amulet from me three months ago for three hundred-fifty baht. She discounted me. I wanted four hundred baht."

"She lied, you mean. . ."

"Japanese man was very rich. Lahu is very poor. He is happy; she is happy. There is no more to say. I think she told a very good story. Foreigner should pay. A story is not free. Next time, I don't let her discount me."

"And she got another five thousand off me," said Breach, reaching down and brushing the dirt off his feet. "She arranged for Snow's release."

"I already fix. She tell another story. You pay like Japanese pay. I think she very good storyteller."

"*Maa moht.*" Breach had meant it as a kind of compliment, calling her a female wizard. In Thai, it was understood to mean old bitch. He could see the reaction in Suda's face.

"*Nahk hoo-uh kry!*" said Suda, in Thai.

"What's that mean."

The pickup swerved out, passing a bus, and two slow moving trucks stacked with sugarcane. Breach's eyes grew big as he watched another truck coming head on in the same lane. At the last possible moment, the driver of the pickup pulled in front of the second truck. As if not losing beat, Suda continued.

"It means heavy on whose head. Who is anyone to judge another person's life. Life is heavy for each person. You cannot say your life is heavier. So you say nothing."

"Or you reach for your gun," said Breach. He crossed his legs and watched the highway.

Chapter 13

The pickup turned off the highway and into a large, open dirt lot fringed with smoky food stalls, metal push-carts and a gray concrete squat building with his and her pissholes cut into the cement. Swarms of flies buzzed overhead as they commuted from the toilets to the noodle bowls. Peasants milled around, holding plastic shopping bags as they waited in small circles of shade for a bus to carry them north to Chiang Rai or south to Chiang Mai. Suda bought two bottles of water and a plastic bag filled with overripe watermelon. Breach walked like a cripple as he balanced on his heels; the dirt was so broiler-plate hot, and he regretted the impulsive action of giving away his shoes. A few minutes later, a Chiang Rai bus pulled in, the driver hard breaking, discharging a mushroom cloud of thick brown dust over the food stalls, scattering the peasants, who choked and coughed into their handkerchiefs until tears streamed down their faces.

A few Chiang Rai passengers climbed down, stretching, and ran through the thick clots of black flies looking for food or a place to piss. One couple stood out from the others. A green-eyed middle-aged *farang* in blue jeans and a white shirt with pale blue piping sewed on the front pockets and collar; he stood in a spot of shade, with an arm wrapped around the waist of a teenage Thai girl. She looked eighteen. She looked like one of his language school students in Bangkok, thought Breach. The girl had a fresh, gentle, smiling face; long, shoulder-length hair spilling over a new baby-blue blouse. Her tight white jeans followed the contours of firm, muscular legs and thighs; rock-hard limbs from humping fifty-kilo bags of across vast spans of rice paddies or go-go dancing night after night in Patpong or Soi Cowboy.

Breach, running on his heels, skidded to a stop in the shade next to the girl. He reached down and rubbed each foot in turn, making a hissing noise. His eyes narrow and watery; his face drawn with pain.

"Where are your shoes, man?" asked the *farang*, his mouth open in disbelief as he stared at Breach's feet.

"I gave them to a Lahu carpenter."

"Shit, what did he give you?"

"Ten pounds of deer meat."

The blond-haired *farang* with the weathered Scandinavian face, the slender nose, thin lips, crowfeet around the eyes, broke into laughter.

"Deer meat?" asked the *farang*. "What in the hell were you going to do with all that meat?"

"My thought exactly, so I passed on the meat."

"I don't get it," said the *farang*, who was no longer laughing, and the sound of suspicion crept into the tone of his voice.

His Thai girlfriend reached in her pocket and offered Breach one hundred baht.

"No, I couldn't take your money," Breach said, trying not to look at her boyfriend.

"Christ, I should hope not," said the *farang*.

The blond-haired man pulled the girl's hand down and moved her back a step, as if Breach was dangerous and might attack. Suda, fifteen feet away, in another small spot of shade, turned and spit in the dirt. She had said nothing and looked off into the middle distance. Her lungs were erupting again. She showed no interest in judging the *farang* or his teenaged girlfriend. Some might have expressed moral outrage at a middle-aged *farang* who would use money to exploit youth; but not Suda. If the teenage girl wanted to sleep with the *farang*, then that was up to her. If the *farang* wanted to give her money for sex, then that was up to him.

Within five minutes he told Breach that his name was Wayne, that he was forty-three years old, lived in Minnesota, and had killed nine deer. He was an electrician, and produced his union card from a brown leather wallet fat with credit cards.

"People can tell you any old shit on the road. Make up stories about what they do or who they are. Well, you don't get one of these for nothing. You better believe that you work your ass off for it."

The photograph of Wayne looked twenty years old. Before his blond hair had begun to recede like a glacier, and the rivers and valleys had formed on his face. Breach returned his card and watched him slip it behind a Visa card.

"And you? What the hell you doing here out in the middle of nowhere without shoes or a hat?"

A shaft of light struck Wayne's belt, spinning sparkling wheels of brillant, reflected sun against the windscreen of an ordinary bus with a Chiang Mai sign.

"Learning the price of deer meat," said Breach, making a line in the dirt with his big toe.

"Yeah, sure, like what do you really do?"

"I used to teach eighth grade shop," said Breach. He felt it was the kind of occupation which might satisfy Wayne and he was right.

"I loved shop in school. The rest was like pissing up a rope. But shop? Fucking A-okay."

"I wanted to teach plumbing. How to fix a light socket without tools. How to build a fire with wet leaves," said Breach. He had made a complete circle in the dirt. Wayne's girlfriend squatted down and, using her finger, made a smaller circle inside Breach's circle.

"That's not shop, that's Boy Scouts."

"That's what the school principal said when he fired me. Camping, fishing, and hunting are not urban skills, Breach. He was right. I came to Thailand to be Boy Scout."

"You ain't doing real well so far," said Wayne. Then he snapped at his girlfriend. "What the fuck you doing playing in the dirt, honey," said Wayne, lifting his girlfriend up from behind, both hands under her armpits.

Breach erased the two circles with his foot. "Were you in Nam?" he asked.

Wayne nodded; he had served a tour in Vietnam in '68, a maintenance worker on F-14 fighters; he hadn't been shot at, or shot anyone. He claimed the first time he mounted a Vietnam whore he had forgotten to take out the earplugs he wore at the airfield.

"Don't you ever want to forget about that? Blank out the whole memory?" asked Breach.

Wayne looked reflective, brow furled. "The whores in Vietnam hated our guts. You could see it in their faces. 'Fuck you, yank' written in every bullshit smile." That distressing discovery still caused Wayne's jaw to clench all these years later standing in the dust beside Highway 1019 between Chiang Mai and Chiang Rai. He took a deep breath, winked at Breach, and fished two fingers and a thumb into his shirt pocket. A pair of earplugs lay in the palm of his hand. "You should try it sometime."

Wayne's companion was Noi, and she was from Chiang Rai—and had worked six months at Supergirls, one of the upstairs, entertainment bars in Patpong.

"She don't do the live sex-show shit,"said Wayne, giving Noi a squeeze. "Do you, honey? Fact is, I've got half a mind to marry this little one. Take her back home. She'd cook my dinner, give me back rubs, wash my feet, pour me a drink whenever I wanted. I'm tempted to make that big buy-out called marriage. I've been thinking about it real serious on this trip. While I still got some hair left. She already calls me the old water buffalo. Don't you, sweetheart."

Wayne tilted his head to one side, looked over Breach's shoulder at Suda, who stood in a half slump, her shoulders pulled forward, drinking water through a straw out of a plastic bottle. She lifted her hand to her eyes, blocking the sun, looking down the highway, the long, black hair under her armpits curling in the damp heat. Her dusty feet arched forward in a worn- out pair of fifteen-baht plastic sandals. She saw Wayne staring at her, and flashed a jagged-toothed, Charlie Chaplin grin.

"Where'd you find her?" asked Wayne.

"At the Sunday Market in Bangkok."

"I got a deal with this one," he said, half cupping his hand, whispering in a loud voice, pretending Noi couldn't hear. "I pick up her expenses, and 500 baht a day pocket money. But then I can afford to wear a pair of shoes."

He waited for Breach to say something. Perhaps a compliment on his business accumen, but Breach only curled his toes in the sun and grinned at Noi. About that time, the Chiang Mai air conditioned bus rolled in, and Wayne and Noi's bus honked—the final call for passengers.

"You mind me askin'," Wayne began. "How much you are paying your girl?"

Breach scratched the back of his neck and stared at the highway as if confused. The face of the aged Viking looked angry; his teeth on edge, eyes small bore; the lines in his face webbed in shadows as he stepped into the sun.

"She pays her own way," said Breach.

"Figures. That poor, fucking girl don't have squat."

"She's wearing shoes," said Breach, a grin spreading over his face. "Gonna miss your bus."

"Noi hasn't had a vacation in what—what did you say it was, honey? One, two years." Noi pretended not to understand the question, and stared at her feet where Breach had made the circles. "Get your act together. Do the right thing by that one. She ain't worth big bucks. So you got her cheap. But cheap ain't always right. What goes around comes around is what I always say."

He gave Breach a hard slap on the back, doubling him over; then he winked at Suda, and disappeared into the bus heading back to Chiang Mai. Breach ran after them, stopping Noi before she boarded the bus. He reached out and grabbed her arm. He stood out of breath, his feet burning on the hard ground.

"You take this?"

"Why you give me your watch?" she asked, looking at the Seiko with a gold band in the palm of her hand.

"Sell it and buy yourself a real vacation," he said.

"Maybe you crazy. Or maybe you have a good heart."

Breach didn't have a chance to reply as Wayne reached down and pulled her on the bus. "Don't talk to that deer meat fool. He's a nut case."

She giggled and hung out the window with the watch hanging loose on her wrist. "Maybe I go home tomorrow," said Noi. Wayne arm-wrapped around her neck like a serpent, squeezing her and dragging her back inside the window. A moment later the bus was gone.

"What did the *farang* say?" Suda asked, as they settled in their seats on the Chiang Rai bus.

"His name's Wayne. He's an electrician from Minneapolis. And he mugs barefoot strangers at remote bus depots."

" 'Hectri'," she said.

Breach wrote out the word electrician on a piece of paper, looked up electricity in his English-Thai dictionary; and she pored through her Thai-English dictionary. A couple of minutes minutes later she had a fairly good idea of what Wayne's job was. She, of course, had no idea where Minneapolis was.

"Near Norway," Breach said.

"Norway?"

Breach waved his hand at the window. "Out there somewhere."

"Electrician is a good idea. He makes much money. Not like English teacher in Bangkok. Like Crosby. He's always poor. Maybe you learn to be electrician."

"You have discovered the irony of our times. We live in the heart of a new Dark Age. We have an abundance of electricians. They have switched on the lights throughout the world," he said. "Now man can control the night with a flashlight. But he cannot escape the darkness of his age."

She stared at him, tilting her head one way and then another.

"*Poot len,*" she said, smiling and curling up in her seat, closing her eyes and trying to switch off her mind, escape the elusive ghost of the last few nights, as the bus to Chiang Rai gathered speed, overtaking an old truck filled with bleary-eyed Thais in bare feet. Suda leaned over Breach, pressing her hand against the window. She pointed at the Thai men.

"Just like you. No shoes."

"And the next carpenter who will trade me five pounds of deer meat for my shirt has a deal," said Breach, waving at the men in the truck. But it was too hot, and most of them were sweaty, and sleeping; they didn't see the *farang* waving both hands at them in the window of the bus. They were sleeping in exhaustion and heat, dreaming, if at all, thought Breach, of moonlit nights, game moving along the side of a mountain, and a single gunshot which pierced the darkness.

"At some point, you understand it is all connected: your life, the price of bread, the Prussian War, the prostitute buying a miniskirt, and who wins the debate at Oxford

Union next week," Dr. Holmes had said to Breach half a life time earlier.

On a bus to Chiang Rai, Breach remembered Dr. Holmes, a history don. Dr. Holmes had stood before the fireplace in his college rooms, and Breach sat on the couch reading an essay on the ethics of political torture, which Breach had subtitled: "The relationship between torture, the disappearance of whooping cranes, and the retail sales of the Big Mac." Out the bus window a motorcyclist steered onto the shoulder of the road, as the Chiang Rai bus, overtook a small, slow-moving van, and barreled straight toward the motorcycle.

Dr. Holmes had been a university reader and attached to a college other than Breach's; he had served in British military intelligence during World War II. He had been stationed in France, and developed a view of the Flemish as disloyal, difficult, dangerous, with an unbroken appetite for senseless destruction and violence.

Dr. Holmes wore silver-rimmed half-moon-shaped glasses midway down a prolonged nose eroded by thousands of hours of sipping the finest port in the college cellar, talked about his enormous satisfaction in witnessing the execution of Flemish collaborators. He had been involved in a risky operation, working with little support deep behind enemy lines. In isolated farmhouses, prisoners were tortured. Dr. Holmes believed that in any essay on the ethics of torture a first-class mind would always conclude: a Flemish traitor could never suffer enough. And he had racked his brain thinking of new and novel ways of extracting confessions before he had them shot.

"One evil bastard had taken a family hostage. Pulled up the wife's skirt in front of her two small children—a boy six, and girl, seven, eight, I forget the exact age of the girl—and played with her. I mean to say, Breach. He sexually abused her. She sat on a wooden chair, her legs spread apart, until she couldn't bear it any longer. She struck him in the face.

And he shot her three times in the chest. I jolly well enjoyed executing him. Before I personally put the bastard against the wall, I asked him one question. 'How could you stand her screaming; the kids bawling, and still keep an erection.' The sonofabitch smiled. 'Earplugs. I wore earplugs.' Standing against the wall, his hands shaking, he pulled a pair from his pocket. We looked at each for a long moment, then I nodded. I let him put them in. The bastard didn't want to hear the rifle shots. One of my few regrets, letting that evil bastard stand against the wall with the same earplugs he'd worn the night he killed that family." Then Holmes stared down at the essay and marked it a B+ and handed it to Breach.

Breach repeated Dr. Holmes's lecture to his tutor, Thomas Pierce. Pierce knew Dr. Holmes's reputation telling his pupils stories of slashing the wrists of Flemish Nazis. "Earplugs? Maybe, I hadn't heard that story before. He saw a lot of blood in France, and suffered in a way that devours him today. He plays this past over and over, coming up with new material, transforming the old, dropping one incident and picking up another. He says he's trying to get it right. What happened? Who was at fault? Why no one had been warned in time? What explanations were more credible than another? That's why he became an historian. So he had some cover to study the records, the newspapers, the dispatches, the diaries, the reports, interview survivors, pickup leads on those still in hiding, knowing he's out there looking for them and programmed to make them pay the price."

Pay the price. Breach remembered those words, as his tutor sat in his overstuffed chintz chair, sucking on the stem of his pipe, teeth mark scratches glistening in the fireplace flames a few feet away. Outside, on the quad, a light snow melted as the flakes struck. An undergraduate in mufflers wrapped in thick coils around his neck shuffled, paused outside the window, his eyes half-lidded, sticking his tongue out and catching snowflakes, swallowing, smiling, and passing on. His personal tutor, Thomas Pierce, an historian, who was light-years away from death then, relit his pipe with a match, filling the air for a second with the smell of sulfur. He instinctively drummed the fingers of his left hand on the arm of his chair. From tutorials over many months, Breach knew what Pierce was thinking; like a blocked writer, what next, what condition, what truth, what meaning. His teeth worked on the pipe stem as he drummed.

"I have read your essay and have been given considerable thought to Dr. Holmes's mark," he said, looking up, the hand with the drumming fingers, now forming a rest for his chin. "About captivity in the past. The past of World War II, his past, mine, yours. After you reach ten or eleven, if you're halfway clever, read the usual newspapers and magazines, you know the score. What's risky, what gets confiscated, worn-out, used up, thrown away, who is abandoned, destroyed, or enslaved. You understand that life is a prolonged exposure to certain general principles with fixed elements that repeat themselves over and over again. In many countries, the spring floods destroy crops, livestock, and people. And every year, it gets reported as if it were some isolated, freakish event. Same with volcanoes—though their timing is less predictable. Earthquakes, tornadoes, typhoons, hurricanes, much the same can be said."

"People steal, cheat, lie, murder and their victims are inevitably inconvenienced, upset, hospitalized, medicated, prescribed therapy, testify in court, have nervous breakdowns, leave their spouses."

"Once you understand that principle, then you begin to wonder why people bother with newspapers hour after hour, reading endless examples of a general principle. A bloody waste of time, and even worse, it creates this notion that someone, some government or institutions can do something to change the principle; to control, protect, guide, and produce a programme that provides for escape.

Any half-clever ten-year-old should see right through this piece of fraud, and cry out: sham! sham!"

"So what should be done?" he paused, watching the falling snow. He refilled his pipe, and shifted in his chair, crossing his leg, stretching his shoulders like a cat waking from a long nap. A broad smile briefly fell over his face.

"You read the kind of books that make no big promises, you believe in people who make no big promises. You seek out books and people who aren't filled with endless examples or sweet talk. Books that recognize you're a big enough lad to accept the impermanence of yourself and your world without false footholds. Books that give insight into the heart and passion at the moment a character knows that nothing can or ever will last."

He rose from his chair, walked over and stood in front of the window, staring at the six-hundred-year-old quad covered in a light blanket of snow.

"That's why I feel for him. My dear colleague who is faithfully leading the life of a newspaper reader," he broke off with a sigh. "I would have judged your essay an A. Why, you may wish to ask? Because you understood the link between fast-food and extinction of a specie—the whooping crane. What cannot be manufactured has lost its place in this world. And that torture is not about ethics and never was. Torture is the application of technology to inflict pain and discomfort for an immediate profit, or as your essay has it, the flip side of torture, then is the Big Mac which has adapted the same technology to produce hamburgers and to create a mass of self-torturing consumers. And so good-bye Mr. Whooping Crane."

Breach felt guilty for throwing away the fake sacrificial knives. He had pretended the knives hadn't mattered. He wished he would have sent them by federal express to Thomas Pierce with a note attached: for torture, the Big Mac, or the whooping crane. On the road to Chiang Rai, he began to understand Pierce's request in a different light. The fact the knives were fakes was irrelevant for the purpose intended by Pierce. They might have been the perfect instrument for Pierce to clutch on his deathbed as he sought his release from this world.

Chapter 14

Near the edge of an emerald-green rice paddy that stretched out from the highway, workers poured cement for a condo foundation.

"Local people think development is good," said Suda. "Maybe good for some."

"Development is a neon-sign word. Tradition is a carved-in-stone word," said Breach, as the bus swept past the condo project. "And you can't see stone at night."

"Or in a Dark Age," said Suda.

Breach turned around and stared at her for several moments. She returned his smile. "You think I don't understand?"

Not any more he didn't. It was the kind of chance remark that could make a man fall slightly in love with a woman. She not only had listened, she understood the connections—she was making them before him.

The women and men behind them on the construction crew also understood: the some who benefited from the Neon Sign World did not include those who poured the cement. She feared the rapid change, and disliked what she witnessed happening: families breaking up, the new creed of selfishness, and young girls hustling bars and street corners. The old family compounds—and the values they had nurtured—were disappearing, sold to developers; villages in the North dissolved into the soft blur of suburban sprawl. Suda coughed, doubling over in her seat, her forehead pressed against the windowpane.

"My grandfather became an anarchist. How did the family know? When he tiled the kitchen floor with pancakes," said Breach.

Suda thought about this for a moment. "Your grandfather put food on the floor?"

Breach nodded. "Not to eat. I tried to understand why he was doing this. At six years old, you walk across a floor covered with pancakes and you know your family is different. He did his pancake flooring gig three, four times. Grandfather blew his pension cheque on boxes of pancake mix. He worked at it in the dead of night. Everyone else was sleeping in their beds. The house filled with the smell of fresh pancakes. About four in the morning Mother caught him on his hands and knees wearing an old bathrobe, glueing each pancake in place. Hundreds and hundreds of pancakes. I was only six. I ate two before mother smacked me and sent me to my room. Grandpa was feeding every cockroach and mouse in the neighbour. Mother had a lock installed on the fridge and stove. She thought the battle was over. But it had just begun. In February, he opened the bathroom window in the middle of the night. He filled up the tub. In the morning, the water was frozen solid. The third time, the tub cracked. And Grandpa was put away in a nursing home. He chuckled when they put him in the straitjacket."

On the outskirts of Chiang Rai the air-conditioned bus passed row after row of new car lots.

"Your father didn't help him?" asked Suda, eyes watery from coughing.

"He was already gone," said Breach.

"He went where?"

Breach shrugged. "My father was the best con man England ever produced. My uncle said that Father never worked a single day in his life. He only played cards. He lived for high-stake poker games. The house that my grandpa tried to carpet with pancakes?"

Suda arched her eyebrows.

"It was a rental. Dad lost our family house in a poker game. And all the fittings and furniture as well which was hauled out and loaded into a truck. Mother left him. It was too much for her. Now that was saying a great deal because she had been born into a family of con artists. The entire family had existed for generations on various scams and schemes. Grandpa had used mother in the street along with my uncle when they were still kids. He instructed them on how to sell flowers. He gave them acting lesson so they could look hungry and sad-eyed and adorable. They pulled in customers, who felt sorry for them. With perfect timing, grandpa jumped out of the shadows with his armed loaded with books. His game was flogging fake rare family Bibles to the customer who had just bought flowers from my mum. Mum thought it was God's will that Grandpa went batty using pancake mix as lino. She told me that Grandpa was kept in a padded room and with Father vanished, she had replied to an ad for mail-order brides. A correspondence delivered over six months. And before I was seven, we had left England and immigrated to Canada. She married a Breach in Vancouver."

"Did you think your grandfather was crazy?" asked Suda.

Breach shook his head. "Nah, it was another of Grandpa's scams. My uncle booked into a first-class rest home, Mum and my uncle footing the bill. Within two weeks he started a bookie operation. By the time we arrived in Vancouver, he had fifteen phone lines connected into the rest-home basement. When the police raided the place, they read his medical history. Pancakes on the floor, said the files. No former charges ever brought. Grandpa had transfered most of his assets from the bookie operation offshore to Gurnsey. For the last nine years of his life, Grandpa lived there in a small villa surrounded by two wives and three small children. In his will, he asked to be buried with a recipe for pancakes."

❖

Highway 1019 wound through a landscape of red dust, construction sights, peasants in bamboo hats with handkerchiefs wrapped covering their mouth and nose, water buffalo and police checkpoints. Entering Chiang Rai was like passing through the gateway of a nineteenth-century American cow town, smelling of fast money mingled with the dust. It had the feel of a gambler's town, where people asked few questions of where the money came from and where it went next. The bus passed several men wearing cowboy hats; and there were pickup trucks with gun rackets against the back window. The bus appeared to have drifted out of Thailand and into a dreamscape; one that weaved and flowed through narrow streets, dirt alleys, concrete yards, endless series of gray shophouses.

Breach hummed the old Janice Joplin's song, and then sang the lyrics, "Oh Lord, why don't you buy me a Mercedes Benz, my friends all drive Cadillacs, and I must make amends." He unfolded Crosby's note again, read it, balled it up into a wad, and dropped it on the floor.

Turning down the city streets, the bus passed shops with electronic gadgets. Men with mobile phones to their ear as they passed in the opposite lane. A motorcylist with a black plastic beeper strapped to the side of his hip gunned his motor pulling around the bus as it pulled to a stop. There was a thirty-minute layover before the bus went on to Mae Sai. The pneumatic door swung open and passengers poured out, stretching their arms and rubbing their eyes, as they crossed through the dreary bays with smudged diagonal lines, fishing in their pockets for one baht for the woman slapping at flies in a chair beside the toilets. Breach walked beside Suda who sucked on cough drops.

"I'm going out for some pancakes," he said, with a wink.

She looked at him with large, brown eyes. "See you on the bus," she said, disappearing into the toilets.

Outside the bus station Breach looked around for the restaurant. Food stalls ran in rows against the outside wall;

the vendor lowered a small bowl into a plastic tub bubbling, a slime of green suds as lifeless as dead fish in a back soi klong. Across the street, Ross stood in front of an open-air restaurant, and waved at him.

"Hey, you weirdo. Over here," Ross shouted through cupped hands through the snarl of traffic.

Ross stood next to a Thai with a Southwestern American braided rope tie held together with a silver clip shaped somewhere between the image of a cigar and a land-to-surface missile.

"Why isn't that sonofabitch wearing shoes," he murmured to the Thai, as he watched Breach dart through the traffic. "White men wear shoes when they walk on hot concrete, goddamn."

Ross sat behind a dirty table, slurping chicken and noodles, and eyeing a bottle of *Old Grand-Dad* at his elbow. Globules of chicken fat glistened on his lips and rolled off the sides of his mouth. He smiled at Breach. "Pull up a stool and pour yourself a drink. This is Khun Pak." Ross nodded at the Thai in western cowboy clothes who sat at the table. Khun Pak smiled, cracking his knuckles; and Breach could see the street traffic mirrored on two gold-capped front teeth.

"You like those teeth?" asked Ross, watching Breach's eyes. "Khun Pak had the real ones knocked out in a king ass, winner-take-all poker game with Khun Sa."

"Where is Crosby?" asked Breach, looking around the tables.

Ross hooked a thumb over his shoulder, head half-bowed over the soup. About a dozen Thais sat in the restaurant, all facing the same direction, all of them in silence, few of them eating. Three were playing cards at a table with Crosby. The rest watched a portable TV on the wall. But they weren't watching television; they were engrossed in a movie on the VCR. The film was all gunfire and explosions. It was *First Blood*. The first Rambo film.

"And Snow? What happened to him?"

Ross looked up from his bowl. "The godman's making a collect phone call. Now are you gonna tell us what happened to your fucking shoes?" He looked worried.

"I lost them in a card game," said Breach, leaning forward on his elbows, trying to get Crosby's attention.

"The fuck you did. Win, win, win. Don't ever use the words lost or lose," said Ross. He filled his glass halfway with *Old Grand-Dad* and held it up. "You owe me ten grand US." He looked directly at Breach. "Khun Pak kicks ass for a thousand baht. And I'm not certain if I told you last night because I was pretty drunk. But I don't like you. Just because you went to Oxford, you think that makes you better than me. In Chiang Rai, Oxford don't mean shit. You mean less than shit. In Chiang Rai a man's judged by what he's got on his feet. So you ain't got squat."

"Is that a legal opinion? Or more in the realm of a layman's idle speculation?"

"You think you're hot shit," snarled Ross.

Khun Pak rocked on the back two legs of his wooden chair, arms folded, his upper lip cut away to expose the gold caps. He had the look of someone who might kill for much less than a thousand baht; that downward movement of the eyes, the nervous, knuckle-cracking hands, and the kind of shallow, false smile that framed an attitude beyond shame or disgrace.

"I'm in the game," said Breach, after a long pause.

"That's not good enough! You are in the game to win," replied Ross, quickly bringing down his empty glass hard on the table. "To win." His voice sounded mean.

"To win, win, win," Breach said, using the same tone of voice.

"Good. That's what I like to hear," said Ross, not smiling.

Breach had been raised to become a world-class card player. But he doubted that he had inherited his Grandpa's pancake gene. While his execution and play were nearly flawless—he lacked that intangible element, the subtle ability which could not be learned, but was essential for the quantum leap to the big leagues. This missing element was mastery through unpredictability. The appearance of the irrational play was the key to controlling the table. The cold-blooded decision to risk a substantial sum of money simply to throw the other side off guard; snare them in their rational, logical expectation of what should be in his hand. Was he bluffing or did he have the cards? Greatness came with creating chaos as a weapon to destroy your opponent's confidence, distract him, or make him underestimate your ability and intentions. Unless a player instinctively raised such hard-edged doubts, he would never be great; and the great players would always beat him. His Grandpa had it. His father had it. His father had lost the family house: and that was the level of risk required. His father had sat across a table expressionless, no sign of sweat, emotions,or tics, with a losing hand and pushed the deed to the house into the pile. The great card player was the ultimate Zen master. And Breach had lived inside a cave trying to find the connection between pancakes on the floor and the moving van loading all the furniture from the family house after his father's gambling loss.

Snow sat down at the table beside to Khun Pak. "Tuttle wants you to phone him, man."

"Fuck Tuttle," said Ross. "Khun Pak says the man we contact in Mae Sai is a Chink named Tang. You know, like that powdered shit we used to make orange juice from? Get the details. And, Breach," he said pausing, "Buy some goddamn shoes."

Crosby strolled over to a table lighting a cigarette with a Nam-era Zippo lighter he had won in a card game. It was inscribed "Fighting for peace is like fucking for virginity."

"They wanted to watch Rambo instead of playing cards," he said. "Bloody unprofessional, I said. Fuck you, they said."

"When you find out what the fuck is going on, leave a message in our hotel," said Ross. He pulled out a pair of wire-rimmed glasses, and turned his chair around, facing the TV. Rambo removed a large knife and silently moved down the side of a hill.

Crosby and Snow followed Breach across the road to the bus station. They stopped in front of the bus to Mae Sai. The bus passengers who were continuing on to Mai Sae drifted back. Crosby lit a cigarette with a large tongue of flame, and snapped back the top of the Zippo lighter, which he pocketed.

"You didn't tell me Suda was ill. That she probably has a fatal lung disease," said Breach.

Crosby flicked a piece of tobacco off the tip of his top with his fingers. "She's got maybe a year."

"Tuttle gave her one grand US," said Snow. "He told me on the phone. She wants to buy a house for her mom."

"That explains it. Why she helped," said Breach mostly to himself.

Crosby laughed, looking down at Breach's feet. "Did you think it was for the ride? Or your no doubt entertaining conversation about your crazy family?"

Breach was too embarrassed to say that had crossed his mind. "In Thailand most everything is cash-and-carry," said Crosby. "You don't think she helped you because she liked Snow?"

"She loves me, man."

Crosby rolled his eyes at Snow who was grinning like a wild man. He helped himself to one of Crosby's cigarettes as a beggar no more than eleven offered to sell each of them red roses, the stems wrapped in plastic, the petals slightly wilted in the afternoon heat.

"You like her?" Crosby asked him, with a crooked grin.

"She's not a romantic. I like that about her. Practical, no bullshit illusions. She never says, 'Am I pretty?' 'Do you like my outfit?' 'Why do I have to die?'" said Breach. "Never once did she say, 'Feel sorry for me, help me, love me, hold me. Because she knows none of that shit matters a damn."

The bus driver raced the engines and threw the huge stick shift in the floor into gear. Breach pulled off his shirt and handed it to the flower vendor with skinny legs with dirty knobby knees. The young boy nervously eyed the shirt, stuck it under his arm and ran away. Breach boarded the bus, and Crosby flipped his cigarette end into the oily bay.

"Look at that little fucker run," said Snow, watching the flower vendor disappear from sight.

"Disrobing in public makes Thais nervous," said Crosby, wiping the sweat from his forehead. He caught a final glimpse of Breach looking out the bus window.

"You're nuts, man," Snow said.

"Your professional opinion as an ex-Lahu godman?" asked Crosby.

Crosby walked away, leaving Snow to catch up with in the street. In the restaurant, Ross's Thai friend, Khun Pak, was sticking a bowie knife into the tabletop. Sweat rolling off his face, Snow shaded his face with his right hand. He had that wet look of the newly born, and that stunned, disoriented look of being held up in a strange, polluted space.

"Now that's crazy," said Crosby, nodding at Ross's table.

"Okay, okay," said Snow, sweat rolling off the end of his nose. "Why not shoes? Why not shirt, man. I don't get it?"

Crosby scooted across the street in front of a new BMW. A couple of minutes later inside the restaurant, Snow tilted his head far back sucking down a *Singha Gold*. "It's his way of preparing for the game."

"That's wild, man. He's working up a nudist act?" asked Snow, lowering his beer.

Ross stopped his conversation with Khun Pak, and leaned across the table. "Nudist my ass."

214

"He has a philosophy about shedding his clothes. He did it in my school in England."

"Stripped naked?" asked Ross, jaw dropping.

"Once he had me drop my pants in a poker game. I stood on the table with a red swollen dick."

Snow rolled his eyes and sipped his beer. "Yeah, I know the story, man. But why the fuck is Breach doing this?"

"You ready for this? Okay, okay. He says, romantics are militants, they hold themselves hostage and everyone around them. Destroy the self. Throw away everything. Put waffles on your bedroom floor. Or was it pancakes on the lawn. I can never remember. But the bottom line, once you put some strange thing in an usual place, then you're prepared to take any risk," said Crosby. "That's what Breach taught us."

"Crosby, even when you try to speak fucking English, you don't seem to be speaking English," said Ross, slamming his heavy fist down on the table. The bottle of *Old Grand-Dad* jumped from the force of the blow and broke on the floor.

"Breach wants to be like his father and grandfather," said Crosby. "The ultimate Zen card player and con man of the universe. A player with no self and no cards and no opponents and nothing to win or lose."

Ross clenched his teeth and grabbed Khun Pak's bowie knife. Blue veins in his forearm bulged as he waved the knife above his head and clenched his teeth. "He better not fuck with me," he said slowly. "Or I'll give him all the fucking opponents he ever wanted."

Breach tried not falling asleep on the bus. He leaned his head back for just a moment and closed his eyes. He counted to ten, opened his eyes. Then closed them and counted to . . .he lost track around 36, 37. In his dream, Suda ran a small stall, a few tables, shelves, and cabinets jammed up with dozens of other hilltribe hawkers who were separated by a narrow dirt path. It was third from the end of Soi two of the market. The first time Breach saw her, Suda stood behind a makeshift wooden counter, leaning forward over a set of scales. On the left side of the scale, a hollow silver bracelet, bought from the Lahu and Akha; they had a ribbed pattern of etched lines on the outside. On the right side of the scale, Suda added small bronze weights. She looked intent until the two sides balanced. She pulled out her calculator and multipled the number of grams by the price. Her customer was a young English woman in a white tank top, shorts, and sandals, who was an undergraduate at Pembroke College, Oxford.

"That much?" the English girl replied, in a surprised voice. Suda nodded. Crosby used his index finger to scoop the bracelet from the scale. He handed it to Breach.

"It's nearly one hundred years old. Suda sells it by weight. Eighteen baht per gram. You get the design and history for free."

"I wanted to buy four," said the young woman. "I have a friend, and—and, well, I thought they might make nice serviette holders. I'm a student. And I don't have that much money."

She sighed, then drifted away across the narrow dirt lane.

"What she mean 'serviette'?" asked Suda, looking after her lost customer, now looking through a pile of small Lahu handbags.

"Napkins," Breach said. "She wanted to use the bracelet for napkins holders to impress her Oxford friends." He made a pass over the bracelet resting on the palm of his hand, making it disappear. And reaching into Crosby's shirt pocket produced the bracelet.

"He was one of my teachers," Crsoby said, introducing Breach. "Then he lived in a cave in Nepal. And he practised magic in the dark because he's convinced we live in a New Dark Age."

Suda looked up from putting the bracelets back into the case. "A caveman?"

"That's what I write in the space for occupation on the immigration card. The Thai immigration officer nods," said Breach. "Thailand isn't worried about caveman tourists."

Crosby translated into Thai for Suda. She was still distracted by the lost sale, though, and Crosby's explanation about Breach's recent past in Nepal.

"Breach is looking for a set of rare shaman knives," said Tuttle. That caught her attention, her head snapped up from the display cabinet. She gave Breach a smile.

"You collect hilltribe pieces?"

"It's your basic waste of time," he said. Confusion set in on Suda face as she looked over at Tuttle who arched one eyebrow. "But there is an old teacher of mine. He's dying. And he wants the knives. He wants to be buried with them. You see, he had a set, and someone broke into his North Oxford house and stole them. The knives mean nothing. Or everything, depending on your point of view and state of health. Since they mean something to him, which apparently they do, I wanted to help him."

Suda looked solemn. "Why he sick?"

"Cancer."

She sighed, moving to the back of her counter and climbing on a stool next to a fan. Three older women sat on stools fanning and whispering, laughing, and glancing at Breach and Tuttle. Suda translated Breach's story for the women.

"Her father die of cancer two years ago," said Suda, pointing at one of the women.

"Was he buried with shaman knives?"

Suda didn't translate the question.

All the women wore silver bracelets, necklaces, belts, and buttons; in the event of a sudden meltdown—spontaneous combustion—the silver ingot on each would have been the size of a basketball. The old women sat like vultures, wings back, heads bent forward, and sharp eyes looking for a meal. Each weekend the women showed up at the crack of dawn and waited for Suda to unpack her latest bags of silver from the North. They watched carefully that no one ever received a better price than they had paid. They eyed every piece a customer picked up, ready to bounce and make an offer themselves.

Breach climbed onto the stool behind the counter beside Suda. A cousin set down a tray with huge tumblers filled with chipped ice and Cola. Breach took a long drink, the Coke spilling down onto his shirt. The early morning ladies frowned and grumbled. They pointed at his nakedness.

"He even drinks like a caveman," said Crosby. "He runs around naked like a caveman. He comes from a family of criminals. He is the missing link."

Crosby helped her close a couple of sales with *farang* tourists, most of whom couldn't tell the difference between silver and tin. He opened a glass display case and removed a spirit lock from the shelf.

"I save for you," said Suda.

"Fought off a horde of people who wanted it," said Crosby.

"Save. *Jing-Jing*—true," she said, as one of the three early-bird preferred customers handed Suda a large blue nobbed glass filled with coconut milk and shavings and ice. She took a long drink through the straw, watching Tuttle turn the spirit lock over in his hand, and then making a rough guess as to approximate weight by bouncing it in the palm of his right hand.

"You like?"

"Maybe," he said, clutching the spirit lock in a way that even Breach knew she had a sale. "Snow has a problem upcountry," he said toying with the silver lock.

Her eyes lit up. "Everyone has problem in their life," she said.

218

"But not everyone can solve one," said Breach. He put down the tumbler of ice and cola and walked and removed a shaman's ceremonial staff suspended between wooden pegs on the back wall of the stall.

Breach didn't look like the usual customers who asked after *Maw Pee* items; they knew were not looking solely at objects in terms of their decoration value or weight. The occasional professor on a research grant, or on an archaeological dig, even the rare missionary, had come to her stall asking after certain tools of the trade employed by tropical shamans. They bought hilltribe *maw pee* relics for museums, personal collections, resale abroad, or—once or twice, for personal use as an amulet to combat an illness, a broken heart, or a death in the family.

Suda opened her cash drawer, and rummaged through the contents, shoving five and one hundred bahts into a paper ball in a far corner. She pulled out a rectangular wood bar about eight inches long; patterns, the shape of snakes, lions and elephants, had been carved into two sides of the wood. Each design was contained within a self-contained plate with a narrow strip acting as a border. On the end there was a stubby wooden handle with a hole in the end, and a thin leather strap threaded through it. She closed the cash drawer. She stood there for a long moment. Beads of sweat forming on the ridge of her upper lip. Sweat stains forming under the arms of her short-sleeved white embroidered cotton blouse. The image of a fish had been carved into one of the plates; for a moment she ran her finger across the curved fish. On her sarong—a rich, deep tan—there were small green and yellow fish that looked as if they might have been conceived by the same hand.

"You like this or not?" she said, handing Breach the carved wood bar.

"*Maw Pee?*" he asked.

She nodded, as Crosby poked his head over her shoulder.

"Mien?" asked Crosby.

That left three outstanding, unanswered questions in the air. Crosby lifted the wood block, turned it over, and answered his own question, "Mien. The shaman used the wood block to print paper money. When someone died the shaman printed a batch, and the dead person's relatives sat in a circle burning the paper money. That way he's got cash in the spirit world and ashes in this one. The hilltribes are like the Chinese. They like the idea of a large spiritual bank account for that high-stakes table in the sky. Some think it helps laying bets on horses."

Suda found an ink pad, rice paper, and Crosby inked up the wood printing block and printed some money. "That and ten thousand dollars will get Snow back in one piece," he said.

"Why should I help you?" she asked, looking without expression at Crosby, and then at Breach. A cough began working its way up from her lungs, and she turned away, doubling over in the corner. When she finished she wiped her face with a piece of toilet paper she fished out of the cash drawer.

"I tell you why," said Breach.

This took Crosby by surprise.

"We are going to pay you a lot of money for your help," Breach said, pressing the wood block onto the ink pad and then down on rice paper. He pulled up the rice paper and held it out for the three old women to observe. Then he removed a lighter, held it to the tip of the paper, let it catch fire, and then fall to the ground. As he stepped on it, he reached over the counter and opened Suda's cash drawer. He pulled out the wadded-up paper, unfolded it on the counter. This frightened the old women, who stirred from their stools.

Suda grinned. "I like that very much. How much you pay me?"

"One thousand US dollars," said Breach without missing a beat. "And you help me get Snow…and the ceremonial knives."

"Jesus Christ," said Crosby under his breath. "We can't print it."

"Can we get Snow without her?" he asked, pulling Crosby to the side. "Well, can we?"

Crosby gasped, shaking his head. Breach smiled, "It's only money. Shamans aren't the only ones who can made paper money." Crosby looked over Breach's shoulder. Suda was watching them closely. "She's sick," said Breach. "She needs the money. She's going to die. You just said so in the street."

"You spent too much time in that cave," said Crosby. "We already got Snow out. So what's the problem?"

"Are you absolutely sure?"

Then realization struck Crosby; he saw why Suda's eyes hadn't left Breach; nor the eyes of the old women, or his mates in the classroom back in England. Breach knew how to tap into the shaman's monopoly on faith. He understood the process that mystified paper into something of value. He had tapped into the faith of Suda who desired currency for transactions with her own world. And Breach appeared to burn the paper currency, but it was only an appearance. With a twist of his hand the paper currency lay untouched by flame in the palm of his hand. He spread it out. It was a currency that didn't inflate or deflate, or trade on world exchanges, or was subject to devaluation rumors.

The relatives of the dead burnt paper money. But no one had ever seen anyone bring paper money back from the dead. Soon the sky was filled with paper money raining down over the market stalls, people scattered, falling on their knees, elbowing each other for a handful. Breach threw a match and everything was consumed in flames.

"*Ah!-rai!*—What?" asked Suda, shaking Breach's arm. The cap had come off the plastic bottle of drinking water, and was spilling out over his right knee. She grabbed the bottle.

"I was thinking about burning money."

"*Khit mahk mai! dee!*—thinking too much is bad," she said, as Breached mopped his leg and the bus seat where the water formed a small pool.

"What will you do with the thousand dollars?"

"I want to finish building a house in Chiang Mai," she said.

"Or you could go into a sanatorium."

"Like your grandfather?"

"He went into a nut house."

She pressed her cheek against the cool windowpane and watched the highway and the rows of squalid houses with corrugated roofs baking in the sun. Breach drank from the plastic water bottle and leaned back in his seat. She wasn't afraid to die, he thought. It was another bus journey upcountry for her. Her absence or presence made little difference in the larger order of events; like everyone else in the drama of day-to-day existence, she was another faceless, nameless spear carrier. But she hadn't sought star billing in her own life; that was an American romantic lie, he thought. That each spear carrier should want or need, or should be self-compelled, to do whatever was required to star in his own show and then, live forever. Failure was dying. Death showed lack of ambition to overcome mortality and a bad billing.

It was easy to predict what people would blow their money on. Costumes, makeup, health, on anyone or anything that promised top billing. A life that was one long audition. Suda wouldn't have been understood by them. She wanted to buy a house for her mother and two younger sisters before she died. And Breach liked the simplicity of her desire. Like him she was stripping herself down to the bare necessities; discarding the ballast that had been slowing her down. They sat side by side, Breach a half-naked spear carrier and Suda a spear carrier coughing up blood, rolling down Highway 1019, neither one knowing what awaited them in Mae Sai and sharing a common secret: whatever it was, in the scheme of things, it made little difference one way or the other.

❖

"I take a shower," Suda said, as they stood on the road staring down the main street of Mae Sai. She had made semi-monthly buying trips to Mae Sai for ten years. Her tone was tired, unsettled. Breach arched his back, stretching as he turned down the soi to the guesthouse.

"And rest," Breach said, slinging his dirty backpack over his left shoulder.

"Next life," murmured Suda, with a faint smile.

"This life I want to meet Mr. Tang."

"Can do," she said. "I know him many years."

"He likes gambling?" asked Breach, shifting his backpack.

"He likes bluffing."

"Pulling your leg."

Feeling the sun hot on his back, Breach stopped, opened his backpack, pulled out a T-shirt and slipped it over his head. Suda watched his head disappear for a moment, then reappear, his hair sticking out in strange angles.

"Pulling?" Suda asked.

"Pulling your leg. It means *poot len*." *- joking*

"Ah, *poot len*." She nodded and carried on walking. "But maybe Mr. Tang's not like a joke when he gambles."

"Unless the joke is on me," said Breach.

"Maybe sometimes you are too smart," said Suda. "And too smart is more dangerous than being too stupid."

"Old Chinese proverb?"

"Old Suda proverb."

Walking the lane to the Chad guest house, four Akha women approached them; the women carried large wicker baskets loaded with charcoal; smudges of black streaks on their cheeks, and smiling faces. A few moments later, the owner, a young Thai with a small moustache, came out and warmly greeted Suda.

He turned to Breach, looking him over and then up and down. "I want two very cold beers," said Breach, peeling a five-hundred-baht note from his wallet.

"He's okay," Suda said to the Thai, nodding toward Breach. "He's like caveman from a long time ago. They have different way than *farang*."

Breach looked stunted. "How did you know that word?"

"You say in your dream." She grinned and turned back to the owner of the guesthouse.

"*Paa moht* dream *mahk mahk*," she said in Thai-ling, "The wizard dreams a lot."

The owner was impressed and looked at Breach with a renewed expression of respect. Wizards did, after all, dress and behave and dream in a fashion unlike others. His expression softened, and he shouted in Thai for a sixteen-year-old hilltribe girl to bring two very cold bottles of *Singha*. As the beer arrived, the Thai owner had talked excitedly about his trip to Nepal two years earlier. Breach drank and listened, nodding. It had been a family trip. The Thai had gone with his mother, father, and a younger brother. They had a relative living in Kathmandu. He nearly fell dead away when Breach described the small spider tattoo on the back of his relative's right hand.

"You want another beer? It's on the house. No problem," said the Thai. "I think you a good *paa moht* if you know Suda. So where you from?" he asked, in good English.

Breach smiled. "The land of lost smiles," he said, that covered a lot of territory.

"Now you in the Land of Smiles, you very happy," said the owner.

After the second round arrived, the owner joined them at the table. A moment later, his wife arrived with eight photo albums. Suda and the young owner talked back and forth in Thai, as she began looking at the photographs.

"His father die," said Suda, flashing a look of inside knowledge she shared with Breach.

"Photographs of the funeral," said the guest house owner.

In one of the photos relatives were burning paper money. Suda pressed her thumb against the edge of the plastic holder, glanced at Breach, then sipped her beer. Looking at other people's photo albums was like listening to someone explain in precise technical terms how a ceiling fan works. Breach flipped through one of the books. There was a large photograph of an older man, wearing thick black-framed glasses and smiling into the camera. Around the tri-pod stand holding the framed photograph were dozens of flower arrangements. Photograph after photograph of different faces and different groupings of faces in front of the same background. And in one, the son bent forward from the waist over a fire holding a fist of Chinese paper money. The photograph stopped the falling paper money in midair just above the flames.

"Many guest say to me, 'Why you do look so happy? So glad in the pictures?'" the guest house owner began to explain. "And I tell them, because we are happy. No more suffering. Maybe my father will come back to a better life. So we're happy."

The last photographs were of the funeral pyre. The first couple of shots were of the coffin on a slightly elevated platform, with wood stacked beneath. The next photographs showed the coffin at various stages of being consumed by flames. The last shot might have been an autumn bonfire; if one hadn't seen the earlier photos, and had never ventured out of North America and into Asia. Around the bonfire, the relatives were throwing paper money frozen by the camera lens in time. Breach had that strange coming-apart feeling. Suda's use of the word caveman, then the photos of the paper money burning; his dream material flying into the world of consciousness, burrowing deep, and opening slowly like pedals of a lotus. He looked closely at the photos. What did they reveal? Death, ritual, life, belief, and, way of betting at the game table.

Chapter 15

The main drag in Mae Sai was wide enough to allow four tanks to cruise along side by side; and then it narrowed into a two-tank width at the bridge entrance. The Mae Bai River formed the border between Thailand and Burma. One division of tanks divided by water from another, thought Breach. He stood on the bridge, leaning over the railing and looking down at the river below. He thought about the two Lahu villagers who had gone to jail for illegal logging. Snow had been their ticket to freedom. He knew, as everyone else knew in Thailand, that certain logging companies, with the right connections, had pulled the levers of power, and a freshly minted licence dropped into their lap; a licence to take the forest from the land and mountains. Beyond the bridge a band of Burmese mountains were blanketed with a dense bluish-green forest canopy. It was an early afternoon sky.

"Smell that in the air?" asked Breach, sniffing as he turned to Suda, who was also leaning forward on the bridge railing. There was a sweet, cloying smell.

"The smell of trees," she replied.

"The green smell that existed before development," said Breach, his nose twitching. "Before the whooping cranes disappeared."

Suda smiled, cocked her head. "Before *farang* put pancakes on the floor."

"It smells even better than Grandpa's pancakes. I want to be buried with this smell and Grandpa's pancake recipe."

The afternoon light encircled the mountains in steamy mist; heatwaves causing the surface to shimmer, colors break apart, shaking the surface in an unendurable, harsh dance. The wind whipped a large red Burmese flag like a ship's rigging on the side of the bridge. Breach looked back at her, the wind had caught her hair. It didn't look like she was dying. She lifted her backpack over her shoulder.

"Sorry, I didn't mean to talk about funerals. The smell carried me away. You know, I. . .Let's go," said Breach.

They walked across the road and passed rows of shophouses.

"We use the the same word for money—*ngun!* that we use for silver—*ngun!*" said Suda, after a few moments. "And silver has a smell. Everything has a smell. Even death. And I wanted to be cremated in a dress made of silver rings and bells and bracelets."

Breach found himself inside a shabby shophouse. He passed along rows of dusty, half-empty display cases with rows of bronzed snakes, elephants, ducks, and chickens; shelves of opium weights gave that practical Chinese shophouse no-nonsense ambience. Suda immediately ducked into the back of the shop. She stopped and leaned over the roof of an old sun-faded blue VW station wagon. The VW was parked a few feet away from an ancient desk. The drab concrete floors, unpainted cement walls, and high ceiling created a stark interior; Breach looked around, thinking the place could be almost anything from a garage, craft shop, junk shop, bunker, to an abandoned warehouse. It had no single, clear purpose like a feature of nature; it was like a structure without expression, you might read any wish or desire into it, and what you read would be as likely as not found available at some price. With a few bats, it might double as a man-made cave, thought Breach.

An old Chinese man in a sweat-stained singlet, his belly rolling over his belt, a gray stubbled beard and eyes with the filmy gloss of an unkept fish tank, rose from behind his old, battered wooden desk.

"Mr. Tang," she whispered to Breach.

His eldest son, Lip, stood at the right of the desk. A couple of young boys hovered in the back against the wall, and two women shuffled in slippers through a door. Cooking smells and the rattle of pots and pans echoed from the kitchen. The Chinese extended family of aunts, uncles, cousins, grandparents, sons, and daughters accumulated in rows like bronze opium weights. In rumbled clothes they stared at Breach. Their heads turned one way and then another; a chorus of whispers muffled the sounds of old Mr. Tang's fart.

"A Chinese welcome, I presume," said Breach.

He gave a little wave and smiled; a couple of the girls giggled and ran back into the kitchen. No made the slightest attempt to introduce themselves. It was enough that Breach was an object of curiosity; as if the Lahu had brought him a relic of unusual value to barter for clothes. As Breach discovered later, Mr. Tang was, among other sidelines, a clothes merchant.

Once a month Lip drove the old VW to Bangkok and bought a car load of fake Calvin Klein shirts, fake Gucci belts, and fake Polo pants. He stuffed the trucks, back seat, and front passenger seat full with pirated designer clothing, and returned to Mae Sai. A day later, he crossed the border to trade the Burmese peasants fake Calvin Klein for their antique silver.

"You buy VW this week?" Lip asked Suda. He glanced at Breach whose head poked inside the VW. He read the odometer and laughed.

"How much you sell for?" asked Suda.

Lip wrote out a number on a piece of paper, and handed it to her. She read it without expression and passed the note to Breach.

"Same price last week. Too much money," said Suda.

"Very good car. Never any trouble." Lip sounded uncertain, nervous, glancing between Breach and Suda. His relatives tittered in the background.

"The odometers has been turned back so many times the the threads are stripped," Breach said to Suda. She didn't understand, and neither did Lip.

"What's odometer?" asked Lip.

"The record of distance the car has travelled. Normally shown in miles or kilometers. Given the condition of this car, an odometer in light-years would have been useful," said Breach.

"Not so many miles," said Lip, grinning and kicking the tires of the VW.

"In terms of the universe, you are correct. In terms of our planet, known as earth, you are properly incorrect," said Breach.

Suda's eyes narrowed, and she looked up at Lip.

"He your friend?" asked Lip.

Suda hesitated for a second, then nodded. "He's my friend."

"One thousand US dollars," said Breach.

Lip grunted, glancing over at his father who shrugged his old, worn shoulders. "Cannot. Cannot. I sell you good Thai price. Government take most. So all the same. Much tax on car in Thailand. Not so much in your country, I think," said Lip. "Not so much for you. You come from a rich country. So you can be flexible."

"Do I look like I come from a rich country?"

Lip looked Breach up and down and wrinkled his nose.

"Do I appear to you like a man who dispenses foreign aid to help poor Chinese car sellers in Mai Sae?"

"I sell you a shirt very cheap. Good quality. And shoes, number-one quality. I have special shirt for you. Very good cotton. I think you like."

"How much you give me for my pants?" asked Breach, pulling the pockets inside out to reveal no cash.

Lip leaned over and whispered to Suda. "I think maybe your friend very crazy."

The VW was an opening act for Suda's drama with the old man. There was an easy banter between Suda and Lip. The showcase performance was reserved for the antique silver Lip had extracted from the Burmese who walked the mountains dressed in fake Calvin Klein shirts. Mr. Tang, with his old man's candy-mint-sweet breath, emptied a cardboard box of silver on his desk. He leaned over the desk, smiling. On his neck was a brown fleshy mole with a half-dozen black hairs a yard long curling down his throat. It looked like a kind of spider.

"*Ngun!*" said Suda.

"Silver!" said Mr. Tang, an ironic expression on his face. "Maybe I put some aside; maybe not." Loose silver, silver in small opaque plastic bags spilled in a dull tide over his desk. Tangled silver chains the color of gunpowder coiled up through the pile, knotting around small silver boxes, rings, hairpins, and bracelets. From the way he leaned over the pile of silver, the throwaway smile on his face, Mr. Tang stroked the mole hair. He considered himself in the entertainment business as well as the silver trade. Breach pulled a stool up to the desk, sat down hard, and leaned on his elbows, sniffing the silver. Breach, seeing the silver, remembered this was the stuff Suda had wished to be cremated.

"It does have a smell," he said.

Suda ignored him. The "maybe not" qualification was the starter's pistol for her race to beat Mr. Tang. There was a kind of wisdom that created commercial advantage by allowing another to believe they had discovered a hidden cost, hiding place, or secret passage. Mr. Tang liked the set drama of leaving a trail of verbal breadcrumbs to a wall, and then abandoning his customer, who either seized the moment to find the passage through or hit their head against it. Suda was an expert; she had played Mr. Tang's game for years. She understood her part in the script; and, at her cue, she, like the old man, became character actors slightly larger than life—in the fashion of actors on stage or in a film.

"Maybe? I think you hold out the good stuff. Not show to Suda," she said, rising from her chair. "You save the best silver for someone else. For your very best customer. You tell me I'm number one. But I think you are a sweet mouth."

By then she had circled his desk. She sniffed the air, winking at Breach. She played the role of stickup man, and Tang raised his hands above his head like a victim.

"Suda number-one customer."

"I think maybe you have many number one customers."

"Cannot. Only one number-one. You are it!" He held up a square stub of a finger with a dirty fingernail.

Suda held up two, three, and then all ten fingers. "I think number ten."

She pulled out all four drawers of his filing cabinet; pulling out boxes, emptying them on the floor, pulling out folders, scattering the contents in the air. Then she turned on Tang's desk, rolling his chair back, and opened all the drawers, and found a bag of silver hidden in the back. She pulled it out and threw the bag on the desk. Breach opened the bag, nodded, and looked up at her.

"Silver," he said.

"There's more," she said. "There's always more."

"As much silver as miles on the VW," said Breach.

"More," said Suda.

Then she went back to the filing cabinet, where she discovered two more boxes of silver. The last drawer unopened was the center door of the desk. Mr. Tang sat with both palms pushed against the drawer, his feet wedged under the legs of the desk. His fish-tank eyes wide and unblinking, he looked like he had something to hide. The blank look of someone who is telling everyone around the table that he was bluffing; Breach relaxed a little, thinking he would enjoy playing cards with the old man.

Suda, deep into her character as the female armed robber, who knew when a victim was holding out, nudged him aside, and ripped open the drawer which fell into his lap. She tossed two more bags of silver onto the table.

"You hide more upstairs?" Suda asked.

Mr. Tang fumbled with the center drawer on his lap, and slowly nodded his head. He loved her toughness, the way she rolled straight through his act like a tank into battle. She came firing every gun. It made him happy to have such an opponent to defeat. His relatives snickered and joked, lurking in the corners and shadows in the background, cheering on the old man. He played up to his audience, throwing them a glance or raised eyebrow. Someone was keeping score of all this, thought Breach. Maybe it was the old woman with droopy eyes or one of the kids who doubled as delivery boys and waiters.

Mr. Tang exchanged one of those unmistakenly amused, admiring looks with Lip, as if to say: here is the kind of woman I like, fast, small, no warming up to false argument or sentiment. No imitation or fake woman. Give her two hundred men armed with AK47 assault rifles and send her into any town. She would make a Khun Sa—the golden triangle warlord—raid look like a Boy Scout weekend camp out.

She had the photographer's ability to judge light and darkness as they passed through words; what was dishonest, bluster, awkward, or as firm as a needle point. She knew how to inspire and insult; sometimes in the same sentence.

Mr. Tang flashed Lip another wink; as if to say, this is how business is done, you push your weight forward, don't ever take "no" for an answer, search the premises, desks, files, boxes. This is the way you take over an office, over a town,

233

an entire country. You can't intimidate without the use of force; even if it's pretend force, because no one can be certain whether you are pretending or not. No one puts the best things on the table unless they are forced to. Suda knew the first rule. Everyone has something to hide; that was Mr. Tang's message. But not everyone was clever enough to find the hidden thing. And those with the brains often lacked the determination. That's what had made Mr. Tang like Suda: she had both brains and determination, and something else that was difficult to describe. She knew the art of intimidation, employing the lightning raid; her timing was perfect, she knew when to catch her prey off-balance, seek out his hidden cache, then pull out goods, expose everything, before Mr. Tang had time to hide them again. Suda was in a class of her own; a class venerated by Chinese merchants and gamblers.

After all the silver was loaded onto the desk, Suda sat back down in her chair opposite Tang and began the long process of sifting, assessing, accepting, and rejecting each individual piece. There were hundreds of silver pieces of every size, shape, condition, and quality in the piles. Having "found" all the silver, the next hurdle was to shift gears from search and seizure, to careful analysis of what she had pulled in on her fishline.

The mamasan sat with her long, tapered legs stretched out on the rough gray concrete floor beneath a small table, sipping a coke and tapping her pencil on a page of the school notebook. She had with great laborious patience written each girl's name in the left-hand margin. She was thirty-so. Her clothes appeared holdovers from years of whoring, the uniform—skintight jeans, a white tank top, revealing her large pink nipples and a jean jacket with

234

"Badman" stitched in large white thread. She eyed the three *farang* who sat in a row against the far wall. They had been sitting and drinking *Old Grand-Dad* for nearly an hour. And they were no closer to making a decision as to which girls they wanted. She ran the erasure end of the pencil down the right hand column, counting the x's next to each girls' name; five customers had arrived and gone since the *farang* had arrived. She was growing slightly impatient, but continued to smile the merchant's smile of patience, allowing the customer to choose the object of his desire and in his own time.

Ross was coming to the end of a lecture on sexual selection. His theory was the art of the selection was everything and the worst sin was to be hurried. The act was over quick enough. But the actual picking of the partner required concentration, the skill of reading the lips, eyes, mouth; the body language of the girl.

"I don't see why that bitch should rush us," said Ross, nodding over at the mamasan. "Buying a piece of ass takes reflection. And reflection takes time. And we are waiting for a business associate. Bennington Harlow Wallace. You think someone with that kinda of name has ever fucked a brothel whore before?"

"Number 46 likes you, man," said Snow, one leg raised up on the bench, his chin resting on his knee.

"That's a bad number for me. She's more Ben's type."

Ross snapped his fingers. "Mamasan," he shouted. She slowly raised her head. "You think you could get us another bottle of *Old Grand-Dad*." Ross smiled, pulling five hundred baht from his wallet. "And a pizza. Double cheese with extra mushrooms."

"They don't have pizza in Mae Sai," said Crosby.

"Why in the fuck don't they have pizza?" stormed Ross, lifting up on one side and sticking his wallet back in his pocket.

"Because they like rice."

He looked over at Crosby. "And I'm telling you if one of these girls ate a single piece of pizza with ham, double cheese, green peppers, onions, anchovies, and hamburger, they would never eat rice again."

"I take it back, man," said Snow, winking at number 46. She pursed out her lips and slowly applied her lipstick, her eyes looking over the top of her small compact mirror case.

"Take what back?" asked Ross.

Snow nodded toward number 46 in the window. "She wants me."

"She's probably into ex-Lahu godman. She won't eat pizza, but she's impressed you still have your balls," said Ross. "Which cost me ten grand. Now your balls might be worth ten grand to you. But they ain't worth dick to me."

"You know the Thai word for balls, Ross?"

"I don't speak Thai, I've told you that before."

"*Look bpuen*—child of the gun. Bullets. Your balls are bullets in Thai."

"That's pretty good," said Ross. "What about dick. What's your dick in Thai?"

"It's pronounced like *Jew*."

Ross doubled over laughing, his face turning red. He slapped his thighs. "You mean *Jew* like what they have in Israel and New York? Shit, Why didn't I know that in law school. This asshole professor, who said I wasn't dick because I wasn't in the club, he was a *Jew*. And all the time, he was a dick but he didn't know Thai either. I knew he was a dick and I didn't know Thai, but I knew I was right. I learned the law of international transactions from a dickhead."

"You are a total racist, Ross," said Crosby, with disgust.

"Get off my case. The English invented slavery. Started the opium wars in China because the slant-eyes wouldn't sell you enough drugs. Who taught me a dick was just another word for a *Jew*? An Englishman."

Crosby, hands folded behind his head, leaned back and watched the girls. The confrontation ended as quickly as it had begun. A whiff of argument followed by a long, dead period of silence. They sat in a harshly lit, small, narrow room on three rows of bleachers. A large plate glass window separated them from the waiting room. An observation tank arrangement like the seafood tanks in a Chinese restaurant. They were on the menu. Afternoon snack items waiting for the nod, and for the mamasan to mark and x beside their name in the book. Some wore tight, short cotton dresses; others wore T-shirts and shorts. The alternative was either a girl with the city or beach. Ten girls sat facing the customers' gallery on the opposite side of the mirror. Time passed slowly, waiting to be chosen, and in between, hours and hours of dead time, sitting on the wooden bleachers under the buzz of the fluorescent light. They smoked, swore, laughed, gossiped, and touched up their makeup.

"What are they saying about me?" asked Ross, finishing the last shot of the *Old Grand-Dad*, and setting the empty bottle under the bench.

"They aren't talking about you," said Crosby.

"How do you know they aren't talking about me?"

Crosby slowly turned his head and looked at Ross for a second. "Because I can read their lips."

"What are they saying, man?" asked Snow, with a crooked smile. He lit a cigarette with Crosby's Zippo lighter. His lips moved as he read the inscription engraved on the lid: "Fighting for peace is like fucking for virginity."

"This asshole got it wrong, man. Fucking Lahu virgins is like fighting for peace," said Snow, reaching over Ross and handing the lighter back to Crosby.

"I thought you quit smoking," said Crosby, taking the Zippo.

"And I thought your goddamn virgins were diseased," said Ross.

Snow shrugged his shoulders as Crosby lit another cigarette, inhaling deeply.

"I did. And they were," said Snow. "For over five years I didn't smoke. And I dreamed of virgins. But in the village, when I found out that Lahu virgins were more dangerous than cigarettes, I started smoking again."

Ross had gone red in the face. "Who gives a goddamn about why you started smoking or stopped smoking? Or the fake Lahu virgins were whores with AIDS. What I want to know is—what are these whores saying about me?"

A coil of smoke drifted out of Crosby's nostrils. He crossed his legs, and nodded at the window. "Top row, third one from the left. Number 18."

"I like her ass," said Ross. "She looks like she loves to fuck."

"She's from a small village outside Roi Et. When she was one, her mother bought a *dtoke-kaw*—a tree lizard for one baht from a village point. Her mother cut off the head, the tail, the legs. Only the torso was left. She handed the *dtoke-kaw* to number 18. And since she was only one year old, she assumed this was lunch. She put the dead *dtoke-kaw* in her mouth. She chewed off a large chunk. Yellow gut juice dribbled out of the corners of her mouth. The mother turned around and saw her daughter smiling and chewing the dead *dtoke-kaw*. Her mother turned green, her eyes rolled up in her head, and she bent over and puked her guts out along the road. And number 22, just below number 18, said her two-year-old brother found a dead *jing!johk*—a small house lizard—in the corner of their house, and he had eaten half of it before her mother caught him. And. . ."

Ross held up both hands. "Mamasan, cancel that pizza order."

"It gets better," said Crosby.

Ross belched, wiped the sweat off his face. He rose up from the bench and walked over to the window and slowly sank down on his haunches. He stared at the girls, his eyes moving from one side of their sockets to the other in a rapid motion. He splayed his fingers and pressed them against glass, arching the knuckles like a piano player.

"What are you doing, man?" asked Snow, flicking away his cigarette.

Ross didn't reply. He leaned forward, touching his lips to the glass, then opening his mouth, sticking the tip of his fleshy tongue against the glass. The girls began to giggle. "*Dtoke-kaw,*" said Ross. He licked the glass, and made a sucking noise. The mamasan looked alarmed.

"He's a very sick man," Crosby said to her in Thai.

Chapter 16

Suda understood the nature of silver. The word silver became a rich ore in the mines of the Thai language: *ngun* meant silver; *ngun soht* literally translated as fresh silver was the Thai word for "cash"; *ngun cheu-a* literally translated as "silver you believed in" was the word for a personal bank cheque; and *nah ngun* or "silver face" meant a person whose only interest was in making money. But silver was more than words for Suda; it possessed a distinct feel. The pads of her fingertips stroked and caressed an antique piece of silver, turning the feel into numbers; and with the rate of speed of Olympic diving competition judges. Real silver had a weight to it. Her fingers slowly turned black from the touching; and after less than thirty minutes, her hands looked like those belonging to a coal miner. Her aesthetic and commerical investigations occurred in microseconds; within each judgment were separate, smaller judgments: shape, design, weight, age, fashion, origin, rarity, authenticity, quality, and damage. And within each of these categories were further refinements: could, for instance, the damage be repaired, if so, at what cost? There were hundreds of separate pieces in each heaping pile of tangled silver chains—many with dozens of small pendants—bracelets, rings, hair ornaments, earrings, neck rings, necklaces.

In Mr. Tang's silver trade two questions that were never asked were: What is beauty? Or why is an object beautiful?

The only relevant question was how much does it weigh. That's how Suda made her profit margin. She bought from people like Mr. Tang by weight and sold to *farang* who paid cash based on an aesthetic decision. Mr. Tang watched catlike as Suda rejected bad pieces. He picked up a piece out of the reject pile, weighed it in his hand, frowned and throw it back. But he knew that she would take some of the bad pieces. That was part of the price of doing business; keeping Mr. Tang off-balance, confused, and uncertain about the perimeters of the world beyond the weight of silver.

Watching her was a lesson in playing the odds, studying your hand, sorting not only your cards, but the ones your opponent might be holding and what was left in the deck, thought Breach. This was the way his father had played cards. She was a natural. She played the pieces of silver as if Mr. Tang had dealt her a blackjack hand. And she watched him, expecting him to deal from the bottom of the deck at any moment. She was pure concentration and attention. She had that gut instinct of how to bit a hand; what was too little, what was too much, what was obvious. She watched her hand, each individual piece, and kept a running dialogue going with Mr. Tang, Lip, and assorted members of the family; she used gossip, rumor, weather reports, traffic patterns, rice prices, and bus crashes as weapons, all the time dragging out of them what they had paid for the silver, who they had bought from, in what quantities, and what was coming on the market. Then abrupt as it had started, it was over. She looked up from her pile.

"How much I pay you?" she asked Mr. Tang.

The sharp edge of humor that Mr. Tang had been riding dulled when the question of price was raised. The Chinese had no sense of humor about their money leaving their wallet and finding a home in another person's bank vault. Wallet, sure, no problem, hit them over the head later, but money in the bank. Big problem.

Suda sat back in front of two piles; the larger pile on her left was the one she offered to buy; the one on the right, the rejections, that Mr. Tang pondered in silent gloom.

"Twenty-two baht a gram," said Mr. Tang, a small amount of salvia operating like a hinge of spume in the right corner of his mouth. He leaned forward on his elbows, his eyes spoiling for a response.

"*Chaat Naa*—next life time," said Suda, catching Breach looking at her out of the corner of his eye. She knew he wouldn't say anything. Her typical Buddhist response hung in the air. Time was divided into three cycles: *Chaat gorn*—last life; *Chaat nee*—this life; and *Chaat Naa*—next lifetime. Time slots were connected by *kaam*—or karma—and determined the cards you held from life to life and for the Thai explained what bets he could make in this life, what kind of bets he had made in the last one as well.

"Very good silver. Look!" Mr. Tang held out one of the chains from the pile for Suda to observe. She glanced calmly at the chain.

"Eighteen baht. Fair price."

"Not flexible price."

"Fair price is flexible price."

"You should be flexible with me. I give you number one pieces. Not so easy to find."

One of the Mr. Tang's relatives, her flip-flops snapping against the cement floor, arrived with a tray of cups, saucers, coffee, and small sugar-covered biscuits. Mr. Tang poured Suda a cup of coffee, added milk and two heaping soups of sugar and handed it to her. She blew on her coffee, and watched Mr. Tang punch in a series of numbers on a small calculator. He grunted, drank from his cup. The long, wild hairs sticking out of the mole on his throat twitched wildly like a spider crossing a wall. He smacked his lips, and drummed his fingers on the edge of his desk. He picked a bracelet out of the reject pile, showed it to Lip, who shrugged.

242

"Why you no buy this?"

"Broken. Pay ten baht."

"Eighteen baht this?" asked Mr. Tang, sweeping his hands over the large pile. He made his mouth thin and sighed as an expression of self-pity. One of those street-smart expressions. The practised defeated merchant look; part of the drama in a transaction filled with false starts, small complications, many theatrical lines.

"Good price."

"Not good price."

"You sell me."

"Think you sell for twenty-five baht in Bangkok. Make much profit. You tell your customer, price very expensive up north. I know you. Then you tell me, customer don't want pay much in Bangkok. So now, you be flexible."

"I make little, little money. Not enough for VW station wagon. Big shop. Desk and file cabinet. Maybe you be flexible with me."

Mr. Tang glanced over at the car. Lip was polishing the chrome on the door. Suda had caught Mr. Tang with a verbal right hook. He was flat on his back, looking up from the canvas, knowing the fight was over. Besides, he had received the price he had established for himself before Suda had walked in the door. Unless Suda received the full treatment, the temptation was always to believe the price unaltered by long, troublesome negotation was rarely an honest one. The lowest price would not be believed in the absence of protracted mock combat; the lowest price was the climax of the drama, the terms of the peace treaty, an emotional odometer to measure the blurred line between friendship and business.

Mr. Tang turned to Breach. "You help her out. Loan her some money so she can buy. What you think?"

Breach smiled, showing a silver fish he had palmed off the table. The old Chinese man sat back in his chair. Breach cut his fist through the air like a prizefighter, then opened his hands to show they were empty. Mr. Tang looked from one empty hand to the other, and then at Suda.

"You have?"

Breach stuck out his tongue and waited until Mr. Tang turned around, attracted by the giggling that had erupted from a couple of his relatives. The silver fish was on the end of Breach's tongue.

"No good, eat my silver," sputtered Mr. Tang.

Breach set the silver fish back on the desk. "No good, I loan money to lady," replied Breach.

It was a standoff. Mr. Tang weighed the silver. He dumped fistfuls of silver objects onto one side of the scale, to Lip and handed him the bronze weights: one kilo, five hundred gram, and so on, until both sides of the scale were in perfect balance. Suda sat eye-level with the scale, ensuring there was a smooth, uninterrupted imaginary line between the two sides. Mr. Tang marked down a figure, as Lip unloaded the scales. Suda frowned, looking at the number. Once again the silver was weighed. Painstakingly, the heavy items—chains and bracelets making a foundation for lighter pieces—earrings, hairpins, rings. Again Mr. Tang writes down a number, shows it to Suda, who leans down and stares at the scale. No hidden wires or strings.

The weigh-in—like that of a heavyweight boxer—tried to give a number to strength, power, form, and the most elusive of all things, value to a quality of being. Once Suda and Tang fixed the weight, multiplied the weight by eighteen baht, Suda immediately demanded a discount.

"I pay you this," she said, scratching out 45,670 baht, and writing 45,000 baht. "Okay?"

"Okay," he said, eyeing Breach with suspicion. "This time I very flexible. Next time, you help me out, okay."

Suda smiled, then turned to Breach. "Good price. Now go to bank. You stay. Talk to Mr. Tang. And Lip."

"If silver had a speedometer, he would find a way of turning it back," said Breach, leaning forward, whispering to Suda.

"I come back, twenty, thirty minutes." She lifted her shoulder bag, hiked it over her right shoulder and walked out of the back room.

Breach stirred a spoon of sugar into his coffee. He eyed Mr. Tang stuffing the old, unwanted silver pile into a cardboard box. When Lip came around from the VW, he swung his legs around the chair next to Breach.

"You wouldn't happen to know where I might find a card game tonight?"

Mr. Tang shoved the cardboard box under his desk. "Mr. Ross say you no good man. He say you take his money."

"Was that a recommendation?"

"Why you come to Mae Sai?" asked Lip, leaning a little too close to Breach.

"For *ngun!*"

Mr. Tang arched an eyebrow at his son. His shoulders, like the hide of an old water buffalo, shuddered as a fly landed and walked several inches. He carefully stored away the weights. "How much money you play with?" asked the old man.

Breach had one thousand dollars. "Five hundred dollars," he said.

Lip grinned, shaking his head. "Maybe you find a small game somewhere."

Mr. Tang stared hard at back of his hands. His small fingers had polished nails two inches long. He made a smacking noise with his lips. "Two thousand dollars minimum. Cannot play for less. Cannot."

"You stay long time in Thailand. Maybe it not so safe for you any more," said Lip, running his index finger around the rim of Breach's coffee cup.

"Ross will be real disappointed," said Breach, with a wide grin, watching a fly struggle in the coils of the hairs sprouting from Mr. Tang's mole.

"Maybe not," said Mr. Tang, lifting one of his small fingers, and scratching at the surface of the desk like a crab's claw. He eyed Suda's silver. "Your friend can borrow you," he said, beaming. Sometimes fractured English had a poignance, thought Breach. "With your five hundred, and this," he said, glancing at the silver, "you can play with the big boys."

Mr. Tang had discovered a flexible way of keeping his silver and getting Suda's cash. He leaned back in his chair, hands behind his head. "I think your trick with fish very good. Sometimes a very good trick can cause you much, much trouble. You think about that, okay?"

"The practise of law is like trying to fart when you got diarrhea," Ross explained, one arm wrapped around Snow's shoulder.

"How's that, Ross?"

"You need critical judgment and luck to prevent making a fucking mess."

Crosby remained in a kind of self-enclosed trance, staring at the window. His calmness disturbed Ross, who had become bored and had run out of jokes to tell.

"Crosby, what I miss with a whore is foreplay," said Ross, checking his zipper.

But Ross's question didn't draw him out. Crosby nodded, and inhaled on his cigarette.

"Foreplay with a whore is like playing with your food, man," said Snow, combing his hair.

Ross laughed. "Some agencies list whores as non-food entertainment. They are profit centers. I kinda like that. You read this list and you can figure out how much the Japs,

Chinks, Americans spend on non-food entertainment each year. Then you know who the real men are."

The mamasan marked an x after number 46's name—her second one—and another x after number 18, shifting on her chair, as she recrossed her long, tapered legs. Crosby hadn't moved from the bench opposite the window. He was smoking, his head tilted up, looking at the rafters of the low ceiling. A cloud of gray smoke hung low in the small cramped anteroom. He was the first to see Breach, hands in his pocket, standing in the doorway; he saw his reflection dancing across the brothel plate glass window.

"Look what that fruit bat has dragged in," said Ross.

Breach didn't look at Ross. "You should get laid more often," said Breach. "It improves your sense of humor."

"How did it go with Tang?" asked Crosby, smoking his cigarette.

"I'm getting picked up at ten in a VW with half a million miles on it," said Breach, moving through the door and over to the viewing window. He looked down at the smudge marks Ross had left with his fingers and tongue.

"Don't even ask, man," said Snow. "You don't wanna know."

"Ten o'clock," said Ross. "That's good. And now, all you have to do is win twenty grand. I get paid and everyone goes home."

"Ten grand," said Breach, slipping Crosby's cigarette out of his mouth. He held up the cigarette with a flourish.

"And ten grand interest," said Ross, eyeing the cigarette as he moved over to the window next to Breach. "That one flosses with dead lizards. Doesn't she have nice teeth?"

Breach created the illusion of pushing the cigarette into Snow's left ear and slowly extracting it from the right one. Crosby raised an eyebrow as Breach handed the cigarette back. He had seen the trick before in a public school classroom.

"Hey, man, how did you do that?"

"He's a witch," said Ross.

Behind him the girls were on their feet, gathered around the window, staring at Breach.

"Now what are they saying?" asked Ross, his face pressed against the window. The girls were close up and giggling.

"They go with Breach for free," replied Crosby.

"Be careful of a man who gets women for free," said Ross, turning around and looking straight at Breach. "Or pulls cigarettes out of a man's ear."

Bennington Harlow Wallace stood frozen in the doorway watching Ross lick the plate glass window. His blond hair was combed straight back and the sides were even with a small wave above the ears suggesting an expensive haircut. He wore half-moon gold cuff links, a white suit, and a striped pale blue tie. Bennington gave the appearance of someone who had walked into the Harvard Club in New York City. His perfect patrician nose and chin; Bennington Harlow Wallace represented everything that Ross and Breach had—for totally different reasons—wanted to smash. And their methods were different as well. Breach had rejected them as the Lahu had rejected Snow; and Ross had been rejected by the Benningtons, belittled, ignored, and ridiculed. So Bennington offered the opportunity for revenge. He made Ross sweat with anger.

Breach thought he saw Bennington for what he was. Here was the man who represented organized entities; a man who understood and consented to the way rights and privileges were distributed and who led a tactical ground unit on behalf of those interests which commanded. Dark Age or no Dark Age, men such as Bennington Harlow Wallace in their gray suits connected money to power. They were the true face of silver—*nah ngun*. In the world of equivalents, correspondences, and parallels Bennington was recognizable as a being who had corrected for the effects of air resistance—read social change—on the way money flowed between centers of power. Unlike the whooping cranes whose disappearance proved the correlation between evolutionary success and correct wheel alignment on the getaway car leaving the scene of the crime. Or in Bennington's case, having arrived at the scene before the crime was to take place.

Ross caught sight of Bennington's reflection in the window; all the girls stared out at him as if a vision had appeared from the heavens. They looked straight past Ross. Bennington's very presence drained the blood from Ross's face which filled with contempt and hate. Crosby leaned forward, nodding, eyebrows arched.

"Mr. Wallace has arrived," said Crosby.

Ross pulled his face away from the window, turned and stared at Bennington. "You ever owned a pair of bowling shoes?" he asked Bennington. Before he could get an answer, Ross tilted his head to the side. "Or you ever gone into a live bait shop?"

"No, I have not had those pleasures," said Bennington, hands folded in a composed, relaxed fashion.

"In Nebraska, first we would go to a whorehouse in our bowling shoes, then afterwards pick up some live bait and go fishing," said Ross.

Bennington gave a thin smile. "Or go bowling for the fish that got away."

"I never let a fish get away," said Ross.

Bennington surveyed, in a courtroom glance, the small waiting area, looking at the audience that Ross had chosen to witness this humiliation. He recognized Crosby and Snow from their meeting at the hotel in Chiang Rai. He was the kind of self-assured man who knew how to steal Ross's audience.

"Perhaps you are drunk?" he said. "I hired your legal services. You were recommended by Colonel Chao as someone who was, shall be say, reliable. We trusted his judgment. This is a very delicate matter. And I expect you understand our concern that you should remain sober at all times until after the transaction is completed. Then you may drink as much as you wish. Is that clear?"

"This isn't New York." Steam appeared to rise off Ross.

"Indeed it is not. If it were New York, I wouldn't have needed to hire you, now would I?"

He walked over to Crosby.

"And is this your idea of a rite of passage?" asked Bennington, looking at Crosby and then Ross.

Ross smiled. "Only for a guy who's never bought bowling shoes or live bait. You're just a courier, Benny. You pick up a bag and take it back to New York. You think that takes any skill? Any brains?"

"You underestimate me, Mr. Ross," said Bennington, with cold blue eyes.

Ross liked that remark. It encouraged him, reinforced his energy and strength. Bennington stood so tall, erect, and certain; no one in his entire life had ever underestimated him, thought Breach. No one had ever challenged him, defeated, pinned him to the floor.

"I'm just a country lawyer," said Ross in a humorous tone. He pulled out his wallet. "And it's our backwoods tradition to see a fellow lawyer from the big city gets laid."

Bennington had that kind of smile that rides high on the face; the amused delight of someone who had asserted his position, advantage, privilege; a man who measured the practises of Mae Sai like a bad New York neighborhood.

"Everything has been arranged for tonight," said Crosby. "You fly out with the money at one a.m."

"I recommend number 46," said Ross. "She's an experience; and she's already paid for."

For one tense moment, as Bennington studied the girl, glanced at his gold Rolex, and then at his polished shoes, it wasn't clear what would happen. Then Bennington broke into a smile; crowfeet spreading out from his eyes, he slowly pulled off his jacket.

"She's safe, of course?"

"Of course. Check out her card. She had blood test, urine test. They've ground up one of her teeth testing her for germs."

"So long as you haven't had intercourse with her, Ross," said Bennington.

"We didn't have intercourse. She wouldn't give a hick like me any course, any time of day."

"What do you intend I give her?"

Ross smiled. "Give her your *Jew*."

"My what?"

"Try your dick."

"Thanks for the advice. Oh, by the way, please send us a bill for your fee after you return to Bangkok."

Those were the last words Bennington uttered as he disappeared out the door with the girl and for an appointment which had not been scheduled.

Chapter 17

Breach had placed a side bet with himself that the Baht guest house catered to the backpack crowd. He could not have been more wrong, and this flaw in his judgment disturbed him. He prided himself on making the right call about the arrangement of things. Was he losing his ability to identify patrons by their surroundings? Or was the world changing sufficiently that the old rules were no longer reliable guides? It had become fashionable for the middle-class tourist to find a more remote location than the neighbors had found the summer before. For a certain class of person, experience in inaccessible villages and slums in exotic places had become another consumer product. You lost points unless your experience bank account showed a large balance from your last trip abroad.

By evening, the tables on the concrete veranda were populated with well-dressed *farang*, with sunburned arms and necks, freshly bathed, scented, and smelling of talcum powder. Perfumed women in sleeveless cotton blouses, holding tall glasses of beer by the stem, their gold ankle bracelets sparkling as the late sunlight slanted through the coconut trees.

"Not like this before his father die," said Suda, watching the owner take a food order at one of the tables.

"I used to teach children of these kind of people," said Breach. He watched one of the women with perfect teeth fingering a gold chain around her neck.

"What do you teach them?" Suda smiled, finding Breach's eyes moving across the tables.

"That the main difference between the nature of their parents—human beings, mostly—and their parents' money—folding paper, mostly—was that the money was easier to fold in half and stuff in their pockets. Otherwise their parents' lives passed from hand to hand like a medium of exchange. They journey from birth to death just like another large denomination currency and never knew they had spent their life living inside someone else's pocket. And every kid had the same question. 'Why doesn't Mummy and Daddy love me? Why do they send me to this horrible school?'"

He removed a hundred-baht note from his pocket and held it up for Suda to see, then with a wave of the hand, made it disappear from sight, and opened his hand to expose a five-hundred-baht note. She looked at the five-hundred-baht note, touched it, rubbed it between her fingers, and then held it up to the light and stared through it. "How did you do that?"

"I used to turn one-pound notes into fivers. I would take out the note and walk around the classroom. Does this note love you? Can a one-pound note love you? Can a five-pound note love you? Would it make any difference if it could love you? And they would start to titter the way schoolboys do. Then I would tell them why they had been sent to this horrible school. Because the five-pound note was the model for their lives. As soon as they started acting like pound notes, then everything in their lives would make sense. And they would have new questions. How can I get more, where can I spend more, and who has more than me? At that point they would understand their parents; and they could rest at night."

A waitress brought a plate heaped with steaming rice and curry to the table. Breach watched the steam rise from the plate. He leaned over and sniffed the rice.

Suda watched his heavily lidded eyes, and glanced over at the owner. "I sell them in the market. These *farang* good for business. So you think I am a money person? That may I have *nah ngun*?"

"I am not going to the card game and bet with peanut butter sandwiches. So we are all connected to the same thing; we all have silver faces." said Breach, sipping his beer. "And if you are overly educated you connect so many events, places, historical incidents, battles, dates, people, religions, paintings, music, and books you reach a breakthrough. Which is the meaninglessness of the connections. None of it holds any more or better than an alternative arrangement of correspondences."

This explanation didn't quite satisfy Suda. "I think if you have no money, then you no eat, if you no eat, then you die. Five hundred percent sure," said Suda. "Why you not teach your student that? This is true."

"And it is also true that Mr. Tang has enough silver to feed his family for a hundred years, but he still wants you to be flexible when you buy from him."

"That's his game."

"It's not his game. It is *the game*," said Breach, making the hundred baht appear out of Suda's ear. He thought of Bennington disappearing into the back of the brothel with number 46. Silver traded for silver; faces traded for the same. When the dots were connected, it pretty much came out the same design, time after time: a dollar sign.

He pulled out a wad of hundred-baht notes and counted five on the table and pushed the rest back into his pocket. He picked them up and quickly counted them again. Then he tossed two of the red notes on the table, leaned forward and blew them away. Suda made an automatic reaction to recover the notes. Breach pulled her back to the table.

"Let them go."

"You can throw them away," she said.

He counted five-hundred-baht notes onto the table. "There are still five."

She confused and angry. He stuffed three hundred-baht notes in the half-empty glass of water. Immediately they were soaked and wrinkled. He again counted five hundred-baht notes onto the table. A small crowd from the other tables gathered around.

"Does this note love you?" asked Breach. "Of course it cannot. Because it never existed." This time he ripped two of the notes and threw them in the air. And as he counted five notes onto the table, a round of applause rippled through the night air. "Now can you perform this illusion with your mother? Your father? Or on your best friend?" Everyone waited for his answer. "The answer is of course you cannot. Because they exist and you cannot fold them like pretty colored paper on a table."

"Even if they have a *nah ngun*?" asked Suda.

Breach smiled. "Even if their entire body is silver," he replied.

More *farangs* filtered into the dining area for dinner, and those at the table beside Breach and Suda had become friendly after seeing his trick with the hundred-baht notes. They were two young couples from Paris. They sat opposite each other, drinking Kloster straight from the green bottle. They joked loudly in French; laughter boomed across the veranda. Beer flowed and the sun set as the owner set about lighting mosquito coils.

"What they say?" asked Suda.

"They're talking about a video camera. They filmed some Karen girls down by the bridge. Each girl asked for ten baht," said Breach.

"Why that so funny?" asked Suda.

"One girl made change for a hundred-baht note. And she took a two-baht commission from the other two girls."

"Very good business," said Suda, pausing.

"Show business," said Breach. He leaned over and whispered to Suda. "They are filmmakers; not tourists. A lens is a lens. Why should Thai actresses work for free?"

From his smile, Suda was sure he was teasing her. She thought he was criticising Thailand. "In what country do people want to work for free?" There was a hint of anger in her voice. Breach, feeling her unease, let it ride out. He leaned across the table and stuck out his tongue. One of the French woman applauded as she saw Breach's tongue. Soon the others at the table joined in. On the tip was a silver fish. Suda tried to remain serious and upset but couldn't stop herself from laughing.

"Is that your answer?" she asked.

Breach nodded, keeping his tongue extended for a couple of seconds longer, then rolling lizard-like with a flick back into his mouth.

"Mr. Tang very angry he know you steal his silver."

Slidding the tip of his tongue out, Breach picked off the silver fish, reached across the table, carefully unfolded the fingers of Suda's hand, and folded the fish inside.

"Romantic," said one of the French women.

Suda toyed with the silver fish and held it up to the light.

"When you were at the bank, I bought it from him."

"How much you pay?"

"Ten baht a gram."

"Cannot!"

"Okay, twenty baht."

"I think *farang* price twenty-four baht."

The moving force at the adjacent table was a stocky, bullet-headed Frenchman, short-cropped hair, large teeth, and a five o'clock shadow that would have defeated a blow-torch. The others called him Jean-Claude. His heavily bandaged right hand pawed the air as he spoke to the others at his table. With his good hand, he tipped the half-full bottle of Kloster to his lips and finished it off with the kind of belch that appeared to explode from his mouth, nose, and ears like a foghorn. Here was a man seeking courage, thought Breach. Jean-Claude rose from his chair and walked over to a display counter. Behind the counter stood Kik, wife of the owner of the Baht guest house. A small woman with a sympathetic smile, and steady hands, fingers cupped together, resting on a glass display counter.

Jean-Claude's bloodshot eyes and rough, lined face were intent as he carefully unfolded a cotton wrap, exposing half a dozen gemstones, gold, green, blue. He laid them out on the glass countertop. Kik watched him line them up side by side. He smiled, gestured with his hands, glanced back at his friends. She sensed what was coming next; the reason he had come, but she waited patiently for him to make the point himself. Kik didn't wait long.

In broken English he asked her to guess their value. He had purchased the gems after lunch in the main street shophouse. He admitted to Kik what he had admitted to the jeweller, he knew nothing about gems. He had told the truth; in a straightforward fashion, he had disclosed the most important piece of information any vendor on the street wished to know: that the buyer was ignorant of stones. But Jean-Claude knew what he liked, what caught his eye. And he gauged what had attracted his eye (his ego unable to believe for a moment his sense of beauty had no worth) must have a minimum value.

"How much you think I paid for them?" he asked.

She examined the stones, looking up at Khun Jean-Claude, then back at his stones.

"One thousand baht I pay."

"One thousand baht," she repeated in English. Her eyes shifted to Suda a few feet away; but there was no change in expression on either woman's face.

He nodded and a broad smile crossed his coarse, unshaved face. Breach had the idea this was the standard freight local merchants exacted as the price of ignorance in Mae Sai.

"So you think he didn't cheat me?" asked Khun Jean-Claude.

"No cheat." She pointed at the gold-colored stone. "Good quality, I think."

"Yeah? I don't know anything about gems."

Kik eyed him long and hard, but without surprise. Nothing *farangs* said or did surprised her any longer. Her last big surprise was at 4:37 a.m. January 26, 1982, when one of Khun Sa's men fired a couple of rounds from an AK-47 Chinese assault rife through her bedroom window.

"You like to take chance?" asked Kik.

Jean-Claude's face broke into a large-toothed grin.

"You like casino?"

"We love casino," said Jean-Claude.

A flicker of emotion quickly left her face; a hysteria rising to the surface, then at the last moment, as if she were verge of saying something, she held back. She had caught herself from expressing some idea or thought. But what had she censored? An indiscretion, a few words that might have given away too much. And for what reason; Jean-Claude wanted to be sold, gems on Main Street, poker chips, and experience to expand his reputation with his friends.

"I have an idea what's really in her head," said Breach. He leaned over and whispered to Suda.

Suda shook her head, and pushed her half-eaten plate of rice to one side.

"Think how *farang* be so careless. Buy gem and not know."

"That's the best thing about women. They know the real price."

"Always. Always know."

"How much kickback does she get from the casino?" asked Breach, after a long pause. Suda shrugged, giving him the glance that goes with a reply to a stupid question. "Just like the Karen girl with change for a hundred-baht note. Mr. Tang cheat you on the silver fish. It's business." He watched Jean-Claude give the thumbs-up sign to his table; one of the women clapped and giggled like a schoolgirl. "The old man. The one who died. Was he a gambler?"

"Did not like," admitted Suda.

Breach fingered his glass, eyebrows arched. A Chinese-Thai who didn't like gambling. "How did the old man die?"

Suda leaned over the table and formed a gun with her index finger and thumb. She squeezed her middle finger. "He get shot."

"Business as usual," said Breach, with a tone of bitterness.

"*Nahk hoo-uh kry,*" she replied. There was that Thai expression again; the one that goes: in literal translation means "Heavy on whose head?" It was mostly used as an insult. But Breach saw a connection between the insult and the sublime. He had been passing judgment on someone's life. Life was heavy on everyone, and what right did he have to judge the weight on anyone else's life? What right did anyone have to pass sentence on another? The answer was none; but everywhere in the world fingers pointed at the people who were to be executed.

"*Nahk hoo-uh kry,*" he said to himself.

"It is the bad thing to say," explained Suda.

"If you are in the line of fire. It doesn't much matter whether it is bad or good," he said.

He thought about the range of conduct excused by a single phrase: from whores to murderers. He thought about an Oxford don's hatred of the Flemish and the executions he had supervised during World War II. Thomas Pierce said the history don had spent his time seeking forgiveness; though not many saw him that way. And Snow had tried to connect magic and spiritualism with near-fatal consequences. And

Snow who had faced a fake execution had sought forgiveness. Breach tore up more hundred-baht notes and threw the jagged pieces into the night air. If applause were forgiveness, then Breach would have entered the state of innocence and bliss. But he knew that forgiveness, like justice, were close-up magic acts; the water had not really been changed into wine, the five-hundred-baht notes had not really stated the same. But the illusion was enough for most people. For a moment he wished he not left the cave.

"I did all right," said Jean-Claude, stopping at Breach's table. "Can you do a trick with these?"

All eyes turned on Breach as Jean-Claude poured the small gems into his hand. Breach looked over at Suda. Her face was expressionless. He made a couple of passes with his hands. Then he opened both hands to show they were empty.

"Where are my stones?" asked Jean-Claude.

Breach reached over and pulled them out of Jean-Claude's shirt pocket. "You must be more careful how you carry your gems," said Breach. There was more applause and laughter and more rounds of beer brought to the tables. Breach was good for business.

Over the years Kik had witnessed countless encounters with guests. Breach mystified her; and she stared at him with distrust. What he had done with the hundred-baht notes and then the gems deeply disturbed her, and the way she thought things. Many *Farangs* had come to Mae Sai for shopping, intrigue, crossing the border, and being on the edge of the golden triangle. It was a town Khun Sa's army had entered and raked with gunfire. Collectively, these foreigners had created an indelible image of *farangs* going from place to place throughout their lives not ever caring or taking the time to discover the value of what they bought. A rational people acting so irrationally with their money.

All that they knew was that some object had captured their attention in the way a child is captivated by a toy. These white children in adulthood bodies automatically reached for their wallet without ever asking the obvious question: "What does it mean that I invite a total stranger, whose business is to sell his merchandise at the highest possible price, to assign his value, his price to the object I want to possess?" Breach's magic seemed to contain an answer to this riddle, and Kik believed that coming up with the answer to a riddle could be dangerous like anything which threatened to exchange confusion for understanding.

In some ways, the *farang* who came to the guest house were no different from the hilltribe people, trusting the first Lahu godman who came into the village, thought Breach. But times were changing. Snow, ex-Lahu godman, had been reduced to another candidate for hostage of the week. A *farang*, a total stranger who bought colored stones at gem prices held himself hostage; that kind always had a standing invitation to play cards at whatever casino was doing business in the neighborhood. Then someone like Breach arrived with his magic to destroy her belief in the meaning of value. She wished him away from the guest house and out of her life. She liked the *farangs* like Jean-Claude the best.

Breach watched Suda twisting the silver fish around and around between her finger and thumb, rubbing the surface, calling up some feeling; she was waiting for the next trick. The one not coming from Breach, but the one that had been prepared for him. And she found herself, suddenly and against her better judgment, liking him, and hoping that he would not become another cost of doing business.

Two rows of wooden cabins, red-shuttered windows opened across a concrete walkway. The sound of a radio filtered from one of the cabins; in another cabin farther down, people laughed and talked in muffled tones. Suda, her hair still wet from a cold shower, slicked back tightly on her head like a cap, sat at a picnic table. Breach, a towel wrapped around his neck, played with a deck of cards; cutting them, shuffling them with one hand, then the other. His concentration perfect against the background clatter of the early evening. The other guest returning from the communal shower on the walkway complained about the mosquitoes, the cold water, and the heat. It was nearly ten o'clock when Breach glanced at his watch.

Suda talked about the antique business. Her eyes were heavy; she was exhausted, having passed the point where sleep could easily carry her from a day jammed with so many ideas and images. The rendezvous with Mr. Tang. Images that cut inward and drove away sleep. She had avoided all evening talking about the silver.

"Why do you laugh?" Suda asked.

Breach shuffled the cards, and quickly laid out the Ace, King, Queen, Jack of Hearts on the table.

"I was just thinking that Jean-Claude doesn't need a minimum to play," said Breach, wearing a Hawaiian shirt, shorts, and a dead man's sandals.

"Never any minimum for man who pay gem price for glass."

"You read that off a Thai T-shirt," replied Breach, picking up the cards.

Her eyes fired up. Didn't he really know, she thought. He was an eccentric, and as such did not fully appreciate the love affair the world had with the ordinary, and the fear engendered by those who loved too far away from the opinions shared and accepted by most.

"Why would a Thai woman who is dying help Tuttle, Crosby, and of course, me? he said. Once again he dealt the ace, king, queen, jack off the top of the deck, and this time they were all clubs. "Why would she risk her savings with a *farang* in a Chinese casino?" asked Breach, listening to a cassette playing *Lucy in the Sky with Diamonds* drifting out from one of the cabins. "What is the percentage for changing sides at the last moment?"

"I think helping you good idea."

Breach rose from the picnic table, paced along the walkway, then spun around. "You are too careful to bet on a good idea."

"Not important," she replied, with a shrug.

"You could die broke."

"Broke or no broke, die anyway."

Sitting on the walkway that night the devil of greed rattled through the cabins. What fascinated Breach was that she had risked everything. Without a whisper of doubt, she had put her fortune in his hands. He had walked into her dreamworld looking for ritual shaman knives for a dying Oxford don. Did she think he had a map and guidebook? Did she want a ticket? Was that it, she was ready to go? None of it fit Suda; this wasn't a sentimental western woman who confused money with romantic ideas that money could never buy.

Suda leaned over the picnic table and, using a small paring knife, peeled the black skin off Chinese truffles—a kind of chesnut. The knife pulled back the thin black skin like tissue. Underneath, a yellow fruit the texture of an apple was exposed to the night air.

"Why you angry?" she asked him, handing him a freshly peeled truffle.

Breach stared at the plum, yellow flesh and popped it in his mouth. "Confused," he murmured, "Why Ross? A Bangkok lawyer finds it so important for me to play cards in Mae Sai. Why a woman who has less than a year to live uses me to roll the dice?" Breach looked tired, the puffy eyes, rimmed with black shadows. He chewed the truffle slowly, feeling the flesh against his tongue. From one of the cabins he heard Jean-Claude's laughter followed by yammering in French.

"Maybe you ask Crosby," she said, with a wan smile.

"There's a man who has never been confused. He knows the stakes. You know why he's always losing?"

She shook her head and peeled another truffle.

"He is greedy but does not understand fear. So he never knows when to fold his cards and walk away. What he has is never enough, and he is never afraid of losing it."

"He not lose this time," said Suda, popping the truffle into her mouth.

Breach whipped the towel from his neck and threw it on the table. He scattered the cards over the walkway. "That's it, isn't it? There is no risk. This isn't a card game," said Breach, clapping his hands together. "It's a business deal. Something between Robert Tuttle and Colonel Chao. An unresolved debt."

"Colonel Chao did a bad thing," said Suda.

He stopped himself, smiling, as he spread the cards out across the table. "Of course, he did. It's all been fixed in advance. Now it's Tuttle's turn. Right?" Suda picked one of the cards and turned it over. It was the jack of hearts. "Ross might be possibly the best actor to drink from a bottle of bourbon. The sonofabitch. But I may have a surprise for him."

Breach scooped up the cards in a single motion, fanned the deck, and dropped them into his towel laid on the table. Suda looked at the cards and then at him. He was like a child, she thought.

Jean-Claude, whistling *Feelings*, strolled up the walkway wearing a navy blue silk shirt unbuttoned to his belly, and tight white pants. His hand had been wrapped in fresh bandages, and behind him came his wife, and the other couple. They were dressed for a night out in Paris.

"I think I have the luck tonight," said Jean-Claude, as he stopped beside Breach.

Breach pulled the ace of spades out of Jean-Claude's side pocket and handed it to him. "Keep it."

Jean-Claude looked at the card. "You are amazing." He walked off with the other French people, who passed the ace from hand to hand and spoke in rapid French.

"I remember first time I see you. You did a magic trick," said Suda, as the French couple passed down the driveway to where Lip stood waiting with his VW. She turned over another card, the queen of diamonds. "Maybe you are a little like Snow. *Farang* shaman good at fooling simple people. But who was the fool?"

As Suda finished, Lip came up the walkway. He panted from the heat and wiped his face with a handkerchief. He had the same uncleaned fish tank eyes as his father.

"No room. I come back fifteen minutes," said Lip. "You wait me."

Lip turned and, without waiting for a reply, walked off. "Start the game without me," called Breach after him. "I've changed my mind." Lip's only reply was a slight twitch of the shoulders. He got into the car, with the two French couples, gunned the motor, and pulled out of the driveway.

"He come back," said Suda, leaning forward on her elbows.

Mr. Tang was in the same business as the guest house owner, the gem merchant, and Suda; selling experience; dream material manufactured to fit the customers' image of the good life. Jean-Claude had come for the experience of Asia; and no one had the slightest intention of disappointing him.

"I go to my room now," said Suda, packing away the truffles, her knife, and the peelings. "I very tired. Cannot talk any more."

Breach picked up the queen of spades from the deck. He found her small knife and stabbed the tip of the knife through the black spade.

"Why did Tang ask for your money?" He looked at her, smiling down at the punctured playing card.

"He want to know how far you go. If you take money from woman who die soon, then you do anything."

"He said that?" Pulling an ace of spades from the deck.

She shook her head, looking at the card and trying to figure out how Breach had given the Frenchman the same card a few minutes earlier. She looked away from the playing card.

"Crosby said many things. But he never told me about your magic. If you can do this with cards and money, maybe you can make another me. One that will not die," she said.

The two coffin-sized single beds in Breach's room at the Baht guest house had been pushed against opposite walls, making the room look like a cheap morgue with a narrow walkway. Both beds had thin, lumpy mattresses and damp pillows like objects that had already been buried and unearthed for reuse. Moonlight and mosquitoes streamed through the cracks in the walls. Breach crawled beneath the mosquito net and lay on the bed. The plastic blades of a small table fan rotated on a corner table. He stretched out on the bed, waiting. He knew that Lip would return.

He listened to the fan in the near darkness. Thai music from a radio in a nearby cabin travelled through the night. Voices seeped through in half-whispered tones. He heard a woman's voice, the tones rising and falling. Another voice liquid with drink joked, then became serious, pleading and sobbing as if some great loss had been realized.

Breach thought about Suda; she was so small, fragile, working the knife to peel back the black skin of the Chinese truffles. Talking about business and death as if they were the same activity. Why had he allowed her to put up the stakes? Wasn't she gambling away families, dreams, and houses, part of his blood? What had he been trying to prove? Why had it mattered so much that afternoon to play in the poker game? Odd connections filtered through his thoughts.

Whooping cranes and Lahu godmen; Tuttle and Colonel Chao; and nature and magic. The Flemish executioner who became an Oxford history don. His thick glasses, red nose, and spittle in the corner of his mouth ready to topple, creating the suspense of a major spill. Mr. Tang's mouth, at a crucial stage of the price negotiation with Suda, formed a bubble of spit in precisely the same place. Once he had written an essay for Thomas Pierce about the connection between scholars and murderers. He had concluded one created the logic, drew up the blueprints for the other. Lenin, Stalin, Mao, and Hitler had solid theory for committing murder.

Why had the Flemish killer turned history don become so strange, distant, unstable? While scholars turned into murderers, it rarely worked the other way: murderers turning into scholars. Or had the don been Breach's first encounter with an ex-Lahu godman type. An Ex Lahu godman made an unsettled academic. The experience had come during the war. The don had been part of an intelligence unit in northern France, and had ordered the execution of many collaborators. After the war, back at Oxford, this don discovered that killing Flemish collaborators was on a different order of things than marking examination papers. The men he killed helped the Nazis because they hated the French not because they loved the Germans; but never mind, that was a detail of no consequence in war, thought Breach. He saw the larger picture, the grand sweep of armies and nations, and his central role in a supreme struggle of good against evil. He could never let go of that feeling, that God feeling of a killer. And what he had taught Breach was a murderer's theory of scholarship. Breach wondered if the same thing had happened to him in Mae Sai.

Real tragedy for humanity was found not inside history but among the people who had lived outside of history. Those on the inside had lost the ability to make sense of what had happened. Those on the outside exploited and used their ignorance. The insiders found themselves in the realm of easy violence; not only did they survive, but they flourished, and loved the terror and fear dancing in the eyes of those around them in the way a merchant loves money. Images were everything and nothing: the rows of tanks and soldiers; the history don signalling a firing squad; Snow tied up in the Lahu village; and Mr. Tang, taking Suda's money and shoving the silver into a box. The same threads to the same moving picture, thought Breach. Breach had drifted into, applied for, had been elected to, or otherwise landed the vacant Lahu godman role.

His entire life, Breach had wandered from school to school, trying to stop the avalanche of students disappearing inside history. He understood why he had failed. Inside history was where the murderers had succeeded in covering over the vast killing fields. His students ran right past him, and finally over him in the safety of that bunker. It wasn't that they didn't understand or believe him; but they feared being left outside like Breach, they would be left alone to wander with the executioners through the graveyards, watching most people pick their plot, thinking that they had chosen life when they had selected death.

So he fled; first into London, using Crosby to win easy money, then running out of England and into Asia. He thought he didn't have the slightest chance of winning, and Asia was the place such people disappeared into. He fled to a cave where people saw visions and went mad, thinking someone who had visions and was already mad might be cured. And each morning as he watched the sun come up, he knew that was a failure too. Because the sun was rising for another day as business as usual. As much as he railed against himself and the world, it pulled him back, hooked him, reeled in back. Nothing had changed; not the game, not the stakes, not the players.

❖

A rapid series of hard, booming knocks on Breach's cabin's screen door broke through and grabbed him hard. He bolted up in bed and glanced at his watch; it was nearly midnight, and he had a strange feeling of being lost inside one of those Russian doll-like dreams. He threw back the sheet, and checked his money belt. It could be an anxiety dream about money, he thought. The pounding on the door continued. In the pitch dark, he swung his legs over the side of the bed, walked four steps to the door, and opened it. It wasn't a dream, thought Breach. It was a fucking nightmare. Ross, smelling of *Old Gand-Dad*, his hair oiled and combed straight back on his head, wore a fresh linen safari suit. Lip, grinning his nervous used car salesman grin, stood next to Ross. He had appeared in the same outfit Breach had seen on him earlier in the day inside the shophouse.

"Christ," said Ross. "You sleeping?"

Breach looked around the walkway; but there was no sign of either Crosby or Snow. Two cabins down, a door opened, and a cassette playing *Chicago's* song *Hard Habit to Break*. He smiled, he hadn't heard that song since watching a cremation in Kathmandu.

"Where's Crosby, Snow?" asked Breach.

"They go already," said Lip. He was impatient, shifting from foot to foot. "Go now. We late. Go, okay?"

Ross reached inside the door and flicked on the light; a naked forty-watt bulb that hung from the ceiling. "Not the kind of room I expected to find an Oxford man," said Ross.

"I've changed my mind. I'm not going," said Breach, through clenched teeth.

Ross put an arm around Lip. "Why don't you wait outside?"

After Lip left the room, Ross removed a silver flask from his jacket, took a long drink, passing his sleeve across his mouth. Then he sat down on the edge of a bed. Ross opened a bag and began taking out a set of clothes. An expensive silk shirt, white trousers, matching jacket, socks, and polished shoes were carefully laid out on the bed. Ross picked up and admired the necktie before putting the flask back to his lips.

"Remember earlier in the whorehouse? That guy from New York. Bennington Harlow Wallace. Nice name. Benny-boy."

Breach remembered Bennington's eyes when Ross has asked if he had ever owned a pair of bowling shoes.

"It seems Benny-boy had an accident in the whorehouse. Brothels can be dangerous places. You need expertise and know how to handle yourself. Ben is—was—an international lawyer who went to a famous Ivy school. But he skipped the course on how to watch your ass in a Mae Sai whorehouse. One of the girls drugged his drink. In twenty-four hours, he's gonna have an exploding headache. He's back in his hotel room sleeping. Since Ben's kinda tired, we thought you might like to take his place. By the way, you get a cut of the action. Twenty grand for an evening of playing cards isn't a bad payday even for an Oxford man."

"And what do you get?"

Ross smiled, emptying his flask. "Controlling interest in *Old Grand-Dad* shares," he said, looking at him hard. "What in the fuck do you care?"

"And Suda?"

"Tough lady. She could bait a hook with you or me without changing her expression. Catch a fish, eat it, and sleep like a baby afterwards," said Ross, handing Breach the silk shirt. "Put it on. You're about Bennington's size. A New York lawyer doesn't show up looking like a coolie."

"What's Suda's share." Breach insisted on an answer.

Ross sighed, shaking his head; he was uncertain whether Bennington's jacket would fit Breach. "We're arranging a house for her mother."

Breach began dressing in the back seat, kicking off his shorts. He ran his hand across Bennington's monogram stitched over the left side of the silk shirt: BHW. Breach had wanted to believe in Suda; he had wanted to find some quality that was resistant to the fires of poverty, the cold, the grave. He slipped into the shirt, found the buttons in the dark, and wondered if Bennington was still alive. Earlier Breach had been walking around in a dead man's sandals; by evening he had an entire wardrobe from a man who had been Ross's client.

❖

A few minutes later, they were on the road. Lip drove, while Ross sat in the front. Breach doubled up his knees in the backseat, looking at the dark thatched houses that slipped past in blurred shadows. "It wasn't your ten grand, was it, Ross?" he asked, watching the headlights from an oncoming ten-wheeler approaching from the opposite direction.

"Possession is nine-tenths of ownership," said Ross. "Ever hear that? In Thailand, it's ten-tenths of ownership."

"It was your fee from Bennington or Colonel Chao," guessed Breach. Suda had all but come out and explained that much. "Or maybe you didn't tell the Colonel about Bennington's fee. You stuck it in your pocket. Undisclosed business. Secret partners. Large sums of cash. And you are the man in the middle."

"Lawyers are professional middle men," said Ross.

"And I thought this was a *teeoh*—a party."

Ross smiled as the huge truck screamed past, the high beam lights bleaching the color from his face. "You know what I like about you, Breach? You're fucking smart. And you like whoring. I like whoring. In fact, I like to tell people I like whoring. It is expected of you. A social obligation to whore and to like whoring. I'm suspicious of any guy who doesn't like to whore. Saying you're a whoremonger is like telling someone like Bennington Harlow Wallace that you know about French wines. Ben's impressed. Because you

271

know your business. And business is whoring, and whoring is business."

"Ben's dead," said Breach in a low, soft voice.

"Sleeping."

"Like the parrot in Monty Python," replied Breach. Ross had never seen British TV, and shrugged his shoulder, then looked in the glove compartment for another bottle.

"I hate fucking parrots."

"I'm wearing a dead man's clothes," said Breach.

"They say a dead man's clothes are lucky for playing cards."

"Who say that?" asked Lip.

"The fucking Chinese," said Ross. "They put it inside fortune cookies."

Breach shifted in a borrowed suit watching the VW shoot down the dark side roads. The lights from Mae Sai disappeared, and they were alone in their thoughts. And Breach began to think of the whores he had known; where they were at that moment, with whom, and if they were in a winning position, going through the gears, pretending to catch fire so they could make an early escape into the night.

Chapter 18

The headlights of oncoming traffic twisted Ross's face into a grim mask with long shadows sweeping away portions of his chin and neck. Ross had shifted his weight around in the front seat and leaned one arm over the top as he tried to read the expression on Breach's face.

"You know what I really hate?"

"What do you hate?" asked Breach.

"Street vendors who sell ice cream in hot-dog buns. They make me break out in a cold sweat. There's something scary about a sweet-assed Thai girl licking a hot-dog bun loaded with three scoops of vanilla ice cream melting down her fingers."

"Cultural shock, Ross."

Ross laughed, coughing and shaking his large head.

"After twenty years living in Thailand, it's not cultural shock. It's cultural negligence. We didn't teach them right. Or they weren't listening the day we explained the function of hot-dog buns. Take, Lip, here, he would eat noodle soup out of a hot-dog bun if he thought it wouldn't leak."

Lip shot Ross one of those Chinese smiles meaning, "I like to kill you, fat white man."

"And you know what else I really hate?"

Breach said nothing, thinking Ross had the manner of an executioner passing time before it was time to do the job.

"Travelling with an ugly woman. There can't be more than ten ugly women in the whole country. And you ended up travelling all the way to Mae Sai with one of them."

"You ever lived in a cave, Ross?"

"Is that some kind of trick question?"

"No," said Breach. "Living alone in a cave you start to see things that aren't really there. You start to smell and hear things which can't place. And after a year or so you start to believe what isn't there and what you can't place is like magic. You begin to understand the prison created by light, shadow, and distraction."

Ross clenched his jaw. "So, what does that have to do with an ugly woman like Suda and eating ice cream in hot-dog buns?"

"Or with a harelip on a chocolate bunny?" replied Breach, leaning forward, and pulling a queen of diamonds from Ross's ear. "That since the beginning of time people have been massacred to restore normality. Mass murderers claim those who were killed with abnormal. Always travel with an ugly woman, Ross. Always eat ice cream from a hot-dog bun. Then you will avoid washing your hands in other people's blood."

Lip stopped at a police road block. A ten-wheeler had flipped over on the side and the cargo of small pigs which had not been slaughtered in the crashed squealed and ran through the night. Some villagers were in hot pursuit. One other car had been turned away by the police. Lip spoke to the officer, who pointed his flashlight at Ross and Breach. The conversation was in Thai and neither Ross nor Breach could follow the exchange. Lip, cursing under his breath, reversed and returned to the main road. Lip was sullen and refused to explain what had been said or the meaning of the reversal. Ross was agitated and became angry.

"Your job is to deliver us to the game, Lip," said Ross. "You are fucking up."

"Truck crash."

"And the driver has fled the scene. But the game will go on," said Ross.

"Screaming at him won't help," said Breach.

"Get back in your fucking cave. I'm handling this," said Ross.

Three kilometers down the road, Lip turned off the road following a loud bang which exploded from the VW engine. Breach felt the vibration, and looked back to see smoke billowing from behind.

"We're on fire," said Ross, opening the door. "Bail out."

"He's thrown a rod," said Breach.

"It's like being on an Indian reservation. Lip, don't you understand cars need oil and water. It's car food. Very important. If the car doesn't eat, the engine fucking blows up."

Lip ignored the lecture and steered the car off the road and onto the shoulder which sloped down to a field. He switched off the engines and the lights. The VW belched smoke. Ross got out, waited for Breach to emerge, and slammed the car door.

"Where are we?" asked Ross, looking at the total darkness.

"You got a plan?" Breach asked Lip, who looked troubled as he surveyed the smoky engine.

"We walk," said Lip. "Not far."

"I hate walking," said Ross. "Lip, get me a taxi."

Lip showed his teeth in a tight smile. "No taxi."

He plunged ahead carrying a flashlight with black electrician tape on the handle; it had a well-used look, and Lip grunted as he stepped into the rice paddy. He didn't look back as he started wading in the cool, black water covering the vast sea of rice.

"Lip, where the fuck you going?" shouted Ross.

The sound of Lip's splashing stopped. "To put ice cream in hot-dog bun. Not worry, not so deep."

"Fuck. You're not sore because of what I said about the buns?" Ross threw up his hands and brought them down hard against his legs.

"This only good way left," said Lip out of the darkness.

Ross pulled off his shoes and socks, and rolled up his trouser legs. "I don't think the game come to you, Mr. Ross."

"I think he's got you, Ross," said Breach.

"I broke my own rule. Never piss off a Chink after he sees a turned-over truck full of dead pigs."

Breach slipped out of Bennington's tailor-made trouser, and folded his shoes and stuffed the monogrammed socks inside, tied a knot, and then lifted the bundle onto his shoulders. As he walked in the rice paddy, his feet made a sucking noise like two fat bellies thumping against one another. Ross had enough trouble walking sober on dry land; in the rice field, he couldn't get his balance, and splashed around, moaning and cursing.

"Watch out for the fucking water buffalo," he said. "I'd hate stepping on one of those mean fuckers in the dark."

"It's the snakes you worry about," said Breach.

Ross stopped dead still. "What snakes?"

"Don't worry, they'd never bite lawyers," said Breach.

Breach saw a bright spotlight ahead of them in the distance, maybe two hundred meters. That was a long walk in the cold, dark water. After nearly twenty minutes in the dark they saw three men in military uniform stationed around the spotlight. The lights were pointed in their faces. Hands riding their service revolver. They recognized Lip immediately and waved him through. Ross shuddered as he stepped back onto dry ground. The police officer at the accident scene had radioed to them, so they had been expecting them to arrive and had used the light to guide them across the rice paddy.

"Lip, are there snakes?"

"Not worry about snake," said Lip. "In China we eat snake in hot-dog bun."

"This is fucking Thailand. Snakes eat people," said Ross, wiping the muck from his feet. "And don't get Bennington's suit dirty. He's a guy who gets pissed off with a mud stain."

"I thought he was dead," said Breach.

"Ben's so, so cool. He was born without a pulse."

"Why did you hire him?" asked Breach.

"He hired me."

Breach looked puzzled. "Then why was the ten thousand his fee?"

"That was your guess."

"Why did he hire you, Ross?"

"For my expert advice on Thai law. For my connections so nothing would go wrong. He didn't want any surprises. And, of course, to guarantee his safety."

"But he's dead."

"He fucked up, didn't he?"

On a side dirt road which had no streetlights, dozens of expensive cars parked on both sides, Breach slipped back into Bennington's socks, shoes, and trousers. Ross leaned against a black Mercedes, the heel of his foot resting on the rear fender, supervising the dressing of Breach. He rocked back and forth, slinging the rice paddy mud off his calves.

"That's a general's car," said Lip.

"A man who beat the pig crash to roll the dice. And because you forget that car maintenance is ninety percent of car ownership, I was forced to make a death march through a sea of snakes," said Ross, looking down at his leg. He screamed and began jumping and thrashing around the side of the general's car. Quickly rolling up his pant leg above his knee, Ross grabbed the flashlight from Lip and shone it on his leg.

"Snakes," he shouted, kicking at the air.

Breach started laughing.

"It's not a snake. It's a leech." The black wormlike creature wiggled as Ross kicked his leg. "You can't kick it off. You have to be burn off."

"Oh, God. Do it. Do it," screamed Ross. Lip squatted down with a lighter. "Don't you dare touch me." He grabbed the lighter and tossed it to Breach.

Breach was laughing so hard he had trouble holding Lip's cigarette lighter to the head of the leech. Ross howled and his face turned red; he held his leg stiff and rigid, as if it were a foreign object, against the trunk of the Mercedes. Breach touched the flame to the head of the leech; it shriveled and collapsed like a piece of cut rope. Breach flicked it away from Ross's leg. He burnt off two more, throwing each one in the road. "Death is everywhere," Ross whimpered and cursed Lip who stood on the side quietly staring at his feet. Breach held up a dead leech so that Ross could see it. Slowly Ross opened his eyes, stared at the leech, shuddered.

"That's the last one," said Breach.

Ross reached down and touched his leg. When he brought his had up, he shone the flashlight on his fingers. There was blood. He howled again, slamming his open fist against the trunk of the Mercedes, setting off the alarm. "First a pig massacre. Followed by a VW exploding like a space shuttle. Then I'm attacked by man-eating snakes. And you think a lawyer doesn't earn his fees?"

A soldier came running up with a rifle, poked a flashlight into Lip's face. Everyone inspected the black Mercedes; there was no damage. The soldier stuck his finger on a lump of mud Ross had left behind and frowned, looking at the three men. He gestured at Lip. They spoke in rapid Thai. A hint of anger broke through the soldier's voice; his angular jaw set firm and hard.

"Tell him a band of Chinese snakes fucked up the car," said Ross.

"He want money," said Lip.

"Tell him I have an important appointment," said Ross, a gleam in his eye. "And *Old Grand-Dad* transfusion with Colonel Chao." Ross eyed the soldier who was shining the flashlight on Ross's bloody legs. "The colonel's my friend. He's waiting inside."

The soldier waved Ross pass. "I'm his lawyer," said Breach, walking over to Ross.

The soldier, handout, waited until Lip peeled off a five-hundred-baht note. Lip kicked at the dirt, and walked away. The soldier slowly folded the purple bank note and slid it into his side pocket. Lip made straight for the entrance to a cave illuminated with strings of Christmas tree lights. Ross walked two steps behind him.

"Look at him," Ross said, gesturing at Lip. "He's pissed off at me. He can put fifty baht of oil in his car. That would be a waste of money. Now he gets hit for a five-hundred-baht bribe, and there's no question in his mind that I owe him the money. *Farang* pay. Why? *Farang* have money. *Farang* flexible. Tell me, Breach. You think this is rational? You think these people have their head up their asses or what?"

"Or what," said Breach. He looked distracted, lost in thoughts as he stared at the cave entrance.

Ross stopped him. "Now what does that mean?"

Lip had already disappeared grumbling to himself into the cave. "What if they know I'm not Bennington."

The idea of fear excited Ross. His *Old Grand-Dad-* saturated blood pumped through his viens. "Yeah, there's always that remote possibility," he said. "But you need fear or you lose your edge. It's the same in darts. If you won't defeat the opposition your edge must be sharper than theirs."

"You think any customers inside believe they are a clitoris?" asked Breach, leaving Ross to scratch his head.

Inside the massive cavern, the domed ceiling disappeared into a vast churning darkness; the flutter of bats diving and darting as if the darkness was one living thing in motion. Three passages led out of a central chamber. Men in expensive tailored suits passed in and out of the chamber. Emerging from a small group of customers, Mr. Tang offered his hand to Breach; baffled by Mr. Tang's transformation, he accepted his outstretched hand.

"Mr. Wallace, how good to see you," Mr. Tang said to Breach with a firm, even voice.

"You can call him Bennington," said Ross.

Breach glanced at Ross, who had taken a drink from a waiter's tray. "Bennington went for a little swim. He was on the Harvard rice paddy swim team." Ross sipped his drink and smiled at Mr. Tang as if they had shared an inside joke.

Mr. Tang's tailoring had improved remarkably from earlier that afternoon. He wore the freshly ironed white cotton shirt, red striped necktie, black pants and wing-tipped shoes—the wardrobe of a pit boss. Like the rabbit in Alice in Wonderland, Mr. Tang scurried ahead on the central walkway, bouncing, tapping his fingers on the handrail as he walked.

"There never was a minimum," said Breach, stopping on the walkway.

"It evens the score for taking my money for those fucking Lahu," said Ross.

"The money you took from Bennington."

"For service beyond and above the call of duty," said Ross.

Breach looked around the cave. "Where is our table?"

Ross hummed to himself, looking Breach over. "That suit fits you too good. Look at it as fate. You return to the cave dressed in someone else's clothes." He walked off, leaving Breach to follow him.

Every fifteen feet they passed an electric light fixture. Security men in blue blazers walked around with walkie-talkies, escorting clients down the passageways leading off the main path. Someone had gone to a great deal of planning and expense to convert the cave into a casino. Off the main walkways were gambling rooms. As they walked down the lit passage, Breach stuck his head in one of the rooms running off the main passage. He saw Jean-Claude and his friends from the guest house playing dollar slot machines. There were fifty or more people, mostly middle-aged Chinese, milling around six rows of slots and a three gambling tables where people were playing blackjack. Mr. Tang waved to Breach and continued walking on the walkway with Ross.

"Lip, he very angry with you," said the old man, with the full smile that revealed the upper gums.

"I'm not exactly thrilled with Lip," said Ross, as Breach caught up with them. "Or that flamethrower he called a car."

"This doesn't look right," said Breach, looking around at the people coming and going, escorted by guides dressed like Mr. Tang.

"Not enough bats for you?" asked Ross. "Don't be nervous. These people are not your usual cave dwellers."

"No one plays a big game in a crowd like this," said Breach

Mr. Tang swung the lantern around, a look of admiration crossing his old face—the same look he had seen in the exchange with Suda—and he stared at Breach. "You are smart. Mr. Wallace he want big game. And knows this place is for tourists."

"Cut out the bullshit, my name's Breach."

The old man glanced over his shoulder. "You pretty good," said Mr. Tang. "You fool me. Fool Lip, too."

"Bennington's no fool," said Ross. "He trained at Harvard in the occult arts of black magic. Then he got his advanced degrees in multiple personalities."

They followed Mr. Tang, who raced ahead holding an oil lantern out at eye level, and expertly jumping from one platform of rock to another. From the ceiling the rock appeared as if frozen waterfalls were clinging to the surface and tumbling down a distant wall. On the floor of the cave were the strange objects found in most caves; objects that appeared like fried eggs. Mr. Tang held the lantern in front of a small entrance that required Breach to squat down as he waddled through.

"Fat man have problem here," said Mr. Tang, his eyes wide open and yellow as he held the lantern for Ross.

"Get a haircut for your mole," said Ross, stooping down, groaning as he followed Breach through the narrow passage.

Two large formations shaped like women's breasts complete with erect nipples made a kind of natural archway. "You have the feeling we've walked out of Thailand?" said Breach.

"Thailand? Burma? Who the fuck knows, or cares? No one is asking for a passport," said Ross.

Near a grotto, behind an outcrop of rock, a ladder rose out of sight. Mr. Tang went directly to the ladder and began climbing. Breach followed a moment later. Having reached the top, Mr. Tang rapped his knuckles on a trapdoor. It slowly opened and flashlights pointed in Mr. Tang's face were quickly replaced by hands helping him to the top. They waited until Ross had been pulled through the trapdoor. "Where is this fucking place?" asked Ross.

Breach looked at two soldiers who unlocked a side door. He tapped the side of a Bentley. "We're in someone's garage."

Six months earlier, the newspapers in Bangkok had run stories about certain influential people in the north who floated the idea of an "Atlantic City" in the Gold Triangle. The idea was attacked in the press, then certain politicians took up the cry seeking an opportunity to embarrass the government, and as quickly as "Atlantic City" of the north had appeared, it disappeared from the press and public discussion. Nothing more was mentioned in the newspapers; the minor party politicians stopped releasing statements about dark influences. Like most controversies, it left the consciousness of the public, leaving only a slight trace in the memory of a few people who had covered the story.

Li Chin, a Chinese high roller, with family connections in Hong Kong, Singapore, Taipei, had thrown his support behind the original idea, but suddenly changed his mind.

He had a brilliant idea adapted from his son; the boy had returned from a school outing to Chiang Dao caves, with postcard photographs of the chambers. Li Chin heard a tiny voice whispering, "Go underground. Open a casino under the earth." He dreamt of caves for several weeks. What worried Li Chin was no high-ranking Chinese would want to gamble in a cave. Such a low place for people of power and influence. Then the tiny voice whispered again to Li Chin.

"Built in the cave. Not for the Chinese but the *farang*. Let them gamble in a low place. Then use this underground casino for your cover. What is a cave? But a tunnel. And where does this tunnel go? To a place known and not known. A place above and below ground. A place no one could ever locate. Build your house in this place."

There was a great deal of family money to wash and dry before it circulated in Asia, Europe, or America. What better place for a Chinese money laundry than in a large fortress compound accessible from the Thai side through a cave located in no-man's land, a region where the border was fluid, and money controlled those with the guns. A police colonel named Chao was phoned and he recommended a lawyer in Bangkok to put together the deal; a man who understood the contractual complexity of running a laundromat for cash. Colonel Chao found him playing darts. His name was Ross. In return for the favor, the colonel had some cash of his own that could use a little dry cleaning.

And Li Chin had his dream compound built. Marble lotus ponds stocked with turtles. Rooms with brocaded chairs, Persian carpets, and Ming vases. Twenty rooms for antiques, shrines, teak floors walled off in a compound of manicured lawns and palm trees.

The playing room was on the second floor. The curtains were drawn over a wall of windows. A ceiling fan rotated over a round table. Except for a bar in the corner, the room was otherwise empty. Breach glided in his stocking feet across the parquet floors and stopped at the entrance.

"See that guy dressed like a bat over there?" Ross pointed.

In the center of the room, seated at the table, was a *farang* dressed in black with pure white hair parted on the side and combed back with a thick-toothed comb in '40s style. He wore gold-rim glasses with half-moon lens. The sleeves of his shirt were rolled above his wrist and on his left pinky was a gold ring with a huge rectangular green emerald. Breach watched him shuffle cards, looking at each man at the table as he handled the cards. The man was a professional. He had a haunted batlike look about him, like some of the Hindu men who had lived in caves outside Kathmandu. He had the stare of a dead man, dull-eyed, unblinking. A causal smile crossed his lips as he examined his hand. He might have been thinking of something else; that detached expression, unsettling the other gamblers at the table.

"Mr. Ross and Mr. Wallace," said Li Chin. He wore a business suit and blue silk shirt open at the neck. "We have our precautions. Please indulge an old man. Go with these two boys who help all our guest, and make us all feel comfortable in our heart."

"Nice place you got," said Ross, his eyes looking over the miles of polished floors.

"Welcome to my humble home."

"If this is humble, then be sure to invite me around when you get rich."

Li Chin nodded his head only slightly, and the two guards immediately escorted Ross and Breach into a smaller living room where a TV broadcast a CNN about teenage girls dying from a watermelon diet in southern California. The guards spoke no English. They motioned and gestured to Ross and Breach as they searched them in a no-nonsense show of diligence. Mr. Li Chin was not an employer one wished to disappoint with negligence. Each guard, in turn, went through each article of clothes, looking into pockets and examining buttons. They were equipped with the latest airport electronic security scanners. One guard ran a hand-scanner up and down Ross's legs.

"It was batman's idea to bring Bennington here," said Ross, giggling. "That tickles. Hey, watch out for my balls."

The other guard was still turning out the pockets of Ross's jacket.

"You mean the old Chinese guy?"

"No, I mean the dealer," said Ross.

"Who is he?"

"Batman? He doesn't have a name. But you can call him the dealer if it makes you feel better," said Ross, pulling on his jacket.

Breach stepped ahead, his hands raised over his head, and slowly turned around as the guard searched for a hidden microphone. He thought about how the dealer had handled the deck, that professional's light-fingered touch, his fingers moving like colorless, positively charged electrons, everywhere at the same time. "I want his name, Ross."

"Edward Ward. He's kinda good with his hands."

A big smile broke over Breach's face. "What's his job?"

"Paymaster," said Ross. "He's been waiting. Bennington's picking up a million dollars for Colonel Chao's brother. Let's say the colonel's brother had a difference of opinion with the IRS on application of American tax laws."

"What's that mean?" asked Breach.

"The colonel's brother believed the tax laws in America didn't apply to the Chinese. Why should America be different? The Chinese didn't pay any tax anywhere else. They weren't going make an exception for Americans."

"And Bennington's job is what?"

"He collects the cash for to bail out his brother. Then Benny flies to Hong Kong, deposits the cash in the Marine Midlands Bank, then on to New York in time for the Opera and drinks at the Harvard Club."

"Only the money never makes it to New York. Which settles a score Tuttle has with the Colonel," said Breach.

Ross said nothing until Breach pretended to pull one of the dead leeches out of Ross's ear. "Goddamn, don't do that shit."

When they were allowed back into the gambling room, the private poker game had gone seriously quiet, and a large pile of money was in the middle of the table; six men sat at the table in high-back chairs with red velvet seats. The dealer was *farang*; but the gamblers were combinations of what appeared Burmese, Thai, Shan mixed with the general Chinese stock. They huddled over their cards with small, black eyes; nursing drinks in long-stemmed crystal glasses, three slim, long-legged women in short skirts silently refilled. It was a Chinese family annual shareholders meeting, Chinese style, where the idea was to pass out accumulated profits.

"Bingo night for the families," whispered Ross. "Hong Kong, London, Rome, Vancouver, Los Angeles, and Manila are at that table." Breach looked at the bosses sitting around the table, holding cards, smoking, drinking, spitting on the cave floor. There was one empty chair. Ross grabbed a drink off a passing tray. He nodded at the chair.

"That chair is reserved for you, Mr. Wallace," he said.

It was the New York City chair; and it was missing Colonel Chao's brother. The gamblers had already won before they sat down; identical briefcases of hundred-dollar bills had been placed to the right of each chair. These were the winnings. Before a card had been dealt everyone was a winner.

"We can start the game now," said Ed Ward, looking up at Breach.

Breach leaned back in his chair and watched the dealer shuffle the cards. And the dealer didn't take his eyes off Breach for a moment; his large gray eyes in the half light staring right through Breach. This old man with the funny white hair opened the bidding with a thousand dollars.

❖

"After the war, I dealt into a big game with a man. It was three in the morning, and everyone else had dropped out. I watched him deal out five cards. I saw his face; no expression as he looked up from his hand. He had no more money left. He asked if he could put up his house. What can you say to a man who would risk his house on a hand of cards? You say, go ahead.

"You must have some kind of special hand; or your blood runs so cold you have come out of place that isn't this world. He writes down the details, signs his name, and throws the note in the center of the table. And he says, I guess it is going to cost you to find out. And I says to him, don't you have a wife and kids. He says, if he loses the house, he will drop up a note for them next.

"He has the sickness or he has an unbeatable hand. He has a way of shaking your confidence, looking at a winning hand and thinking that you are about to lose. The game is all in the mind. Who controls the mind controls the hand, and who controls the hand, takes the pot. Only a few can ever master the art of living without regret and without sentiment. Those are the two bastards that spoil the pudding for most. It's a simple principle that's been true since man learned to walk upright on his hind legs. So there was a choice to make. Do I call the bluff or do I fold my hand? Do I risk standing eyeball-to-eyeball with someone who isn't afraid of betting his house? He had to be called. The situation demanded it.

"And when he laid down the cards, they came up short. You know what his words were to me? Nice call. No bitching, crying, and pissing around. Just two words. Nice call. He had lost his house. What was he going to say to his wife and kid? The other guy made a nice call, and I didn't have the cards? Or maybe he said, one day I'll make it up to you. Somewhere, somehow, I'll square things with you and the kid. Not because he felt regret; he had made the right bet. Not out of sentiment. But there was a balance outstanding and unpaid. He wasn't the kind of man who left debts behind.

"The years screamed past, and he never got the chance. People moved away; got lost in the great shuffle of things. Names changed, remarriage, new countries, God knows how things never play out the same way twice. That's why I wanted you to come tonight, Mr. Wallace. I had some information a few months back, my son might be in New York. He'd be about your age. I have details in an envelope. Take them with you. If you could make a few inquiries I would appreciate it. And, if you find him, I have a message. I made the right play. I would do it again. Tonight.

"I was in Bangkok about a month ago, and found myself in a friendly game in an upstairs Patpong bar. I told this story around the table. An Englishman claimed to know my son. Said my son had been his history master at an English private school. My son told him the hand I was holding that night. The hand I bet the house on. Two aces and three jacks. He remembered after all those years. He had been only five. And I said to this Englishman, that boy must hate his father's guts. And the Englishman shook his head. No, your son thought you were the perfect father. How can that be, I asked him. And the Englishman said because you taught him the most important lesson in life: Unless you can bet your house against the house, don't bother playing.

"Take a schoolteacher's job, or whatever you think makes you feel safe. But if my father taught me anything, it is this: no place is safe. No bet is certain. No table cares whether you play or walk. No person can be relied on to stop this emotional free-fall through life. And the ultimate truth is never in wanting the big kill, wanting to win. Winning makes you numb and stupid. But riding that raw edge of losing, getting mowed down at three in the morning with a full house and losing your last two bucks—then you came to terms with who and what you really are. You suddenly realize you never lost the house, your wife, and son because you never had them.

"And then this Englishman tells me a story about how my son got him to drop his pants on a bet in the back of an English pub. And that he took the winnings and disappeared. A month later the English schoolboy gets a letter and the money from my son. He had bet on a horse. The horse had come in. And my son paid off his debt. Maybe you think it was selfish to drag you all the way here from Bangkok to hear this story. But it sounds better in a cave; around a table, where no one else speaks three words of English, in the heat of action. It's nearly time for your plane. One more hand. Just the two of us, Mr. Wallace. You deal five cards from a cold deck. And you bet the house; and I bet the house. One of us leaves homeless. Are you in or out?"

Breach rapped his fingers on the new deck of cards. The dealer waited, his eyes watching Breach's hands. Breach picked up the top card from the deck, held it face down inside his hand, sighed, and threw the card into the darkness of the cave. "A lawyer never bets with his client's money," said Breach.

"Colonel Chao's brother is a lucky man," said the dealer.

Ross bent down, whispered something to the dealer, looking over at Breach. The dealer nodded and pushed back in his chair. Colonel Chao, along with his two bodyguards, approached the table. He reached down and picked up the card that Breach had thrown away. He looked at it.

"Why would a man throw away the ace of spades?" Colonel Chao asked, looking at Breach, and then Ross. "Unless the game is over."

"We have a flight to catch," said Ross nervously.

"Patience, my friend. It is a virtue." Colonel Chao eased in a chair next to Breach. The other gamblers at the table had disappeared like the bats into another part of the cave. "In Chinese tradition, the family is very important. We stick together; we show one face to outsiders. We are one house with one door. So when my brother gets into trouble with the police, I worry about him. I worry for our family. Do the police beat him? Torture him for a confession. What might he say about the family in that case? Would he bring shame and disgrace on our house? Tell me what you think?"

Breach swallowed hard, his eyes rising to meet his father's across the table. "I think if your brother was dishonorable, he would have hired a crook for a lawyer. Someone who would have gambled away his money. But I know that he needs this money for bail. That like you, he relies on the family in a moment of crisis. Once he's out of prison, he will go over the border to Canada, and then onto Hong Kong," said Breach, turning to his right and trying to judge the meaning of Colonel Chao's smile.

Ross finished two of the drinks left behind by the other gamblers. He didn't drink them so much as he tossed them straight down his throat as if there were some monster screaming inside for alcohol.

"You go now," said Li Chin then, as Breach began to rise from the table. "One more little thing. My brother has a tattoo here." Colonel Chao rolled up his sleeve, and pointed at a spot halfway up the forearm. "You wouldn't happened to know what it is?"

"A small, red dragon," said Breach. "About three, four centimeter. The tail is curled off the right almost like a scorpion ready to strike its victim dead. The eyes are a perfect dull black like the eyes of death watching you examine your cards. Dragon eyes that look straight through the heart of any man."

Crosby stood at the foot of the hotel bed looking at the body. Two uniformed police officers watched him staring

290

down. One of the officers held Breach's wallet with driver's licence, passport, expired membership card at a health club. There was enough of a likeness between Bennington and Breach that local police who thought all *farang* looked alike didn't question the ID. Crosby frowned, wrinkled his nose, and looked away.

"That's Breach, all right," said Crosby, lighting a cigarette. "Just like I found him an hour ago."

"You sure he your friend?" asked one of the officers, looking at Breach's passport photo.

Crosby glanced back at Bennington's body curled up on the bed, and nodded his head, looking over the officer's shoulder. "An old picture. Breach looked different in every photo ever taken. But if you knew him, then you'd never forget Richard Breach."

"Doctor say he take too much drug." The police officer shook his head in frustration. "No good for image of Thailand. *Farang* eat drugs and die here. People think we do the bad thing."

Crosby looked at Bennington's face; he might have been sleeping. "Learn to say no, I always told Breach. He claimed being normal was a disease. See how wrong he was?" Crosby asked, as the police officer tried to interject a word. But Crosby ignored the officer. "The danger of destruction. The risk of self-annihilation, not to mention the problem of the company you are often forced to keep." Crosby stopped, inhaled deeply on his cigarette, turned and put it out. "But he wouldn't listen to me."

"You know how we contact his family?"

Crosby shook his head. "He had no family. They are all dead. Buried in caves. Drugs flowed in through the blood of the Breaches."

The twin engine commander with the wing lights flashing was waiting as the black Mercedes pulled to a stop at the edge of the landing strip. Ross got out of the car, shaking his foot, complaining that it had gone numb. He limped over to the plane. Francis, an American pilot and dart person, leaned out of the window smoking a cigarette. "You're late," he said to Ross.

Ross looked up at the sky brilliant with stars overhead. "How's the weather holding?"

"Clear all the way to Bangkok. I'm missing a dart tournament at the Stokey Pub and Grill tonight. We are second in the league, Ross. You should have seen my clusters last night. Man, I was unstoppable."

The dealer and Breach, talking in low voices, stopped two feet away from Ross.

"I've tried, goddamn," said Ross, clenching his hands into fists. "But I don't understand how you knew about the red dragon, Breach. I sure as fuck didn't tell you. Bennington sure as fuck didn't tell you. Crosby didn't fucking know. I look up at these stars and I ask myself how in the fuck did he do that?"

"Do what?" asked Francis, hanging out of the cockpit of the airplane.

"Shut up, Francis, I'm not talking to you," snapped Ross.

Small blue veins curved across Ross's nose illuminated by the lights from the cockpit and wing. Breach looked quickly over at his father, who nodded. "When I was five years old I heard my father talking with my mother. Their bedroom was next to mine. He told her that he'd lost our house. That we had to move out. That he'd lost it to a Chinese gambler with a small red dragon on his forearm. It was two or three centimeters in length and had this funny scorpion-like tail and dull black eyes that bored through a man's soul. I heard him tell my mother, this man had cold-decked him. I remember her crying. And Father told her that with the Chinese you never express anger. You learn patience; you wait, and you wait, and you find an opportunity somewhere down the line to get even."

The dealer climbed into the plane. Ross followed him inside and sat in a window seat, reached under the seat and found a bottle of *Old Grand-Dad*. Standing in front of the door, Breach pulled off Bennington's tie, dropped it on the ground; then peeled off the jacket, shirt, trousers, socks, and shoes. Underneath, he wore his stained, torn singlet and jogging shorts. He said nothing, watching his father lean back in the seat next to Ross, the briefcase open in his lap. Ross, his eyes wide open, gripped the whiskey bottle by the neck, as he watched the dealer remove one hundred thousand dollars in ten wrapped bundles. He then closed the briefcase.

"We're off," said Ross. "Get the door."

The dealer rose out of his seat, and with one clean movement tossed the briefcase out and shut the door. Breach caught the briefcase and stood on the landing strip watching the plane begin to roll away. He saw his father look out the window for a moment, and then his face was gone.

"What in the fuck are you doing," shouted Ross. "Francis, stop the goddamn plane."

The dealer threw a ten-thousand-dollar bundle up to the cockpit. "Time to move out, Francis," said the dealer.

"Why in the fuck did did you give him my briefcase?"

Edward Ward, the dealer, smiled as the plane taxied down the landing strip. "Like Colonel Chao said, there's only one house. One bank. Family. You've got your fee." The dealer flipped two of the bundles on Ross's lap. He smiled, looked out the window as the plane left the ground, and turned back to Ross. "Here, take another one as your Christmas bonus," said the dealer, throwing one more bundle of ten thousand to Ross.

At four in the morning, drenched in sweat, Breach rolled out of a twin bed, checked the briefcase under his bed. The sheets were damp and stuck to his legs. The fan had stopped working. In the airless room he couldn't catch his breath. Heat blisters had popped out on his chest. He slipped into shorts and walked out to the landing. Suda sat at the picnic table. She leaned forward on her elbows, her chin balanced on top of her cupped hands. Her eyes were glazed over as if she were a million miles away. A full tropical moon split through the crooked tapered fronds of a palm tree a few feet away, casting a spiderweb of shadows and light on the table and Suda's face.

As Breach lowered himself to the table, he noticed her trembling.

"You okay?"

She didn't say anything, her head bent down, she stared at the table with red-rimmed eyes.

He went around to her, hooked a leg over the bench, lowered himself down and put his hand on her shoulder. He wanted her to feel that he cared. Just for a second to think he was not part of her job; another client whose function was to earn her money. She had trouble accepting human compassion from others. It made her suspicious as to what lay behind the gesture. Suffering was a natural state of being. He remembered her expression in front of the starved Buddha. His suffering reflected a kind of serenity in her face, he thought. For the first time, he understood what he had seen in her face as she gazed at the Buddha—it was a shared understanding about the order of things. Something he had tried to find in his self-imposed exile in Nepal.

Her body stiffened at his touch, but she couldn't stop herself from trembling. She wanted him to hold her; but she didn't. Compassion could be a mask that you couldn't see behind. Suda had been taught compassion was a family matter; don't take chances with compassion offered by a stranger. Her feelings were raw and open; like the alive darkness toward the ceiling of the cave. Something was moving at rapid speed, taking away her breath and she felt blind and helpless to recognize or control the movement. She couldn't begin to sift through what might be in someone else's mind when she was so confused inside her own.

"Are you ill?" he asked.

She nodded and stared down at the ground.

"Nightmares?"

"Ghost. *Jing! Jing!*—really. You don't believe me?"

"I believe you. It's a night for ghost circling," he said.

Her teeth chattered and she shivered. "Ghost very bad in this place."

"Ghost very bad in most places," he added. "English ghost and Chinese ghost. The ghost of Christmas past. The ghost of a red dragon. They were holding a convention in my room."

She relaxed against his arm. Her head touching his shoulder.

"Khun Toa, he come to my room."

"You're sure it wasn't a dream?"

She nodded. "We always joked together. But I scared because he's a ghost. I no want to joke him any more."

Breach remembered Khun Toa and the Chinese paper money. He was the old man in the funeral photographs. The paper money was in flames, thrown in the air, as his family stood around in a circle. Money was something they could not avoid even at death. It was the sendoff for the show business in the afterlife; where there would be new connections, rivals, enemies, scores to be settled, plans to be laid. Suda had known him. They used to talk, banter, joke together at the same table—Breach thought of them at the same table.

"Maybe you learned something from me after all," his father had said as they had strolled over the landing strip to the waiting plane.

"I learned a great deal," Breach had replied. His father had liked the pun.

They walked a few steps more in silence, then his father had turned and asked him. "Did you actually set the headmistress's Christmas decorations on fire?"

"Crosby told you."

"Your act of arson made a lasting impression on him."

"He said that?"

"That boy thought you were a mountain ten miles high. He said you had been the only person who had never once let him down."

He thought of awkwardly shaking his father's hand, then hugging him. His father turned and climbed into the plane.

"Come on, let's go," Ross had shouted, standing in the door.

As the small plane taxied down the landing strip, Breach had seen his father in the window. He gave Breach the thumbs-up sign and, a moment later, the wheels lifted off the runway and all that was left were the flashing red lights on the wings, and the lights quickly faded into the night sky.

Suda grew excited, thinking about the ghost.

"He come to my room. And tells me, No good not have car. Good you have boyfriend," said Suda.

And they would go round and round for hours, eating and drinking and joking late into the night. Khun Toa's eyes in one of the photos taken before he died reminded Breach of old Mr. Tang's eyes. That same sense of eyes bursting with amazed joy, as Suda rifled through Mr. Tang's drawers as he looked on, pretending to be helpless. She was afraid Khun Toa's ghost had slipped into her room, and if she fell asleep, then she couldn't stop him from wandering into her private thoughts and dreams, smelling of burnt paper money. She liked him, but she had no use for his ghost, or any ghost, which were beings that human beings should fear and avoid. Because a ghost is the cost of a life that has not been completed. A ghost comes back for something left behind. Suda wanted nothing to do with the business left over by the dead.

Mae Sai called the ghosts from the hallow of every memory that had been locked away. They roamed freely at the picnic table until three, when they returned to their separate room. Breach drifted off thinking of Edward Ward shuffling cards, cutting the deck, dealing, and how his eyes never betrayed that one single, common human emotion: fear.

Suda watched his face. "It over now."

He nodded. "You earned your money."

"I not care about that."

This wasn't the response he had expected. "You can go home now. You don't have to do anything else. Ross will pay you like he promised."

"I think money, dirty money."

"What did you expect? No, no. What do you want, Suda?"

She opened her fingers and inside her hand she held the silver fish. She held her hand out to Breach.

"I want you to keep it."

Chapter 19

On the bus to Chiang Mai, Suda slept; her head slumped against Breach's shoulder and rocked gently with the motion of the road. He thumbed through the pages of his new British passport; it had contained his day, month, year, and place of birth—and his name at birth: Richard Ward. Every date, place, time was true. The British passport had been part of the new documents for Richard Ward. His new identity and class ranking were stuffed inside an envelope which had been neatly wrapped with an elastic and placed at the bottom of the briefcase. A British driver's licence, a membership card in the Foreign Correspondents' Club, a library card, a Visa card. The documentation of a middle-class Briton with some passing connection in Thailand. Each document or card included an address in England; one he had not thought about for many years—the address of the house his father had lost during his childhood in a poker game.

Richard Ward had been born and lived before the red dragon; this has been his identity back in a postwar England when everything was ruined. But that name, with Suda sleeping nestled beside him on a bus in the north of Thailand, seemed as strange and alien as the terrain outside the window. He studied the name, said the name to himself, listened to the sound inside his mind, and tried to remember the last time he had heard anyone call him Richard Ward. A Patpong forgery factory had done a first-rate job in re-creating the life that had once been his. His father must have paid a substantial sum for the documents. He had a purpose in mind; not so much to reclaim the past—because the past was as dead as Bennington—but shift the weight of one poker game for another, and extract, for a moment, a bittersweet memory. He had gone to the poker game with the single-minded mission of redeeming his only son; a way of making a gamble that one could go back in time with a hand of cards and change the odds, the bet, the stakes, and come out as if nothing had happened. He had desired the impossible, what everyone sought—the stuff of which magic was made: a chance to grab a past mistake, to hold it, to alter the image of the red dragon until it transformed into a harmless memory and fell away. He had wanted what every father wanted for his child: a second chance to reverse the grievances and errors as if it were possible to reprogramme the past, to undo the conditioning that had made the child which made the man.

There had been a real death in Mae Sai; Bennington Wallace was found dead. Cause of death: drug overdose. He had been discovered in his hotel room, curled up in a fetal state, blue-lipped, his teeth clenched from the final death rattle. Crosby had been gone along with the police to identify the body as that of a *farang* named Richard Breach. His father had explained the details of the entire operation this as they had slowly walked toward the airplane on the landing strip. As the plane had circled overhead, his father leaned back in his seat, ignored Ross's curses and threats, and thought that it had been the same game as before, the same bet, the same people, only this time the gamble had paid off.

Breach shifted his legs in the narrow, hard seat, opened an eye and stared at a small framed photo of an old, smiling monk, his watchful, kind, trusting eyes looking out above the driver's head. Suda was still sleeping. He watched her breathing. He looked back at the photo of the monk. Everyone sought protection against evil, disease, pain, and death that raced down the road, weaving across the line of life, always waiting around the corner; a compressed fist of ten thousand pounds of steel aimed chin high. But if there was a monk's picture, the fist might miss; strike another, or fall harmlessly away along the side of the road. If only life clothed in such hope would open a broad, level, expanse of confidence and trust and all the grandstands were filled with spectators cheering you on, and there was never again a need for a shield because the battlefields had emptied. Breach knew the lie, and he knew the achy, twitchy need to clutch an amulet. Under the seat, Breach's heels brushed against his backpack stuffed with one million dollars in hundred-dollar bills.

He looked down at the forged library card for a library in England he had been far too young ever to explore or use. Had his father ever gone there? His father made a habit of fiddling with the radio, telling him the magnetic fields caused interference of the signal. Then one day he was gone; the house was gone, and a year later they were living in Canada as if they had always lived in Canada. His father had expressed no sorrow; the world had turned out pretty much the way he figured it was designed to turn out—correspondences which only corresponded in the mind—connections which could be disconnected or reconnected and people who believe the new arrangements with the same determination as they had believed the old; and illusions showed that all patterns which were taken for granted were fragile, momentary, and what vanished did not necessarily reappear. . .or disappear, even though one swore they had.

The trump card hadn't been the kind of playing card one would have expected. It had been a calling card, a tattoo on a man's hand, a memory that stained the innocence of his childhood. A small red dragon tattoo—that's what had bridged the past to the present, a repeated image heard through the wall of a parent's bedroom. Of all the education, all his development, reading, study, and searching, it had been that simple, short nucleus of memory that had saved his life; the life of his father, Ross, Crosby, and Snow. No sleight of hand, no kernel of wisdom, no bright, burning insight into the secrets of man or the universe. He stared at the old address in his passport and his own picture; a picture snapped of his childhood into his mind. He remembered his father sleeping during the day, and how he had to tiptoe and not make noise to wake him. His father hadn't been sleeping last night, thought Breach.

All that money, he thought, nudging it with the heels of his feet. Had his father tried to discharge the past, remove the old files? Strange ideas surfaced all night and that morning on the bus. There was a video club membership card from Manila, with address, phone number, and in his name. It occurred to Breach this was his father's way of telling him how to find him. Looking through the cards again and again was like reeling raw silk from a cocoon in a clandestine place. How many years had his waited for last night? And when he had won the struggle, held the fruits of victory, he turned the role over to his understudy and flew offstage. He had recognized his paternity in the only way he knew how.

The first lesson his father had taught him that one could always bet the house, lose, and survive. The second lesson, from the night before, was harder; having won the value of the old family house with substantial interest and penalties attached, what was Breach to do with the potential to buy a new life to go with his old identity? There had been a glint in the old man's eye, as if he knew, which Breach had read as a warning. Breach might use the hard currency as a rope to climb into a new life, to tie around his problems, to forge a new shape of living in his old life, or to slip around his neck and surrender to the basic truth behind magic.

"Shuffle the cards, take a card, any card," Breach would instruct someone. Breach would watch as the person took the card and carefully put it back in the deck. He shuffled the deck. He let the other person cut the deck and, a moment later, showed the card.

"But how did you know it was the ten of hearts?" asked the voice.

"Magic," he would say. Then he would make the card disappear from his hand. He would ask the other person to check their back pocket. The card was inside.

The illusion always amplified the basic fear that human beings possessed senses which were unreliable, they easily betrayed and tricked, no matter how many times the same card disppeared and reappeared the eyes deceived the brain. People laughed because it was like a joke; but inside the mind the terror of such deception was unavoidable. Because it wasn't just a card that was at issue. Breach knew the day he left the cave in Nepal that what lay at the heart of all magic was the ritual slaughter of the tangible, the visual and the logical premises connecting them into some unity. The only real card in the deck was the joker.

The loss of his childhood was as much an illusion as the win had been in his middle age; and his father had returned in his life for a single name not for a card game, not for the money, but to perform for his son the ultimate task of the best of wizards: the ceremony of deliverance.

He looked out the bus window at the flat land already heated like a forge. And then he glanced up at the framed photo of the monk. There was no escape on the roads in Thailand from the traditional belief that everyone needed access to the gods. The spirit world, like the everyday world, was a question of finding and balancing the right connections. Life without them was nasty, hostile, and unpleasant; and all the bad of this life was a debt left over from the last, and any hope of a marginal progression in the next was closely tied up with magical relationships which promised hope. A monk for the driver to Chiang Mai, he thought. A small red dragon on the arm of a Chinese gangster for his father, he thought. For Thomas Pierce, his Oxford mentor, who lay dying inside his North Oxford house, the magic of deliverance resided in a set of ritual shaman knives. No matter what the object, there was a pre-condition of belief in the power of rescue. That was a reason he never believed in a house, a home, a mother or father as instruments of rescue; how could he believe in something that could be gambled away?

Breach shuffled in his feet under the seat ahead of him and tried to stretch. Suda moaned softly, shifted, and turned towards the window. She twisted around, trying to get comfortable, and a moment later, her head again rested on his shoulder. Suda believed a house for her mother would rescue her. Rescue her from what, she wasn't precise; perhaps she didn't know, or hadn't cared to share her knowledge, or more likely, as with most beliefs, there was no rational reason, only a gut-level feeling that it would save her.

He watched Suda sleeping, her head having shifted to the window from his shoulder. For her, she found protection in a silver medal worn on a silver chain around her neck. An ancient silver medallion—a weaved design symbolizing seven gods—the wind, earth, air, water, fire, plants, and animals—had been given to her by an old Mien *Maw Pee* when she was fourteen; a year after she had been sent by her father to live with her aunt. It hung to one side on her throat, moving slightly as she breathed in her sleep. A piece of silver was her way of cutting through chaos, he thought. Death was not a perfectly normal, acceptable, expected event; but a situation of ultimate chaos, with everyone scrambling to clutch onto something which might rescue them.

He thought about what Thomas Pierce had once told him over a high-table dinner at Oxford, "Everyone searched for the right armor to do battle with death. And no one ever won. But it never stopped everyone in their own lifetime from trying. Until at the end, a harsh realization came home—death of self was an overcooked and soft split-pea pudding with a sharp knife hidden inside and nobody had the appetite or the guts to eat it alone."

Pierce's remark was made one evening in Oxford after the port and brandy; when all assembled in the senior common room, portraits of dons like themselves handed down from the eighteen century stared across the room. Pierce had been standing in front of such a portrait, sipping his port. "A right bloodly overcooked split-pea pudding, all right," he repeated to himself quietly, throwing a glance at his former pupil, Richard Breach.

❖

It was early afternoon when the bus arrived in Chiang Mai. They decided to go their separate ways for a couple of hours. Suda had business to transact; she set off for a silversmith shop to collect three or four pieces of silver jewellery. She had left the jewellery for repairs and the shop owner, a friend of her mother's sister, had promised the pieces would be done upon her return from Mae Sai. Breach, his backpack slung over one shoulder, carrying the business briefcase in the other, went in the opposite direction, walking to the main market. This was his last time on the trip to buy the ritual shaman knives; the next day he would return to Bangkok. He would fax Thomas Pierce either way. And either way he knew that his former tutor would understand that Breach had tried his level best; and even the best magician, like the best gamblers, can be ambushed, having given their best performance. On the last train stop in life, Pierce wanted his own illusions made real.

The plan was to find Kaeng, the old Mien man, who had sold Ross the set of fake knives. Kaeng had quickly closed his stall and vanished. What Breach didn't know was Kaeng had slipped away under cover of darkness that night, using Ross's to finance two days of non-stop drinking and gambling.

Only two or three customers wandered in the vast area of wall-to-wall stalls in the early afternoon. The market had a deserted, sleepy, dreamlike atmosphere. It did not appear as a place where objects were bought and sold; but an empty warehouse where none of the people inside appeared conscious. Several Akha girls spilled off their wooden stools, slumping forward, heads propped on hand-stitched pillows. Their eyes closed, they breathed in slow, dull deep sleep rhythms. Breach crept past as a stranger in someone's bedroom.

After winding through the market, toward the back, he caught sight of Kaeng. After the two-day binge, the old man looked pale and feeble. Breach came in on his blind side. Breach seized the opportunity to catch him like the Akha girls, in an unguarded moment. Kaeng stood inside his stall with his wobbly knees wedged between two wooden display tables. He smoked a cigarette, sucking in deeply, and talked with a couple of overweight women, faces lined and wrinkled, who squatted in some shade behind the stall. Smoke curled out of his nose and from between the crooked, yellowish stumps that looked like teeth which had been logged.

Breach out-flanked the old man, moving in slowly, as the old man continued talking with the women. A small electric fan with a black cord snaking to the ceiling ruffled the dresses of the women. A couple of feet away, Breach saw a crumpled set of shaman ceremonial clothing in a tangled pile; the stall had the appearance of a Savalation Army collection point. It smelled musky and old. A shaman's staff lay against the pile of clothing, and to one side, the flies flew sorties among a set of ritual knives half exposed in old newspapers reeking of fish and garlic.

"*Tao!ry!*—how much?" Breach asked, gesturing at the staff, pausing for a moment and moving his hand over one of the knife blades.

Breach picked the largest of the knives, turned it over carefully, running his index finger down the length of the blade coated with red rust. Breach looked mean, angry, twisting the knife in the air as if he had stuck through the belly wall of an enemy. He created the illusion of cutting a piece of ribbon into pieces and then, as if by magic, showing the old man and the women, the ribbon was still intact.

"Very good knives," said Kaeng.

"Maybe fake. Like the other knives you sold to the fat *farang*."

Kaeng shook his head and sucked in on his cigarette, the end burning a bright red.

"Not fake this time. Suda want fake first time. I sell fake. No problem. Fake easier to get. Not so expensive."

A cloud of smoke hung in the still air around his nose and mouth, and with a gnarled old hand he picked up one of the smaller knives. He ran a hand down the blade, as if lost in thought, then looked at Breach; his eyes narrowing as he tried to determine what Breach planned to do.

"Suda told you to sell fake?"

"She tell me."

They stood opposite one another as two extras in a sword-fighting scene. It was a question of who would strike the first blow; and who would ultimately emerge from this hand-to-hand combat victorious.

He had clearly remembered Breach from their brief encounter several days earlier—though his attention had been diverted by Suda. She had looked deeply into the old man's red-rimmed eyes, and had explained that a fat *farang* and a thin *farang* would come and barter for the knives. She asked him not to tell them the truth. She told him that the man with her would return later for the real knives, and he was to sell Breach those knives.

Kaeng remembered every word. And he had waited and waited for the strange *farang* to return. He took the offensive and opened his price at double the price of the fake ones.

"*Neung meun baht*—ten thousand baht," he said, holding out the knife, holding like a man who had drawn blood before. He nodded at the other knife held by Breach.

"*Hah Pahn! baht, krahp!*—five thousand baht, sir." Breach smiled and stuck out his tongue, revealing a silver fish amulet on the tip.

This shook the old man, who, with the look of fear and guilt, began backing away from the table, to the back of his stall. He barked in his native language something to the women, who stared at Breach as if he were a ghost or a wizard.

"No like," Kaeng said. "I go home now. Not sell. Not want money."

"I threw the fake knives off a mountain," said Breach, guessing his English wasn't good enough to understand. But that he was smart enough to worry about what he had failed to understand.

The old man studied him, then slowly nodded.

"Are these genuine, or more fakes?" asked Breach, coming around the table, with his backpack and ritual knife. "Because if these are fakes, that will be very bad. My friend Mr. Pierce in Oxford knows the difference. He will sad in his heart unwrapping a load of old rubbish. And my heart would hurt if I send him knives he can not use." Knives he could believe in was closer to the truth, thought Breach.

The old Mien had followed almost nothing that Breach had said. With a blank expression he pressed one finger against his right nostril and shot a long wick of snot onto the floor. He touched one of the knives, and waited. It didn't matter what Breach said or didn't say; all that mattered was the price.

"Just tell are these like the ones you sold to the fat *farang* two days ago, or are these real? Would Suda give you money for these knives?" asked Breach.

The old man sucked on his cigarette, looked at the knives, then at Breach. "They real. No fake. Suda, friend you want me sell fake to friend you."

His appreciation of Suda continued to rise. She had set up Ross with the fakes. She had been brilliant, letting Ross defraud himself; it was an appropriate Buddhist way of allowing the other person to make the choice. Kaeng returned Breach's smile, with a weary grin revealing a mouth of bad teeth. Not unlike Ross allowing Bennington to make the choice in the brothel. He could have walked away; it was his choice not to; he could have chosen another whore, but he chose the one Ross presented him; he could have refused the drink, but he drank it straight down.

Breach picked up each of the knives, one by one, examining the handles, blades, colored ribbons, and wondered what Thomas Pierce would make of them. He thought about him lying in his North Oxford sickbed. His thoughts shifted to the million dollars in the briefcase. It was surprising how light so much cash was. If only the old Mien knew how much cash was on this customer, then what? Would he have used one of knives to rob him? Inflate the price tenfold? Blow a line of snot from his other nostril?

What were the knives worth? Suda had said the old man was honest, fair, and the maximum price was five thousand baht. From the way Breach held the knives one grasped in each hand, he knew that Breach wouldn't leave the stall without them. The old man held up both hands and wiggled his fingers. He wanted ten thousand baht; double the fair price or, another way of looking at it, the old man had given Breach the *farang* price.

"Suda *bawk wah Kaen seu dtrohng! laa! jy! dee*," Breach said in broken Thai, or roughly what he said was, "Suda told me you were honest and had a good heart." He didn't know how to say, "And while it was all right to let that dickhead Ross cheat himself, you shouldn't cheat me."

"Suda *poot koon! bawk wan rah-kah sawng pahn! hohk! rawy baht, jing!*" Or what Breach thought Suda had said, "The price for the knives is 5,000 baht." But a red traffic light lit up in the old man's eyes; that should have ripped Breach off that something had gone terribly wrong at this stage in fixing the value.

The mistake was thinking he could pull off another illusion—fluency in a language he imperfectly understood. Breach had thought using Thai, like cutting the ribbon with the knife and the silver fish on the tongue, might scare Kaeng, and force him to submit. But he fouled up the tones and ended breaking the illusion. He made himself human again. The fear was gone from the old man's face. Instead he had that expression that says, "Do you have any idea how you've fucked up your bargaining position in my language? Are you crazy? Or crazy like a fox? Are you toying with me? Or are you stupid."

This was not the cut and thrust the old man had expected. When someone came after him with a sword he had reason to believe they knew how to use it. What it is intended for. The old Mien smiled that smile of someone who had witnessed his opponent fall on his own sword. No one had ever played the game that way with him before. Except, of course, maybe another *farang*. And they generally looked at the rusty old knives as junk. That's what confused Kaeng; a *farang* who desired objects that only Thais—and only a fraction of them—understood, and Breach couldn't make his position on the price understood.

Breach's mistake had been in the pronunciation of "*bawk wan*." Two words that cost him his credibility and destroyed his entire performance. From the moment, his relationship with the old man changed. He thought he said *bawk wah*, which meant, "Suda says." It never occurred to him that the difference between an "h" and "n" might carry such a heavy weight of negative implication; one that Thais, a smile wrapped on their face, used to cut down someone. Breach had told Kaeng that Suda, in her heart, thought he was someone who used his sweet words to create an impression that was false. It was a polite way of calling someone a fucking crook, a thief, a fraud, someone whose words were used to obtain an advantage rather than communicate the truth. Kaeng knew Suda and her family, and knew she would never use such an expression about him with a *farang*.

The old Mien had heard Breach repeat the same phrase; there could be no mistake. He stood firm on his price, turned away from the stall, and sat in a beach chair beside the fan. The old man lit another cigarette, put his head back, and stared at the canvas ceiling of his stall. Breach pulled out his wallet and counted out ten thousand baht, positioned one a shaman's staff over the notes, wrapped up the knives, and began to walk away.

"I no bullshit," the old man said, as Breach walked away.

One of the worst indictments by a Thai, in reply to something you've said, is *"Bawk wan."* Breach knew he had lost the battle with a single phrase, and learning how much damage he had done to his negotiating position, he smiled to himself, turning a corner, and he glanced back and watched Kaeng counting the five-hundred-baht notes.

As if on cue, Suda appeared in the market.

"You pay how much?" she asked, looking at the dirty, torn newspapers with the blade of a knive sticking out.

"It's okay," Breach said.

"Five thousand, okay."

"Ten thousand."

"Too much!"

"Five thousand for the knives. Another five grand for a Thai lesson."

Suda leaned over Kaeng's stall and rattled off a few phrases quickly in Thai. The old man shrugged. He explained what Breach had attributed to her about his character in establishing the original price. She might have rolled her eyes and thrown up her hands. What could she do? There she was with a guy who had given away his shoes and shirt; who had a different name coming back than he had going; a man whose father had bullshitted one of the most powerful, dangerous influential men of the North. And he had accused Kaeng, without even knowing he had done so, of being a fraud.

She nodded Breach's direction. "*Thii len thii jing,*" she said. "He is half-playing, half-telling the truth." This was the Bangkok style of getting one's point across, which came across as aggressive and hard for those in the North.

Another woman might have thrown up her hands. Not Suda, who exchanged some light banter with Kaeng, smoothing over the misunderstanding. She smiled and said, in a soft, lilting tone, "*Mai! bpen! rai!*—it doesn't matter."

"*Mai! bpen! rai!*" she repeated several times again in the taxi, as Breach leaned back, grim face, slowly turning over each of the knives wrapped in last year's Thai newspaper. "Crosby sent you a message. It's at my sister's house."

"What did he say?"

Suda glanced out the window, watching a young girl pass on a motorcycle, a shopping bag hung over one of the handles.

"You can read it later. First you can take shower. Then we can eat and afterwards you can read his letter."

Breach looked around and found that Suda had disappeared. Fah, her elder sister, steered him to the shower in the back. At the end of narrow wooden walkway were the outhouses. Two doors were partially opened. Inside was a gloomy darkness. Mosquitoes and black flies with emerald-colored wings buzzing the entrance for a food source found Breach.

He walked inside, slammed at the mosquitoes, and closed the door. He undressed, finding two hooks in the wall for clothes, and took a cold bucket bath in an outhouse filled with insects hungry for blood. He soaped up with a tiny wedge of white soap stuck to the bottom of a plastic dish. Filling the bucket with cold water, he rinsed off, slowly pouring the water over his head.

"It's useful," he said, spitting out the water that should never enter a human system. Magic was the most useful of all activities, he thought. And what was magic other than a special effect suggesting a hidden power? He couldn't wash away the vision of his father dealing cards. It had been the first time since a child he had confronted the man who had let a red dragon tattoo make his life disappear.

Standing naked, pouring cold water over his head from the plastic bucket, eyes closed, he thought of sitting in the back of the Mercedes with his father. He tried to remember every word that he had said in the brief time they spent together. Each word and phrase held the possibility of illuminating his father's *true motive*. All that Breach needed, he had thought the night before, was to fit together the words into some discernible pattern; one that commanded a pattern more valid than any other combination, and point to the reason for his actions. He poured another bucket of water over his head and shoulders, leaned against the wall, looked down at his toes on the concrete floor.

"King died, then the queen died," he remembered was the formula he taught his students. This was an example of a story. "King died, then the queen died of grief," though, was more than story; it was plot—the emotional guts of why one event caused another. E.M. Forster had written the first was a story and the second a plot. All he had to do was determine what had moved his father to go to Mae Sae and to hand over a briefcase of money. If he knew this one piece of information, then the pattern of his life would clear; and become much more satisfying, and he could look at himself, and his choices in a meaningful way. The illusion of the past would give way to the reality behind the illusion, or so he thought. To estimate, contain, understand how that trick was done had been the basis of almost every significant move in his life. Forster's simple formula required a confession of motives; otherwise, how might blame be assessed, punishment carried out, and how judges go about judging.

He ran the formula through his mind again, "Father lost big in game of chance, then Father won big in a game of chance." But where was the motive or the verdict? Everything squared off, balanced out, and came off in perfect order. But Breach knew the pieces only appeared to fit together like in a puzzle or a movie. He was certain that his father hadn't known his *real motive*. It had to be sheer luck—an image of a red dragon tattoo planted in a child's mind thirty-five years earlier, which he had pulled out of a hat when his life and his son's life depended on it. That was a cool, detached bet. But it scarcely mattered. Edward Ward's action had been improvised; an accident, an unpredictable blind leap from one foothold to another. Ross and Crosby had been enlisted to help. That suggested more than was actually the case. There had been no vision, plan, diagram, charts. Nothing fundamentally had changed from the moment his father had bet away the house. The small margin which separated the loser and the winner was the way they managed to play their hand.

"*Mai! bpen! rai!*—never mind," said Breach, towelling himself and shivering.

Dogs scattered and barked outside the outhouse as he emerged. On the walkway, he passed the outside kitchen; the gray sink overflowed with large pots and pans, all turned upside down. He tossed a ragged piece of beef at the dogs. Being Thai dogs, seeing his hand jerk back, they instinctively expected Breach to hurl a stone and they scattered, heads down, claws rapping against the wooden walkway. The piece of meat landed with a dead, sucking sound. The dogs sniffed the air and barked from the near distance.

"*Mai! bpen! rai!*" Breach said, turned and walked back to where Yai was putting the finishing touches on the T-shirt.

Suda had disappeared into the main shop where she had spread out half a dozen small rugs before an American from Santa Fe. He ran a craft shop in Santa Fe, and was on a buying expedition. She patiently explained the design of each rug, the price, tribe, age, and fabric. Breach toyed with a shaman's paper money printing block; he half-listened to Suda's pitch, thinking of paper money burning at a burial ceremony high in the mountains.

Reaching into his pocket for their rail tickets, he stumbled across a page torn out of a glossy magazine. He smoothed out the wrinkles, and held it up to the light. Suda had written her name and phone number on the page she had stuffed in his shirt pocket one Saturday at the Market. A Saturday long before he ever thought they would travel north. Long before he had spoken a single word of Thai. He looked at the page again. A smiling young African woman, dressed in traditional clothing, a silver bracelet on her right wrists, balancing a large gray water bucket with a rusty bottom on her tunic-covered head. Suda's name and number were on the side of the bucket.

The African woman had perfect, white teeth, and at the corners only a small rim of reddish-yellow color to set the pupils off from the rest of her face. Suda thought the woman was beautiful. The traditional headdress, the silver bracelet, the rusty bucket, and a winning style—her grammar for the words "beautiful woman." And the more Breach studied the page, and Suda off to the side bargaining with the dealer from Santa Fe, the more he understood how she defined beauty.

After the customer left, Suda strolled over to Breach.

"Remember," he said, holding out the page with the African woman.

The smile came off her face. She pulled an envelope from her pocket and handed it to Breach. "I read it already. Maybe you angry."

Breach put down the shaman's printing block and took out Crosby's telegram. It was addressed to Richard Ward in care of Suda's sister, Fah. "I spoke Tuttle on the phone. He was very upset to learn of Breach's death. They cremated you this morning at eleven. Tuttle had a message for Breach. It from Oxford. Thomas Pierce died at midnight on Sunday night Oxford time. Signed Mrs. Pierce."

Breach, emotion filling his face, leaned back against the wall; he looked at Suda standing in the shadows of a large display case.

"I try to find you before. But you already pay for knives."

"Find me another mountain to throw them off," he said, bowing his head and finding himself laughing for motives that he could only guess at.

On the Chiang Mai rail station platform, Breach walked ahead with his wrapped knives buried under one arm and the backpack slung over one shoulder. Suda said nothing, walking one step behind. It was then Breach heard a woman call out his name.

"Richard! *ah-jahn*—teacher. *ah-jahn!*"

He spun around, his knees wobbly, as a young Thai woman in tight jeans, blue tank top, and sneakers came running up. His heart thumped hard against his chest. No one knew Richard Ward. And Richard Breach was dead.

It was too late. Noi had spotted him and jumped up and down with excitement like a child. He turned and exchanged a worried glance with Suda. They looked each other over with headlamp eyes.

"What are you doing in Chiang Mai?" he asked, a funny rattle in his voice.

"Come with *farang*. Over there. Him name Roger," and she pointed at a balding man with a bushy moustache sitting on a bench some distance away. He was eating chicken, and a dab of grease had touched his nose so when the sunlight struck his face as he looked over it looked like a lighthouse beacon.

She pulled a notebook out of her hip pocket, flipped through the pages, then shoved it forward proudly. "See, my "G's" are good now. I practise, practise everyday, everyday in Chiang Mai."

Suda looked over Breach's shoulder, took the notebook out of Noi's hand, and flipped through all the pages of the letter "G."

"Very nice," said Richard.

A disappointed look came over Noi's face as she looked away from her notebook.

"He not teacher," Suda said to her in Thai, pulling Breach along, hooking her arm around his.

"She's one of the students in his English class," he whispered to Suda. A look of terror crossed Suda's face.

"He teach us good," said Noi, holding up her thumb, running and keeping pace with Suda. "Teach English, *dee mahk! mahk!*"

Little Noi was one of his star students. Always the first to give an answer. Always smiling. Always so full of hope and happy. She was a star go-go dancer at the Heartstop Bar in Soi Cowboy. She had brought her English exercise books. No matter what, Noi wasn't going to fall behind. Being the star student on Saturday mornings had become something she liked. She was part of the visible westernized prostitution industry which had started with the go-go bars during the Vietnam war before she was born. The G-strings and rock 'n roll had created the illusion and myth that the *farangs* had begun the flesh trade. When all that had been brought into the production was a new script. Noi had taken the modernization the next step: an auditioning for a speaking role in English so she might, with the magic of English, transform herself into the queen of hearts. With the right word or phrase the performer might get a better part next time out.

In pencil, she had written out the entire English alphabet. She could not read or write Thai. Noi had great difficulty making the "G" letter. Each letter "G" tumbled over, line after line of them, like curled-up fetuses. Noi produced another copybook filled with simple and mainly useless English words such as rat, hat, map, mat, man—vocabulary builders. There was nothing about the white spaces between words that worried Tuttle. This was a start. A beginning. Maybe a road to somewhere else. No one knew, but no one would stop Noi from trying to find another way. And now the teacher who had given her hope, was running away from her; pretending not to know her; and she was confused. What possible motive could he have to flee the scene? She had relied on him; felt he was different. How could she have been so wrong about this *farang*?

Her middle-aged boyfriend Roger finished his chicken, threw the bones in a steel trash barrel. Noi, arms hanging limp at her side, sobbed. She had lost face in the rejection. She was his star. And he denied she existed. Roger waddled over to Noi and put his arms around her from behind, clasping his hands together under her breasts. Breach looked out from the train. Roger flashed him one of those clown-faced winks.

"She made a mistake," said Breach.

Roger laughed. "We all look alike to them," he said.

Breach moved back from the window, leaned his head back and thought about a Wednesday night in Bangkok, not long after started teaching at Tuttle's school. He sat with Crosby, drinking Kloster beer and watching Noi in a see-through top, bikini bottom, red high-heel shoes, twisting, shaking the dance of those who sell themselves for money. He had seen Crosby's face in the ovals of her eyes; and his own reflection in the mirror behind her. He remembered what had passed his mind at that moment.

"And you ask yourself is this a career choice she would make, given free choice? And then you ask yourself who is worse off? The Nois serving the sexual needs of the Rogers and Waynes; or the Nois working in a Chinese sweatshop packing the tins of baby corn? Or do we leave the Nois like perfectly ripe fruit on the ground where they fell? Peasant by birth, peasant on death. That depended on your grammar for a large number of words: hope, love, logic, dreams, health, and God. And what you decided became largely a product of your attitude about these things. How you think about sex; how you think about business—and any connections that form in your mind about where the line blurs."

Suda had gone back to the platform, comforted Noi, and explained that Breach wasn't Breach. Walking down the corridor of rail car fifteen, bag over his shoulder, he counted the numbers to berth 25. A heavyset Thai in his twenties sat on the seat. The obese man introduced himself as "Lek." His name, in Thai, meant "little" or "small" and demonstrated how grammar could come apart as the body of the baby progressed from a two- or three- day-old infant to adulthood.

The return tickets to Bangkok were for separate berths. At the time, the rail official informed Suda that it was impossible to give two berths together. There had been no choice but to split up. Given the nature of their relationship, this alternative should have caused Breach only minor disappointment. By the time they had returned to Chiang Mai, something had changed in the way he felt about her; the kind of gradual realization that some crest had been reached together, and in getting there, the worst ridges and spikes had not stopped them. In the heart of that disorderly pitch of life when the crunch had come, when she could have stood at the crossroads and watched, she had entered into regions where the currents were something other than money. Besides, they had grown accustomed to fighting off each other's ghosts from nearby quarters.

In Suda's absence, Breach began to negotiate with Lek. The deal was simple; Lek would take Suda's berth three rows down in the same car, and in exchange, she would take his. Lek smiled throughout Breach's explanation. He sweated. With a handkerchief he wiped his brow, brushing back his hair on a purple scar that ran an inch below his hairline in a jagged line across his head. After Breach finished, Lek pulled out a silver chain with a half dozen amulets; mainly Buddhas images inside tiny gold-coffin-shaped cases with raised polished glass covers. One fact stood out in his mind about the proposal. He had been asked to sleep in a lower berth beneath a woman! When Suda arrived back with bags of food, she immediately understood the man's plight.

"He says, he can't sleep beneath women. His amulets are no good then." Suda explained his fear.

Lek made a gesture of throwing them out the window. Because of his weight problem, Lek believed that his weight would be too much for an upper berth in the sleeping car of a Thai passenger train; that he would come crashing down in the middle of the night on the hapless person sleeping below.

Lek had stopped being "lek"—or small, around eight years old, when he started putting on a lot of extra weight. After that, he said that he had been "fat."

So fate demanded Breach be placed in the compartment above the amulet-guarded young Thai, who had undergone major brain surgery eighteen months earlier. He explained the entire procedure to Suda, who ate slices of mango, nodding her head as he spoke, turning and translating fragments for Breach. The doctors had opened Lek's skull and poked around. A small tumor had been removed, and the doctors said he had fully recovered.

"*Maw*—doctor think maybe he fat because of problem," Suda said, touching her index finger to her head.

The tumor had caused him to eat too much? Produced the wrong chemistry? Created pressure on the "hunger center" of the brain? None of these questions could Breach ask in Thai, and ultimately left feeling satisfied that Lek wasn't bunking above him. Why did the conversation always come around to food? Snow, prior to becoming a Lahu godman, had patrolled the aisles of Foodland in Patpong. Every major street and soi in Bangkok was congested with food vendors and their charcoal fires and boiling pots. Noi's customer had stuffed his face with chicken on the railway platform.

Breach stretched out in the upper berth, switched on the nightlight, and opened his backpack. He touched the bundles of hundred-dollar bills; ran his finger down the ends like a deck of cards. What fork in the road had his father taken? He would be in the Philippines along with Ross. One would be drinking *Old Grand-Dad*; the other shuffling a deck of cards. A hot wind swept across the landscape outside the train, rocking the train. They had entered the open country. But in the womb of the upper berth, Breach traveled deep into an underground vault—returning in his thought to the cave where he had slept and eaten in aloneness.

He unfolded the note Crosby had sent and read it again. Thomas Pierce died at midnight on Sunday night Oxford time. Breach worked out the time difference in his head. Thomas Pierce had died around the time the Lahu had herded Crosby, Snow, and himself into the small clearing; and the shaman had pointed the old rifle at Snow and the report of the gun echoed off the mountains. That had been about midnight Oxford time. The time when he had pulled a live snake from Snow's ear.

Chapter 20

"Abracadabra," said Breach in a hushed tone, holding out two clenched fists. Across the aisle in an upper berth, a small face peered out of the curtains. The small boy's eyes judged the location of the coin. His mouth was firm and eyes bright as he tapped Breach's right hand. Then another child's head popped out above the first boy. Brothers, thought Breach, as he slowly opened his hand, showing that it was empty, then reached out as a porter passed and pretended to pull the baht coin out of the air above the porter's head. Four large brown eyes opened wide as Breach made the coin disappear again.

"Say the magic word," said Breach.

"Abracadabra," said the boy.

Breach snatched the silver baht coin from his ear.

The boys disappeared, giggling, behind their curtain. Children loved magic and illusion because it corresponded with their own feeling that the world was not as it appeared. For children the world was a magical shelter. There could be invisible friends, and humanoid robots, and talking animals. Children were like pagan cave dwellers who would paint their bodies blue—if given half the chance. Cause and effect had been planted in their reality but had not taken root and destroyed their refuge in the mysterious. In ancient times, children were sacrificed for their innocence and purity. Their tender throats slit open in rituals and their blood drained into a stone altar. Breach propped himself up at one end of his berth and examined the blade of one of the ritual knives.

Pierce was dead, he thought. He laid the knives out on the white sheet. He lined them up in a row with the blades pointing away. He grabbed the handle of the largest one and held it to the light. It was difficult to move around the cramped train berth. He ran the blade of the knife along the edge of the curtain. He closed his eyes and thought of a wizard chanting charms and spells. Toward what unresolved end had the wizard's arm swung in a down motion to extinguish life? He felt the sweat on his face and neck. Again he ran the knife in a circle around his berth. The tip of the blade snagged the sheet and cut it. The purpose of all sacrifice, all magic, all ritual had always remained the same: it was an act of faith. "Faith in what? Banana ice cream and Tarot cards?" he had asked Pierce as they walked along the lake. And Thomas Pierce smiled at his star student. "Faith that we can find a way out of the existence to which mankind is condemned. And still exist. There's the problem. How to bridge existence and nonexistence and move freely between them?" Breach watched ducks glide across the unbroken surface of the lake. "The roller coaster only goes one way," Breach had said. "And that's to the bottom." Pierce, closing one eye and squinting with the other, slowly traced the contours of the lake with his outstretched finger. "But some people have always believed it rises back to the top," said Pierce. "I can create a lake with my finger and the heavens with my eye."

Pierce had believed that with our absorption into the world of magic, we escaped complete solitude and—this was the important part—behind the illusion was our wish to explore the infinite—the place where thought was unmade, unborn, and the unconditioned. The place where Pierce could draw a lake with his finger, and claimed the authorship of the lake; where he could trace a finite pattern of life and never lose sight of the infinite. Then, faced with the terror of death, Pierce had wanted the ritual knives not to spare himself from death but to trace the infinite. Children instinctively behaved as if all life and the universe were a magic show, an illusion unfolding, evaporating, coming and going, and standing still. In the world of abracadabras one word resolved the unresolved. Breached rolled the knives inside the pillowcase, and pushed them into the corner of the berth. He stared at the backpack stuffed with packets of US$100 notes and began to laugh until the tears fell down his cheeks.

❖

The interior of the rail car looked like a third-rate magic show after the provincial fairgrounds had closed for the night; with the lights turned on, and the public gone. Children's heads popped out of the curtains; then an old man with gurgling throat, a fat woman with a hairnet over her head. Head after head pulled in and out of the curtained berths accompanied by giggles, whimpers, moans, and whispers. The matted hair, suspicious eyes, blurred in the hard prisonlike caged ceiling lights, looking out, seeking the source of the farting, the belching which had showered the car with rancid smells of half-digested garlic, mekhong whiskey, and overripe pineapple.

Above the clickety-clack of the train a child moaned that he had already brushed his teeth and had to take another pee. The train softly rocked back and forth. Breach lay back in his berth, clutching the ritual knife. He had a feeling of being locked inside a chamber buried deep in a void, a place beyond destiny and self; the place where Pierce had gone. Or was this only a feeling fostered when people are trapped inside a common object hurling through space with other people's children? Or was there any difference between the train, the classroom, the whorehouse, the gambling casino?

Everyone tried to make the best of yelling, belching, scratching, running, talking, grunting, laughing, and spitting beyond their curtain. He peered through a crack in the curtain, watching his neighbors pass. Breach had seen these kind of expressions before; in the classroom on students, at the end of a crucial examination, when walking up and down the aisle a face would look up with that hard-shelled, depressed look of someone whose life was nourished by either too much or too little intelligence. Either one guaranteed a certain kind of defeat.

Stewards in red vests, with the curt manner of prison guards, brought around coffee and tea with tan clay cups and saucers on small trays. Cream-filled biscuits on the side. In the berth beneath Breach, Lek shifted with heavy grunts, rattling his amulets. He had brought his own box of biscuits. Breach lay and listened to Lek eating biscuits, and drinking tea. Overhead fans circulated the thick, stale air; it was like breathing an invisible curtain in and out of the lungs, the feeling of a heavier-than-air fabric dragging across the nippled ridges. He thought about Suda's tuberculosis and the slow burn of that hot air swelling through her lungs. Screwing a tongue of fire down the central tube of her body, he thought, his hands folded behind his head.

For the first time in a long time, Breach thought about his mother. Her presence had been at the gambling table in the cave and again later in the car, she hovered near as he spoke with his father. A felt, silent other sphere in the constellation that exploded all those years back. When he was twelve, she had returned home early from work and found his stepfather buck-naked chasing an old girlfriend around the living room. He had caught her near the couch. She was bent over and his father, standing upright, entered her from behind. He leaned forward and grabbed her breasts, then brought his hands back along her back and thighs. She was groaning, her breasts flopping up and down on the cushions. His mother had watched him from behind, his hips thrusting back and forth; the giggles and sighs growing in volume; and straight ahead on the fireplace mantel were the family photos lined up like ducks in a row. The naked woman, her head arching up with each thrust, stared straight at the photos. Of all the places where Edward Ward might have taken the woman, he had taken her there on the couch with a full view of the family.

That same night she crept into Breach's bedroom; the windows overlooked the back garden showered in moonlight. She was beyond distraught as she sat on the edge of his bed and wept in her hands. He had seen her hurt, sad, crying, miserable, frustrated, depressed before, like every kid. But he never had seen her with this worn, stripped-down to the brass plate kind of despair; the gloom at the bone level of the soul. The little girl who had sold flowers on the streets of London suddenly realized she had no control over her life. Her eyes were wild with fire and her mouth liquid from drinking half a bottle of gin. Then she told him a story.

❖

"Even in the most civilized, intelligent, stable woman, there is something semi-wild. Something a man can never know. We are born with this virus of fear. The worst part is we don't know why we are so afraid. I'm vulnerable like a deer on the highway. You know, with the high beams of a big truck coming down on it. So I married your father. Why did I marry that crazy sonofabitch who would gamble away our lives? Because I thought he would always be there. I would be safe and protected. Only a couple of years later, I found out like most women find out looking at him as he slept on night. Vapors of steam pouring off his head on a hot July night. Here was that high beam that terrified me; it wasn't on the horizon, it was beside me, around me, on top of me. I couldn't catch my breath. I started to panic. I knew I had to be brave. But that's easy to say. I leaned over him as he slept and whispered, catch me before I fall. He rolled over and grunted. A month later, he lost the house. Then you and me come to this godforsaken country, and your old mum marries a sonofabitch who fucks old girlfriends while I work. So I'm a little drunk. So what? I've a right, don't I? You know what I whispered into his ear two nights ago? The same as I whispered to your old dad, catch me before I fall. You'd think your old mum would learn. Ain't no one ever go string out a net to save me. I'm just gonna keep on falling and falling. Why do you think people drink? So they can pretend for a while they're all right. Yes, sir. You can forget what's really happening in your life. Because a woman knows she like a can beer. Some bloke is waiting to drink her down to the bottom of her toes, and then toss her out the window of his life. Freaks of evolutions, that's what we are. Fragile, vulnerable bodies; throwaways passed from hand to hand, until we are all used up, dry, hollow, not worth two cents. Until the magic's gone, then nothing can ever break our fall again."

When Breach recounted this speech to his father, the old man smiled, shook his head, and said, "Your mother was better than most. Marriage works for men who are ignorant, zombies, saints, or just plain scared. They manage for a little while to keep a woman from falling to pieces. But your poor mum ended up with someone who was slack for the part. So like she said, it all came down to who made the first move to escape. Maybe she did whisper in my sleep, 'catch me.' I don't know and I don't care. She's dead now and it doesn't matter. But we both had the same idea. If I had won that hand when I bet the house, we were going to split the money and call it quits. So it didn't much matter in the end. Except we ended it poorly. I made a bad bet in a game I should have known was fixed."

Ross had his head bent back drinking from a bottle of *Old Grand-Dad*. "We're programmed to fuck and die just like toads and ants," he said, with a sigh, looking straight ahead at the oncoming lights of the limo. Breach sat silently as his father had finished the story. Ross waited for one of them to respond. When neither did, he carried on, because he knew that he had the answer. Whether they wanted it or not, he was going to tell them.

"Mindless, relentless fucking is the name of the game. And if you ask Henry between your legs, he'll tell you that it's the only game in town," said Ross. "I have a little song I would like to dedicate to the dealer and his son. Something special for the occasion."

He took another drink from the bottle and began singing, "Froggie went to market to get laid. Froggie went to market to screw a tart. Froggie went inside a hot-dog bun and down a Chinaman's gullet did he slide, singing, Froggie went to market to get laid. Froggie went to market to screw a tart."

After Lek belched on the sixth biscuit, Breach shoved the backpack in the corner, swung his legs over the top and climbed down. In the next car, Suda sat reading in the lotus position in her upper berth. Breach poked his head through an opening in the curtains. She wasn't surprised to see his face appear unannounced in her compartment. She let him lean in an awkward bent over position for several minutes before acknowledging his presence.

She lowered the travel magazine opened to a story on Paris. There was a night photograph of Sacre Coeur washed in warm light.

"Where you go now? Cannot go back to Bangkok," she said.

"Why not Bangkok?"

She frowned. "I think dangerous for you. Like that girl, Noi. Someone will see you. Then maybe the bad thing might happen to you." She cocked her head to the side. "You're all right now. No problem. But you must be careful. Never forget it is not like before."

And at that moment, Breach smiled, thinking about what Ross had said, leaning over the seat in the car, looking first at him and then shifting his gaze on Breach's father.

"Shit, you don't have a goddamn thing to worry about. No one knows fuck all in Bangkok. It is a city of ten million people but they've got yellow pages smaller than Omaha, Nebraska. Four million people live in houses without addresses. Forty percent of the population is off the books. No one knows where anything is or where anyone is. Just keep off Silom Road, Sukhumvit; Patpong, Soi Cowboy, Nana. Grow a beard. Dye your hair. Fuck, you don't even have to do that. We all look alike to them."

Breach had started to laugh.

"I don't think so funny," said Suda.

"I was thinking about what Ross said in the car."

"Man who thinks he knows doesn't; man who thinks he doesn't know, knows," she said.

"Oriental wisdom," said an English-accented voice, "is strictly forbidden in upper berth sleepers."

Crosby reached under the curtain and tapped Breach on the shoulder. He jumped, pulling the curtain up and looking at Crosby's smiling face.

"Thought I conductor?" asked Crosby.

Crosby swung underneath the curtain at the foot of Suda's bed with a lit cigarette in the corner of his mouth. He plopped a canister on the bed, and pulled the cigarette out of his mouth. He looked at the magazine. "Paris. What a lovely idea."

"Crosby, have we ever talked about whose side you're on?"

"I would have thought you'd be grateful. I did pull a rabbit out of the hat. One that had been lost for many years. A man should know his father."

"I don't recall asking for an introduction." Breach looked hard at the dull metal canister. Crosby flicked an ash on the top. "What is that?"

"This?"

"That!"

"Richard Breach's ashes," said Crosby, flicking a long, grey ash into his cupped left hand.

"What are you doing with them?" asked Breach.

"Obviously, travelling with them. Though it is a bit strange. I've got your ashes and you apparently are not dead."

Slowly Crosby snubbed out his cigarette against the top of the canister, shaking his head. "I'm sorry about Pierce, old boy."

Breach rapped his knuckles against the side of the canister. It made a dull thud, and with a sleight of hand caused the appearance that Crosby's Zippo lighter had been removed from inside. Breach turned it over and read aloud the inscription on the other side: "We are the unwilling led by the unqualified to do the unnecessary for the ungrateful."

Crosby smiled, brushed his fingers over the top of the Zippo and gestured at the canister. "I buried you and yet here you are risen from the dead." Crosby paused, and leaned with an elbow on the canister. "I thought you might like to hear the eulogy I gave?"

"Who was there?" Breach was suddenly interested.

"Snow and a couple of monks."

Breach tried not to appear curious. He waited for several moments. "Okay, what did you say?"

"Richard Breach burnt Christmas decorations when I was a child. That was told us he was the child of a red Chinese dragon and a London flower girl. Such an offspring was destined to become a wizard, a magician, a teacher in second-rate English public schools. He told us that magic showed us that our first lesson was to demonstrate the illusion of life was the deception of death. The secret was to release ourselves from false knowledge and the bonds of religion, family, and country and to be reborn to the wisdom of the universe. Mr. Richard Breach lectured that we should never build our lives around sentiment. That to burn your bridges was to find your path. Then I said, he once bet on a horse named *Roger Dodger* in the running in the fifth race and won. He bet to win, and I left it at that. The monks were sleeping and Snow has started to flirt with a sixteen-year-old street vendor who had wandered past selling watermelon."

Crosby flicked the Zippo and the large flame danced, throwing shadows across the interior of Suda's berth.

"Did he buy watermelon from her?"

"He took her short time," said Crosby.

"A perfect eulogy."

"I want to go to sleep," said Suda, turning over on her side, facing the wall.

❖

Crosby paid Lek a sum of cash to switch berths. A business transaction that took about thirty minutes to close. Lek went cheaply into that dark night with one thousand baht and a Thai paperback on ghosts. Crosby spent another ten minutes sweeping the cookie crumbs from the bedding. Another hour passed before Breach returned. He said nothing to Crosby. He lay stretched out in the darkness of his upper berth, feeling the movement of the train on the track; holding the canister of ashes on his chest.

He heard Crosby shifting position. He rattled ice in a glass. And Breach remembered his face from fifteen years before; he thought about Crosby's baby face, the double chin, the shy, awkward, doughy face; the way he breathed through his mouth, and touched, without seeming to know that he was touching, his forehead. He thought about Bennington standing in front of the window next to Ross looking at the rows of young girls, and he thought about Thomas Pierce, diving into that overcooked split-pea pudding without his ritual knives. He thought of a water buffalo with eyes wild with fear, thick red tongue swollen, watching the blurred movement of a shaman who lifted a knife above his head. His hand arched high. The sun catching the blade edge in a blinding flash on the downward plunge.

Breach sat bolt straight up. He stuffed the canister with Bennington's ashes into the backpack with the money. Pulling back the curtain, he dangled one arm down and banged against Crosby's berth. A moment later, he heard Crosby strike a match, and the pungent smell of cigarette smoke curling upward.

"It was a brilliant eulogy. I'm proud of you. You bet the perfect game. You arranged the perfect setup. The one with no holes or flaws. It was a master blueprint," he said, as Crosby appeared at eye level.

Crosby's hand involuntarily touched his forehead as if he had switched channels inside his brain before he could give a direct answer. This act was in character. Crosby's strange, boyish mannerism had not altered since he was a boy.

"It had been a fantastic plan," said Crosby. "Like that time in London when you had me dropping my drawers to display my diseased cock. It was a revelation to think my dripping penis could win a bet. The money appealed to me then, and, of course, the money did enter into things again this time. I have flesh; and this flesh has its needs. Sometimes I think you forget that real trinity is the gullet, the anus, and the cock. But I have another reason. You see, back in school I had this idea your family was an optical illusion. A magic trick. Mine was always so boring, so predictable, really so English. My mum and dad were so fucking normal they made me insane. They rarely raised their voices. They were permanently settled in this arrangement you convinced me was meaningless, an outright fraud. You said we needed the strength to strip all that away and stand up in the world the way it really was. Anything that promised security or safety or peace was a lie, you said. Only the mad believed someone or something could stop their fall into bottomless ignorance. That the magicians of our century had been mass murderers; they had a trick of turning their victims into their own executioners.

"That first couple of weeks when I was in your class, I kept saying to myself, what the fuck does he know? Then, like a lot of other kids, I started believing you did know something; something important, and we were these dumb, backward imbeciles who thought about nothing other than jacking off at night. No one had ever said such things to us before. We wanted to be like you. We wanted to follow you. But every time we tried to get close, you pushed us away. It was unreal, and I was confused.

"We would have done anything for you. And did. Showing my dick around a table of strangers in that pub gives you an idea how far we were willing to go. And then I got you to come to Bangkok. That was a true victory. I thought, the old magician was still alive in you. You had done what you told us to do. You'd burned your bridges. You'd gone and lived in a cave. And all the time, I kept asking myself, what is he really looking for? Leaving one country, then another, one job, then another, one relationship, then another.

"After I met your father in a card game, it suddenly occurred to me. You had never really told us anything about yourself. Your family. But in essence you had told us everything. Your father was a red Chinese dragon and your mother a flower girl in the streets of London. Such a child wanted to burn his own nest. And you were all for us burning up the paper houses. That made you famous, of course. But whenever anyone asked you to tell them more about your parents, you never replied. Why, why, I asked myself. What had been imprinted inside your head, that was flying the room and trying to get inside our heads? When I met your father, I figured, this was the personality that had set the type. You had taken on his identity without ever knowing him.

"He was a kind of Chinese dragon, those eyes of his, the way he coiled himself around his cards. I mentioned in passing about the red Chinese dragon to him, and he smiled and laid down his cards. Maybe we can do business, he said. Why me, I asked him. He looked at me for a long time. Because the dragon is back, he said. What if, just what if, Richard Breach had to do what the rest of us had to do our whole lives, I thought. What if Richard Breach confronted himself in the dragon one more time? And I could be there to witness that confrontation?"

Breach shifted in the shadows, trying to make out the expression on Crosby's face in the dim berth light. He thought about this confrontation of father and son for a moment. Stretching out his legs, he touched his backpack, smiled, and waited as Crosby lit another cigarette.

"So how does it feel to be reborn again?" asked Crosby.

"It doesn't quite work that way, Crosby."

"Then how does it work?"

Breach started singing. "Froggie went to market to get laid. Froggie went to market to screw a tart. Froggie went inside a hot-dog bun and down a Chinaman's gullet did he slide, singing, Froggie went to market to get laid. Froggie went to market to screw a tart. Froggie. Froggie. Froggie. Come back!" He tapped out a tune on the urn. Then Breach's voice died away.

Crosby listened to the muffled noise of the train. A few berths away someone breathed like a foghorn; and there were whispers and clearing of throats. Those nocturnal sounds of slumber from the throats and noses of many people confined in small, cramped, strange spaces. He sucked in on his cigarette, watching the red glow in the dim light.

"You can stay at my place for as long as you want," Crosby said.

"Thanks, but—"

Crosby interrupted him. "No buts. You can stay." Then he paused; he had the look of something awkward on his mind. "And, I want to ask you something."

"Ask."

"Did he stiff you for the ten grand he promised?"

Breach smiled, shaking his head. "No, he didn't stiff me." He paused for a moment. "Who actually killed Bennington?"

Crosby sighed, lighted a cigarette. "The guy was a button man for the mob in New York. Not an occupation you put on the immigration card. So his cover was that he was a lawyer. An Ivy lawyer."

"To work up Ross," said Breach.

"Never take away another person's object of hate. Rob him of his object of love. He can survive that. But don't tamper with hate. Isn't that what you told us?"

"Who did it?"

"He capped himself. Didn't know it, of course."

"I played the part of a hitman playing the part of a lawyer," said Breach.

"One of your all-time best illusions."

A couple of minutes later, Breach heard Crosby snoring in the berth below. He reached up and switched off his light, and felt the motion of the train, rocking gently, softly, like a mother's arms wrapped around him. Soon he was sleeping, and he saw the high beam lights shining off the large red eyes of a deer, ears erect, frozen on the double yellow line running down the center of a road with forest on either side. He felt his hands on the steering wheel and his right foot press the accelerater pedal to the floorboard.

When the truck struck the deer two 12-foot strong warriors with wings, flowing beards, body armor, holding 9-foot spears in their stone fists tumbled out of his ribcage. They marched to a large, rectangular door into one of the buildings at Wat Po and stood guard. The concrete entry-way was cluttered with gym equipment. Workout benches, and barbells with fixed, concrete weights that looked as if they'd been moulded in old water buckets. Seven or so young Thai boys with dirty feet and scraped and nicked ankles and calves sat huddled on the workout bench, watching the monks pass. Staying close to the yellow door, in the shadow, out of the killing afternoon sun. A monk blesses them by dipping a thick batch of bundled switches into a large black water bowl carried by an assistant, and flicking the bundle at them. He came in closer, and began hitting them on the shoulder, neck, and head.

The boys stretched out like cats, holy water sparkling on their cheeks, lips, all the way down to their feet.

Suda and Breach sat in a sea of people on the hard concrete courtyard under a large blue and green canopy stretched like a tent top over a superstructure of steel rods Everyone sat with their shoes off; spreading out Thai-language newspapers to keep their clothes from touching the concrete.

Above their heads, and as far as the eye could see, there were long white strings, hundreds and hundreds, each tied to a roof of strings anchored to the steel rods beneath the canopy. And each string could be followed back to an individual who sat with holy water, oil, incense, and with saffron and red flags to ward off evil spirits. They sat with a small plastic bag squeezed between their legs. There was a pair of penny loafers next to a pair of blue sandals. Across from where we sat a young Thai girl, in a yellow blouse with the words Sam's Club written across the front, scooped chipped ice into a plastic bag, then filled the bag with coke, handed it to an old woman with betel red lips.

Some gesture, some expression appears familiar in her next customer. He is an army officer dressed in a brown uniform; a big, black-handled pistol inside a leather holster is strapped to his hip. She gave the officer a Sprite, and as he

335

turned around, Breach recognized him. He's Mr. Tang. He nods at Breach, who looks behind him and see Lip selling fake Rolex watches. Mr. Tang taps the heel of his pistol with the palm of his hand, smiles, then walks on drinking the Sprite.

Ceiling fans rotated in a series of interconnected rooms across the courtyard; rooms obscured by metal grating with white paint peeling off under the sun. Everywhere from the rooms to the open courtyard, each string is connected by a vast, expansive white web; each person connected to every other person. The temple grounds curved, and narrowed, opened up, then fell back on themselves like a labyrinth with a hundred passageways. Strings pushed by the wind in one way, were straight elsewhere, and billowed in another direction in yet another section of the courtyard. Monks sat at tables. Loudspeakers blaring their voices, their jokes. People, hands folded in a prayer, their string between their fingers, laughing, crying, yawning, drinking water, nodding off, talking, eyes closed, or looking off into a void.

Monks, shifting their robes in the heat, walked barefooted on the sunbaked concrete. One monk, an old man, with a gray stubbled beard the same length, texture, and color as the hair on his head, passed smoking a cigarette with one hand; and collecting money sticks decorated with colored paper. Ten- and twenty-baht notes were wedged inside the crack at the neck of each stick. He stuffs the sticks, scores of them, fistfulls of money sticks into a large pink plastic shopping bag.

Suda nudged Breach, "Around your head," she said. "*Wy! Jai!*—trust me."

She coiled the string around her head forming a slender band over her forehead. All around Breach, everyone had wrapped string around their heads and ears. Encircled were friends, relatives, and strangers—all connected in the same latticework of wrapping. The loudspeakers blared with shouts, chants, strange, unearthly groans, shrieks, and cries—of pain, of horror, of abject fear. Suda smiled as Breach removed a deck of cards and began shuffling them, and doing some simple tricks for the boys who rushed beside him from the weights. Each time they picked a heart or diamond, he rewarded them with a bundle of hundred-dollar bills from his backpack. He had just finished shuffling the card for an old monk with the gray stubble when his right hand glittered with gold specks. He lifted his hand, opened it, and examined the whorls and lines as if they were canals on a strange moon. The palm of his hand, thumb, index, and middle finger were clustered with a dense layer of tiny specks from the gold leaf Buddhists use to paste on statues of Buddha. He reached over and showed Suda, and she smiled, her hands still folded in a prayer, the string wrapped around her head and hands.

Breach frantically resumed his card tricks, trying to shake off, then ignore the accumulation of gold. He shuffled and began throwing his bundles of money into the crowd; but no one noticed the bills softly raining down on their head. But the gold leaf grew heavy and thick and he couldn't shuffle the cards; the cards began dropping on the ground and breaking like glass into a million shards. He looked around at the other people; but there was gold leaf nowhere to be seen; it wasn't flying off a Buddha statue and no one else had a speck of gold on their hands, face, or clothing. The faster he tried to shuffle, the more the gold flew in like a blizzard, until he couldn't move his hands and the ace of spades was frozen against his hand by the gold. The gold came like a blizzard, until he had been buried up to his neck in a gold drift. He no longer could move and no longer even tried. Only then, did the gold leaf storm stop.

A fat, elderly monk, with bowed legs, gnarled toes, and a fierce face—the same face as the stone warriors—stopped before the crowd ahead of where Breach sat in a shroud of gold. He looked up between the monk and the statue; one of stone, one of flesh. And he recognized the expression—

it was Thomas Pierce, who slowly stuck out his tongue. On the tip was a small red dragon with shafts of fire blowing out of tiny nostrils.

The elderly monk, his face without expression—a blank, totally detached look—tipped the bundle of tied sticks into the holy water, and began throwing the water over a vast area. As he came closer, his eyes fell on Breach and the gold flecks. Again, with no visible expression, Pierce stood above Breach, and struck him repeatedly with the tied sticks that suddenly had turned into a shaman's ritual knives. The water soaked Breach's hair, shirt, and trousers. Only when he had emptied the water bowl did he move on. The water had melted the gold in a thin sheet over his lower body and both hands. There was no pain. But Breach could only move his head.

As he glanced back at the giants, they began climbing out of the heads of people around him; giants with faces that he knew. His students from years past, the old Mien who had sold him the knives, crooked antique dealers, hilltribe women singing from the fields, Ross drinking from a bottle, Crosby dancing naked on a casino table, his mother and father making love under a full moon under the headlamps of an old Austin. Breach instinctively reached down for the deck of cards. Then he remembered his hands couldn't move. He couldn't shuffle the deck. One of the dirty-faced street kids took the deck from him and ran, darting like a rabbit, through the crowd.

Breach could only observe and be observed; and as the ghosts collected around him, they watched, like the monk, without expression, feeling, emotion. There was no place to hide. No money left to shelter beneath. No tricks to run into; and as he turned to Suda, Breach watched the ghost that had come out of her; he was still attached to her string. He had the same face as the stone warrior, as the monk. Pierce's face smeared with split-pea pudding. Those faces were all waiting, looking for the same thing: for Breach to finally look at the giant that had climbed outside of his body. But he closed his eyes and refused to look. Or he didn't want to. He sensed something had shifted. He looked out, and he was back in that field with Snow and Crosby and the hilltribe shaman. He saw the shaman aiming a pistol and squeezing the trigger. No bullets came out; only the melody of Ross's song about Froggie goes to market and ends up in a hot-dog bun. The voice was Ross's, then his father's, then his own, and finally with a chorus of voices sang the Froggie song. Bennington's knees crumpled and he pitched forward into the dirt. Next the shaman pointed the gun at Breach and pulled the trigger. Breach dived to the ground beside the giant.

And when he looked face-to-face at his own giant, the one that climbed out of his throat, he screwed his eyes closed. But the image floated in that sea of darkness within. Wayne, the electrician, from Minnesota, and Breach opened his eyes, and the face had changed feature by feature, reconstructing into a new mask. Wayne smiled and vanished. And in place of Wayne, the last headmaster in England who had fired him for sleeping with his wife. The speed of the transformation increased. The old Mien from the market at Chiang Mai; the Akha woman on the bus; Crosby, Snow, a Chinese man with a red dragon tattoo— and, the last mask, Suda. Her face, expressionless, lingered on the giant's face.

He glanced left, then back, and she was gone. He searched everywhere, back and forth, but the giant had gone, Wat Po, the strings, canopies, monks, and temples vanished. And in this great solitude with everyone having abandoned him, he felt an intolerable loss as if fallen into an inaccessible distance with no words, signpost, name, face, and gate in or out. Breach had the feeling of moving in a lightless space; he no longer appeared to anyone; including himself.

❖

He called out, first in a whisper. Then louder his voice carried through the berth curtains and throughout the sleeping car.

"Suda, *Thii len, thii jing!*—a game of the truth."

No reply. The car was dead still as if afraid to acknowledge the nightmare of one of its members.

"Suda, for godsakes. *Poot len!*" he shouted. And shouted louder, until he heard the panic choking in his throat and felt tears coming from someplace.

Crosby leaned into his berth and shook his shoulder. "You're dreaming in Thai, that's a good sign."

Sweat rolling off his face, Breach bolted straight up, hitting his head on the low ceiling. He winced. "Where am I?"

"On your way home," Suda said. *"Thii len, thii jing."*

A train steward with eyes the color of old cheese drew back the curtain of Breach's upper berth. He stared at disoriented *farang* and shook his head.

"He ate some bad pineapple," Crosby told the steward in Thai.

Breach reached forward and pulled a pair of dice from the steward's ear and held them out. The steward clutched his amulet and backed away from the berth. A moment later, Suda's face appeared under the curtain. And standing next to her, Crosby unwrapped the set of ritual knives, admiring them one by one.

"*Mai! sa-by!*—Are you ill?" Suda asked.

"A Bad dream."

"Too much *Maw Pee*," she said, running her fingers over the handle of one of shaman knives which Crosby handed to her.

The train steward returned with a higher ranking officer and they shone a flashlight in Breach's face in that kind of we-know-who-you-are-fella kind of motion. Suda rattled off an explanation in rapid Thai and he switched off the flashlight, ducked under the curtain and vanished, muttering about crazy *farang*. After the two stewards left, Crosby looked at Suda, then Breach, arched his left eyebrow, touched his chin, before slipping without a further word back into his lower berth. The background sounds from the other curtained berths quickly died away. Soon, order restored, the motion of the rocking train pulled them all back into that place Breach had crawled out of screaming. Suda gave him a smile.

"What did you tell the steward?"

"I say him you eat too much Chinese truffles. Make you sick. Maybe they make you a little crazy. Pull dice out of the air. But you okay now."

"How did you know? You were in another car?" Breach asked, resting back on his elbows.

She shrugged, looking down at the mess of sheets, backpack, and a couple of bundles of hundred-dollar bills spilling out in the shadows. "I not sleep. So I go for a walk. That's all. I come inside this car, and I hear you calling my name."

Breach saw her eye line leading directly to the bundles he had kicked free during his nightmare. "Couldn't sleep? Ghosts in the train?"

"No problem for ghost. They go on train, airplane, but poor one go on bus," she said. "You sleep now. No more shout: 'Suda, *poot len.*' Conductor report you to the police. That not so good, I think."

"*Bahng tee*—maybe."

"You speak Thai very well," she said, smiling, as she looked away from the money.

She removed the silver chain from around her neck. Hanging on the chain was the silver medallion he had seen around her neck as she slept on the bus. The one she had worn since she had been fourteen and sent away from her family. Breach flipped over the medallion. The border had three overlapping braids, and in the center were seven interconnected stars. The stars looked like seven attached Stars of David. But the silver piece was not Jewish; it was Mien. It was a Mien spirit house; one worn around the neck to guarantee the protection of the seven gods who occupied the seven stars of human fate.

He knew it was very old and rare, and that over the years, she had had many offers for it. She had always refused. It was her private spirit house. The place where business stopped. The one thing she believed had protected her on the road in Mae Sai—on every road. She carefully took the chain from Breach and put it around his neck.

"Now you okay," she said.

Breach slept through the rest of the night waking about six. For thirty minutes he lay in the berth, looking at the silver chain and Mien spirit house. Touching the seven stars. He decided how much he should pay her for the piece. Or, alternatively, he would return it to Suda. He wondered whether in a moment of emotion she had really intended to give away something she had treasured for years. He climbed down from my berth, nodded to Crosby, and showed him the spirit house on the necklace.

"How much that set you back?" asked Crosby.

"Don't know yet," replied Breach, twirling the interlockings stars around his neck.

"If I'm not mistaken, I think she's rather attached to you. God knows why," said Crosby, with a grin.

Breach walked through the next car and leaned under the curtain of Suda's berth.

"How much do I owe you for this?"

"Souvenir of Thailand. You keep." He pulled out one of the bundles of hundred dollar bills and tossed it at the foot of the berth.

"Ten grand enough?"

"*Fawng*—listen. *Poot*—say souvenir. Understand?"

"Okay, then. I thought you were the one who said. Business first; business last. *Farang* not ever understand the Thai. So keep the cash. You saw it last night. You earned it. Otherwise, I have to give this back," he said, beginning to unfasten the necklace. "Understand? You should wear. You should keep."

"No longer mine. It's yours." She bent forward, scooped up the bundles of hundreds and stuffed them down the front of Breach's T-shirt.

"Business first; business last, yes, I say." Suda paused, studying Breach's face. "But some things are never for sale; you can't own; your can't buy. I thought maybe you understood. Maybe I was wrong."

When he went back to his car, berths had been collapsed back into seats and Crosby sat holding Breach's briefcase on his lap, looking out the window at the moonscape of fields that had been savaged, broken, abandoned to the rain and wind. Breach sat opposite his old student, saying nothing for a long time.

"She wouldn't take any money."

Crosby looked away from the window. "You must be careful who you offer money. Some people might get the impression you consider them a whore."

Half an hour later, the barefoot steward had folded away the berths and the seats emerged again. Suda came into the car, sat next to Crosby, opposite Breach. She said very little. Then, three stops from central station, as Breach was about to apologize, she climbed out of her seat, holding her two bags, and vanished off the train.

He followed her to the door. Just before she climbed down, she turned to him.

"Go now. Closer to my home." That's all she said.

When he looked out of the window, he saw her walking with her back toward him; the bag with the kilos of silver slung over her left shoulder, looking like Charlie Chaplin. He stuck his head out the window.

"Suda," Breach shouted through cupped hands, as the train started to roll.

She made a half-turn, a crooked smile on her face.

"Thanks," he said. "Thanks for everything."

"You're no electrician. But in a dark age, maybe they are not so important." Wayne, the guy at the dirt field that passed as a bus depot between Chiang Mai and Chiang Rai, had worked as an electrician. The way she said "electrician"— a nearly impossible word for a Thai—suggested that she'd spent hours repeating the word like a mantra out loud to herself, over and over, as night fell, and as she passed into sleep. Somehow it was very important to her that she could express herself. Wayne's occupation in Minnesota.

The train made hissing sounds but didn't pulled away immediately. As Suda disappeared from sight, Breach returned to his seat. As the train stood still in the station he looked out at the open fields, palm and banana trees, water buffalo, and children playing half-naked in dusty yards with chickens, he read the note that Crosby had left behind stuck to the canister with a label which read: Remains of Richard Breach. Breach pulled off the note and read it again.

"Trust me, you'll get back what I owe you soon. There is this horse named *Son of Roger the Dodger* running in the Fifth race at Epsom. I have it on good authority this horse will win."

Breach's backpack was gone and the ritual knives laid out in a neat row on the seat around the canister. And the travel magazine was open to the story on Paris. Breach smiled to himself. He remembered a similar note many years before he had written to Crosby about a division of spoils. But he didn't want to think about Crosby or the money. He pressed his face against the window, and for a second, he thought about running down the aisle, jumping off the train. Suda's leaving had been so sudden. It started to make more sense; as did her presence when he started crying out in his dream. She had been beside Crosby in the bottom berth the entire time. Only a moment before, he was thinking how he should grab his backpack, climb off the train, and run after her, catch her from behind, spin her around, swing her off her feet. They would go to a small restaurant with an early morning tropical sky above, and sit across from one another, looking as if they had found the emotional bond people use to bridge the gap between each other. This horrible void that had trapped his mother; he wanted to tell Suda how wrongheaded his mother had been.

But he didn't get the chance do that. Maybe he never could do that. Perhaps that was the answer his father had called him to Mae Sai to deliver in person. There are certain journeys you can only make together, and then only once, for a short period of time, he thought. And if you make the mistake of trying to go back, the hard reality filters in: something essential has changed, and if you examine it too closely even the memory gets spoiled, fractured, blown to pieces like the playing cards in his dream. No matter how hard anyone tries, they can't find the names or addresses of the emotions you left along the way.

He had discovered something important, the way he had underestimated her; himself, his father, Crosby, and just about everyone else who had crossed his path. What they wanted, their motives for wanting it, and where they hid the truth about themselves. The margin of error had been even greater in his assessment of the things people dreamed of, looked for beauty in, and understood the nature of suffering in. Despite it all, he believed he had found a bond of trust. He wanted to believe Suda had cared—for a moment, maybe on the railroad platform in Chiang Mai, when Noi was convinced she had seen a man who was dead. The blade of doubt penetrated deep as he wadded up Crosby's note and threw it on the floor. He thought that within the scope of this bond they had touched as well as any two people can hope to; for a while, at least, and what better use of life could there be, than to live a fragment, here and there, with a deck of cards, a sleight of hand, a spirit house at the throat.

❖

The last words he saw forming on Suda's lips as the train pulled out were, perhaps her favorite, her strength, the anchor of the Thai people, "*Poot len*—telling a joke."

Like that deer frozen on the highway of his mother's stories, he was very still, alert, and every muscle in his body told him that whichever way he jumped it would make no real difference. As the train began to gather speed, Crosby emerged out of the shadows of the station, the backpack with the money in his right hand, and stood next to Suda, waving with a cigarette. He bolted from his seat, and ran to the back of the train car, the canister tucked his arm. He rattled the window locks on the door and managed to pull the window down. Breach picked up the canister and hurled it out the train. It bounced on the siding, shattering into thousands of fragments and sending up an ash-gray cloud of power. Then he threw the shaman knives off the train. Pulling them out of the pillowcase, he threw them like a carnival performer, in a long, looping arc. At the end, the empty pillowcase blew out of his hand, caught in an updraft and fluttered.

"Like a fucking whooping crane," he shouted, looking up at the pillowcase riding the wind.

He glanced back and saw Crosby laughing like hell. Suda stood, head in a half bow, watching the blur of train wheels whirling past. Breach leaned out of the window and shouted but the wind blew his voice away. No one heard his words. Suda moved towards the tracks; and at the last moment,

Crosby pulled her back. He had stopped laughing. She had tried. But it was already too late for her to jump again, the train had gained speed, disappearing down the track. He would soon be in Bangkok. His ashes scattered, Pierce's knives lost. And Breach had appointments to make, assignments to complete, a thousand reasons to invent a new birth from the same red Chinese dragon and to breath fire for a new generation of students, who, like Crosby, had caves of their to discover and make their own.